**VOLUME 4**

TEEN TITANS GO! TEEN TITANS SPIRIT

Paul Morrissey   Heather Nuhfer   Ivan Cohen
Derek Fridolfs   Sholly Fisch
Writers

Marcelo DiChiara   Jeremy Lawson   Erich Owen
Derek Fridolfs ▪ Lea Hernandez
Artists

Jeremy Lawson   Franco Riesco   Erich Owen
Tony Aviña   Lea Hernandez   Pamela Lovas
Colorists

Wes Abbott
Letterer

Dario Brizuela and Franco Riesco
Collection Cover Artists

SUPERMAN created by Jerry Siegel and Joe Shuster
By special arrangement with the Jerry Siegel family
BEAST BOY created by Arnold Drake

BRITTANY HOLZHERR Assistant Editor – Original Series ALEX ANTONE KRISTY QUINN Editors – Original Series
JEB WOODARD Group Editor – Collected Editions LIZ ERICKSON Editor – Collected Edition
STEVE COOK Design Director – Books LOUIS PRANDI Publication Design

BOB HARRAS Senior VP – Editor-in-Chief, DC Comics PAT McCALLUM Executive Editor, DC Comics

DIANE NELSON President DAN DiDIO Publisher JIM LEE Publisher GEOFF JOHNS President & Chief Creative Officer
AMIT DESAI Executive VP – Business & Marketing Strategy, Direct to Consumer & Global Franchise Management
SAM ADES Senior VP & General Manager, Digital Services BOBBIE CHASE VP & Executive Editor, Young Reader & Talent Development
MARK CHIARELLO Senior VP – Art, Design & Collected Editions JOHN CUNNINGHAM Senior VP – Sales & Trade Marketing
ANNE DePIES Senior VP – Business Strategy, Finance & Administration DON FALLETTI VP – Manufacturing Operations
LAWRENCE GANEM VP – Editorial Administration & Talent Relations ALISON GILL Senior VP – Manufacturing & Operations
HANK KANALZ Senior VP – Editorial Strategy & Administration JAY KOGAN VP – Legal Affairs JACK MAHAN VP – Business Affairs
NICK J. NAPOLITANO VP – Manufacturing Administration EDDIE SCANNELL VP – Consumer Marketing
COURTNEY SIMMONS Senior VP – Publicity & Communications JIM (SKI) SOKOLOWSKI VP – Comic Book Specialty Sales & Trade Marketing
NANCY SPEARS VP – Mass, Book, Digital Sales & Trade Marketing MICHELE R. WELLS VP – CONTENT STRATEGY

TEEN TITANS GO! VOLUME 4: SMELLS LIKE TEEN TITANS SPIRIT



DC Comics, 2900 West Alameda Ave., Burbank, CA 91505
Printed by Solisco Printers, Scott, QC, Canada. 11/3/17. First Printing.
ISBN: 978-1-4012-7374-3

PEFC Certified
This product is from sustainably managed forests, recycled and controlled sources
www.pefc.org
PEFC/26-31-02

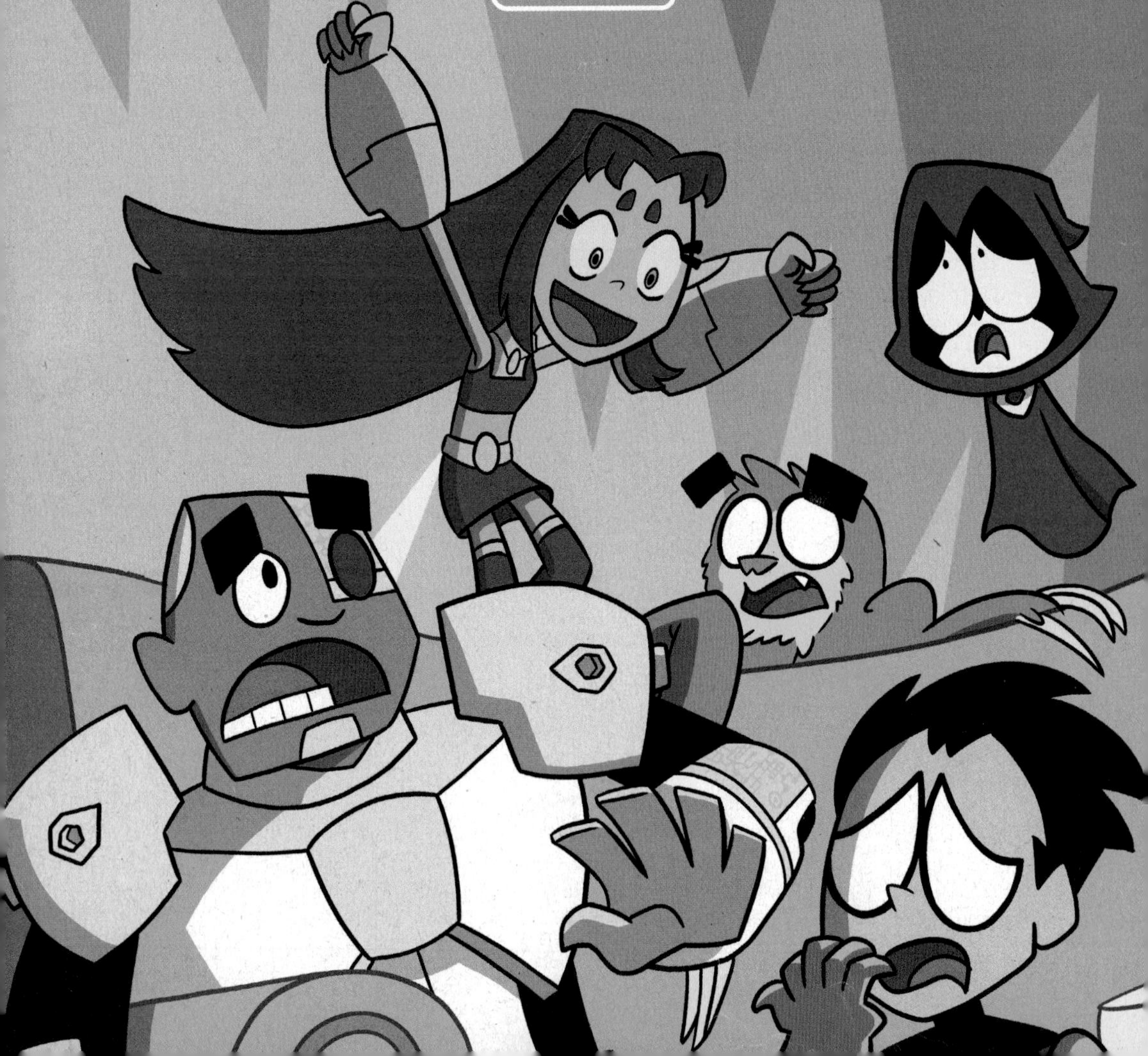

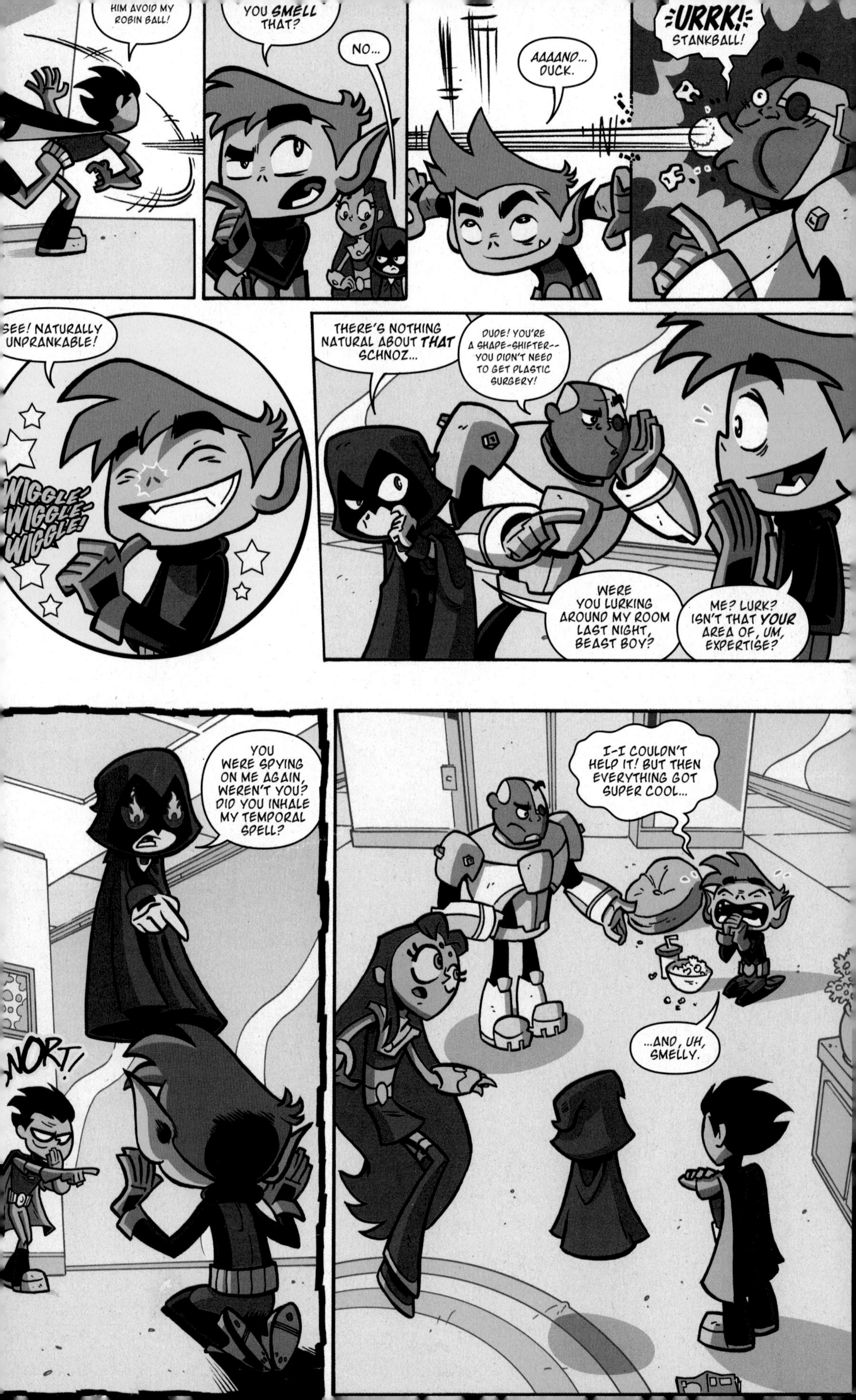

HIM AVOID MY ROBIN BALL!
YOU SMELL THAT?
NO...
AAAAND... DUCK.
URRK!
STANKBALL!
SEE! NATURALLY UNPRANKABLE!
WIGGLE-WIGGLE-WIGGLE!
THERE'S NOTHING NATURAL ABOUT THAT SCHNOZ...
DUDE! YOU'RE A SHAPE-SHIFTER-- YOU DIDN'T NEED TO GET PLASTIC SURGERY!
WERE YOU LURKING AROUND MY ROOM LAST NIGHT, BEAST BOY?
ME? LURK? ISN'T THAT YOUR AREA OF, UM, EXPERTISE?
YOU WERE SPYING ON ME AGAIN, WEREN'T YOU? DID YOU INHALE MY TEMPORAL SPELL?
NORT!
I-I COULDN'T HELP IT! BUT THEN EVERYTHING GOT SUPER COOL...
...AND, UH, SMELLY.

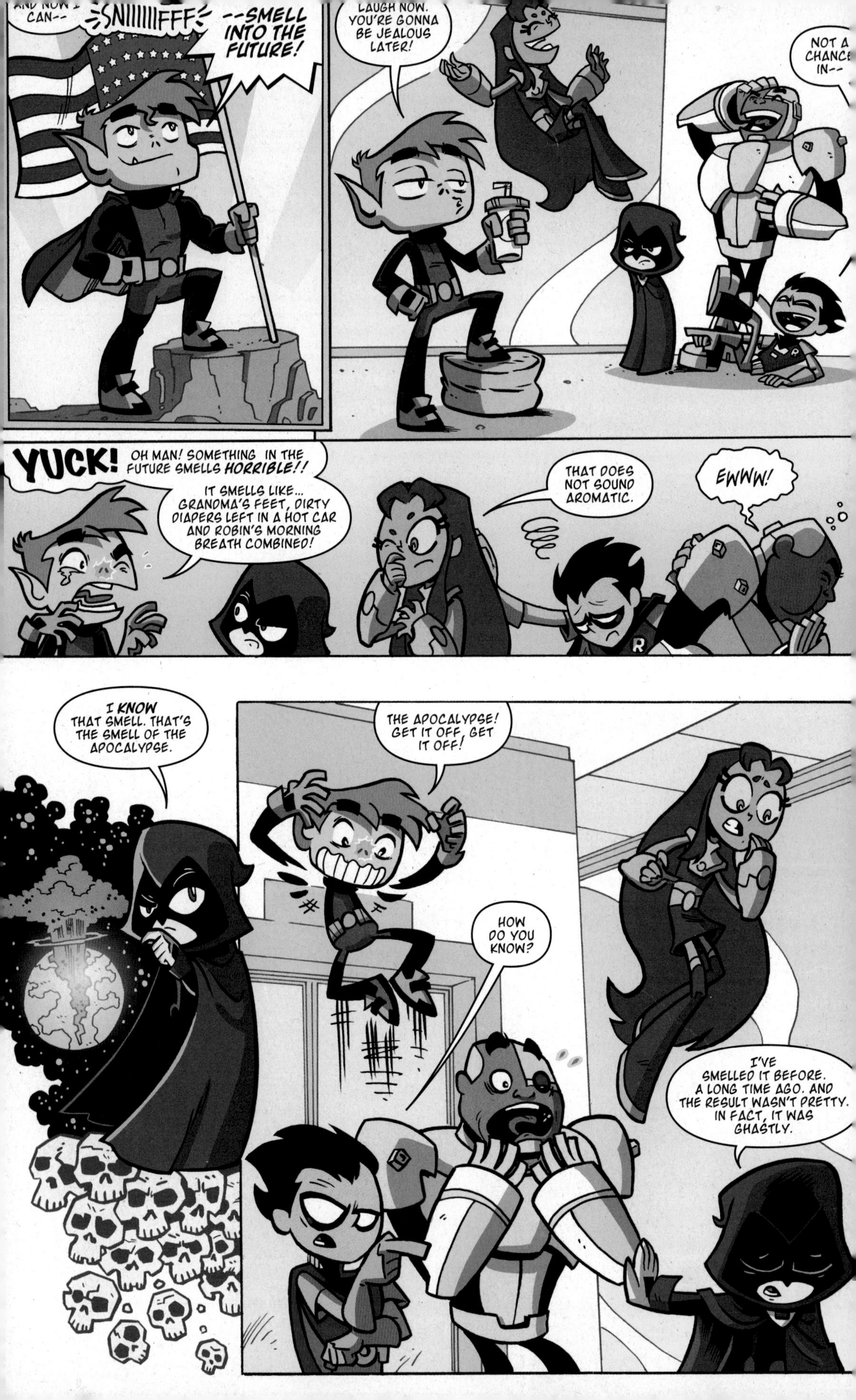
CAN--
SNIIIIIIFFF
--SMELL INTO THE FUTURE!
LAUGH NOW. YOU'RE GONNA BE JEALOUS LATER!
NOT A CHANCE IN--
YUCK!
OH MAN! SOMETHING IN THE FUTURE SMELLS HORRIBLE!!
IT SMELLS LIKE... GRANDMA'S FEET, DIRTY DIAPERS LEFT IN A HOT CAR AND ROBIN'S MORNING BREATH COMBINED!
THAT DOES NOT SOUND AROMATIC.
EWWW!
I KNOW THAT SMELL. THAT'S THE SMELL OF THE APOCALYPSE.
THE APOCALYPSE! GET IT OFF, GET IT OFF!
HOW DO YOU KNOW?
I'VE SMELLED IT BEFORE. A LONG TIME AGO. AND THE RESULT WASN'T PRETTY. IN FACT, IT WAS GHASTLY.

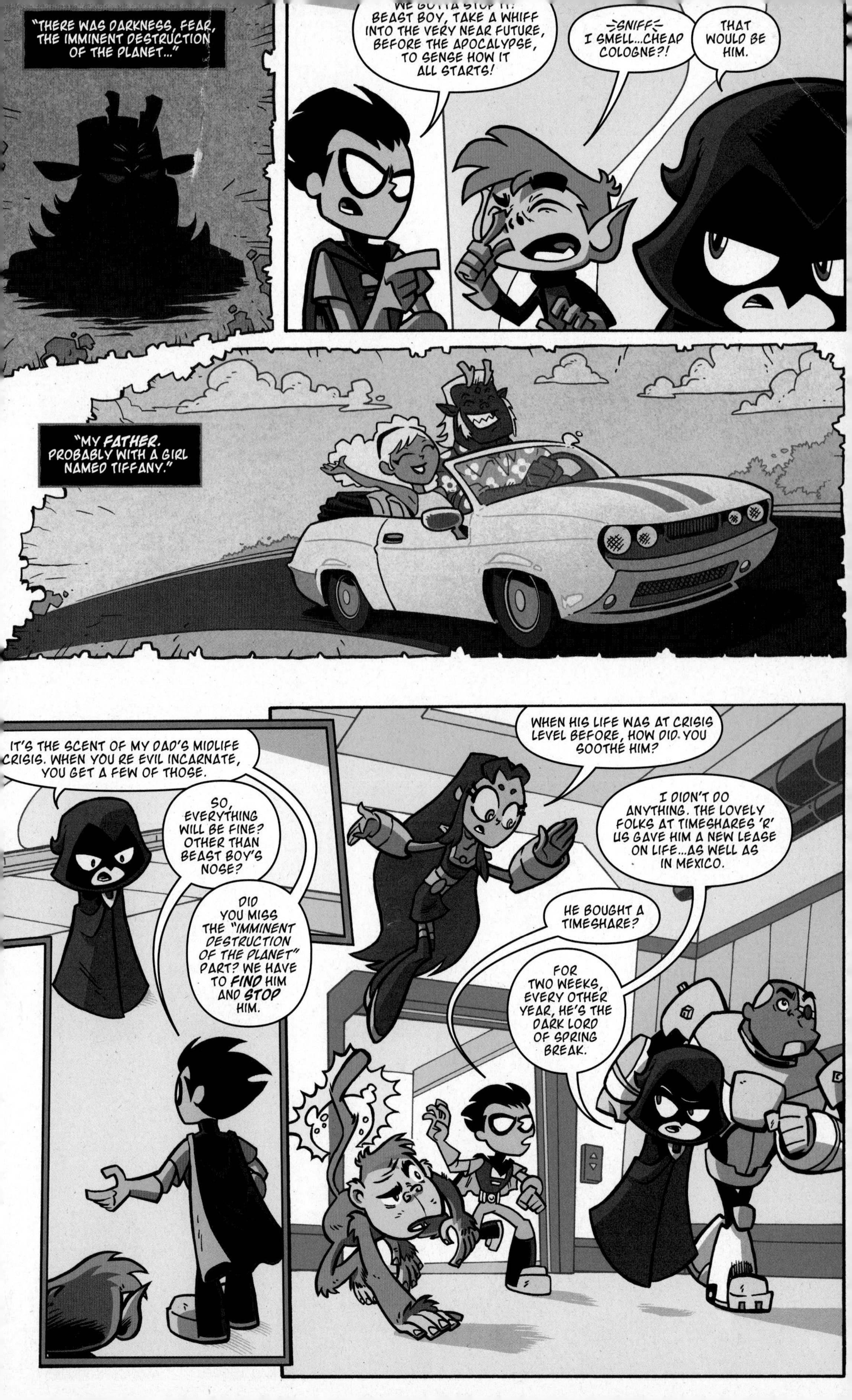
"THERE WAS DARKNESS, FEAR, THE IMMINENT DESTRUCTION OF THE PLANET..."
BEAST BOY, TAKE A WHIFF INTO THE VERY NEAR FUTURE, BEFORE THE APOCALYPSE, TO SENSE HOW IT ALL STARTS!
SNIFF
I SMELL...CHEAP COLOGNE?!
THAT WOULD BE HIM.
"MY FATHER. PROBABLY WITH A GIRL NAMED TIFFANY."
IT'S THE SCENT OF MY DAD'S MIDLIFE CRISIS. WHEN YOU'RE EVIL INCARNATE, YOU GET A FEW OF THOSE.
SO, EVERYTHING WILL BE FINE? OTHER THAN BEAST BOY'S NOSE?
DID YOU MISS THE "IMMINENT DESTRUCTION OF THE PLANET" PART? WE HAVE TO FIND HIM AND STOP HIM.
WHEN HIS LIFE WAS AT CRISIS LEVEL BEFORE, HOW DID YOU SOOTHE HIM?
I DIDN'T DO ANYTHING. THE LOVELY FOLKS AT TIMESHARES 'R' US GAVE HIM A NEW LEASE ON LIFE...AS WELL AS IN MEXICO.
HE BOUGHT A TIMESHARE?
FOR TWO WEEKS, EVERY OTHER YEAR, HE'S THE DARK LORD OF SPRING BREAK.

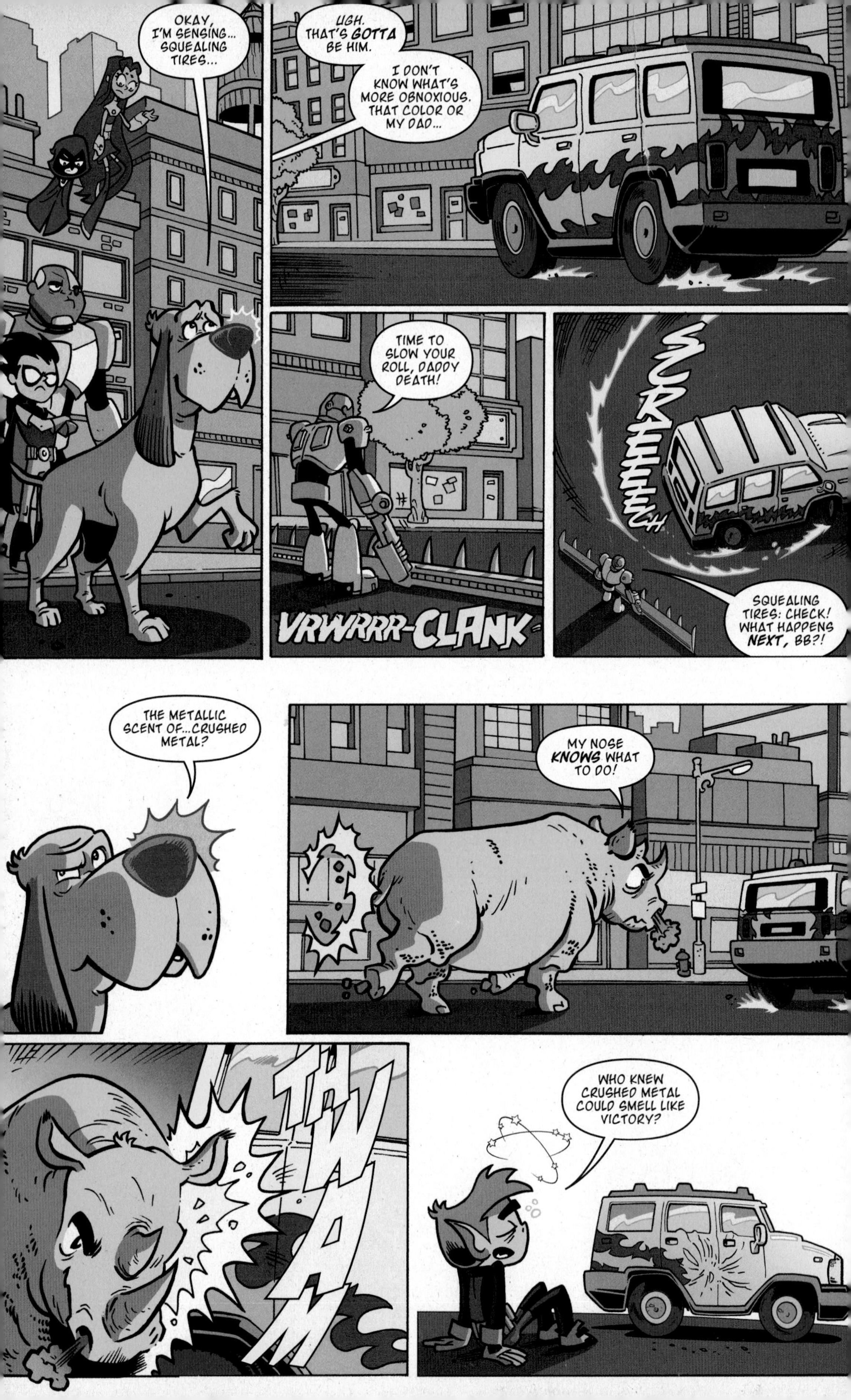
OKAY, I'M SENSING... SQUEALING TIRES...
UGH. THAT'S GOTTA BE HIM.
I DON'T KNOW WHAT'S MORE OBNOXIOUS. THAT COLOR OR MY DAD...
TIME TO SLOW YOUR ROLL, DADDY DEATH!
VRWRRR-CLANK
WURHHHHHH
SQUEALING TIRES: CHECK! WHAT HAPPENS NEXT, BB?!
THE METALLIC SCENT OF...CRUSHED METAL?
MY NOSE KNOWS WHAT TO DO!
THWAM
WHO KNEW CRUSHED METAL COULD SMELL LIKE VICTORY?

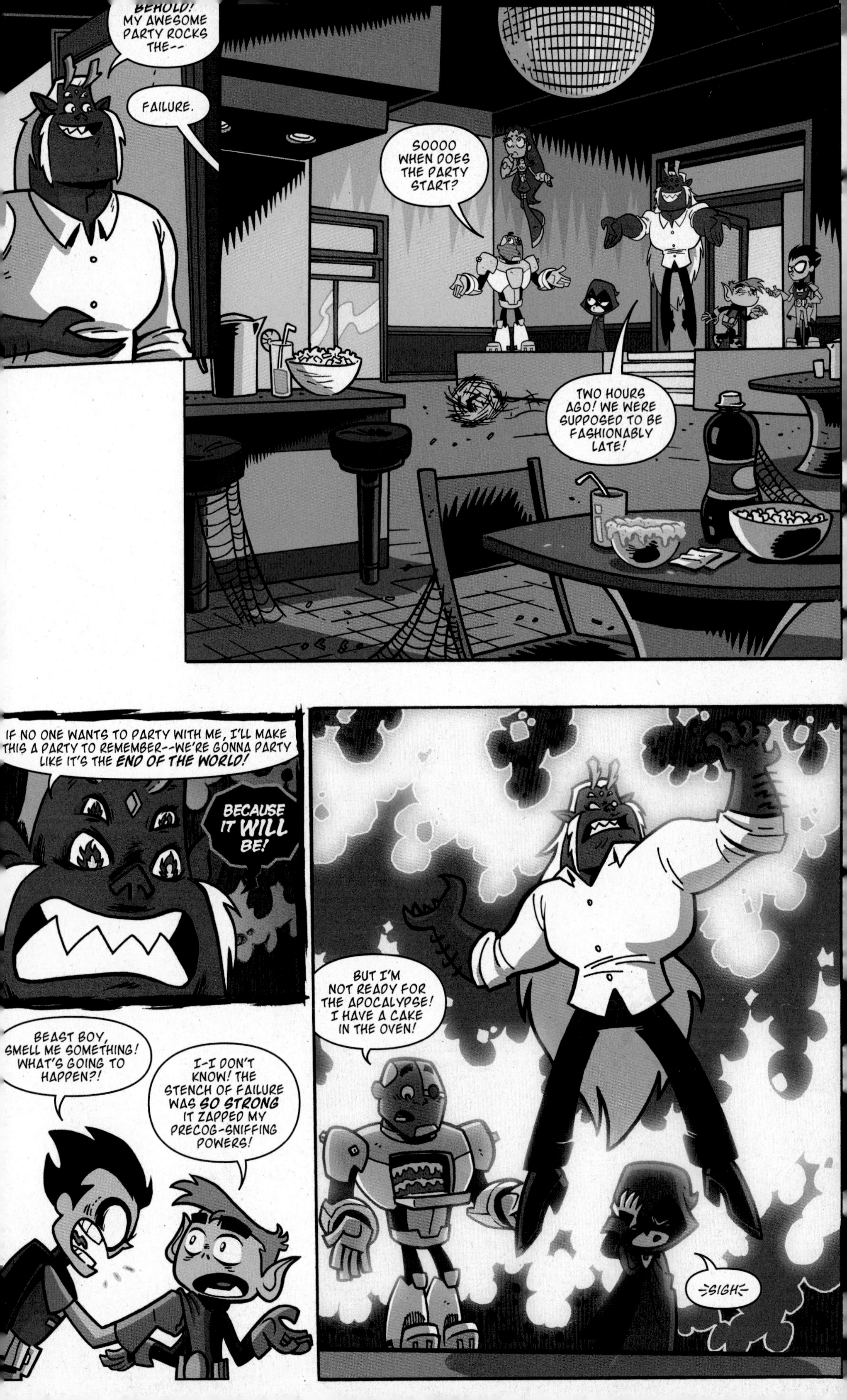
BEHOLD! MY AWESOME PARTY ROCKS THE--
FAILURE.
SOOOO WHEN DOES THE PARTY START?
TWO HOURS AGO! WE WERE SUPPOSED TO BE FASHIONABLY LATE!
IF NO ONE WANTS TO PARTY WITH ME, I'LL MAKE THIS A PARTY TO REMEMBER--WE'RE GONNA PARTY LIKE IT'S THE END OF THE WORLD!
BECAUSE IT WILL BE!
BUT I'M NOT READY FOR THE APOCALYPSE! I HAVE A CAKE IN THE OVEN!
BEAST BOY, SMELL ME SOMETHING! WHAT'S GOING TO HAPPEN?!
I-I DON'T KNOW! THE STENCH OF FAILURE WAS SO STRONG IT ZAPPED MY PRECOG-SNIFFING POWERS!
SIGH

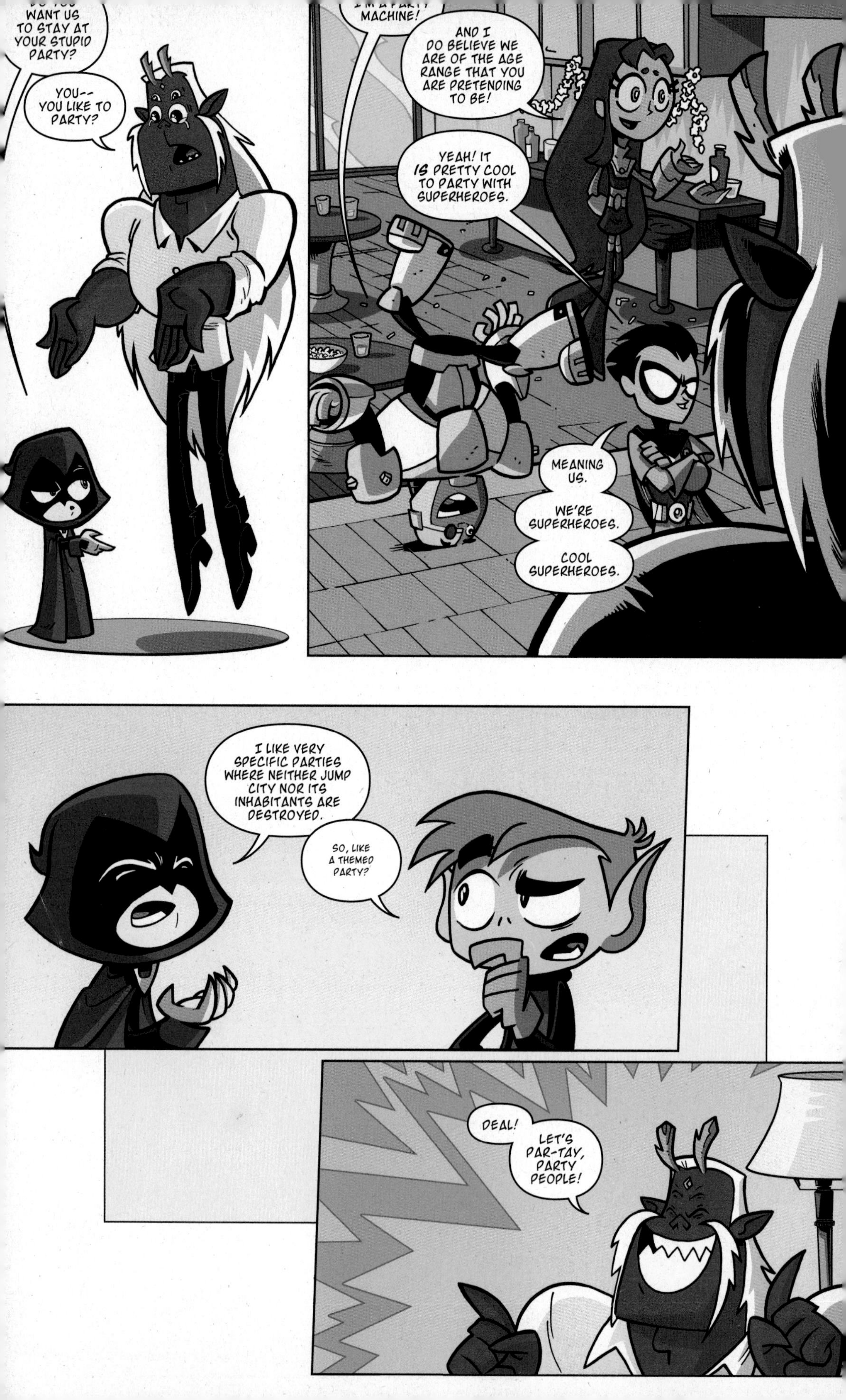
WANT US TO STAY AT YOUR STUPID PARTY?
YOU-- YOU LIKE TO PARTY?
MACHINE!
AND I DO BELIEVE WE ARE OF THE AGE RANGE THAT YOU ARE PRETENDING TO BE!
YEAH! IT IS PRETTY COOL TO PARTY WITH SUPERHEROES.
MEANING US.
WE'RE SUPERHEROES.
COOL SUPERHEROES.
I LIKE VERY SPECIFIC PARTIES WHERE NEITHER JUMP CITY NOR ITS INHABITANTS ARE DESTROYED.
SO, LIKE A THEMED PARTY?
DEAL!
LET'S PAR-TAY, PARTY PEOPLE!

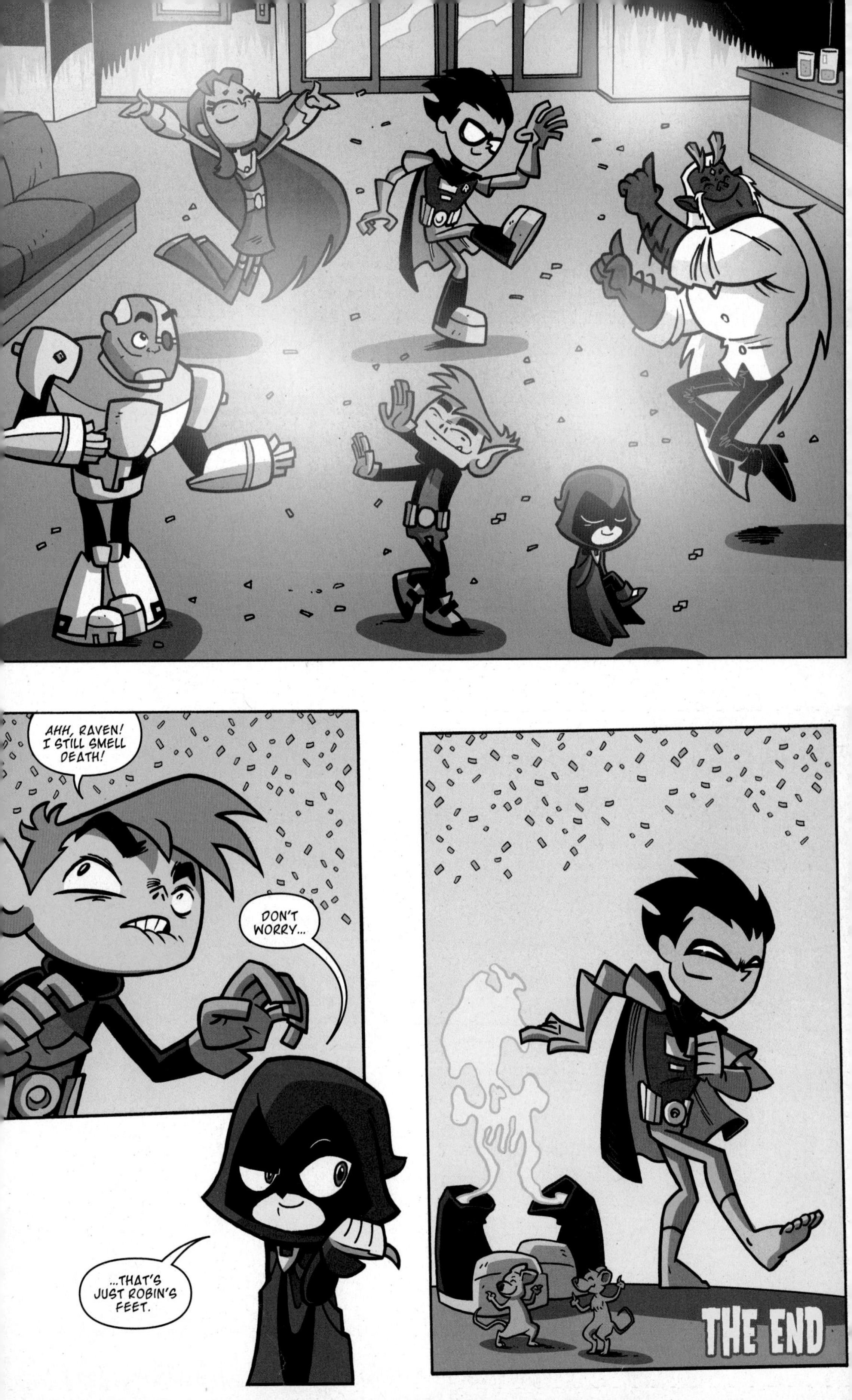
AHH, RAVEN! I STILL SMELL DEATH!
DON'T WORRY...
...THAT'S JUST ROBIN'S FEET.
THE END

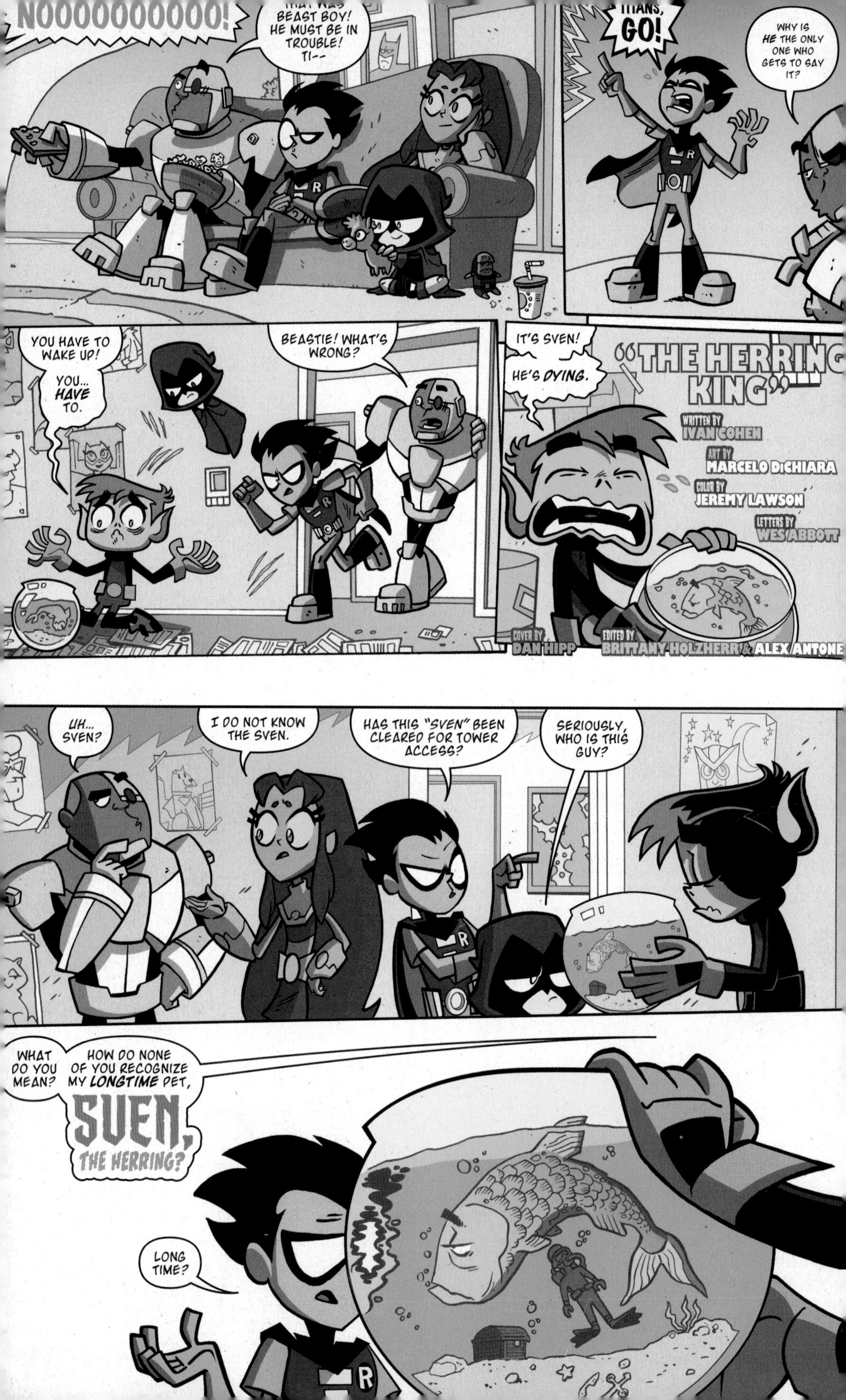

NOOOOOOOOOO!
BEAST BOY! HE MUST BE IN TROUBLE! TI--
GO!
WHY IS HE THE ONLY ONE WHO GETS TO SAY IT?
YOU HAVE TO WAKE UP!
YOU... HAVE TO.
BEASTIE! WHAT'S WRONG?
IT'S SVEN!
HE'S DYING.
"THE HERRING KING"
WRITTEN BY IVAN COHEN
ART BY MARCELO DiCHIARA
COLOR BY JEREMY LAWSON
LETTERS BY WES ABBOTT
COVER BY DAN HIPP
EDITED BY BRITTANY HOLZHERR & ALEX ANTONE
UH... SVEN?
I DO NOT KNOW THE SVEN.
HAS THIS "SVEN" BEEN CLEARED FOR TOWER ACCESS?
SERIOUSLY, WHO IS THIS GUY?
WHAT DO YOU MEAN?
HOW DO NONE OF YOU RECOGNIZE MY LONGTIME PET, SVEN, THE HERRING?
LONG TIME?

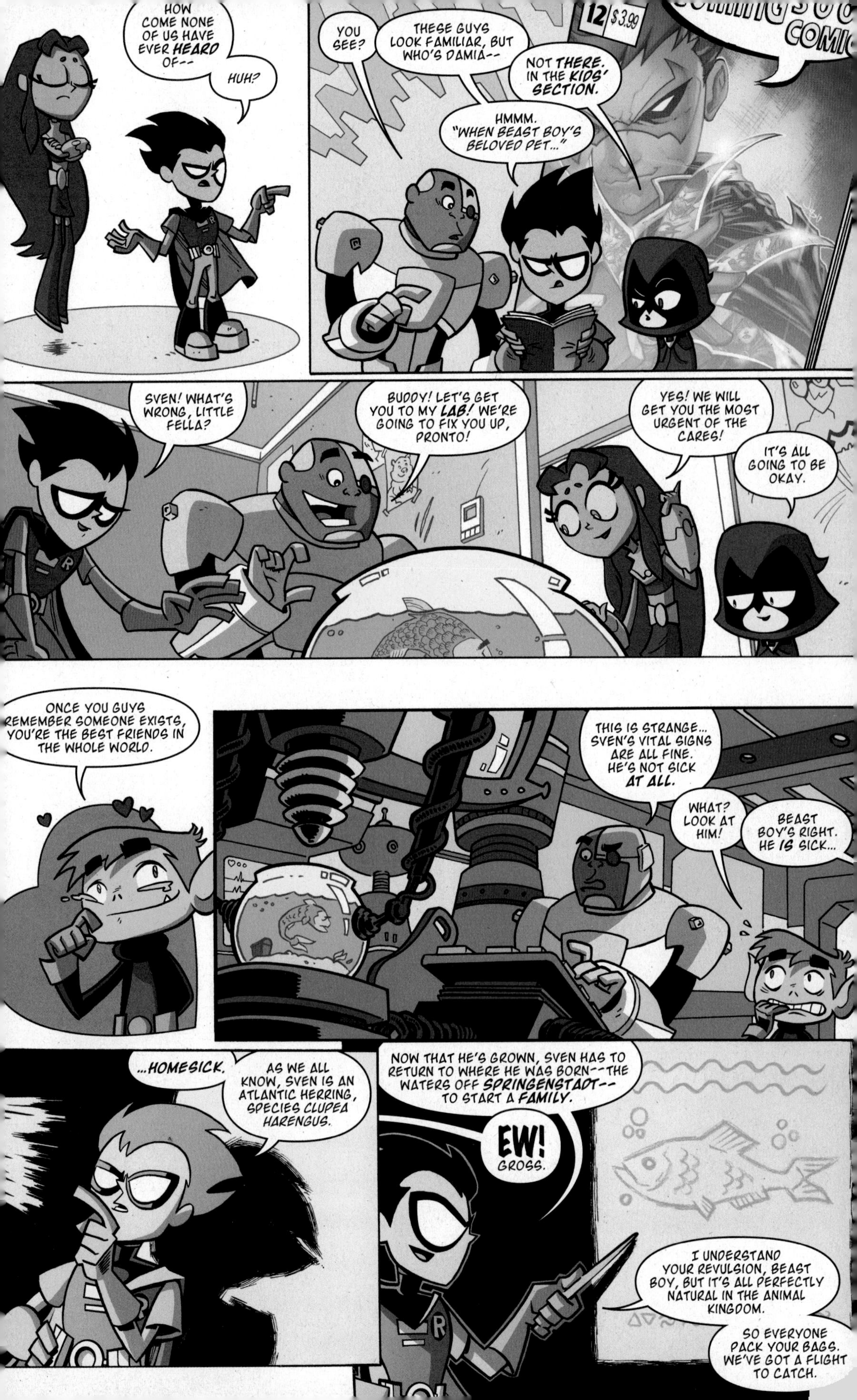
HOW COME NONE OF US HAVE EVER HEARD OF--
HUH?
YOU SEE?
THESE GUYS LOOK FAMILIAR, BUT WHO'S DAMIA--
NOT THERE. IN THE KIDS' SECTION.
HMMM. "WHEN BEAST BOY'S BELOVED PET..."
12 $3.99
COMIC
SVEN! WHAT'S WRONG, LITTLE FELLA?
BUDDY! LET'S GET YOU TO MY LAB! WE'RE GOING TO FIX YOU UP, PRONTO!
YES! WE WILL GET YOU THE MOST URGENT OF THE CARES!
IT'S ALL GOING TO BE OKAY.
ONCE YOU GUYS REMEMBER SOMEONE EXISTS, YOU'RE THE BEST FRIENDS IN THE WHOLE WORLD.
THIS IS STRANGE... SVEN'S VITAL SIGNS ARE ALL FINE. HE'S NOT SICK AT ALL.
WHAT? LOOK AT HIM!
BEAST BOY'S RIGHT. HE IS SICK...
...HOMESICK.
AS WE ALL KNOW, SVEN IS AN ATLANTIC HERRING, SPECIES CLUPEA HARENGUS.
NOW THAT HE'S GROWN, SVEN HAS TO RETURN TO WHERE HE WAS BORN--THE WATERS OFF SPRINGENSTADT--TO START A FAMILY.
EW! GROSS.
I UNDERSTAND YOUR REVULSION, BEAST BOY, BUT IT'S ALL PERFECTLY NATURAL IN THE ANIMAL KINGDOM.
SO EVERYONE PACK YOUR BAGS. WE'VE GOT A FLIGHT TO CATCH.

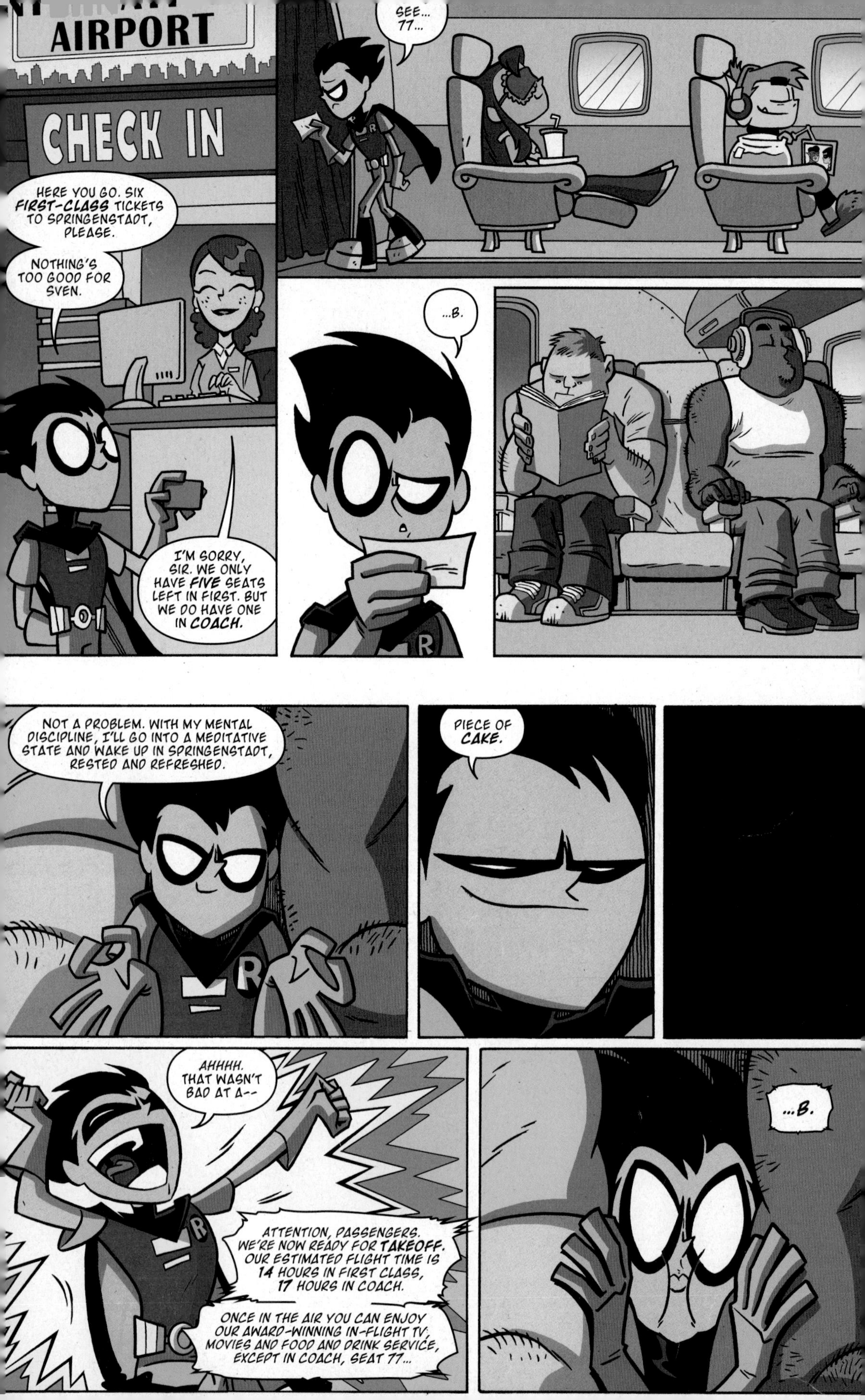
AIRPORT
CHECK IN
HERE YOU GO. SIX FIRST-CLASS TICKETS TO SPRINGENSTADT, PLEASE.
NOTHING'S TOO GOOD FOR SVEN.
I'M SORRY, SIR. WE ONLY HAVE FIVE SEATS LEFT IN FIRST. BUT WE DO HAVE ONE IN COACH.
SEE... 77...
...B.
NOT A PROBLEM. WITH MY MENTAL DISCIPLINE, I'LL GO INTO A MEDITATIVE STATE AND WAKE UP IN SPRINGENSTADT, RESTED AND REFRESHED.
PIECE OF CAKE.
AHHHH. THAT WASN'T BAD AT A--
ATTENTION, PASSENGERS. WE'RE NOW READY FOR TAKEOFF. OUR ESTIMATED FLIGHT TIME IS 14 HOURS IN FIRST CLASS, 17 HOURS IN COACH.
ONCE IN THE AIR YOU CAN ENJOY OUR AWARD-WINNING IN-FLIGHT TV, MOVIES AND FOOD AND DRINK SERVICE, EXCEPT IN COACH, SEAT 77...
...B.

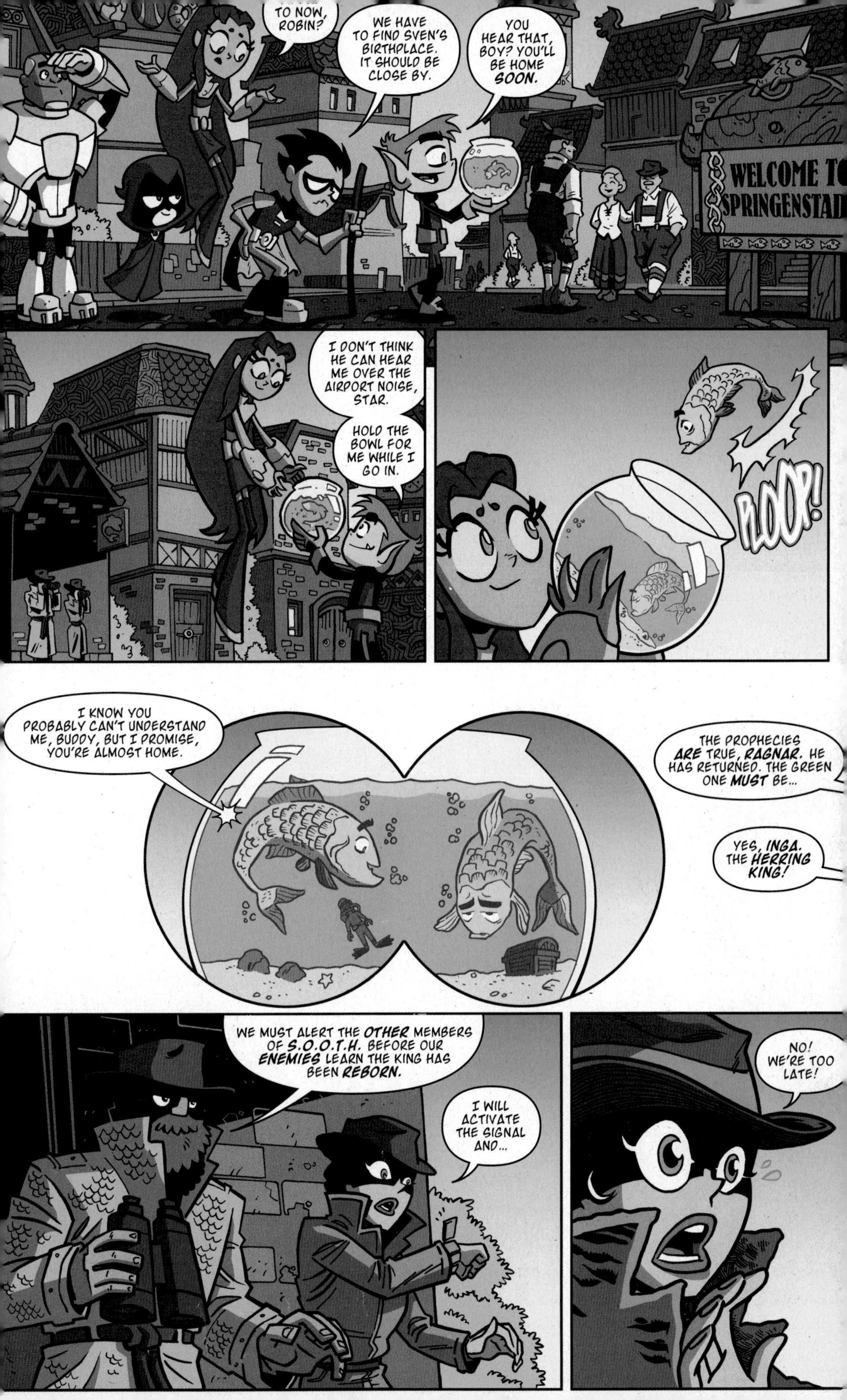
TO NOW, ROBIN?
WE HAVE TO FIND SVEN'S BIRTHPLACE. IT SHOULD BE CLOSE BY.
YOU HEAR THAT, BOY? YOU'LL BE HOME SOON.
WELCOME TO SPRINGENSTAD
I DON'T THINK HE CAN HEAR ME OVER THE AIRPORT NOISE, STAR.
HOLD THE BOWL FOR ME WHILE I GO IN.
PLOOP!
I KNOW YOU PROBABLY CAN'T UNDERSTAND ME, BUDDY, BUT I PROMISE, YOU'RE ALMOST HOME.
THE PROPHECIES ARE TRUE, RAGNAR. HE HAS RETURNED. THE GREEN ONE MUST BE...
YES, INGA. THE HERRING KING!
WE MUST ALERT THE OTHER MEMBERS OF S.O.O.T.H. BEFORE OUR ENEMIES LEARN THE KING HAS BEEN REBORN.
I WILL ACTIVATE THE SIGNAL AND...
NO! WE'RE TOO LATE!

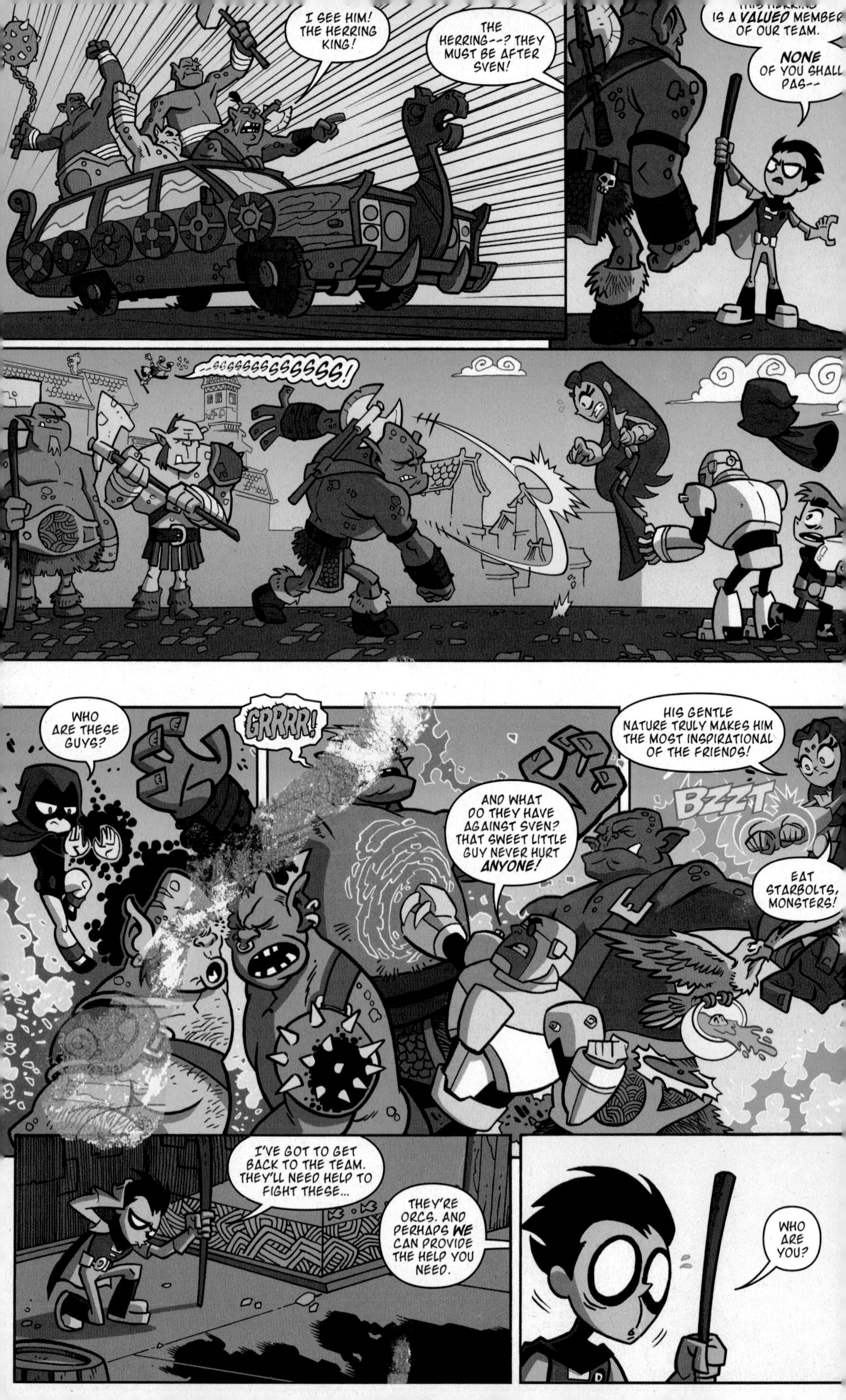
I SEE HIM! THE HERRING KING!
THE HERRING--? THEY MUST BE AFTER SVEN!
IS A VALUED MEMBER OF OUR TEAM.
NONE OF YOU SHALL PAS--
--SSSSSSSSSSSSSS!
WHO ARE THESE GUYS?
GRRRR!
AND WHAT DO THEY HAVE AGAINST SVEN? THAT SWEET LITTLE GUY NEVER HURT ANYONE!
HIS GENTLE NATURE TRULY MAKES HIM THE MOST INSPIRATIONAL OF THE FRIENDS!
BZZT
EAT STARBOLTS, MONSTERS!
I'VE GOT TO GET BACK TO THE TEAM. THEY'LL NEED HELP TO FIGHT THESE...
THEY'RE ORCS. AND PERHAPS WE CAN PROVIDE THE HELP YOU NEED.
WHO ARE YOU?

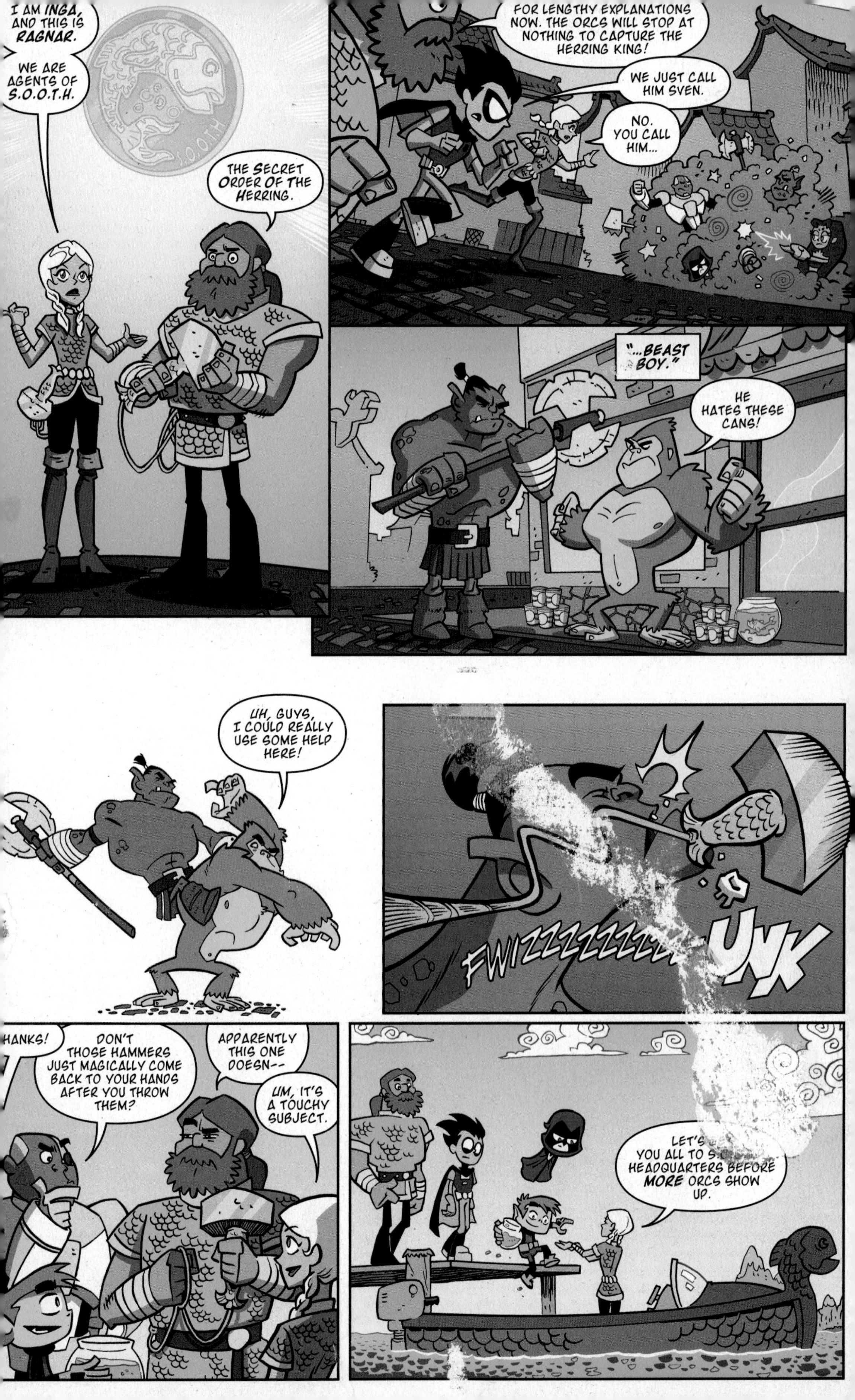

I AM INGA, AND THIS IS RAGNAR.
WE ARE AGENTS OF S.O.O.T.H.
THE SECRET ORDER OF THE HERRING.
FOR LENGTHY EXPLANATIONS NOW. THE ORCS WILL STOP AT NOTHING TO CAPTURE THE HERRING KING!
WE JUST CALL HIM SVEN.
NO. YOU CALL HIM...
"...BEAST BOY."
HE HATES THESE CANS!
UH, GUYS, I COULD REALLY USE SOME HELP HERE!
FWIZZZZZZZ
UNK
HANKS!
DON'T THOSE HAMMERS JUST MAGICALLY COME BACK TO YOUR HANDS AFTER YOU THROW THEM?
APPARENTLY THIS ONE DOESN--
UM, IT'S A TOUCHY SUBJECT.
LET'S
YOU ALL TO S
HEADQUARTERS BEFORE MORE ORCS SHOW UP.

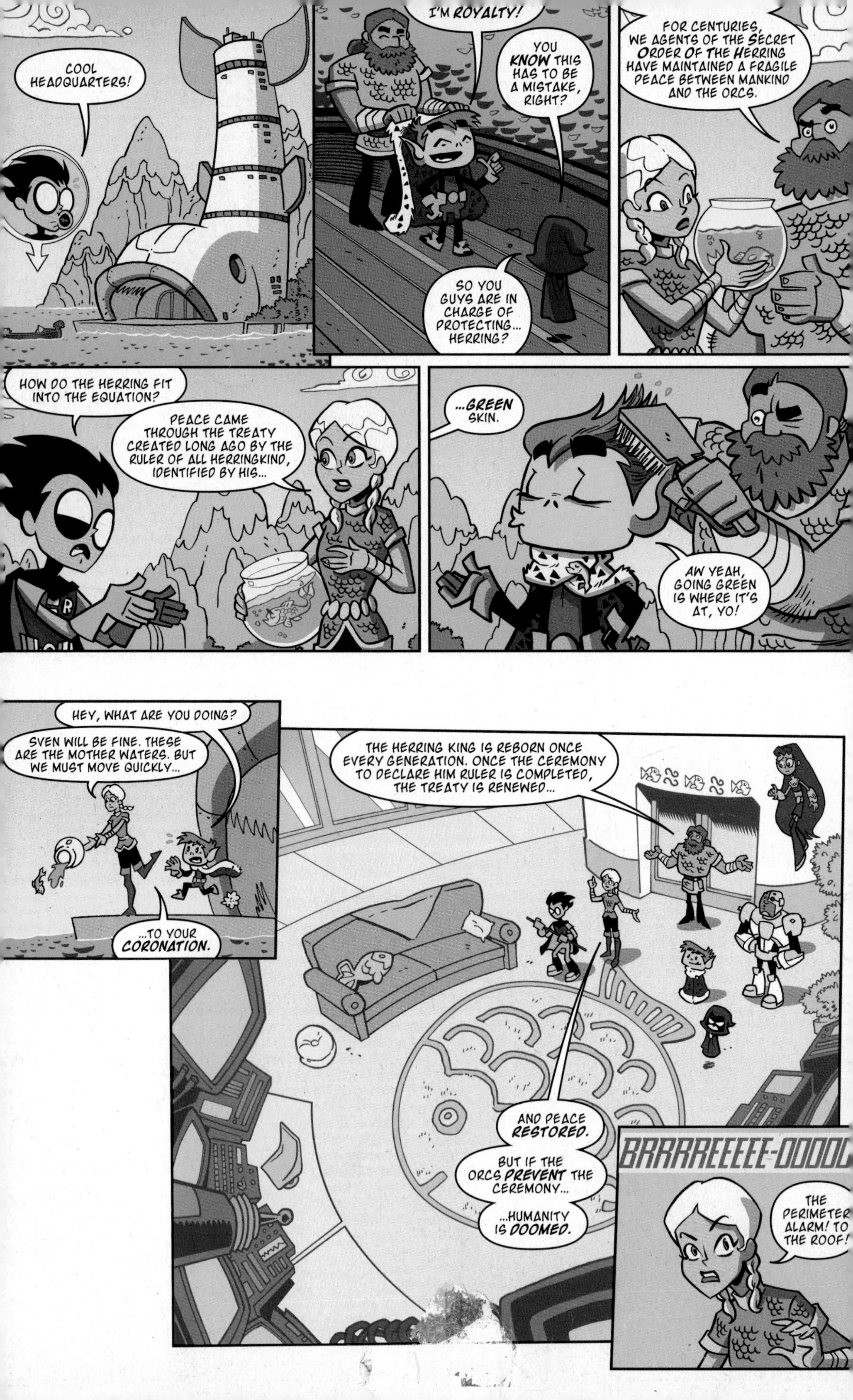
COOL HEADQUARTERS!
I'M ROYALTY!
YOU KNOW THIS HAS TO BE A MISTAKE, RIGHT?
SO YOU GUYS ARE IN CHARGE OF PROTECTING... HERRING?
FOR CENTURIES, WE AGENTS OF THE SECRET ORDER OF THE HERRING HAVE MAINTAINED A FRAGILE PEACE BETWEEN MANKIND AND THE ORCS.
HOW DO THE HERRING FIT INTO THE EQUATION?
PEACE CAME THROUGH THE TREATY CREATED LONG AGO BY THE RULER OF ALL HERRINGKIND, IDENTIFIED BY HIS...
...GREEN SKIN.
AW YEAH, GOING GREEN IS WHERE IT'S AT, YO!
HEY, WHAT ARE YOU DOING?
SVEN WILL BE FINE. THESE ARE THE MOTHER WATERS. BUT WE MUST MOVE QUICKLY...
...TO YOUR CORONATION.
THE HERRING KING IS REBORN ONCE EVERY GENERATION. ONCE THE CEREMONY TO DECLARE HIM RULER IS COMPLETED, THE TREATY IS RENEWED...
AND PEACE RESTORED.
BUT IF THE ORCS PREVENT THE CEREMONY...
...HUMANITY IS DOOMED.
BRRRREEEEE-OOOO
THE PERIMETER ALARM! TO THE ROOF!

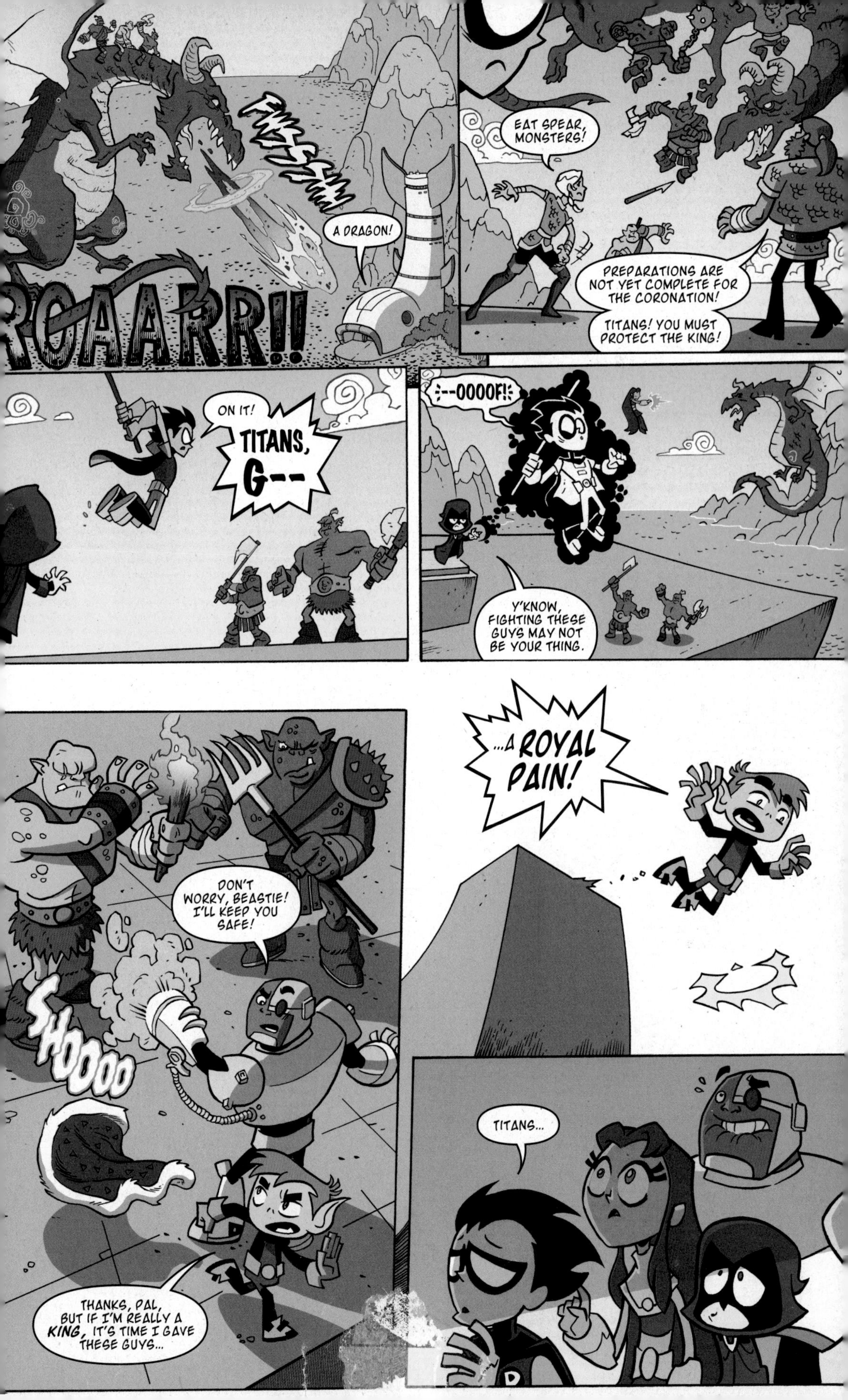

A DRAGON!
ROAARR!!
EAT SPEAR, MONSTERS!
PREPARATIONS ARE NOT YET COMPLETE FOR THE CORONATION!
TITANS! YOU MUST PROTECT THE KING!
ON IT!
TITANS, G--
--OOOOF!
Y'KNOW, FIGHTING THESE GUYS MAY NOT BE YOUR THING.
DON'T WORRY, BEASTIE! I'LL KEEP YOU SAFE!
SHOOOO
THANKS, PAL, BUT IF I'M REALLY A KING, IT'S TIME I GAVE THESE GUYS...
...A ROYAL PAIN!
TITANS...

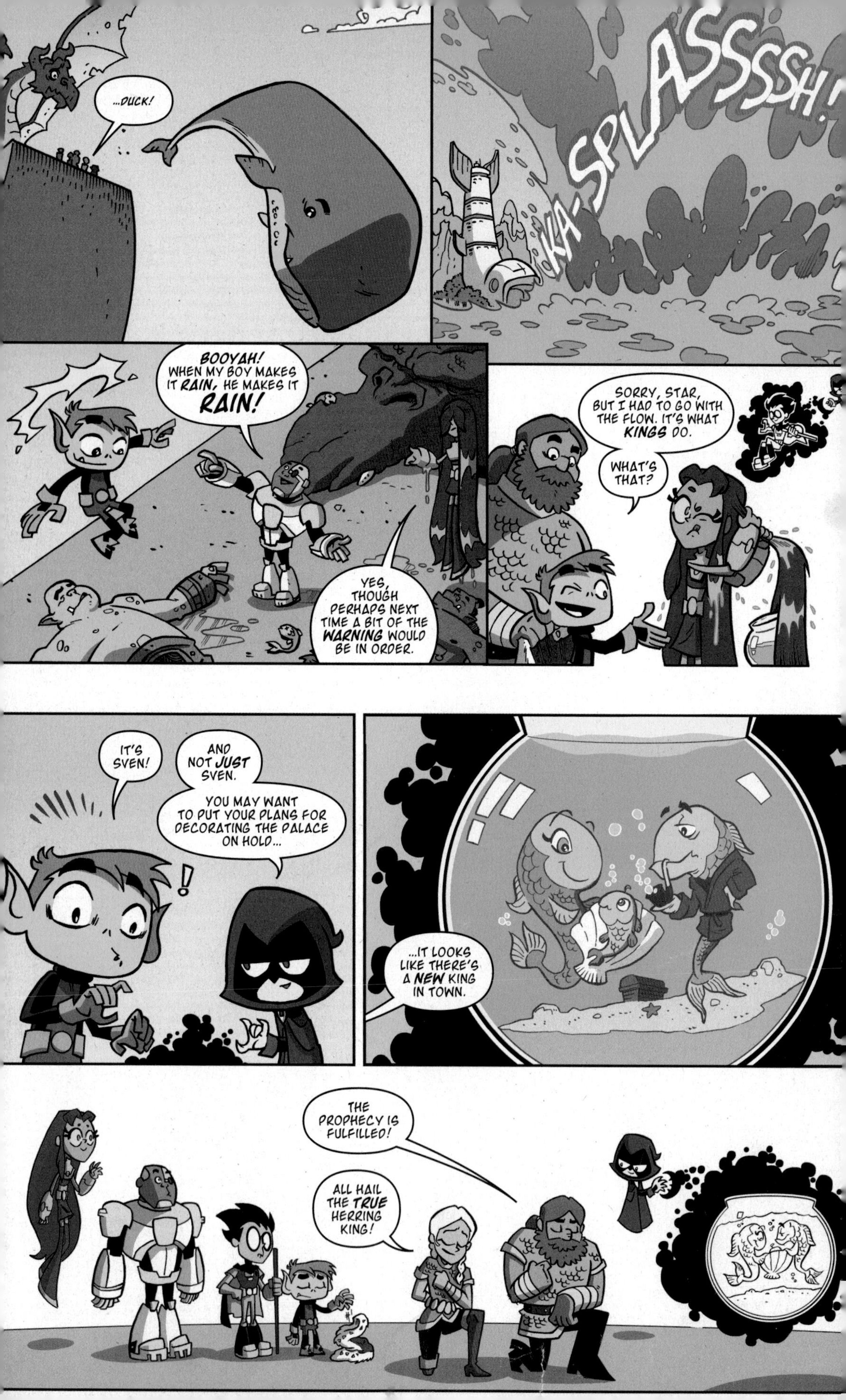
...DUCK!
KA-SPLASSSSH!
BOOYAH! WHEN MY BOY MAKES IT RAIN, HE MAKES IT RAIN!
YES, THOUGH PERHAPS NEXT TIME A BIT OF THE WARNING WOULD BE IN ORDER.
SORRY, STAR, BUT I HAD TO GO WITH THE FLOW. IT'S WHAT KINGS DO.
WHAT'S THAT?
IT'S SVEN!
AND NOT JUST SVEN.
YOU MAY WANT TO PUT YOUR PLANS FOR DECORATING THE PALACE ON HOLD...
...IT LOOKS LIKE THERE'S A NEW KING IN TOWN.
THE PROPHECY IS FULFILLED!
ALL HAIL THE TRUE HERRING KING!

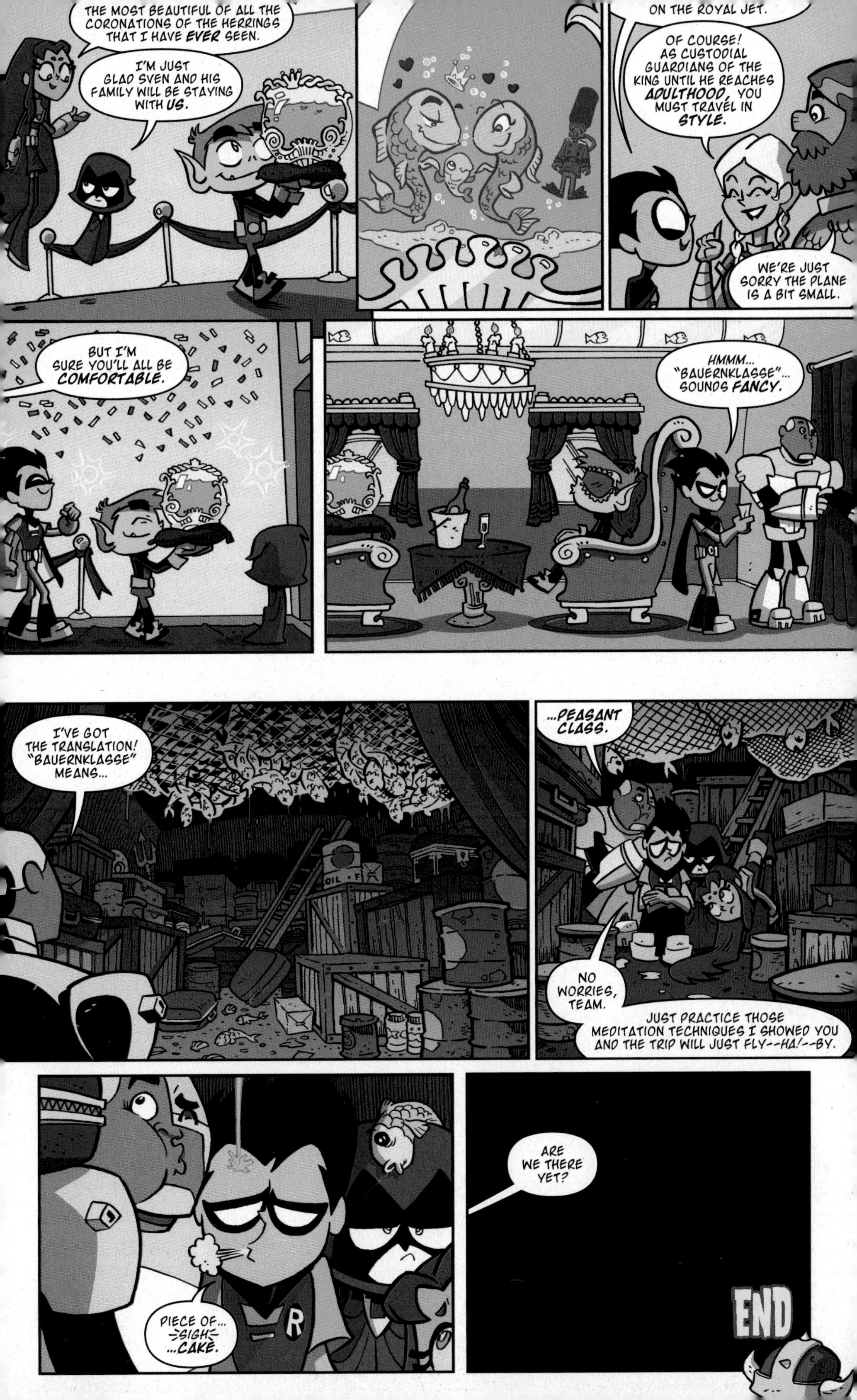
THE MOST BEAUTIFUL OF ALL THE CORONATIONS OF THE HERRINGS THAT I HAVE EVER SEEN.
I'M JUST GLAD SVEN AND HIS FAMILY WILL BE STAYING WITH US.
ON THE ROYAL JET.
OF COURSE! AS CUSTODIAL GUARDIANS OF THE KING UNTIL HE REACHES ADULTHOOD, YOU MUST TRAVEL IN STYLE.
WE'RE JUST SORRY THE PLANE IS A BIT SMALL.
BUT I'M SURE YOU'LL ALL BE COMFORTABLE.
HMMM... "BAUERNKLASSE"... SOUNDS FANCY.
I'VE GOT THE TRANSLATION! "BAUERNKLASSE" MEANS...
...PEASANT CLASS.
NO WORRIES, TEAM.
JUST PRACTICE THOSE MEDITATION TECHNIQUES I SHOWED YOU AND THE TRIP WILL JUST FLY--HA!--BY.
PIECE OF... SIGH ...CAKE.
ARE WE THERE YET?
END

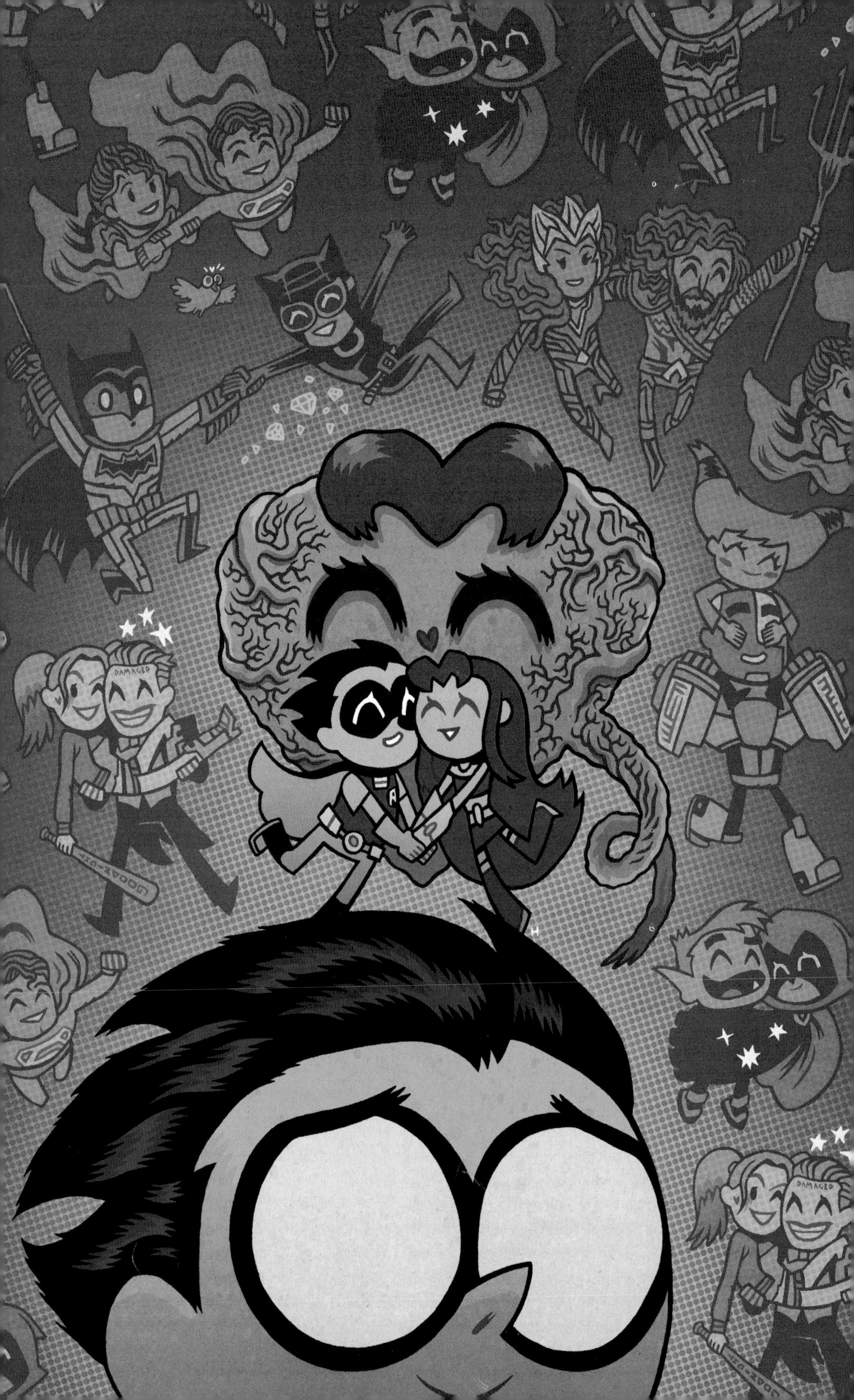
DAMAGED

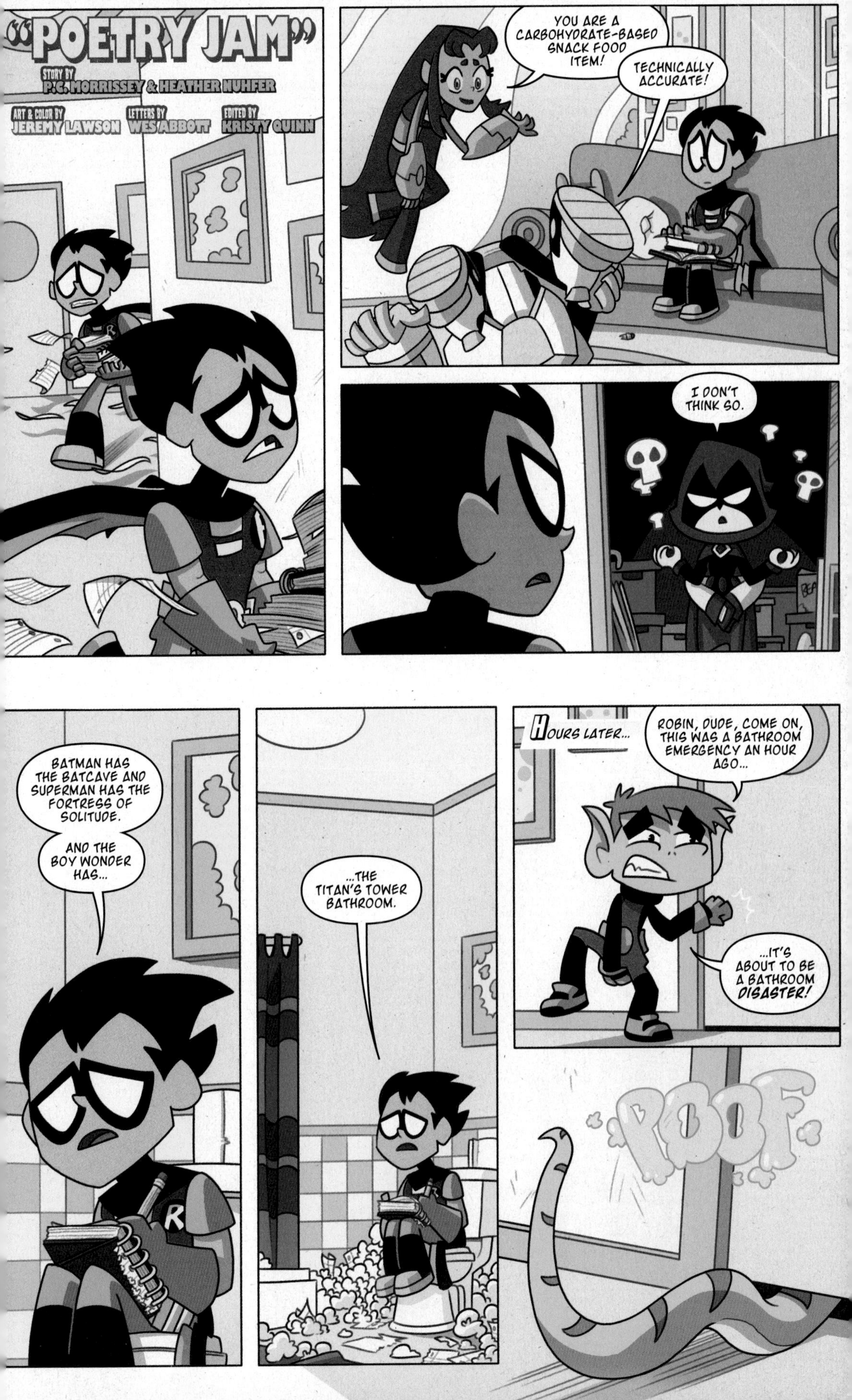

"POETRY JAM"
STORY BY P.C. MORRISSEY & HEATHER NUHFER
ART & COLOR BY JEREMY LAWSON
LETTERS BY WES ABBOTT
EDITED BY KRISTY QUINN
YOU ARE A CARBOHYDRATE-BASED SNACK FOOD ITEM!
TECHNICALLY ACCURATE!
I DON'T THINK SO.
BATMAN HAS THE BATCAVE AND SUPERMAN HAS THE FORTRESS OF SOLITUDE.
AND THE BOY WONDER HAS...
...THE TITAN'S TOWER BATHROOM.
HOURS LATER...
ROBIN, DUDE, COME ON, THIS WAS A BATHROOM EMERGENCY AN HOUR AGO...
...IT'S ABOUT TO BE A BATHROOM DISASTER!
POOF

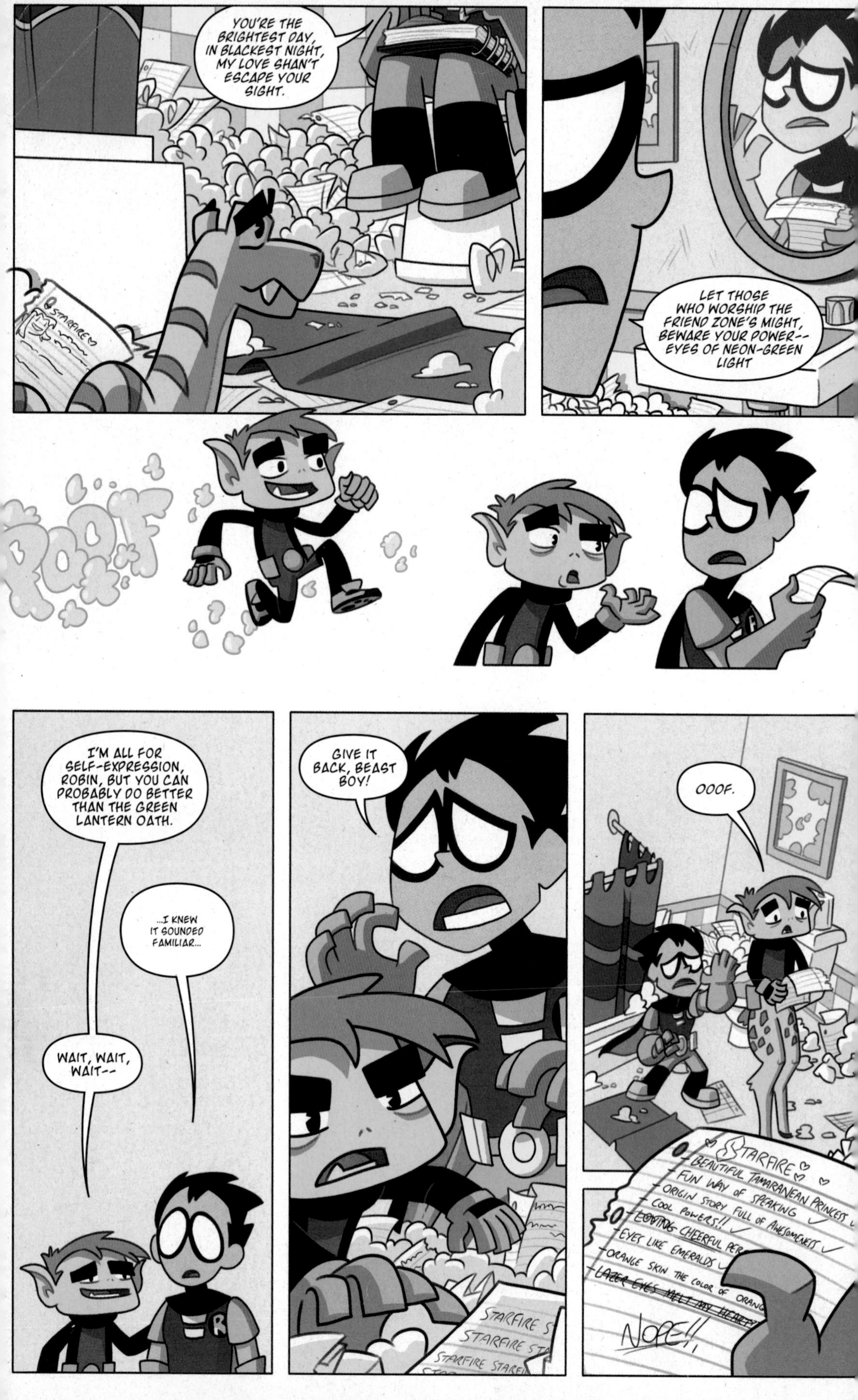
YOU'RE THE BRIGHTEST DAY, IN BLACKEST NIGHT, MY LOVE SHAN'T ESCAPE YOUR SIGHT.
STARFIRE
LET THOSE WHO WORSHIP THE FRIEND ZONE'S MIGHT, BEWARE YOUR POWER-- EYES OF NEON-GREEN LIGHT
POOF
I'M ALL FOR SELF-EXPRESSION, ROBIN, BUT YOU CAN PROBABLY DO BETTER THAN THE GREEN LANTERN OATH.
...I KNEW IT SOUNDED FAMILIAR...
WAIT, WAIT, WAIT--
GIVE IT BACK, BEAST BOY!
OOOF.
STARFIRE
BEAUTIFUL TAMARANEAN PRINCESS
FUN WAY OF SPEAKING
ORIGIN STORY FULL OF AWESOMENESS
COOL POWERS!!
EYES LIKE EMERALDS
NOPE!!

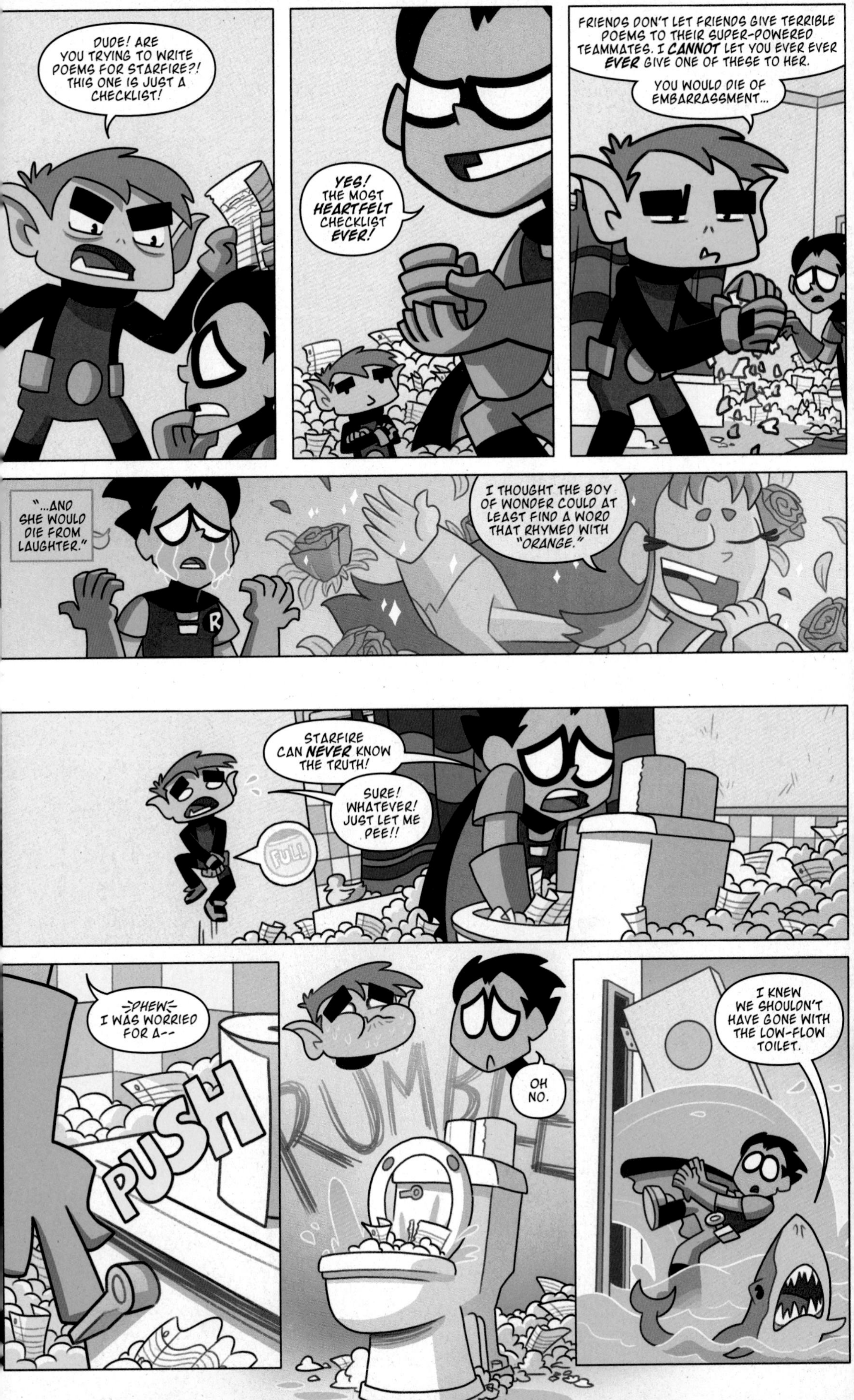
DUDE! ARE YOU TRYING TO WRITE POEMS FOR STARFIRE?! THIS ONE IS JUST A CHECKLIST!
YES! THE MOST HEARTFELT CHECKLIST EVER!
FRIENDS DON'T LET FRIENDS GIVE TERRIBLE POEMS TO THEIR SUPER-POWERED TEAMMATES. I CANNOT LET YOU EVER EVER EVER GIVE ONE OF THESE TO HER.
YOU WOULD DIE OF EMBARRASSMENT...
"...AND SHE WOULD DIE FROM LAUGHTER."
I THOUGHT THE BOY OF WONDER COULD AT LEAST FIND A WORD THAT RHYMED WITH "ORANGE."
STARFIRE CAN NEVER KNOW THE TRUTH!
SURE! WHATEVER! JUST LET ME PEE!!
FULL
PHEW I WAS WORRIED FOR A--
PUSH
RUMBLE
OH NO.
I KNEW WE SHOULDN'T HAVE GONE WITH THE LOW-FLOW TOILET.

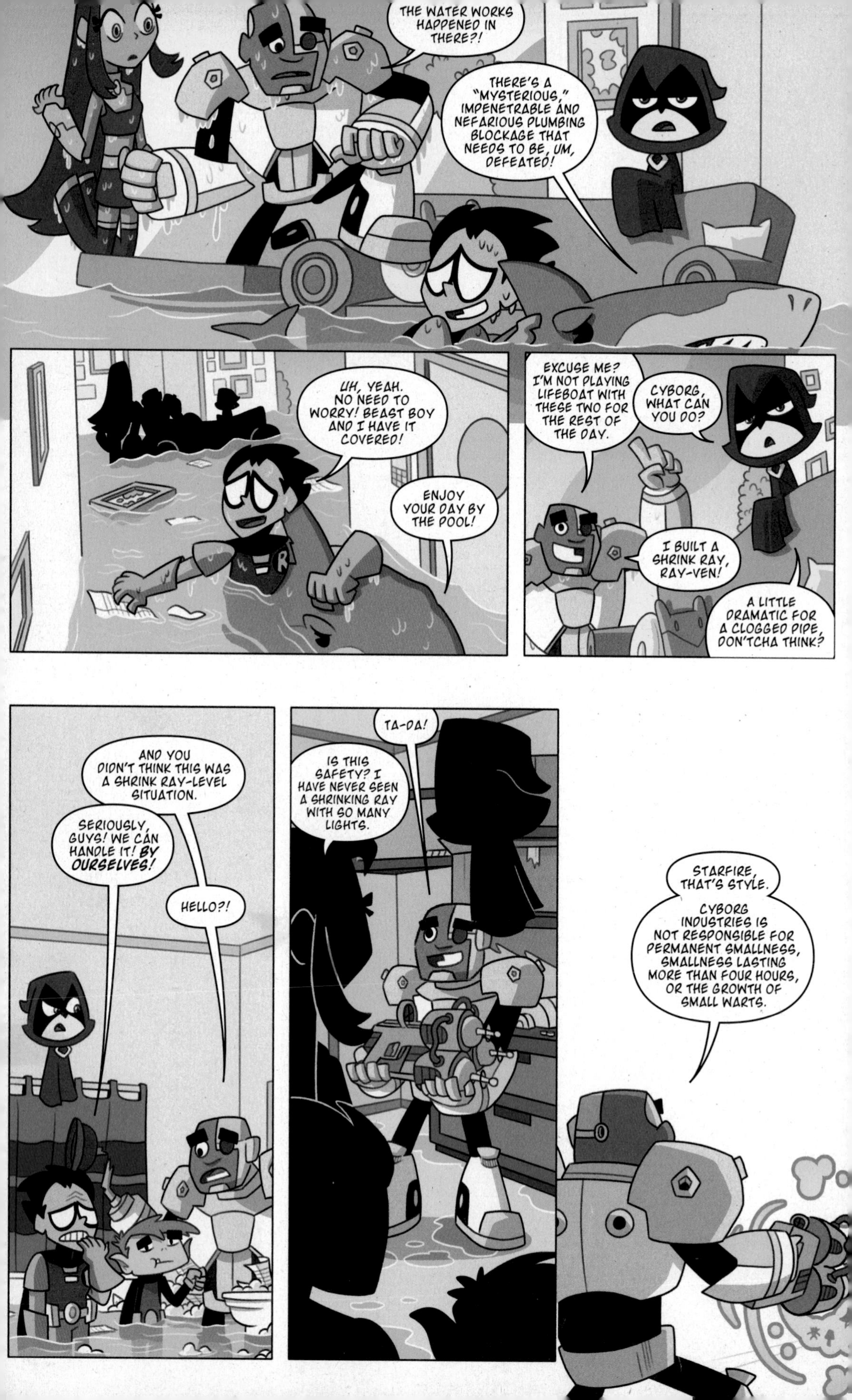
THE WATER WORKS HAPPENED IN THERE?!
THERE'S A "MYSTERIOUS," IMPENETRABLE AND NEFARIOUS PLUMBING BLOCKAGE THAT NEEDS TO BE, UM, DEFEATED!
UH, YEAH. NO NEED TO WORRY! BEAST BOY AND I HAVE IT COVERED!
ENJOY YOUR DAY BY THE POOL!
EXCUSE ME? I'M NOT PLAYING LIFEBOAT WITH THESE TWO FOR THE REST OF THE DAY.
CYBORG, WHAT CAN YOU DO?
I BUILT A SHRINK RAY, RAY-VEN!
A LITTLE DRAMATIC FOR A CLOGGED PIPE, DON'TCHA THINK?
AND YOU DIDN'T THINK THIS WAS A SHRINK RAY-LEVEL SITUATION.
SERIOUSLY, GUYS! WE CAN HANDLE IT! **BY OURSELVES!**
HELLO?!
TA-DA!
IS THIS SAFETY? I HAVE NEVER SEEN A SHRINKING RAY WITH SO MANY LIGHTS.
STARFIRE, THAT'S STYLE.
CYBORG INDUSTRIES IS NOT RESPONSIBLE FOR PERMANENT SMALLNESS, SMALLNESS LASTING MORE THAN FOUR HOURS, OR THE GROWTH OF SMALL WARTS.

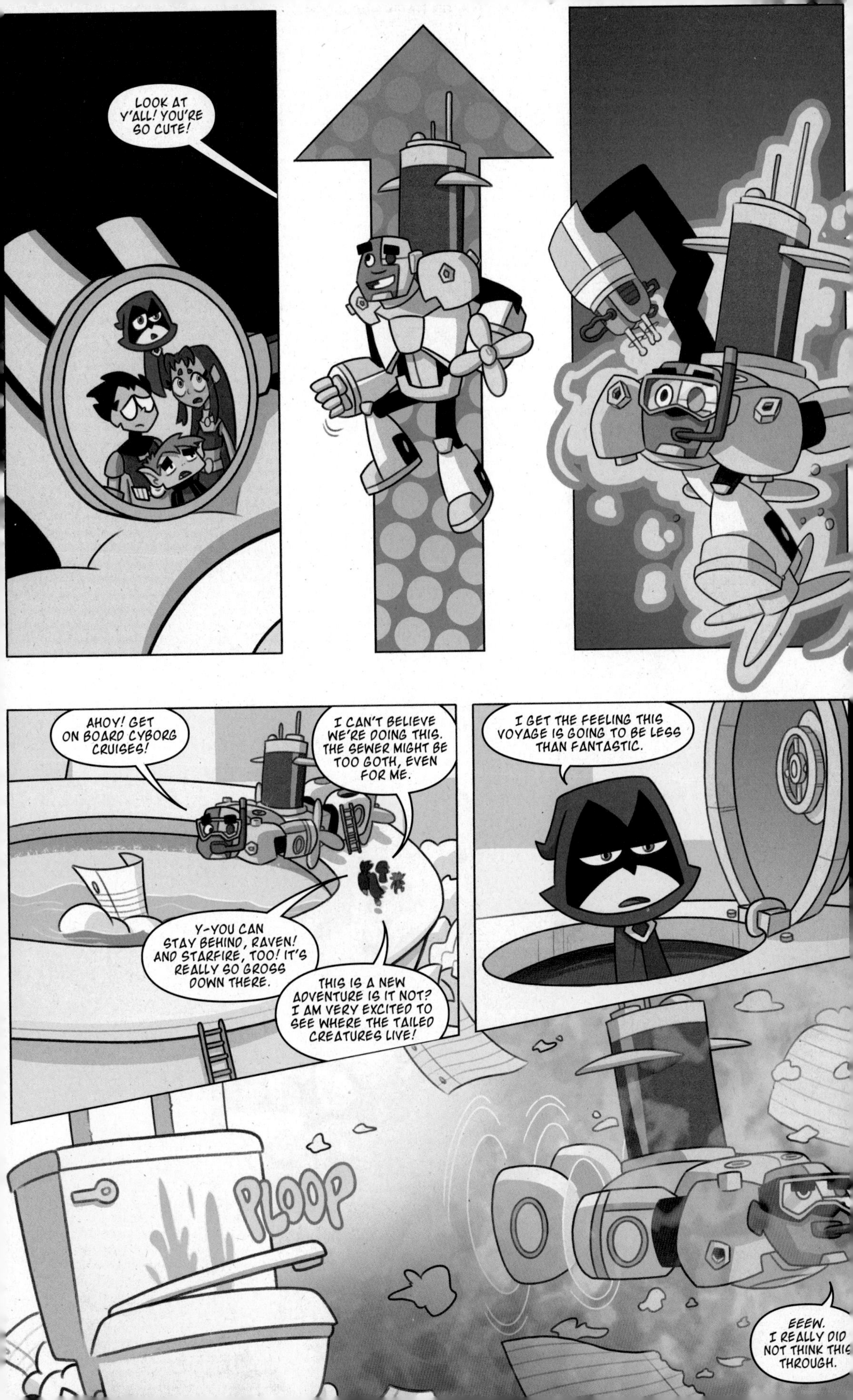
LOOK AT Y'ALL! YOU'RE SO CUTE!
AHOY! GET ON BOARD CYBORG CRUISES!
I CAN'T BELIEVE WE'RE DOING THIS. THE SEWER MIGHT BE TOO GOTH, EVEN FOR ME.
Y-YOU CAN STAY BEHIND, RAVEN! AND STARFIRE, TOO! IT'S REALLY SO GROSS DOWN THERE.
THIS IS A NEW ADVENTURE IS IT NOT? I AM VERY EXCITED TO SEE WHERE THE TAILED CREATURES LIVE!
I GET THE FEELING THIS VOYAGE IS GOING TO BE LESS THAN FANTASTIC.
PLOOP
EEEW. I REALLY DID NOT THINK THIS THROUGH.

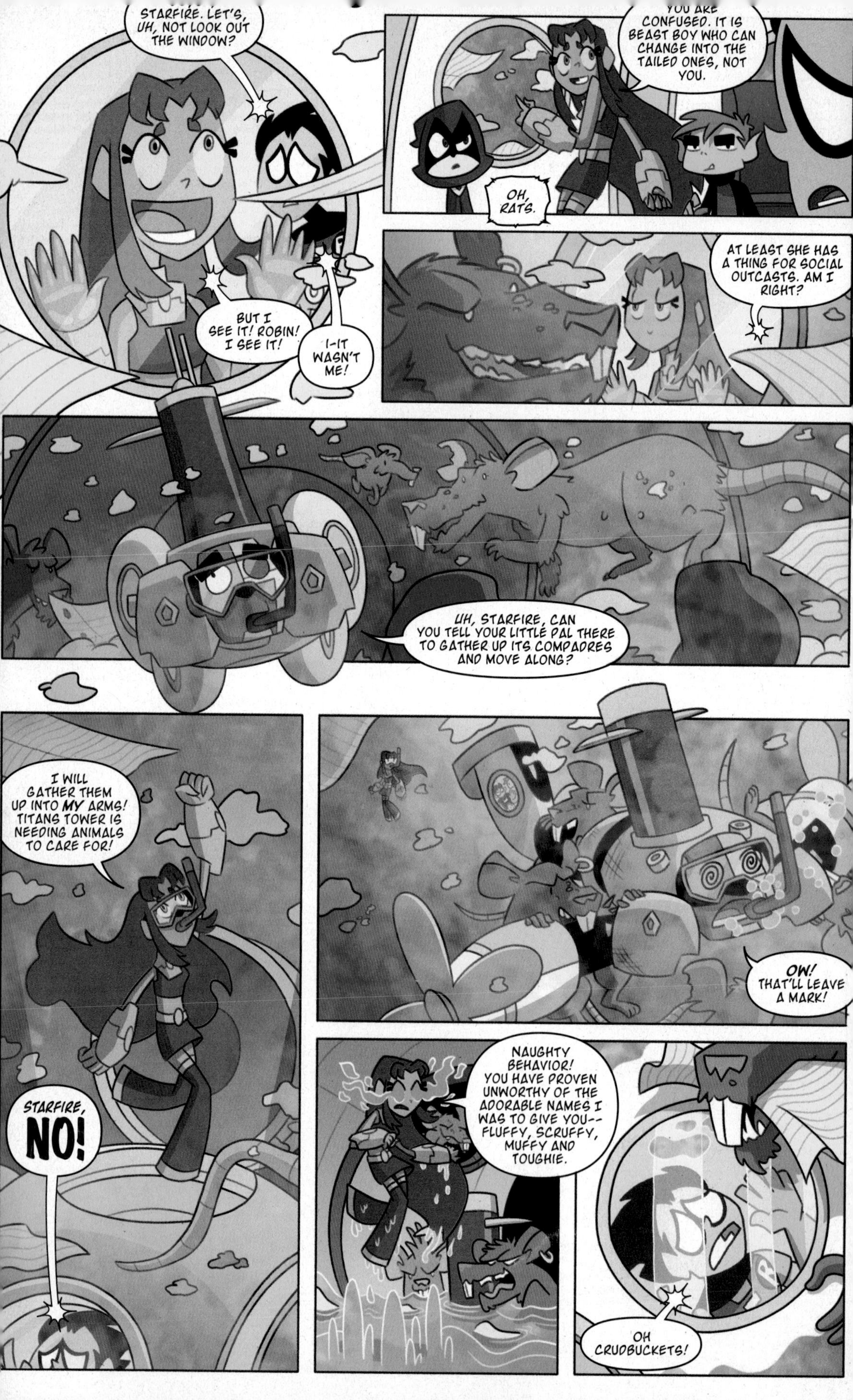
STARFIRE. LET'S, UH, NOT LOOK OUT THE WINDOW?
BUT I SEE IT! ROBIN! I SEE IT!
I-IT WASN'T ME!
YOU ARE CONFUSED. IT IS BEAST BOY WHO CAN CHANGE INTO THE TAILED ONES, NOT YOU.
OH, RATS.
AT LEAST SHE HAS A THING FOR SOCIAL OUTCASTS. AM I RIGHT?
UH, STARFIRE, CAN YOU TELL YOUR LITTLE PAL THERE TO GATHER UP ITS COMPADRES AND MOVE ALONG?
I WILL GATHER THEM UP INTO MY ARMS! TITANS TOWER IS NEEDING ANIMALS TO CARE FOR!
STARFIRE, NO!
OW! THAT'LL LEAVE A MARK!
NAUGHTY BEHAVIOR! YOU HAVE PROVEN UNWORTHY OF THE ADORABLE NAMES I WAS TO GIVE YOU--FLUFFY, SCRUFFY, MUFFY AND TOUGHIE.
OH CRUDBUCKETS!

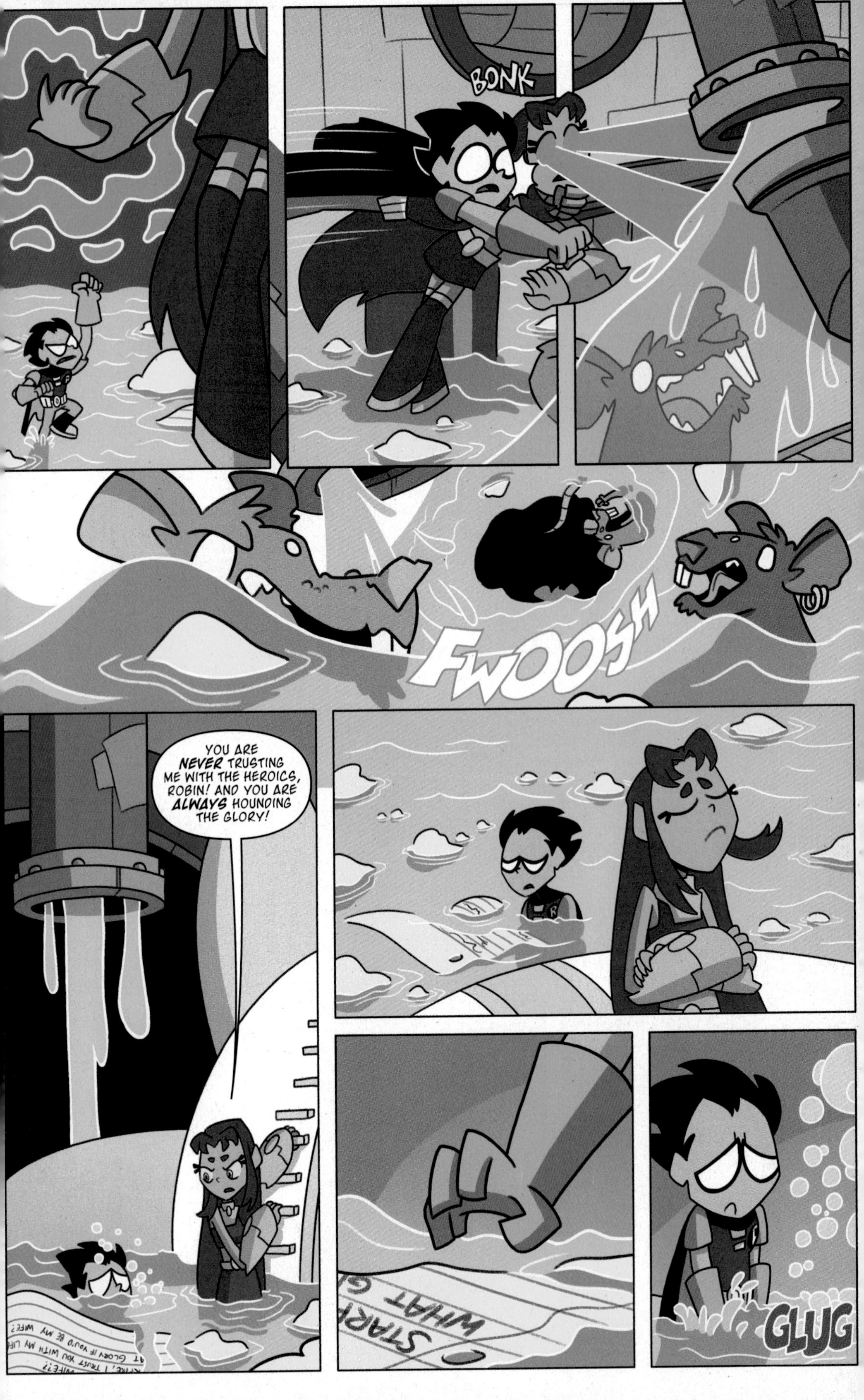
BONK
FWOOSH
YOU ARE NEVER TRUSTING ME WITH THE HEROICS, ROBIN! AND YOU ARE ALWAYS HOUNDING THE GLORY!
GLUG

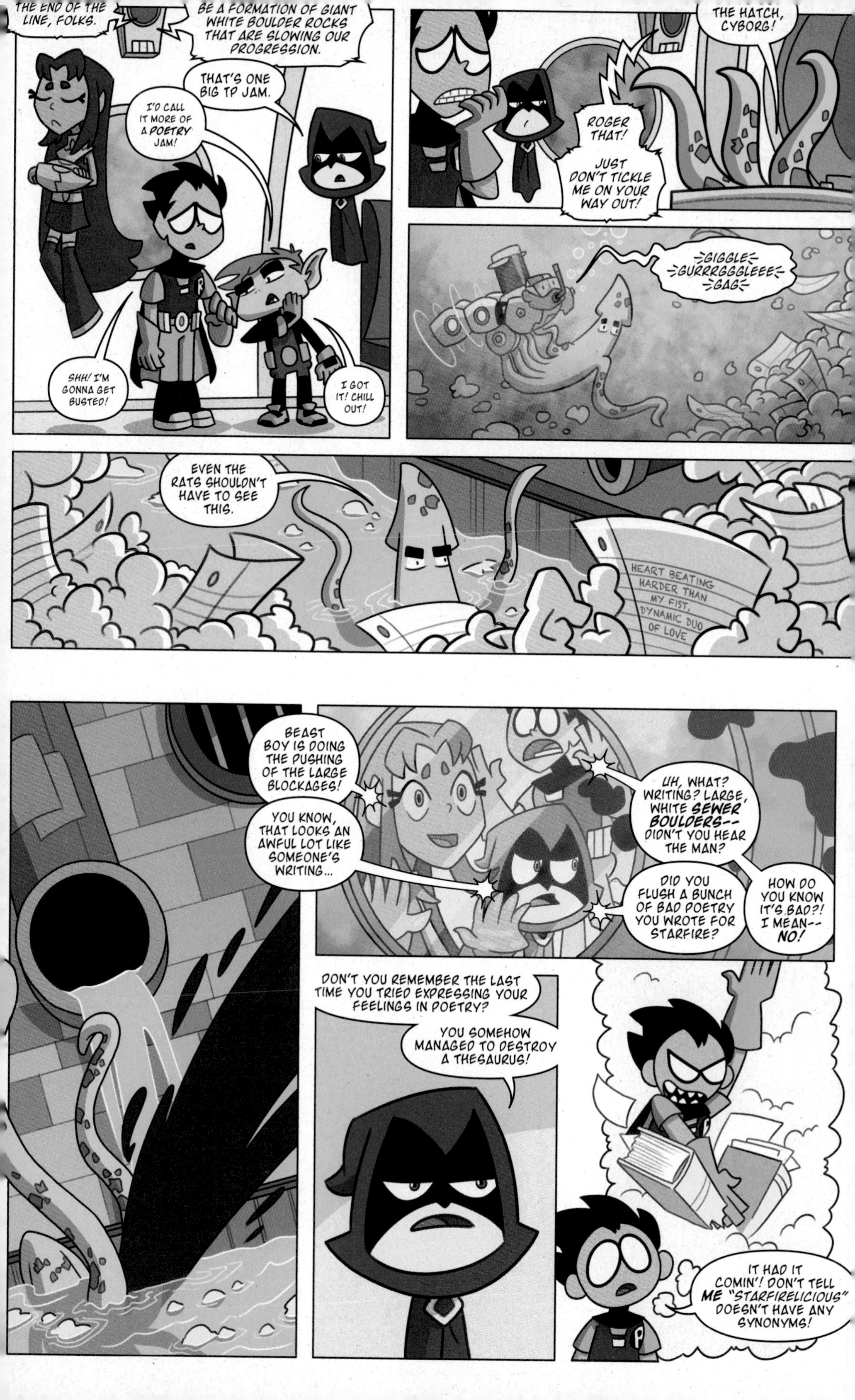
THE END OF THE LINE, FOLKS.
BE A FORMATION OF GIANT WHITE BOULDER ROCKS THAT ARE SLOWING OUR PROGRESSION.
THAT'S ONE BIG TP JAM.
I'D CALL IT MORE OF A POETRY JAM!
SHH! I'M GONNA GET BUSTED!
I GOT IT! CHILL OUT!
THE HATCH, CYBORG!
ROGER THAT!
JUST DON'T TICKLE ME ON YOUR WAY OUT!
GIGGLE GURRRGGGLEEE GAG
EVEN THE RATS SHOULDN'T HAVE TO SEE THIS.
HEART BEATING HARDER THAN MY FIST, DYNAMIC DUO OF LOVE
BEAST BOY IS DOING THE PUSHING OF THE LARGE BLOCKAGES!
YOU KNOW, THAT LOOKS AN AWFUL LOT LIKE SOMEONE'S WRITING...
UH, WHAT? WRITING? LARGE, WHITE SEWER BOULDERS-- DIDN'T YOU HEAR THE MAN?
DID YOU FLUSH A BUNCH OF BAD POETRY YOU WROTE FOR STARFIRE?
HOW DO YOU KNOW IT'S BAD?! I MEAN-- NO!
DON'T YOU REMEMBER THE LAST TIME YOU TRIED EXPRESSING YOUR FEELINGS IN POETRY?
YOU SOMEHOW MANAGED TO DESTROY A THESAURUS!
IT HAD IT COMIN'! DON'T TELL ME "STARFIRELICIOUS" DOESN'T HAVE ANY SYNONYMS!

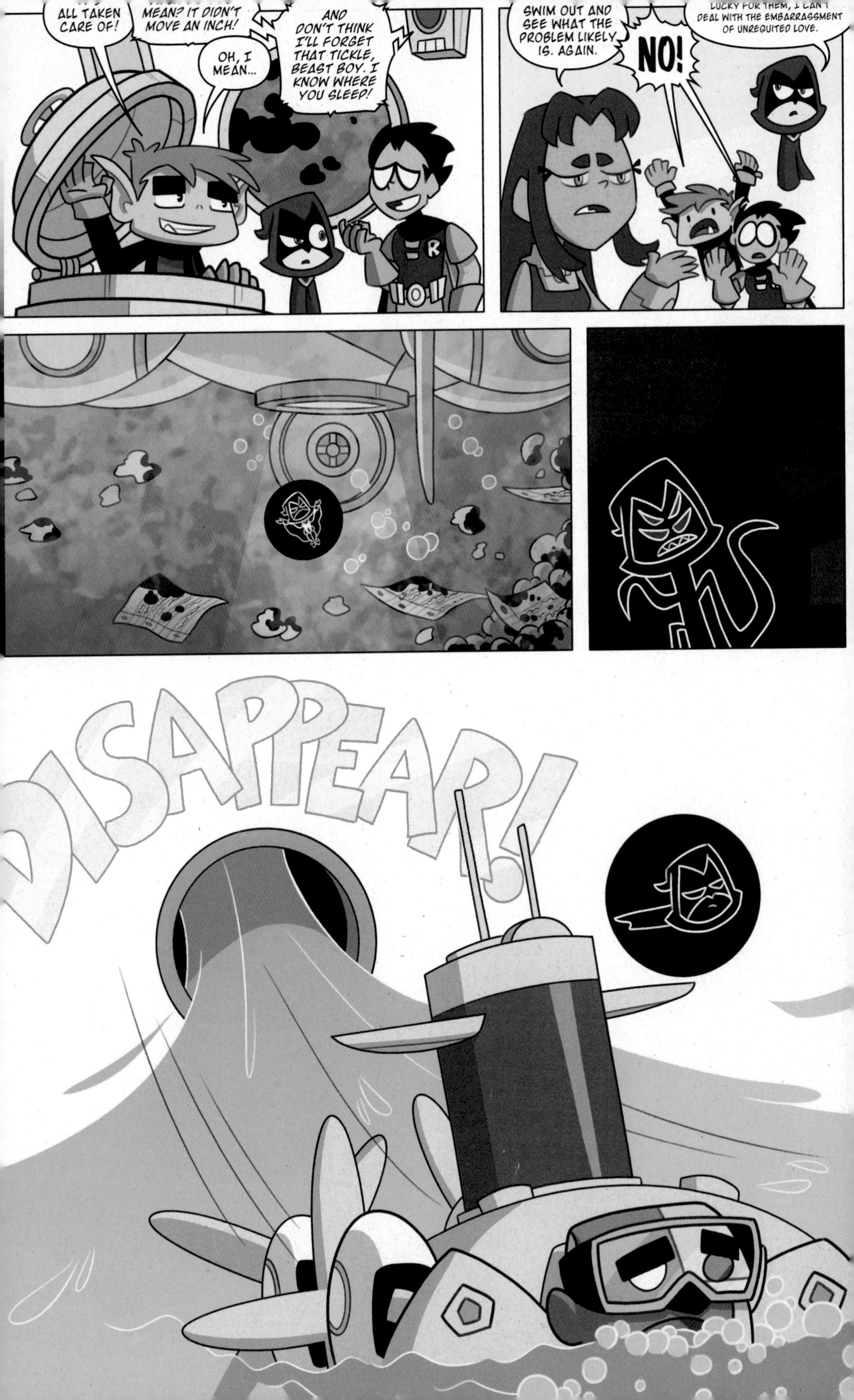
ALL TAKEN CARE OF!
MEAN? IT DIDN'T MOVE AN INCH!
OH, I MEAN...
AND DON'T THINK I'LL FORGET THAT TICKLE, BEAST BOY. I KNOW WHERE YOU SLEEP!
SWIM OUT AND SEE WHAT THE PROBLEM LIKELY IS. AGAIN.
NO!
LUCKY FOR THEM, I CAN'T DEAL WITH THE EMBARRASSMENT OF UNREQUITED LOVE.
DISAPPEAR!

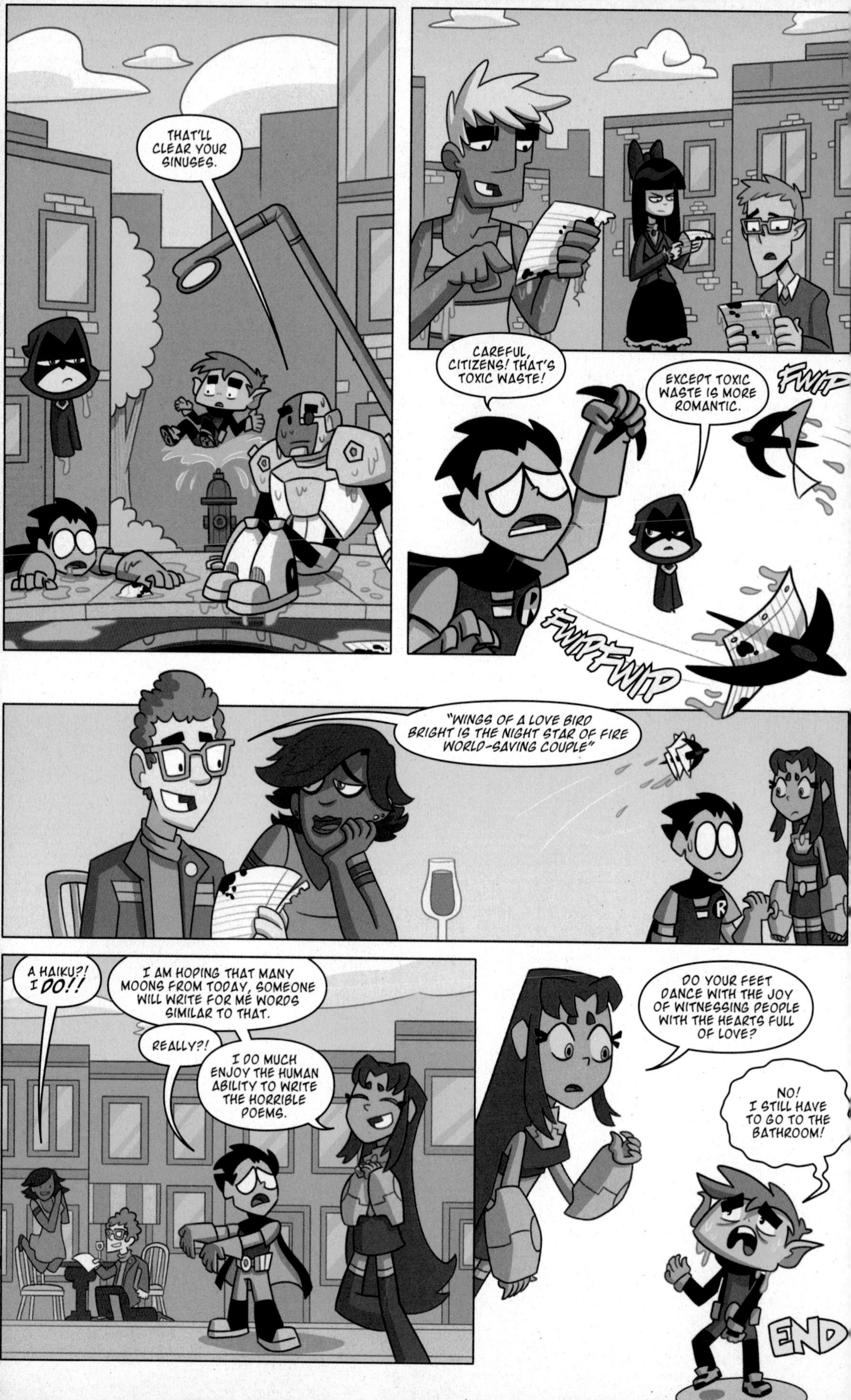
THAT'LL CLEAR YOUR SINUSES.
CAREFUL, CITIZENS! THAT'S TOXIC WASTE!
EXCEPT TOXIC WASTE IS MORE ROMANTIC.
FWIP
FWIP-FWIP
"WINGS OF A LOVE BIRD
BRIGHT IS THE NIGHT STAR OF FIRE
WORLD-SAVING COUPLE"
A HAIKU?! I DO!!
I AM HOPING THAT MANY MOONS FROM TODAY, SOMEONE WILL WRITE FOR ME WORDS SIMILAR TO THAT.
REALLY?!
I DO MUCH ENJOY THE HUMAN ABILITY TO WRITE THE HORRIBLE POEMS.
DO YOUR FEET DANCE WITH THE JOY OF WITNESSING PEOPLE WITH THE HEARTS FULL OF LOVE?
NO! I STILL HAVE TO GO TO THE BATHROOM!
END

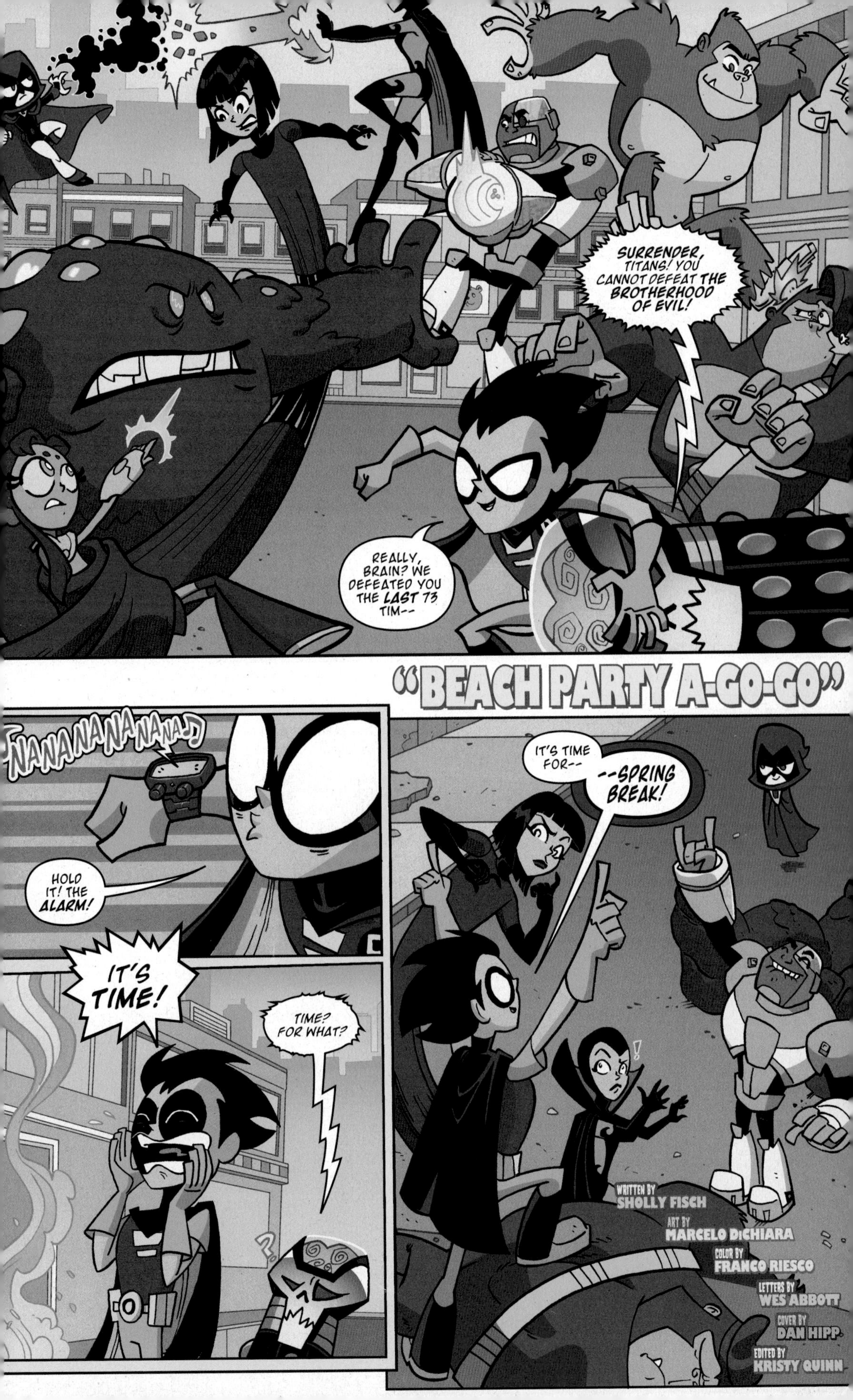
SURRENDER, TITANS! YOU CANNOT DEFEAT THE BROTHERHOOD OF EVIL!
REALLY, BRAIN? WE DEFEATED YOU THE LAST 73 TIM--
"BEACH PARTY A-GO-GO"
NANANANANANA
HOLD IT! THE ALARM!
IT'S TIME!
TIME? FOR WHAT?
?
IT'S TIME FOR--
--SPRING BREAK!
!
WRITTEN BY SHOLLY FISCH
ART BY MARCELO DICHIARA
COLOR BY FRANCO RIESCO
LETTERS BY WES ABBOTT
COVER BY DAN HIPP
EDITED BY KRISTY QUINN

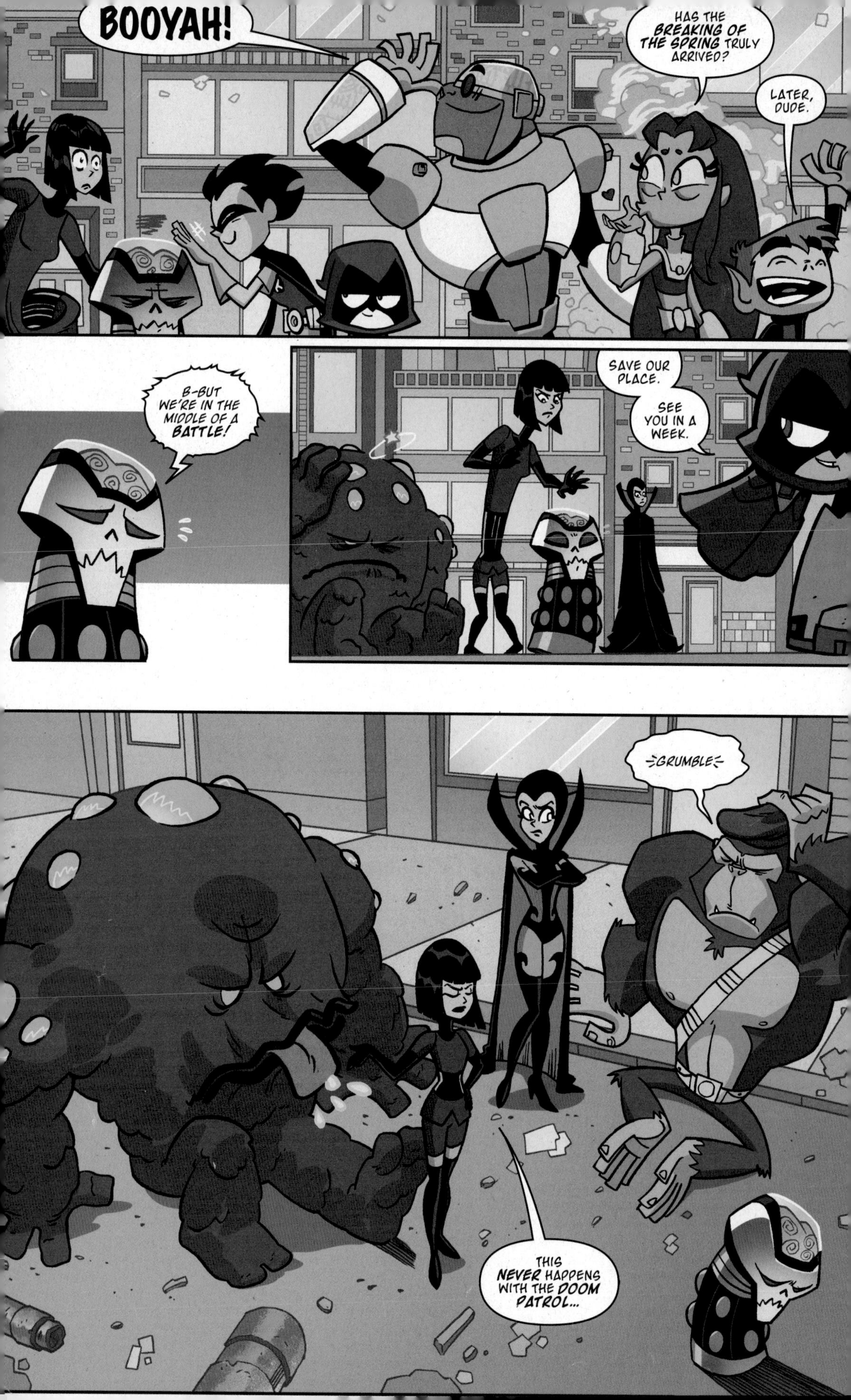
BOOYAH!
HAS THE BREAKING OF THE SPRING TRULY ARRIVED?
LATER, DUDE.
B-BUT WE'RE IN THE MIDDLE OF A BATTLE!
SAVE OUR PLACE.
SEE YOU IN A WEEK.
=GRUMBLE=
THIS NEVER HAPPENS WITH THE DOOM PATROL...

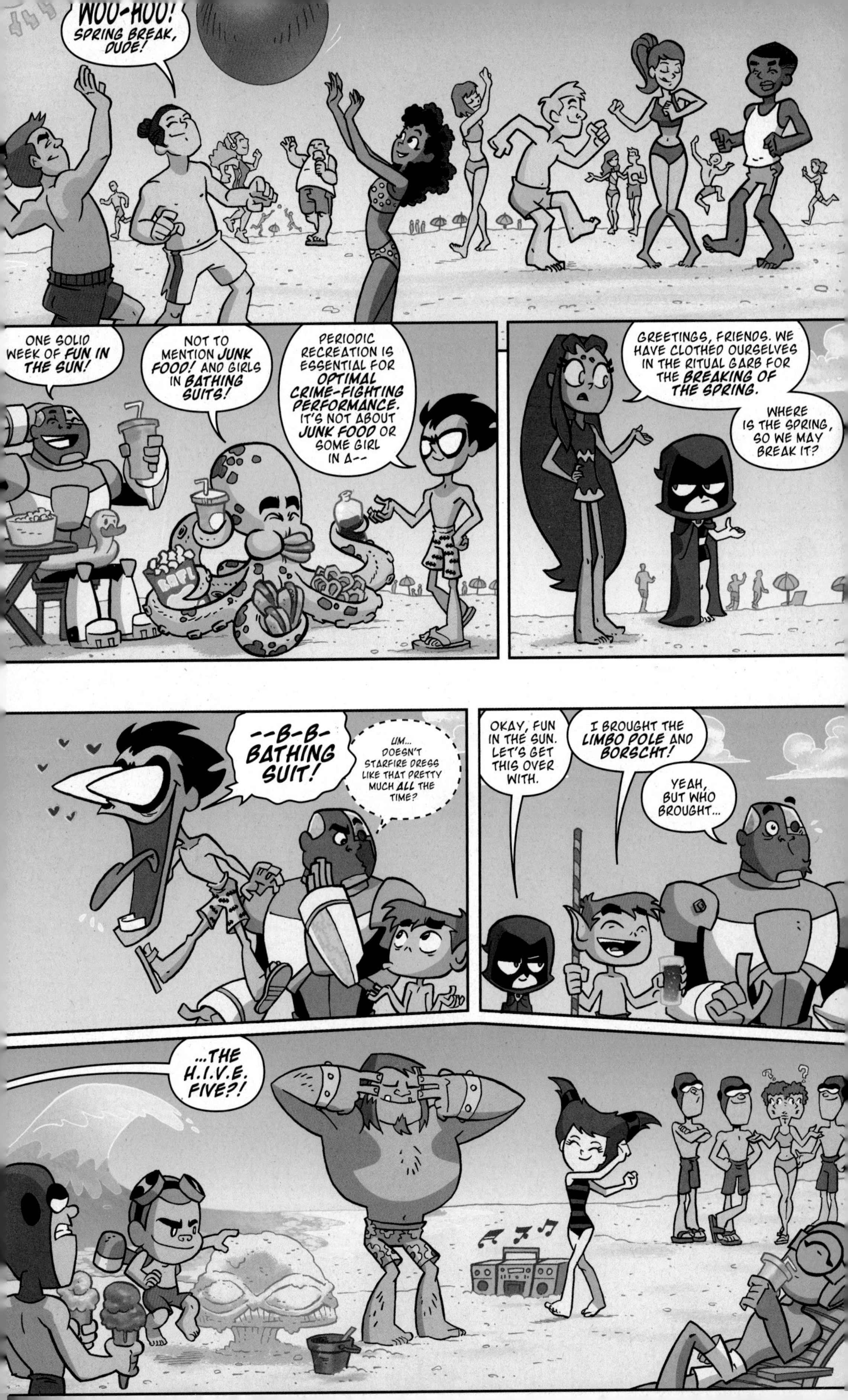
WOO-HOO! SPRING BREAK, DUDE!
ONE SOLID WEEK OF FUN IN THE SUN!
NOT TO MENTION JUNK FOOD! AND GIRLS IN BATHING SUITS!
PERIODIC RECREATION IS ESSENTIAL FOR OPTIMAL CRIME-FIGHTING PERFORMANCE. IT'S NOT ABOUT JUNK FOOD OR SOME GIRL IN A--
GREETINGS, FRIENDS. WE HAVE CLOTHED OURSELVES IN THE RITUAL GARB FOR THE BREAKING OF THE SPRING.
WHERE IS THE SPRING, SO WE MAY BREAK IT?
--B-B-BATHING SUIT!
UM... DOESN'T STARFIRE DRESS LIKE THAT PRETTY MUCH ALL THE TIME?
OKAY, FUN IN THE SUN. LET'S GET THIS OVER WITH.
I BROUGHT THE LIMBO POLE AND BORSCHT!
YEAH, BUT WHO BROUGHT...
...THE H.I.V.E. FIVE?!

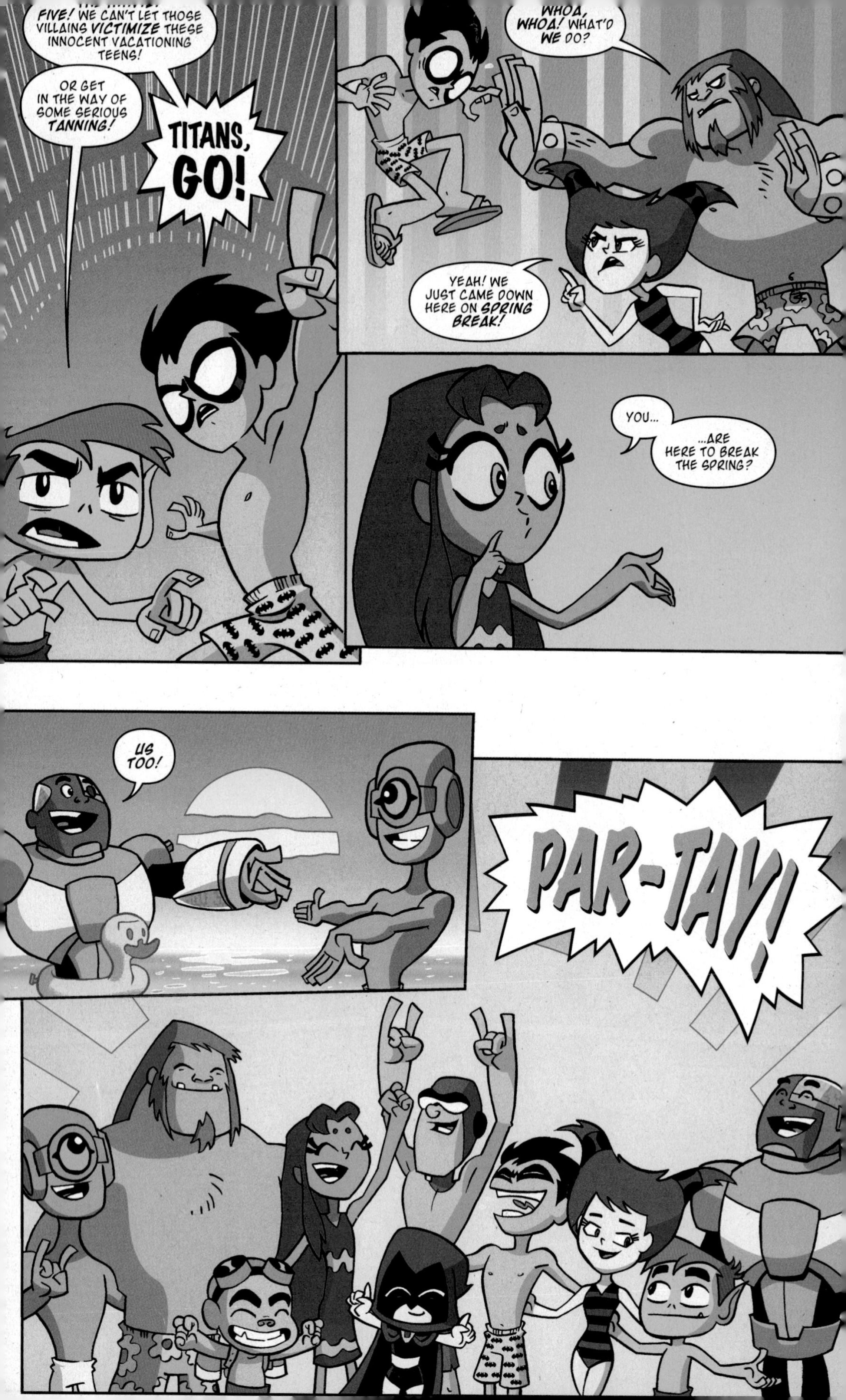
FIVE! WE CAN'T LET THOSE VILLAINS VICTIMIZE THESE INNOCENT VACATIONING TEENS!
OR GET IN THE WAY OF SOME SERIOUS TANNING!
TITANS, GO!
WHOA, WHOA! WHAT'D WE DO?
YEAH! WE JUST CAME DOWN HERE ON SPRING BREAK!
YOU...
...ARE HERE TO BREAK THE SPRING?
US TOO!
PAR-TAY!

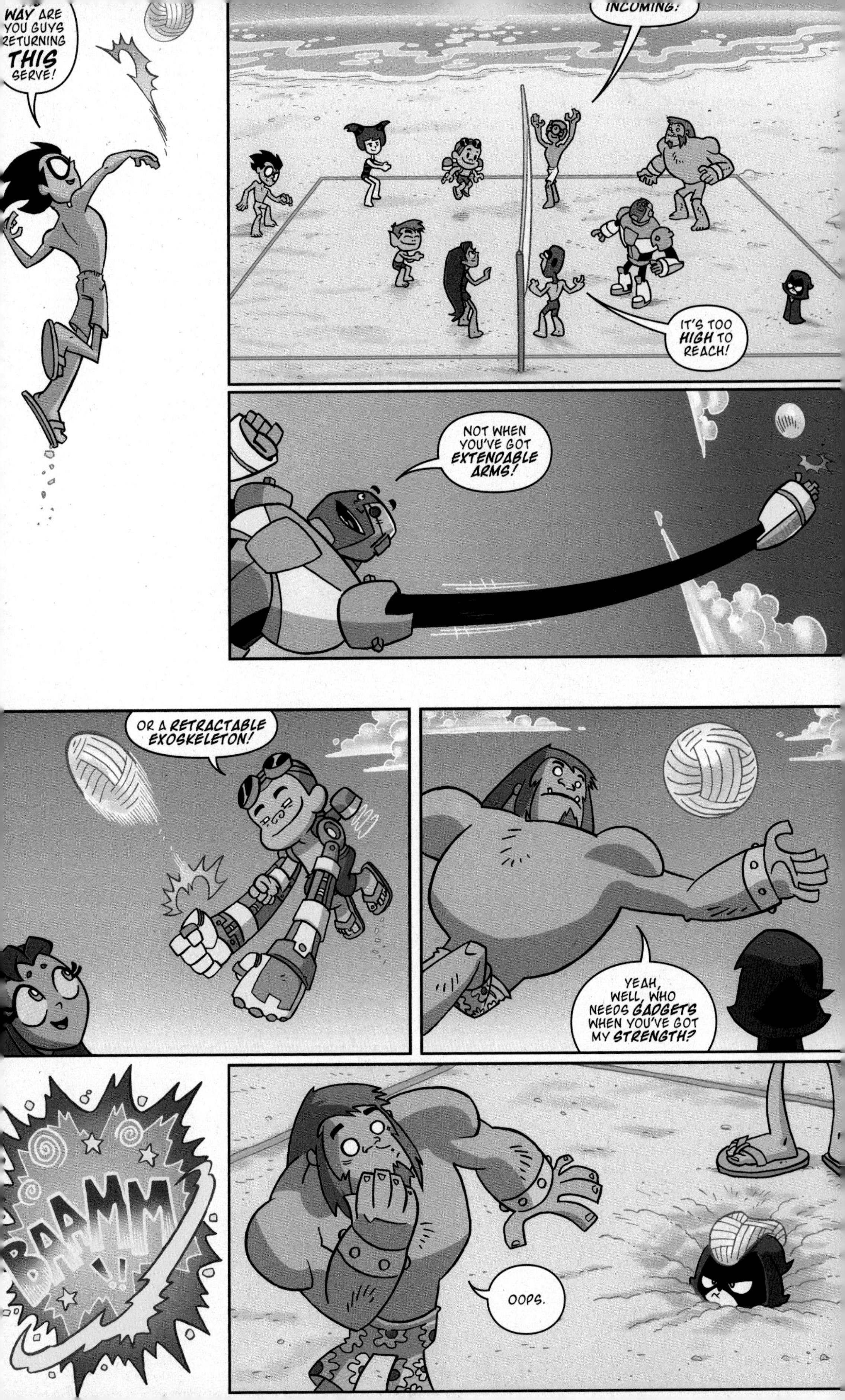
WAY ARE YOU GUYS RETURNING THIS SERVE!
INCOMING!
IT'S TOO HIGH TO REACH!
NOT WHEN YOU'VE GOT EXTENDABLE ARMS!
OR A RETRACTABLE EXOSKELETON!
YEAH, WELL, WHO NEEDS GADGETS WHEN YOU'VE GOT MY STRENGTH?
BAMM!!
OOPS.

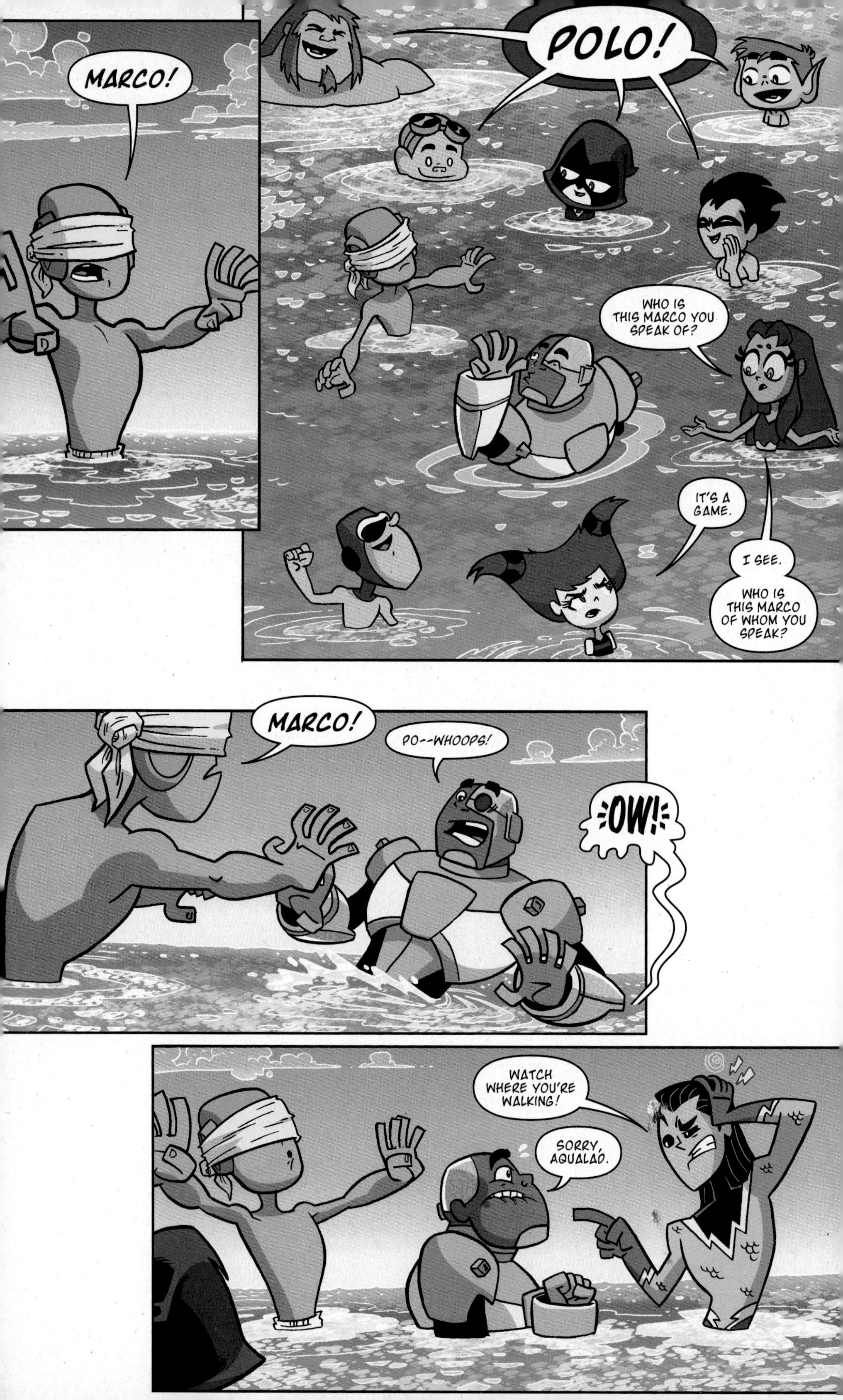
MARCO!
POLO!
WHO IS THIS MARCO YOU SPEAK OF?
IT'S A GAME.
I SEE.
WHO IS THIS MARCO OF WHOM YOU SPEAK?
MARCO!
PO--WHOOPS!
OW!
WATCH WHERE YOU'RE WALKING!
SORRY, AQUALAD.

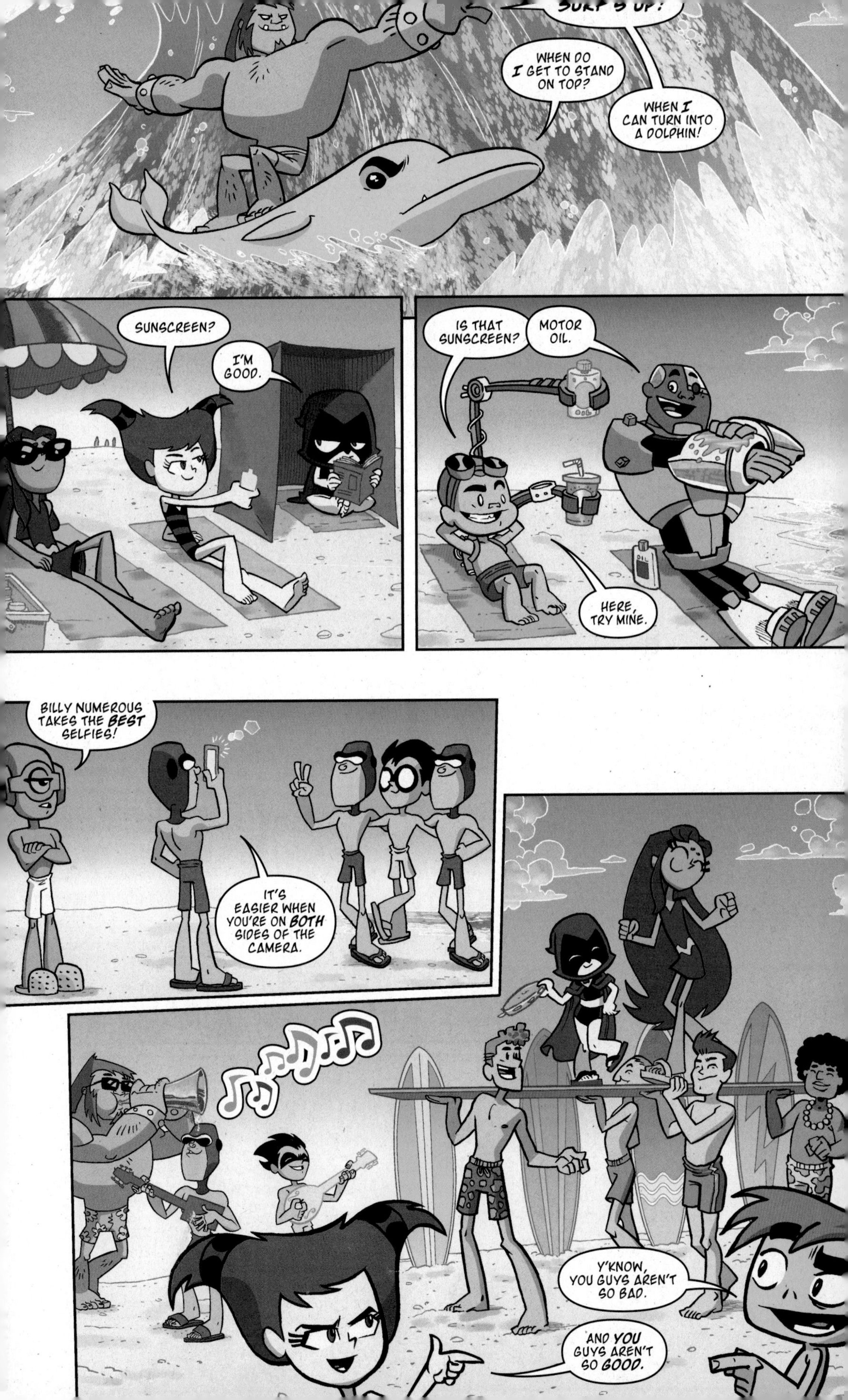

WHEN DO *I* GET TO STAND ON TOP?
WHEN *I* CAN TURN INTO A DOLPHIN!
SUNSCREEN?
I'M GOOD.
IS THAT SUNSCREEN?
MOTOR OIL.
HERE, TRY MINE.
OIL
BILLY NUMEROUS TAKES THE ***BEST*** SELFIES!
IT'S EASIER WHEN YOU'RE ON ***BOTH*** SIDES OF THE CAMERA.
Y'KNOW, YOU GUYS AREN'T SO BAD.
AND ***YOU*** GUYS AREN'T SO ***GOOD***.

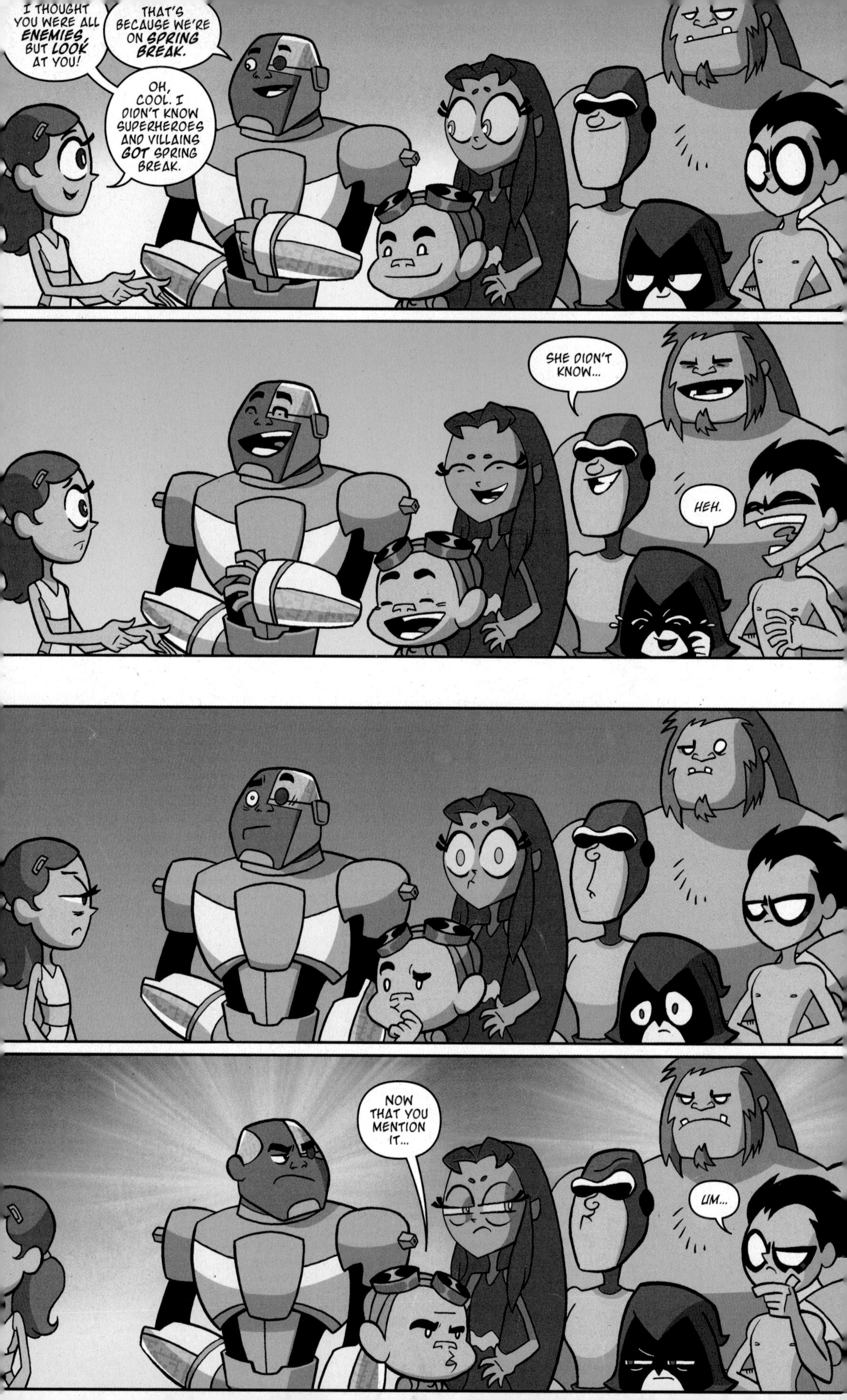
I THOUGHT YOU WERE ALL ENEMIES, BUT LOOK AT YOU!
THAT'S BECAUSE WE'RE ON SPRING BREAK.
OH, COOL. I DIDN'T KNOW SUPERHEROES AND VILLAINS GOT SPRING BREAK.
SHE DIDN'T KNOW...
HEH.
NOW THAT YOU MENTION IT...
UM...

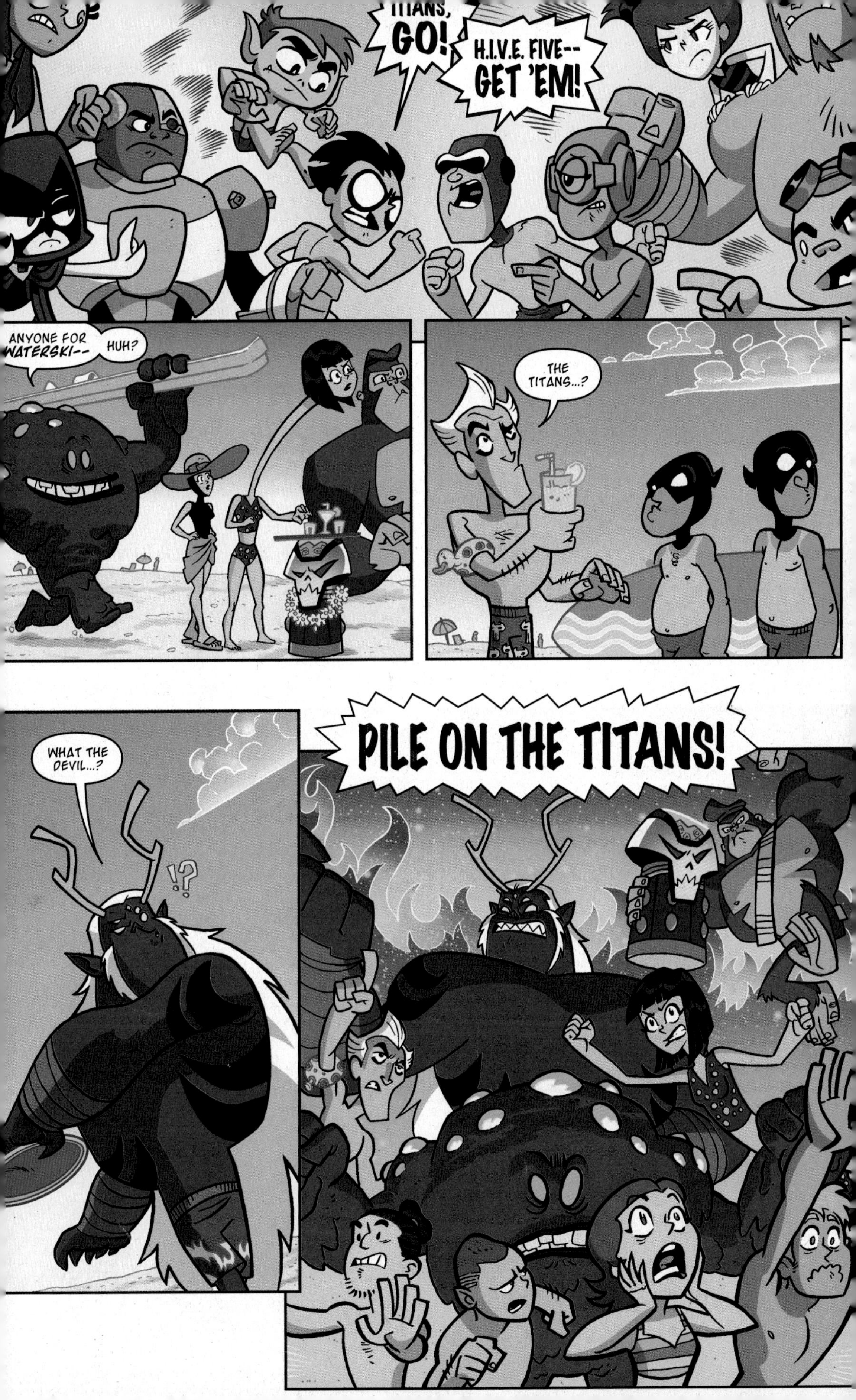
TITANS, GO!
H.I.V.E. FIVE-- GET 'EM!
ANYONE FOR WATERSKI--
HUH?
THE TITANS...?
WHAT THE DEVIL...?
!?
PILE ON THE TITANS!

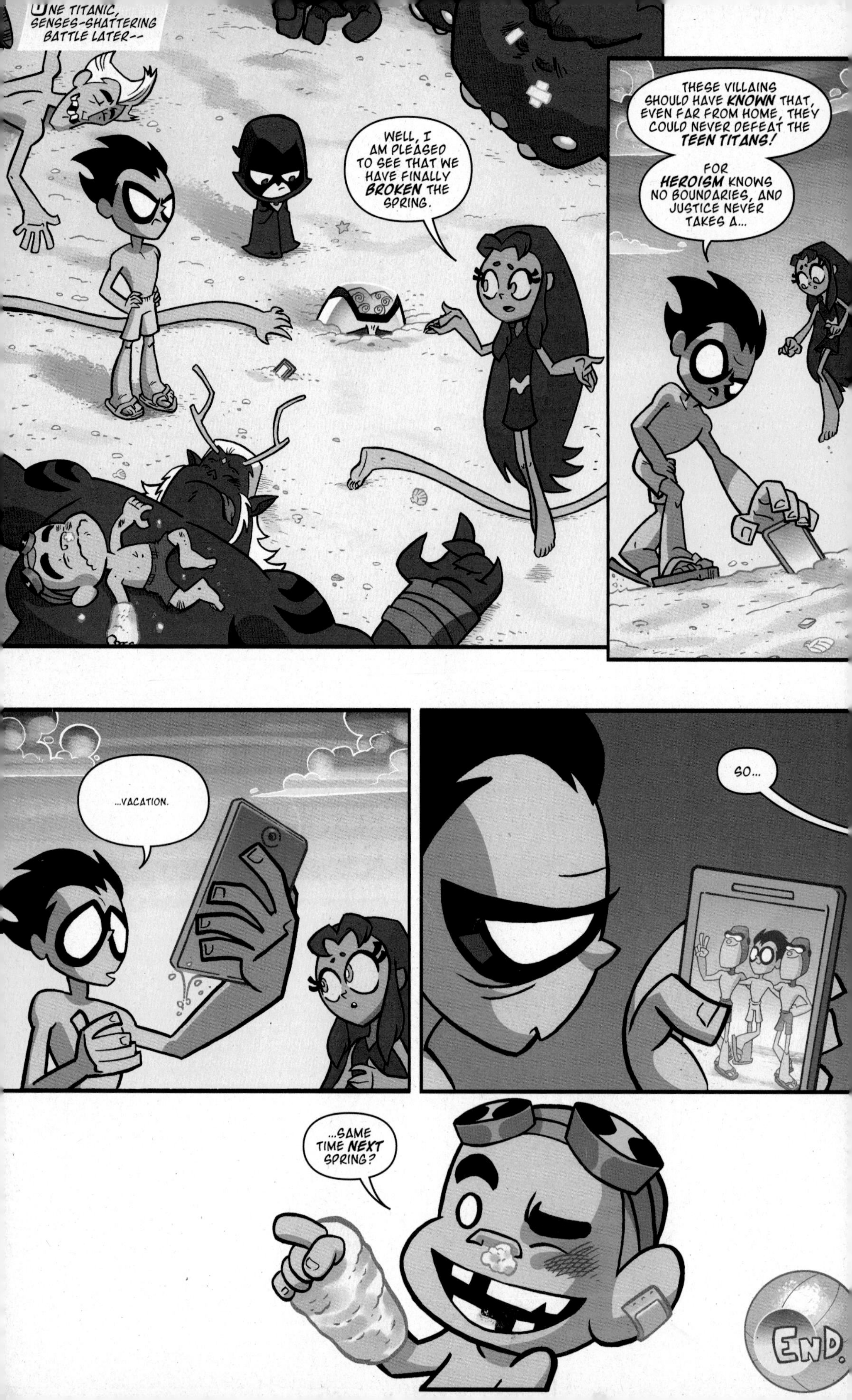
ONE TITANIC, SENSES-SHATTERING BATTLE LATER--
WELL, I AM PLEASED TO SEE THAT WE HAVE FINALLY BROKEN THE SPRING.
THESE VILLAINS SHOULD HAVE KNOWN THAT, EVEN FAR FROM HOME, THEY COULD NEVER DEFEAT THE TEEN TITANS!
FOR HEROISM KNOWS NO BOUNDARIES, AND JUSTICE NEVER TAKES A...
...VACATION.
SO...
...SAME TIME NEXT SPRING?
END.

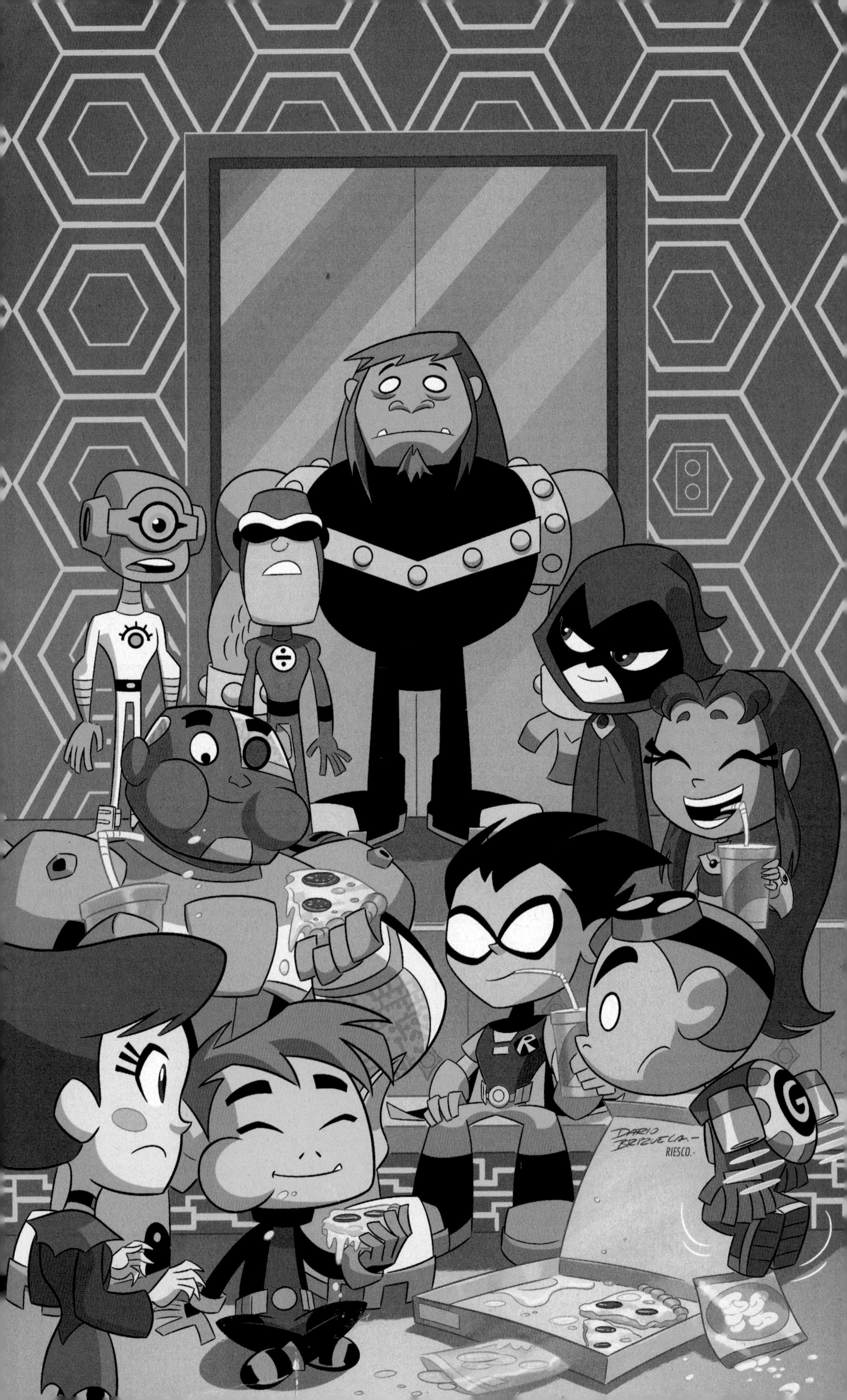
DARIO BRIZUELA -
RIESCO.-

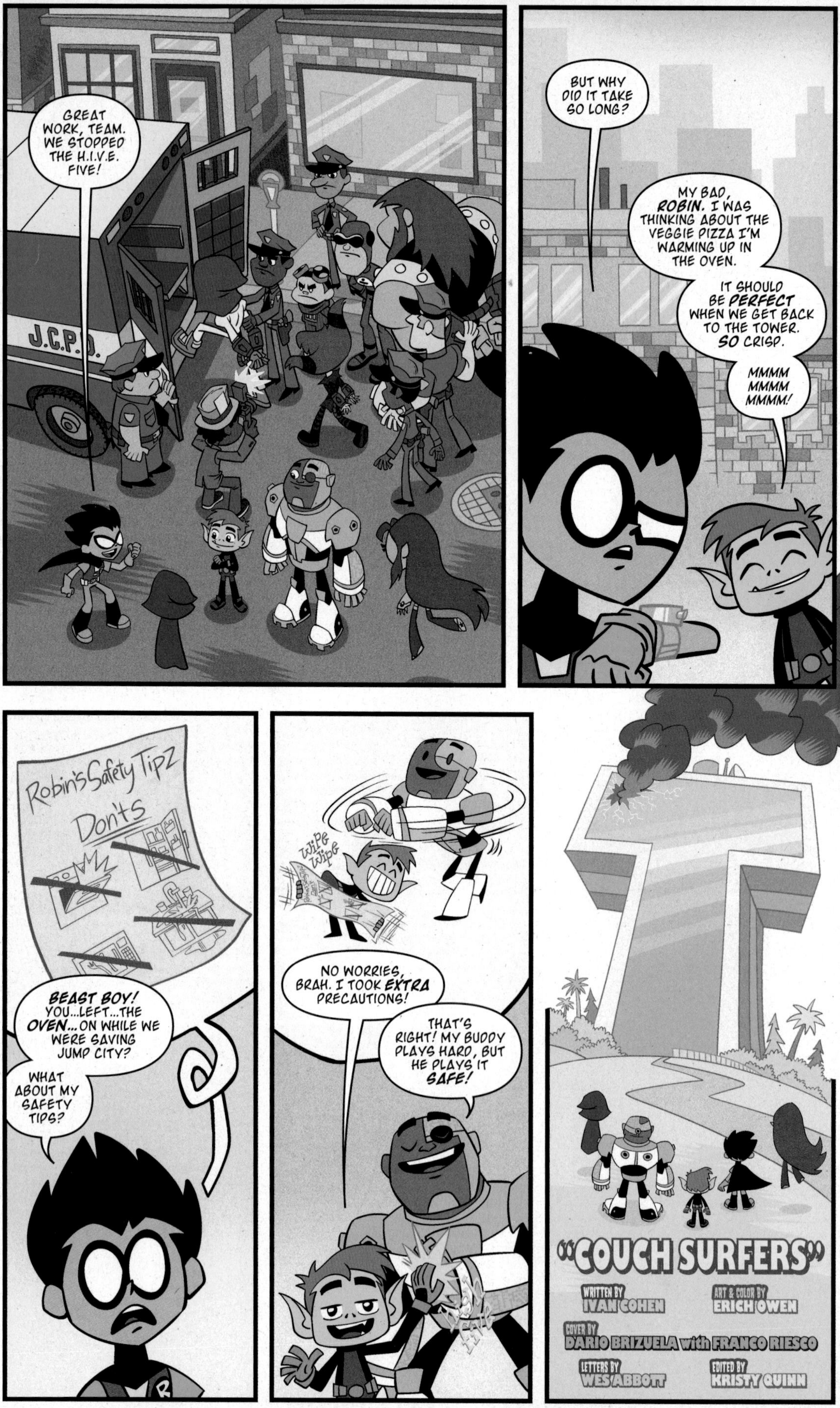
GREAT WORK, TEAM. WE STOPPED THE H.I.V.E. FIVE!
J.C.P.D.
BUT WHY DID IT TAKE SO LONG?
MY BAD, ROBIN. I WAS THINKING ABOUT THE VEGGIE PIZZA I'M WARMING UP IN THE OVEN.
IT SHOULD BE PERFECT WHEN WE GET BACK TO THE TOWER. SO CRISP.
MMMM MMMM MMMM!
Robin's Safety Tipz
Don'ts
BEAST BOY! YOU...LEFT...THE OVEN...ON WHILE WE WERE SAVING JUMP CITY?
WHAT ABOUT MY SAFETY TIPS?
WIPE WIPE
NO WORRIES, BRAH. I TOOK EXTRA PRECAUTIONS!
THAT'S RIGHT! MY BUDDY PLAYS HARD, BUT HE PLAYS IT SAFE!
"COUCH SURFERS"
WRITTEN BY IVAN COHEN
ART & COLOR BY ERICH OWEN
COVER BY DARIO BRIZUELA with FRANCO RIESCO
LETTERS BY WES ABBOTT
EDITED BY KRISTY QUINN

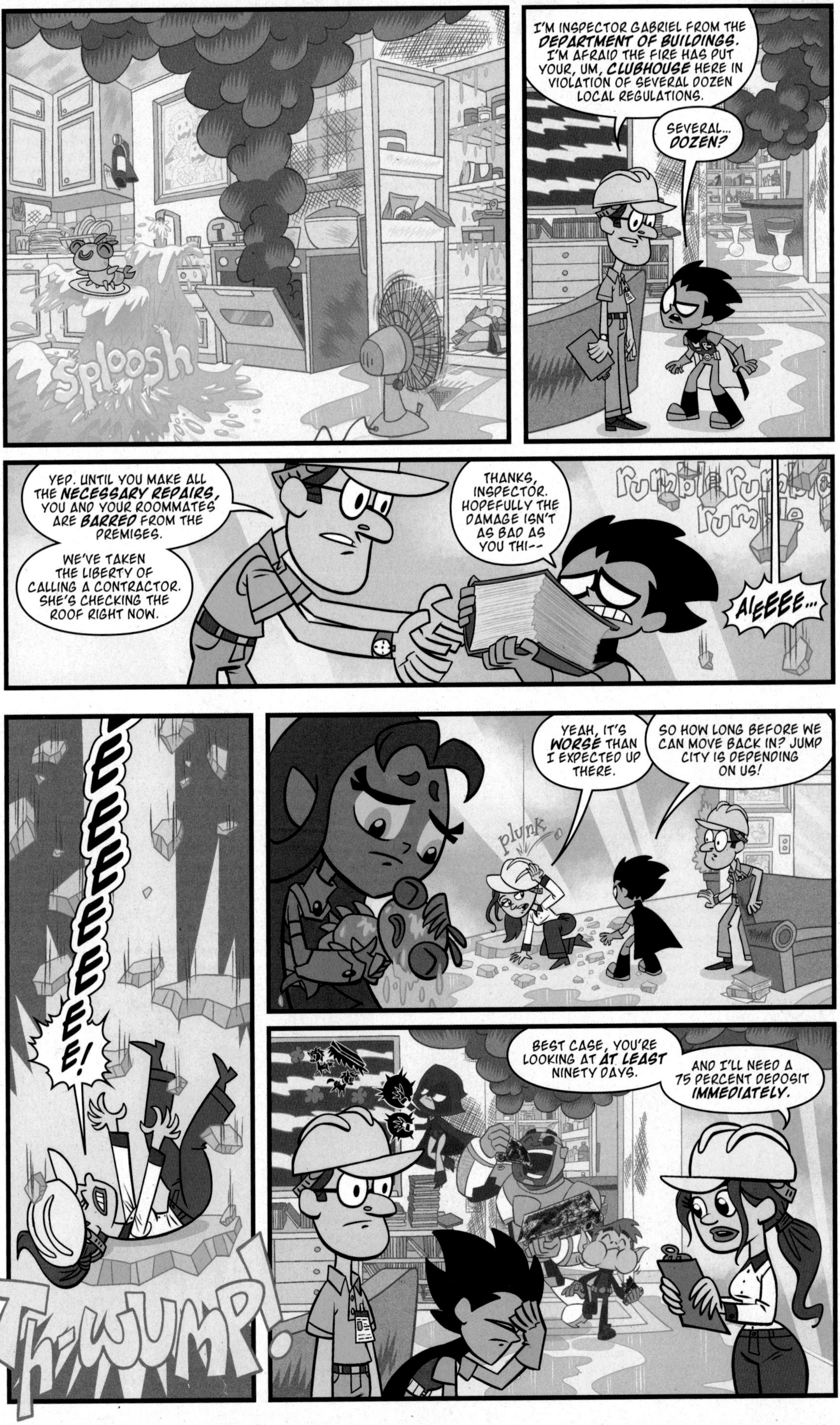
sploosh
I'M INSPECTOR GABRIEL FROM THE DEPARTMENT OF BUILDINGS. I'M AFRAID THE FIRE HAS PUT YOUR, UM, CLUBHOUSE HERE IN VIOLATION OF SEVERAL DOZEN LOCAL REGULATIONS.
SEVERAL... DOZEN?
YEP. UNTIL YOU MAKE ALL THE NECESSARY REPAIRS, YOU AND YOUR ROOMMATES ARE BARRED FROM THE PREMISES.
WE'VE TAKEN THE LIBERTY OF CALLING A CONTRACTOR. SHE'S CHECKING THE ROOF RIGHT NOW.
THANKS, INSPECTOR. HOPEFULLY THE DAMAGE ISN'T AS BAD AS YOU THI--
rumble rumble rumble
AIEEEE...
EEEEEEEEE!
Th-WUMP!
plunk
YEAH, IT'S WORSE THAN I EXPECTED UP THERE.
SO HOW LONG BEFORE WE CAN MOVE BACK IN? JUMP CITY IS DEPENDING ON US!
BEST CASE, YOU'RE LOOKING AT AT LEAST NINETY DAYS.
AND I'LL NEED A 75 PERCENT DEPOSIT IMMEDIATELY.

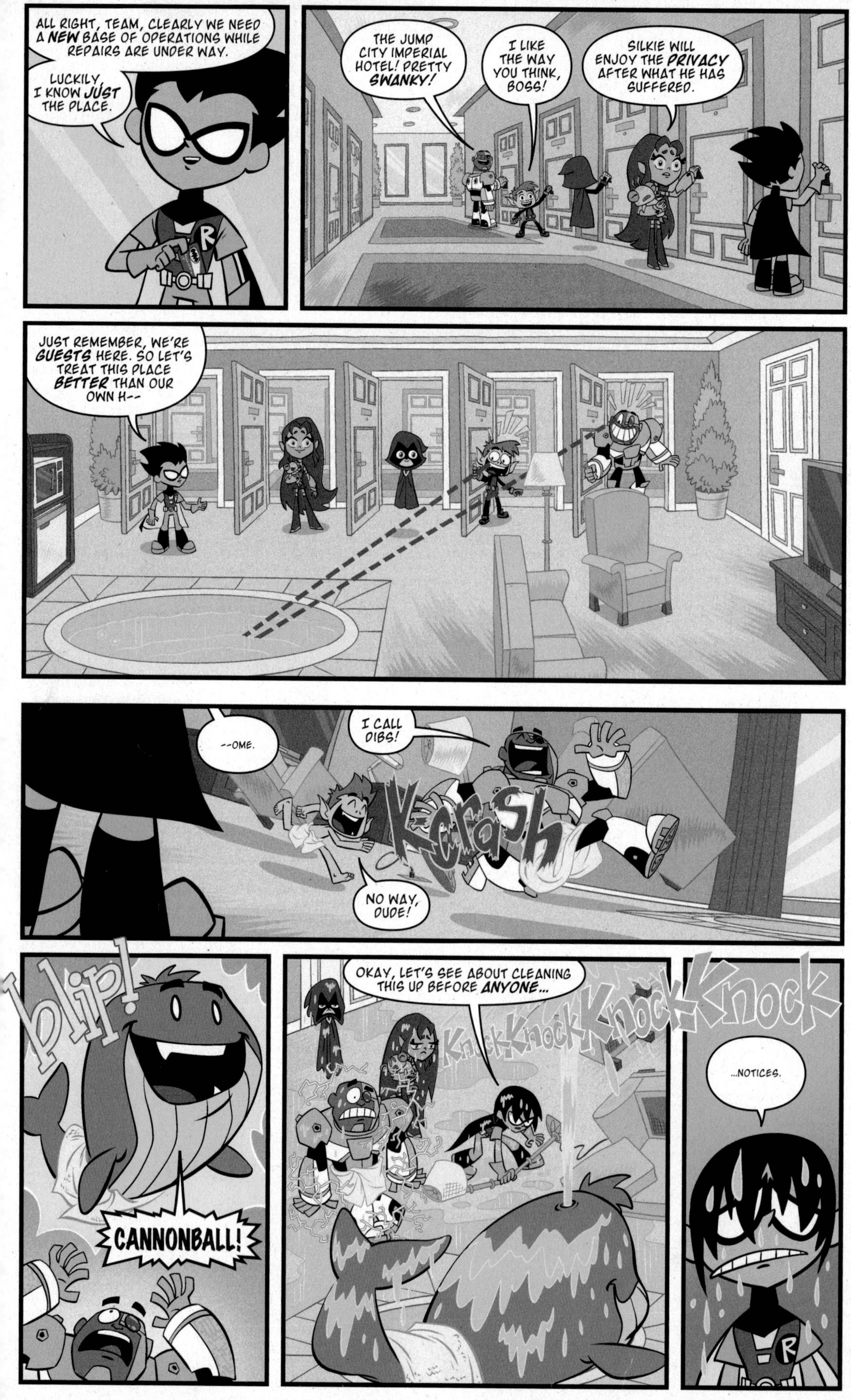

ALL RIGHT, TEAM, CLEARLY WE NEED A NEW BASE OF OPERATIONS WHILE REPAIRS ARE UNDER WAY.
LUCKILY, I KNOW JUST THE PLACE.
THE JUMP CITY IMPERIAL HOTEL! PRETTY SWANKY!
I LIKE THE WAY YOU THINK, BOSS!
SILKIE WILL ENJOY THE PRIVACY AFTER WHAT HE HAS SUFFERED.
JUST REMEMBER, WE'RE GUESTS HERE. SO LET'S TREAT THIS PLACE BETTER THAN OUR OWN H--
--OME.
I CALL DIBS!
KRASH
NO WAY, DUDE!
blip!
CANNONBALL!
OKAY, LET'S SEE ABOUT CLEANING THIS UP BEFORE ANYONE...
KnockKnockKnockKnock
...NOTICES.

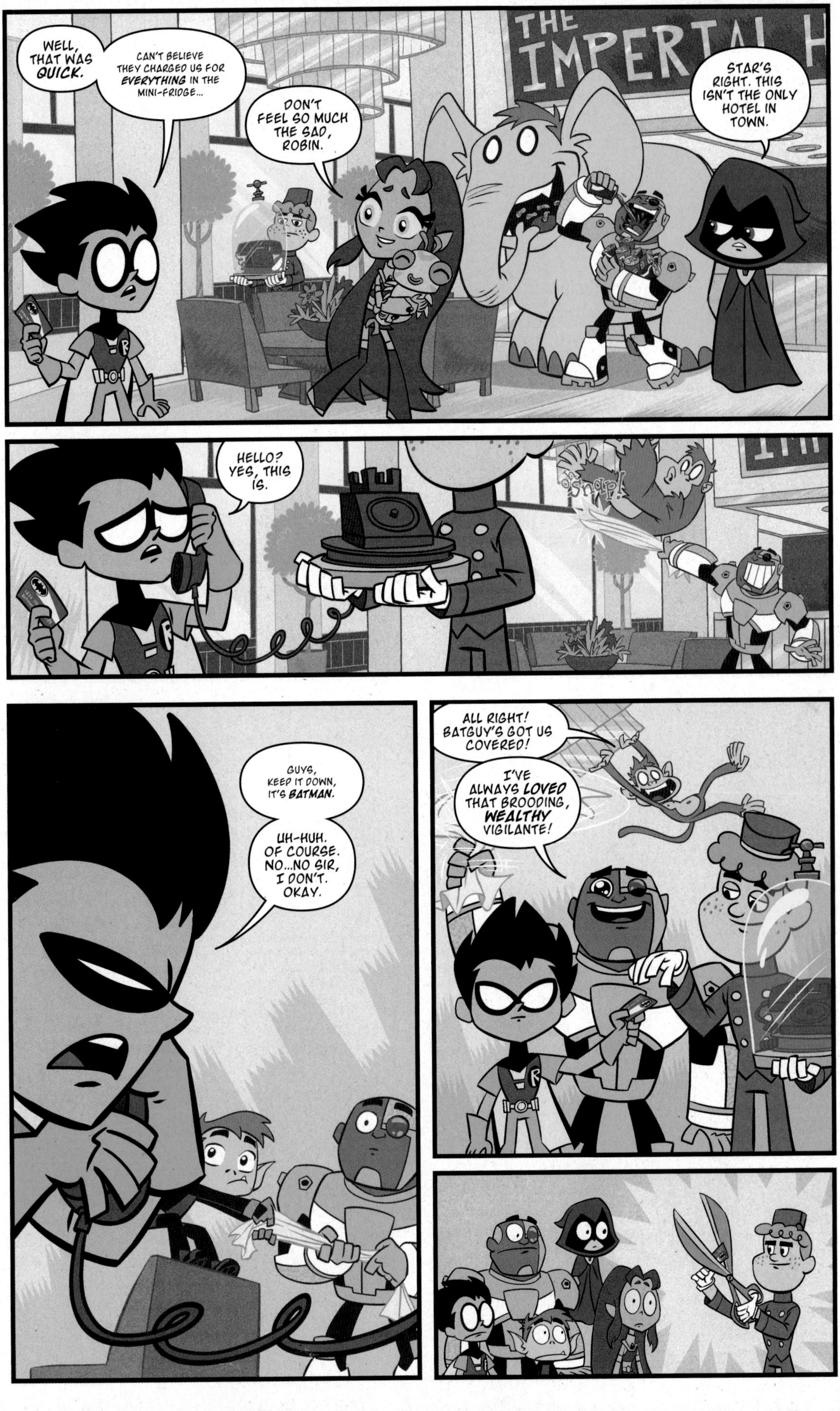
THE IMPERIAL H
WELL, THAT WAS QUICK.
CAN'T BELIEVE THEY CHARGED US FOR EVERYTHING IN THE MINI-FRIDGE...
DON'T FEEL SO MUCH THE SAD, ROBIN.
STAR'S RIGHT. THIS ISN'T THE ONLY HOTEL IN TOWN.
HELLO? YES, THIS IS.
SNAP!
GUYS, KEEP IT DOWN, IT'S BATMAN.
UH-HUH. OF COURSE. NO...NO SIR, I DON'T. OKAY.
ALL RIGHT! BATGUY'S GOT US COVERED!
I'VE ALWAYS LOVED THAT BROODING, WEALTHY VIGILANTE!

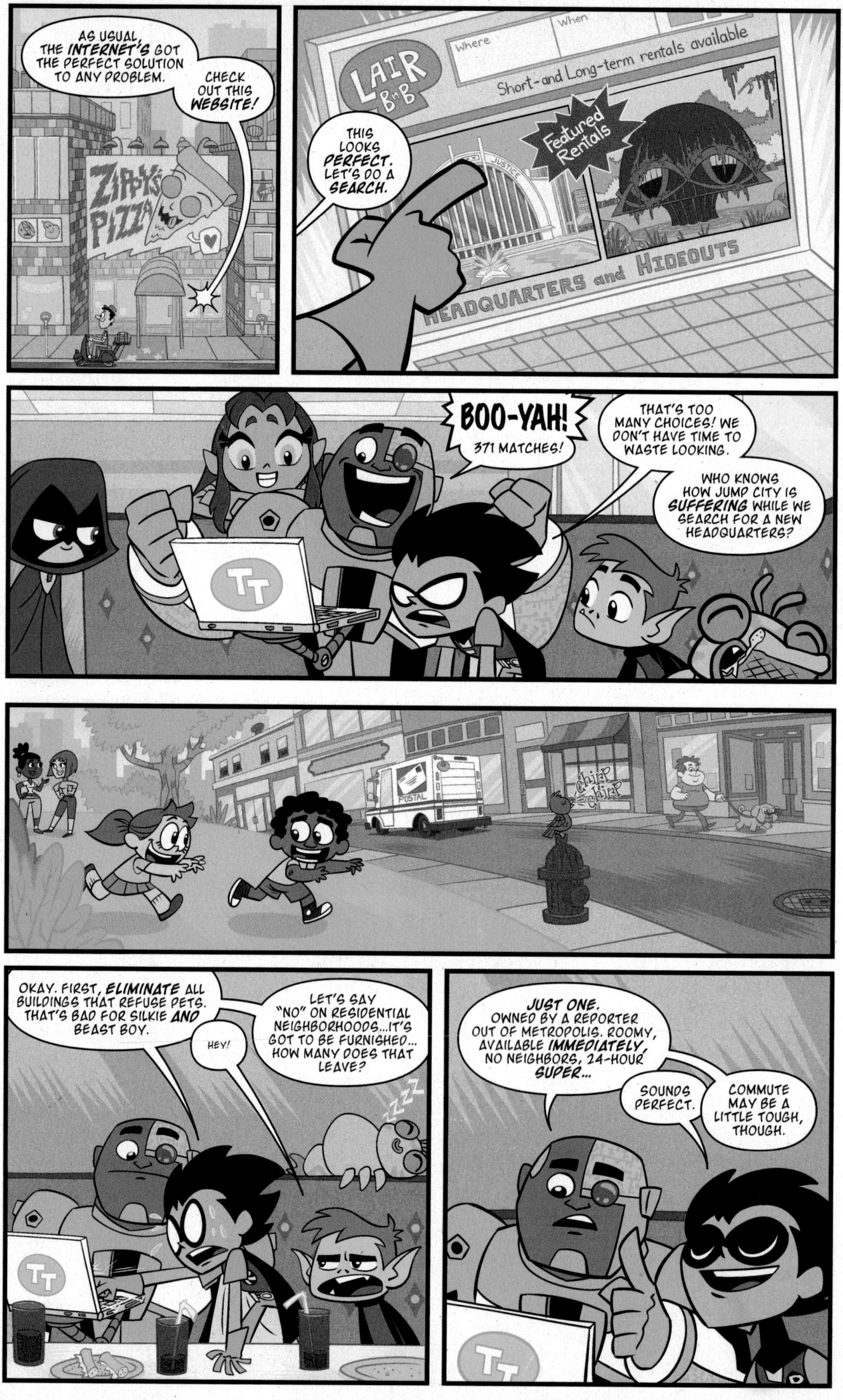
AS USUAL, THE INTERNET'S GOT THE PERFECT SOLUTION TO ANY PROBLEM.
CHECK OUT THIS WEBSITE!
ZIPPY'S PIZZA
LAIR BnB
Where
When
Short-and Long-term rentals available
THIS LOOKS PERFECT. LET'S DO A SEARCH.
Featured Rentals
JUSTICE
HEADQUARTERS and HIDEOUTS
BOO-YAH! 371 MATCHES!
THAT'S TOO MANY CHOICES! WE DON'T HAVE TIME TO WASTE LOOKING.
WHO KNOWS HOW JUMP CITY IS SUFFERING WHILE WE SEARCH FOR A NEW HEADQUARTERS?
TT
POSTAL
CHIRP CHIRP
OKAY. FIRST, ELIMINATE ALL BUILDINGS THAT REFUSE PETS. THAT'S BAD FOR SILKIE AND BEAST BOY.
HEY!
LET'S SAY "NO" ON RESIDENTIAL NEIGHBORHOODS...IT'S GOT TO BE FURNISHED... HOW MANY DOES THAT LEAVE?
ZZZ
TT
JUST ONE. OWNED BY A REPORTER OUT OF METROPOLIS. ROOMY, AVAILABLE IMMEDIATELY, NO NEIGHBORS, 24-HOUR SUPER...
SOUNDS PERFECT.
COMMUTE MAY BE A LITTLE TOUGH, THOUGH.
TT

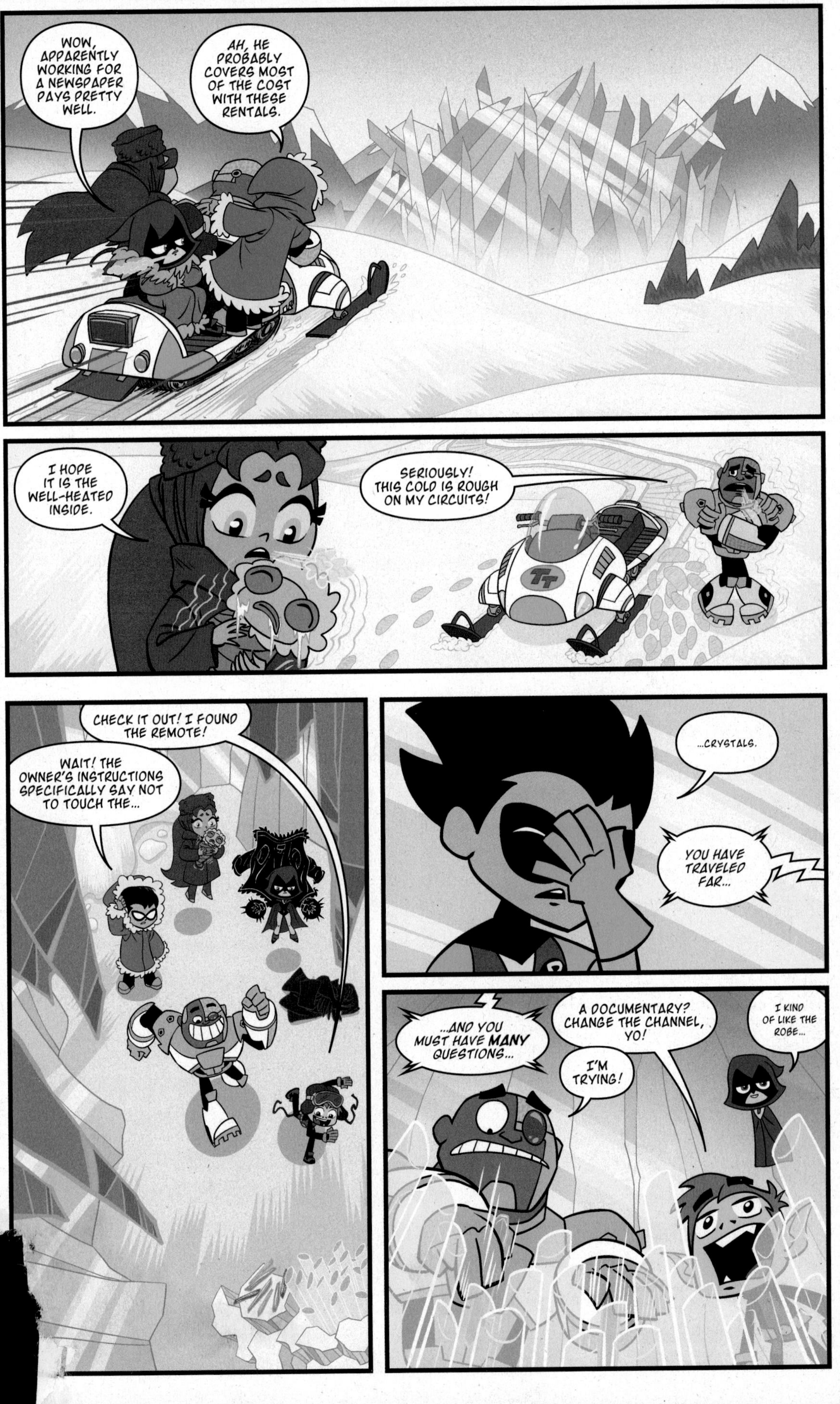
WOW, APPARENTLY WORKING FOR A NEWSPAPER PAYS PRETTY WELL.
AH, HE PROBABLY COVERS MOST OF THE COST WITH THESE RENTALS.
I HOPE IT IS THE WELL-HEATED INSIDE.
SERIOUSLY! THIS COLD IS ROUGH ON MY CIRCUITS!
CHECK IT OUT! I FOUND THE REMOTE!
WAIT! THE OWNER'S INSTRUCTIONS SPECIFICALLY SAY NOT TO TOUCH THE...
...CRYSTALS.
YOU HAVE TRAVELED FAR...
...AND YOU MUST HAVE **MANY** QUESTIONS...
A DOCUMENTARY? CHANGE THE CHANNEL, YO!
I'M TRYING!
I KIND OF LIKE THE ROBE...

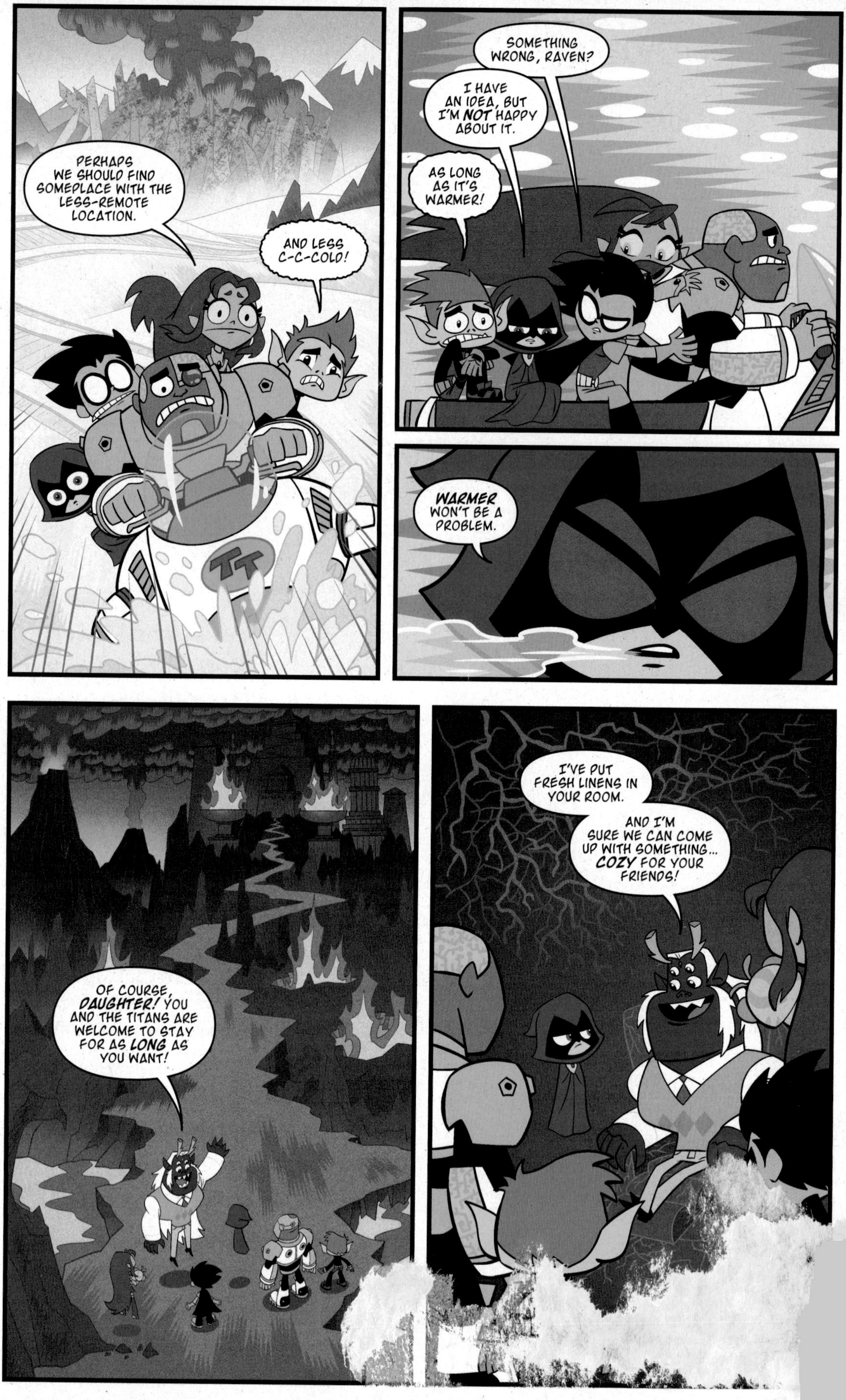
PERHAPS WE SHOULD FIND SOMEPLACE WITH THE LESS-REMOTE LOCATION.
AND LESS C-C-COLD!
SOMETHING WRONG, RAVEN?
I HAVE AN IDEA, BUT I'M NOT HAPPY ABOUT IT.
AS LONG AS IT'S WARMER!
WARMER WON'T BE A PROBLEM.
OF COURSE, DAUGHTER! YOU AND THE TITANS ARE WELCOME TO STAY FOR AS LONG AS YOU WANT!
I'VE PUT FRESH LINENS IN YOUR ROOM.
AND I'M SURE WE CAN COME UP WITH SOMETHING... COZY FOR YOUR FRIENDS!

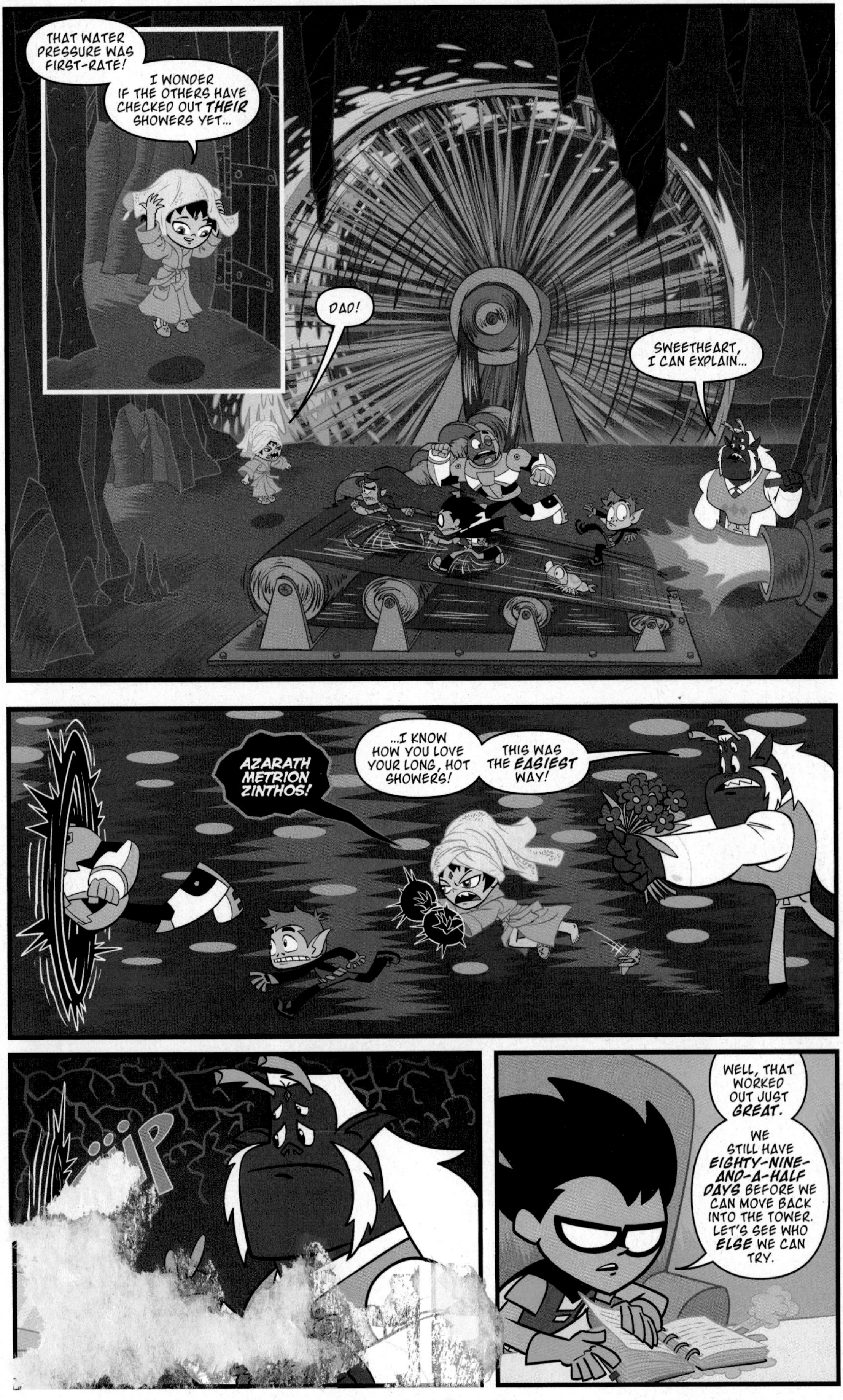
THAT WATER PRESSURE WAS FIRST-RATE!
I WONDER IF THE OTHERS HAVE CHECKED OUT THEIR SHOWERS YET...
DAD!
SWEETHEART, I CAN EXPLAIN...
AZARATH METRION ZINTHOS!
...I KNOW HOW YOU LOVE YOUR LONG, HOT SHOWERS!
THIS WAS THE EASIEST WAY!
WELL, THAT WORKED OUT JUST GREAT.
WE STILL HAVE EIGHTY-NINE-AND-A-HALF DAYS BEFORE WE CAN MOVE BACK INTO THE TOWER. LET'S SEE WHO ELSE WE CAN TRY.

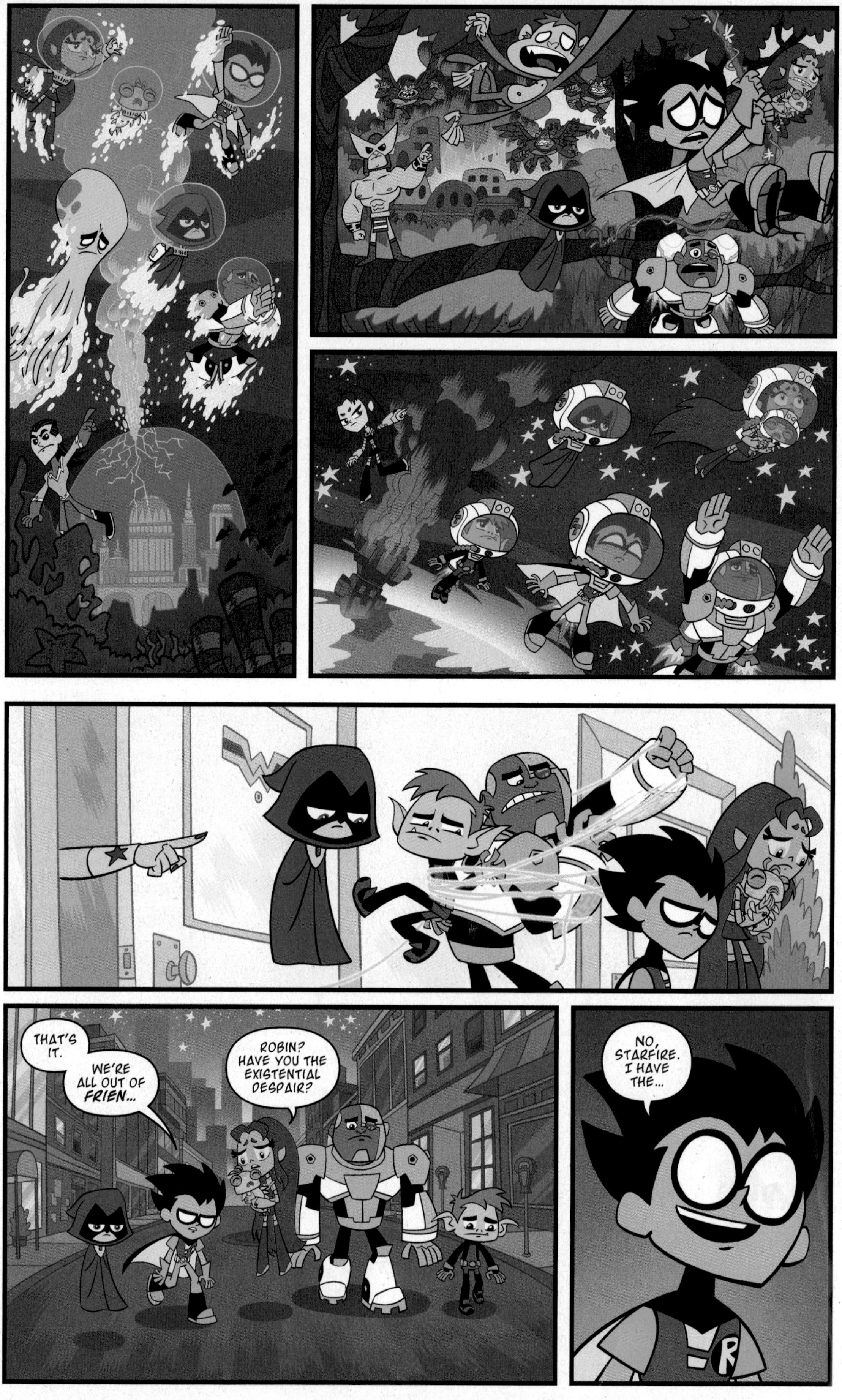
THAT'S IT.
WE'RE ALL OUT OF FRIEN...
ROBIN? HAVE YOU THE EXISTENTIAL DESPAIR?
NO, STARFIRE. I HAVE THE...

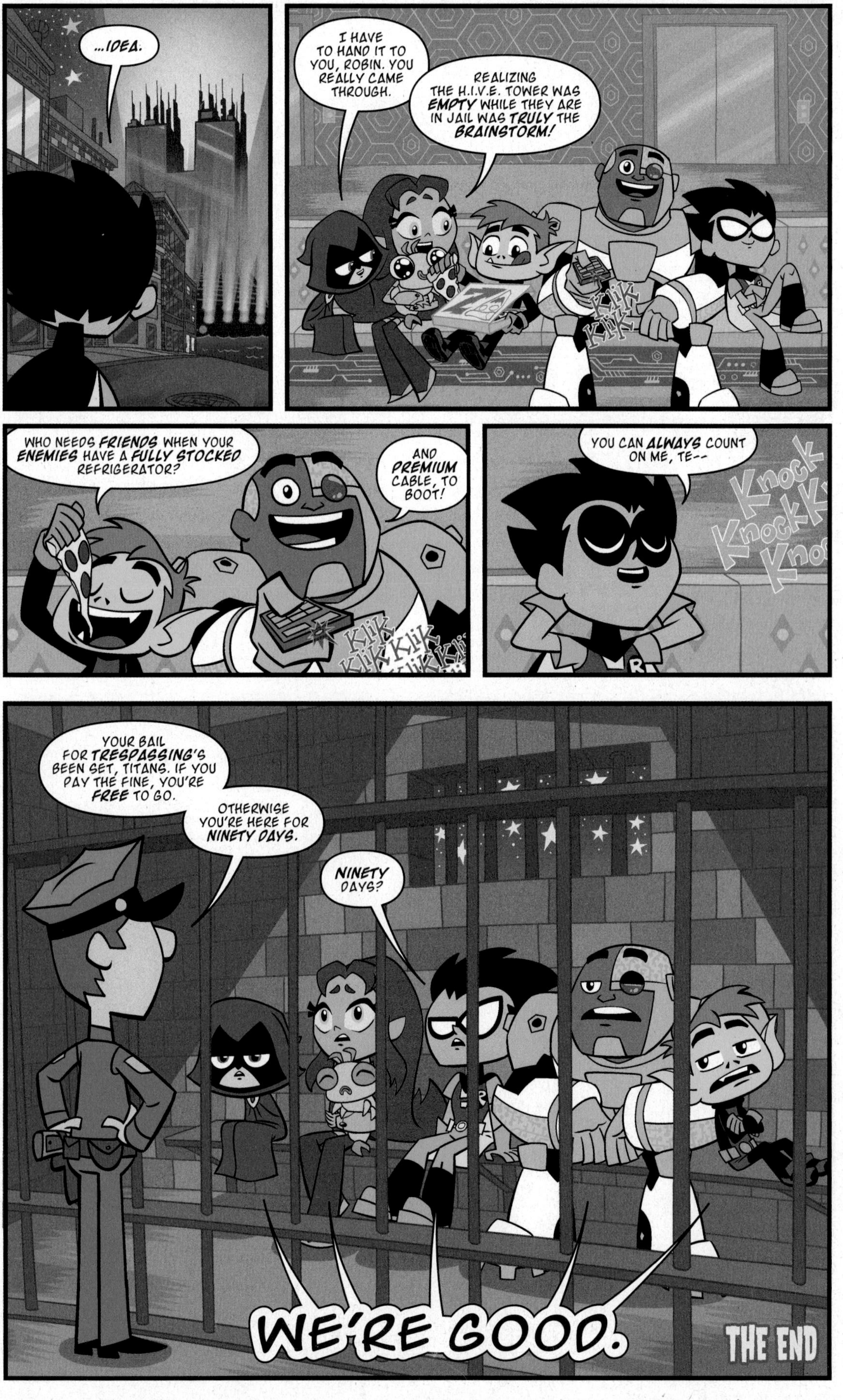
...IDEA.
I HAVE TO HAND IT TO YOU, ROBIN. YOU REALLY CAME THROUGH.
REALIZING THE H.I.V.E. TOWER WAS EMPTY WHILE THEY ARE IN JAIL WAS TRULY THE BRAINSTORM!
KLIK KLIK
WHO NEEDS FRIENDS WHEN YOUR ENEMIES HAVE A FULLY STOCKED REFRIGERATOR?
AND PREMIUM CABLE, TO BOOT!
KLIK KLIK KLIK
YOU CAN ALWAYS COUNT ON ME, TE--
KNOCK KNOCK
YOUR BAIL FOR TRESPASSING'S BEEN SET, TITANS. IF YOU PAY THE FINE, YOU'RE FREE TO GO.
OTHERWISE YOU'RE HERE FOR NINETY DAYS.
NINETY DAYS?
WE'RE GOOD.
THE END

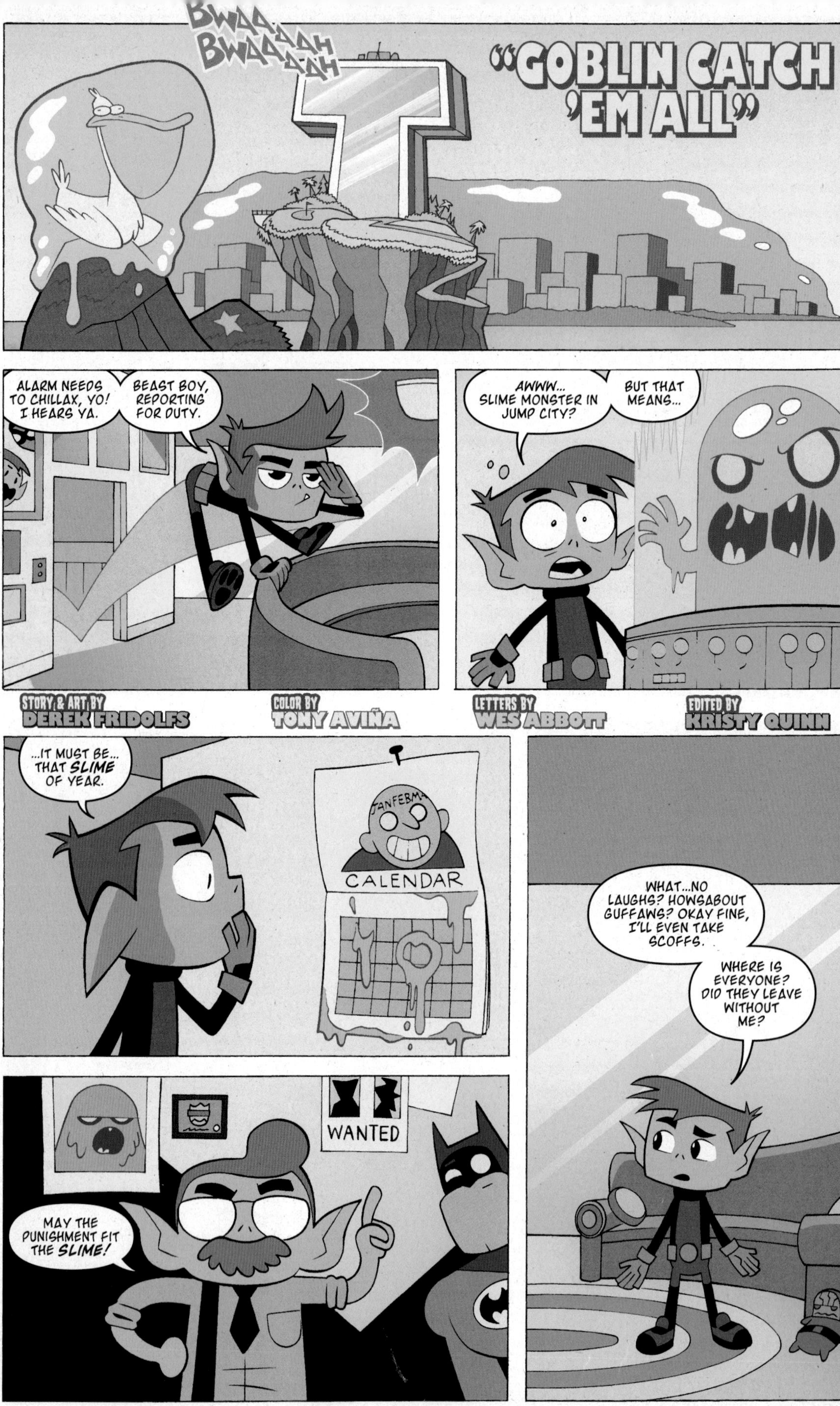
BWAAAAAH
BWAAAAAH
"GOBLIN CATCH 'EM ALL"
ALARM NEEDS TO CHILLAX, YO! I HEARS YA.
BEAST BOY, REPORTING FOR DUTY.
AWWW... SLIME MONSTER IN JUMP CITY?
BUT THAT MEANS...
STORY & ART BY DEREK FRIDOLFS
COLOR BY TONY AVIÑA
LETTERS BY WES ABBOTT
EDITED BY KRISTY QUINN
...IT MUST BE... THAT SLIME OF YEAR.
CALENDAR
JANFEBMA
WHAT...NO LAUGHS? HOWSABOUT GUFFAWS? OKAY FINE, I'LL EVEN TAKE SCOFFS.
WHERE IS EVERYONE? DID THEY LEAVE WITHOUT ME?
WANTED
MAY THE PUNISHMENT FIT THE SLIME!

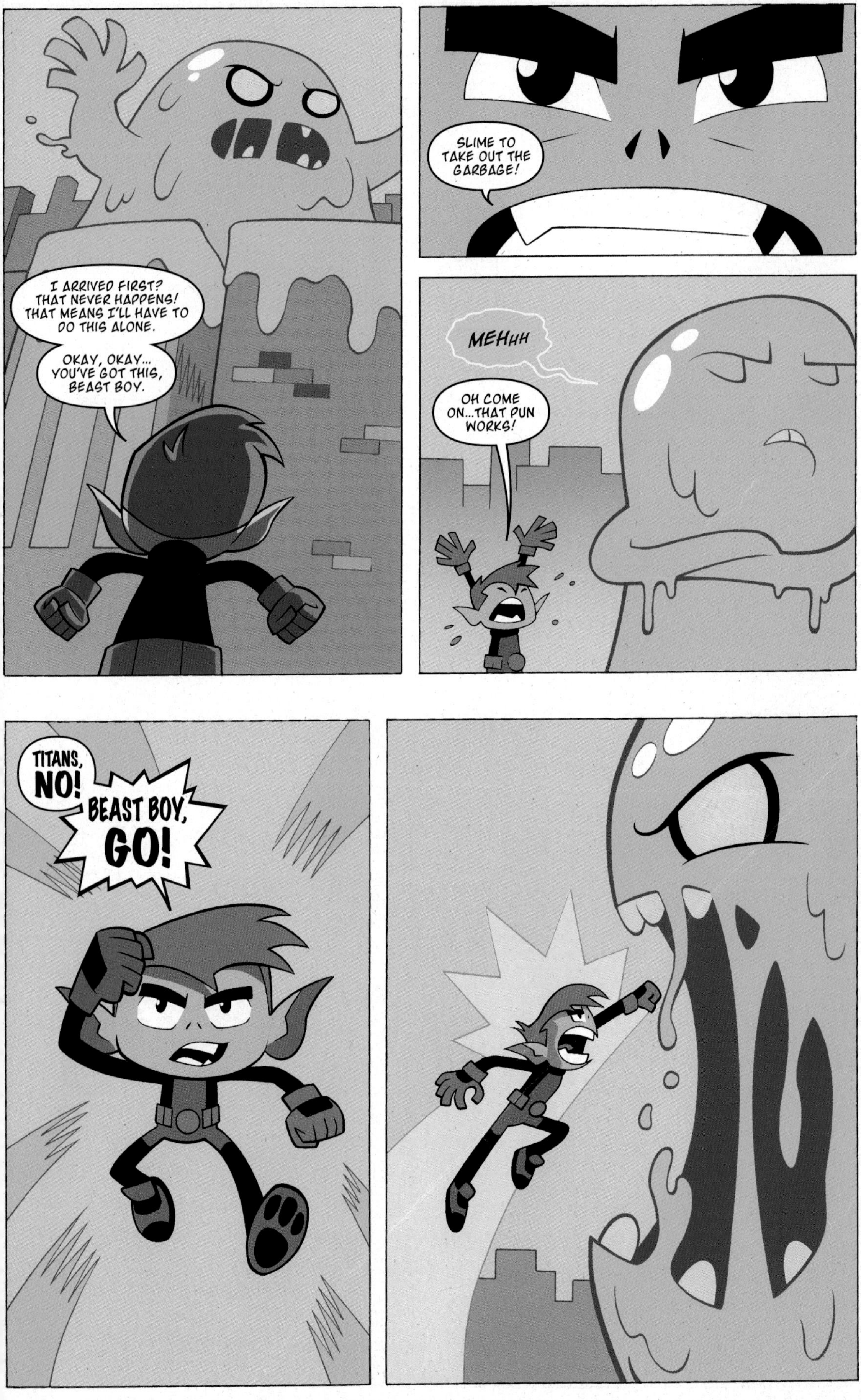
I ARRIVED FIRST? THAT NEVER HAPPENS! THAT MEANS I'LL HAVE TO DO THIS ALONE.
OKAY, OKAY... YOU'VE GOT THIS, BEAST BOY.
SLIME TO TAKE OUT THE GARBAGE!
MEHhh
OH COME ON...THAT PUN WORKS!
TITANS, NO!
BEAST BOY, GO!

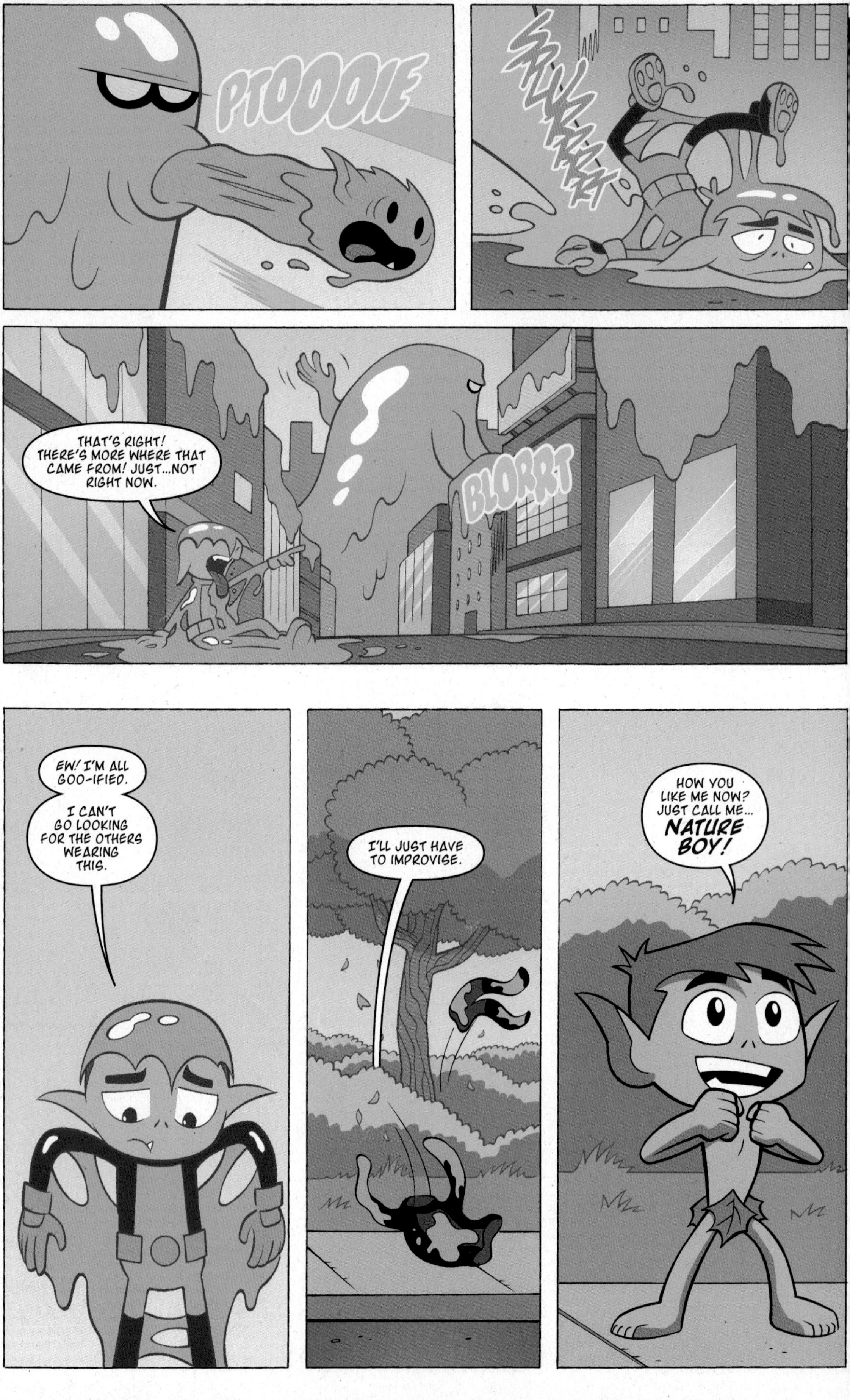
PTOOOIE
SPLAKAKAKAKT
THAT'S RIGHT! THERE'S MORE WHERE THAT CAME FROM! JUST...NOT RIGHT NOW.
BLORRT
EW! I'M ALL GOO-IFIED.
I CAN'T GO LOOKING FOR THE OTHERS WEARING THIS.
I'LL JUST HAVE TO IMPROVISE.
HOW YOU LIKE ME NOW? JUST CALL ME... NATURE BOY!

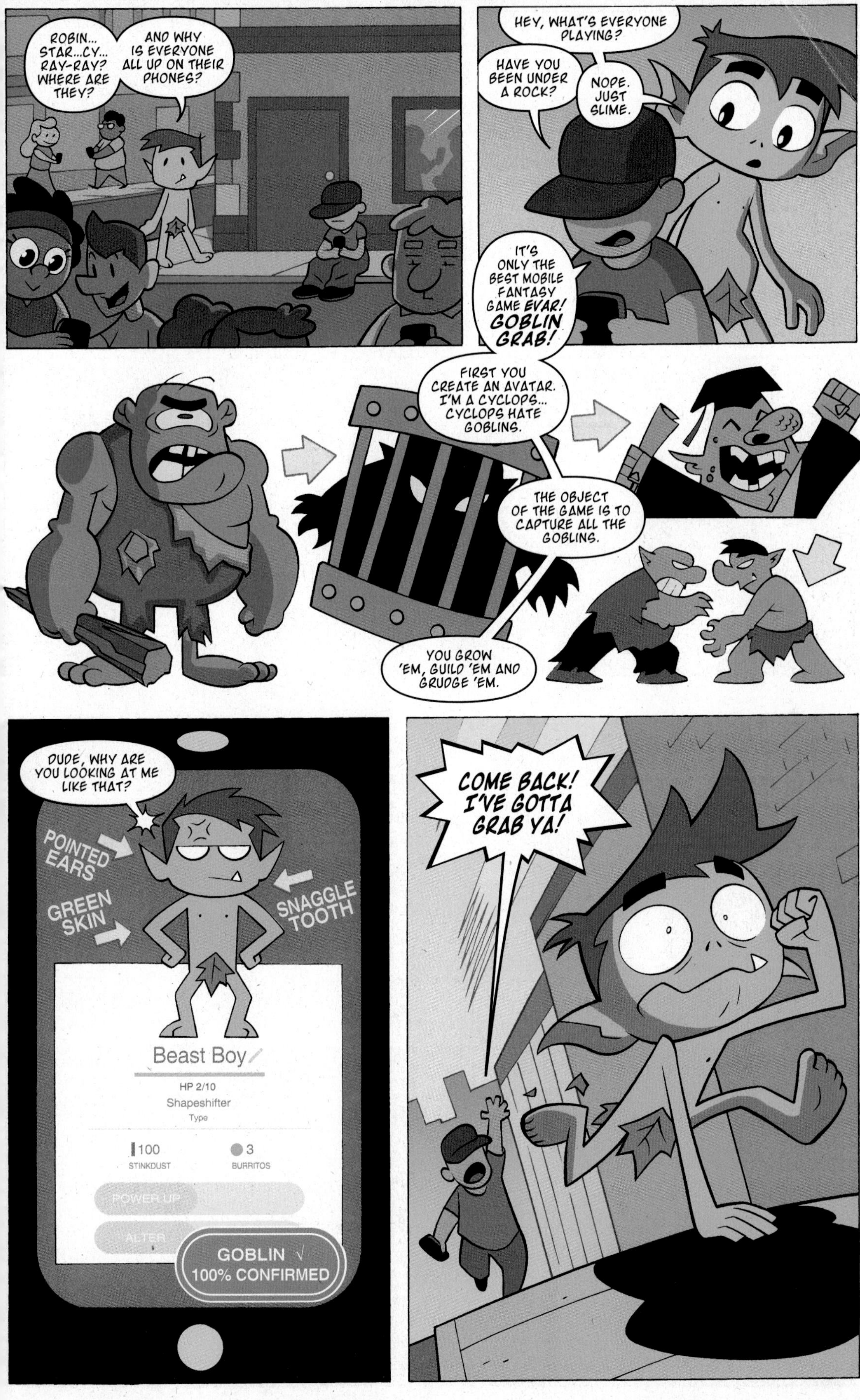
ROBIN... STAR...CY... RAY-RAY? WHERE ARE THEY?
AND WHY IS EVERYONE ALL UP ON THEIR PHONES?
HEY, WHAT'S EVERYONE PLAYING?
HAVE YOU BEEN UNDER A ROCK?
NOPE. JUST SLIME.
IT'S ONLY THE BEST MOBILE FANTASY GAME EVAR! GOBLIN GRAB!
FIRST YOU CREATE AN AVATAR. I'M A CYCLOPS... CYCLOPS HATE GOBLINS.
THE OBJECT OF THE GAME IS TO CAPTURE ALL THE GOBLINS.
YOU GROW 'EM, GUILD 'EM AND GRUDGE 'EM.
DUDE, WHY ARE YOU LOOKING AT ME LIKE THAT?
POINTED EARS
GREEN SKIN
SNAGGLE TOOTH
Beast Boy
HP 2/10
Shapeshifter
Type
100
STINKDUST
3
BURRITOS
POWER UP
ALTER
GOBLIN √
100% CONFIRMED
COME BACK! I'VE GOTTA GRAB YA!

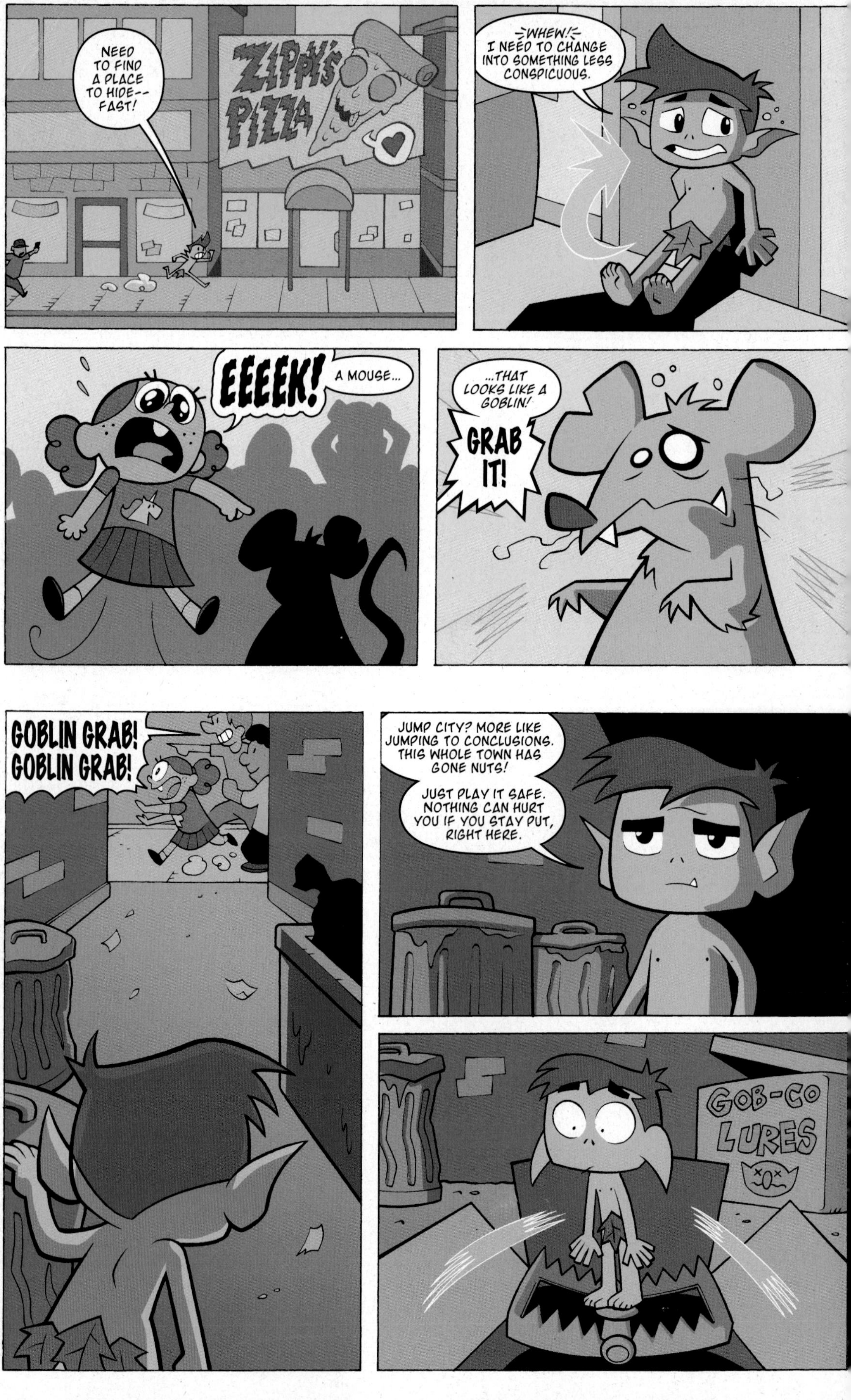

NEED TO FIND A PLACE TO HIDE-- FAST!
ZIPPY'S PIZZA
-WHEW!- I NEED TO CHANGE INTO SOMETHING LESS CONSPICUOUS.
EEEEK!
A MOUSE...
...THAT LOOKS LIKE A GOBLIN!
GRAB IT!
GOBLIN GRAB! GOBLIN GRAB!
JUMP CITY? MORE LIKE JUMPING TO CONCLUSIONS. THIS WHOLE TOWN HAS GONE NUTS!
JUST PLAY IT SAFE. NOTHING CAN HURT YOU IF YOU STAY PUT, RIGHT HERE.
GOB-CO LURES

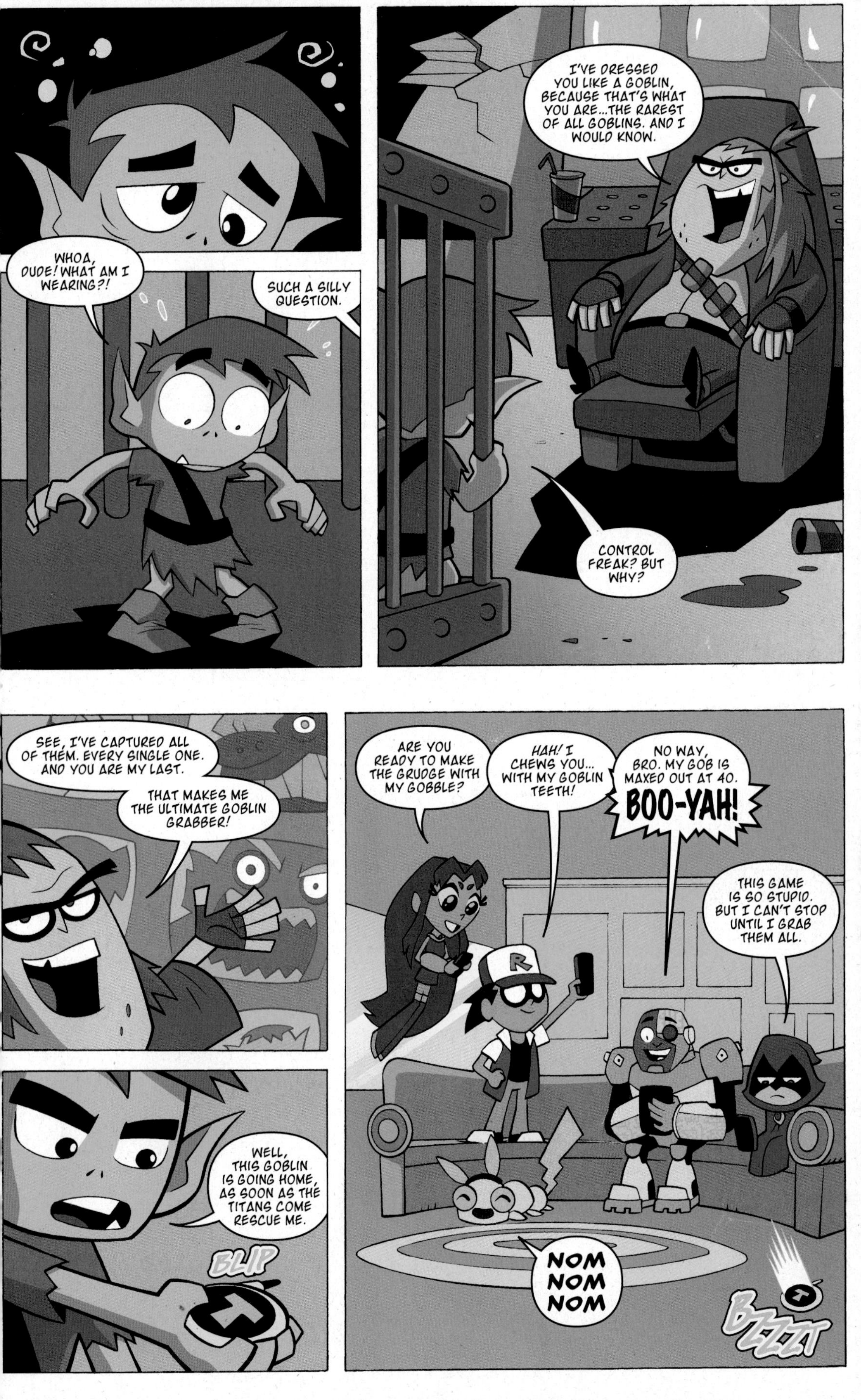
WHOA, DUDE! WHAT AM I WEARING?!
SUCH A SILLY QUESTION.
I'VE DRESSED YOU LIKE A GOBLIN, BECAUSE THAT'S WHAT YOU ARE...THE RAREST OF ALL GOBLINS. AND I WOULD KNOW.
CONTROL FREAK? BUT WHY?
SEE, I'VE CAPTURED ALL OF THEM. EVERY SINGLE ONE. AND YOU ARE MY LAST.
THAT MAKES ME THE ULTIMATE GOBLIN GRABBER!
WELL, THIS GOBLIN IS GOING HOME, AS SOON AS THE TITANS COME RESCUE ME.
BLIP
ARE YOU READY TO MAKE THE GRUDGE WITH MY GOBBLE?
HAH! I CHEWS YOU... WITH MY GOBLIN TEETH!
NO WAY, BRO. MY GOB IS MAXED OUT AT 40.
BOO-YAH!
THIS GAME IS SO STUPID. BUT I CAN'T STOP UNTIL I GRAB THEM ALL.
NOM NOM NOM
BZZZT

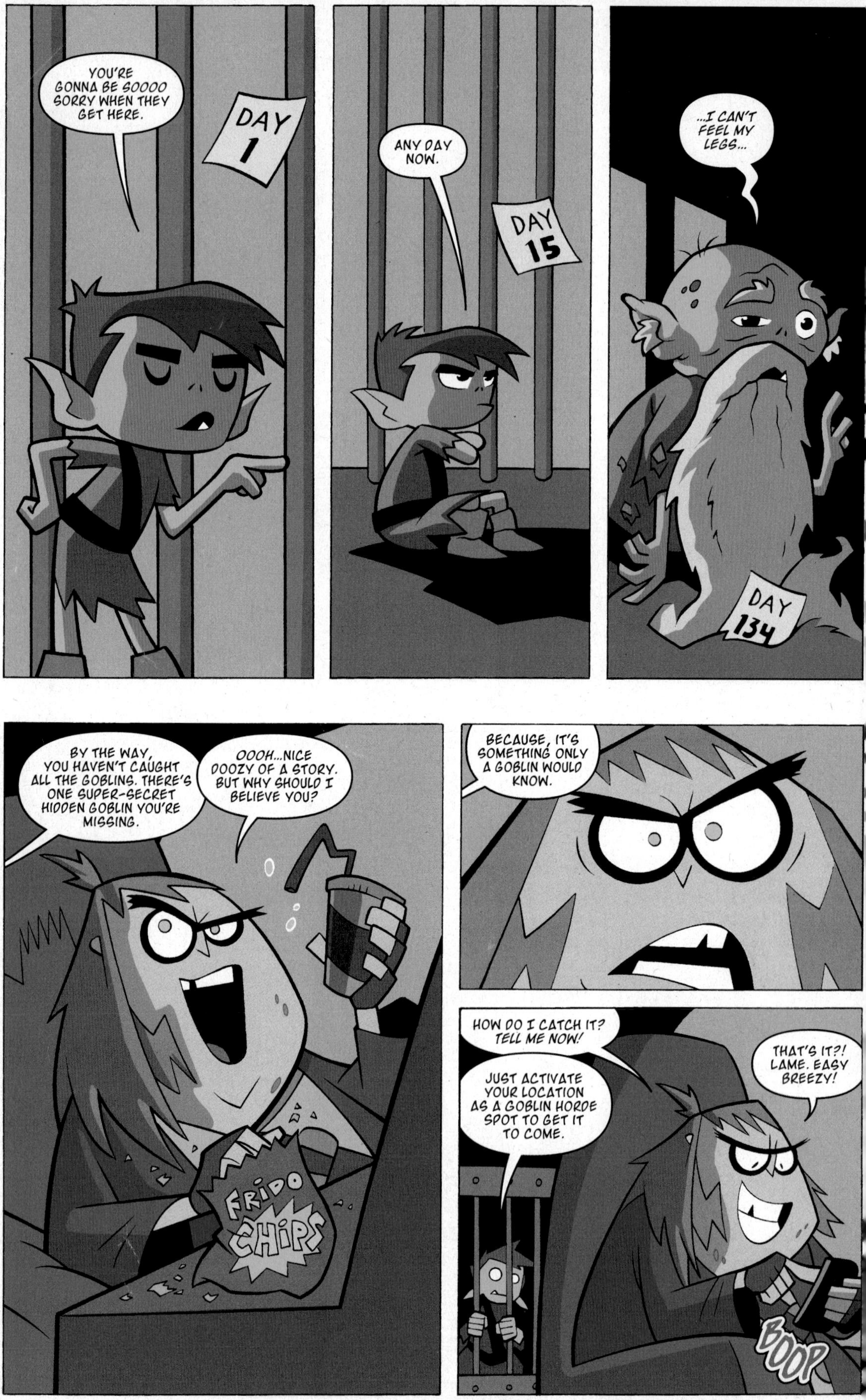
YOU'RE GONNA BE SOOOO SORRY WHEN THEY GET HERE.
DAY 1
ANY DAY NOW.
DAY 15
...I CAN'T FEEL MY LEGS...
DAY 134
BY THE WAY, YOU HAVEN'T CAUGHT ALL THE GOBLINS. THERE'S ONE SUPER-SECRET HIDDEN GOBLIN YOU'RE MISSING.
OOOH...NICE DOOZY OF A STORY. BUT WHY SHOULD I BELIEVE YOU?
FRIDO CHIPS
BECAUSE, IT'S SOMETHING ONLY A GOBLIN WOULD KNOW.
HOW DO I CATCH IT? TELL ME NOW!
JUST ACTIVATE YOUR LOCATION AS A GOBLIN HORDE SPOT TO GET IT TO COME.
THAT'S IT?! LAME. EASY BREEZY!
BOOP

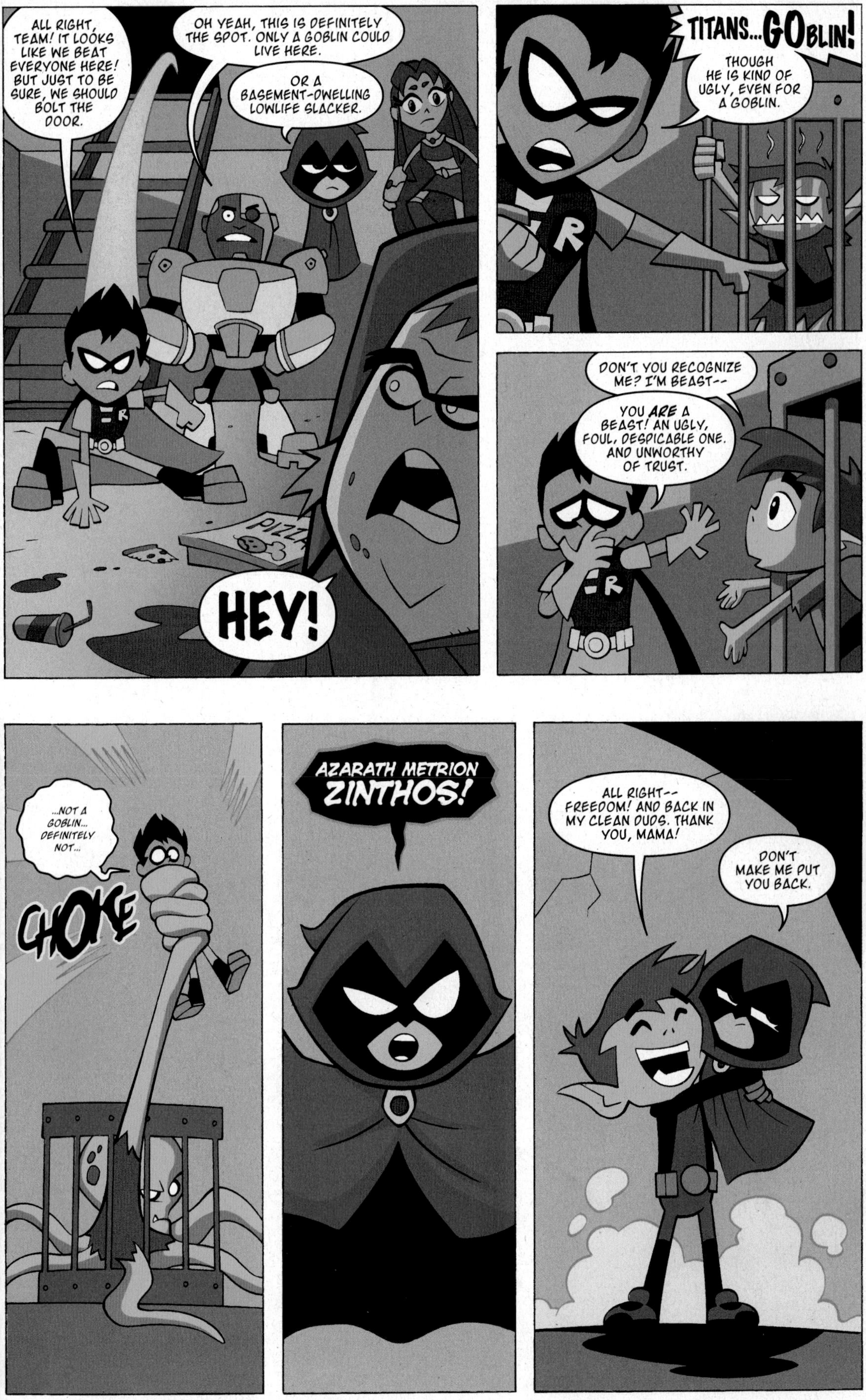
ALL RIGHT, TEAM! IT LOOKS LIKE WE BEAT EVERYONE HERE! BUT JUST TO BE SURE, WE SHOULD BOLT THE DOOR.
OH YEAH, THIS IS DEFINITELY THE SPOT. ONLY A GOBLIN COULD LIVE HERE.
OR A BASEMENT-DWELLING LOWLIFE SLACKER.
PIZZA
HEY!
TITANS...GOBLIN!
THOUGH HE IS KIND OF UGLY, EVEN FOR A GOBLIN.
DON'T YOU RECOGNIZE ME? I'M BEAST--
YOU ARE A BEAST! AN UGLY, FOUL, DESPICABLE ONE. AND UNWORTHY OF TRUST.
...NOT A GOBLIN... DEFINITELY NOT...
CHOKE
AZARATH METRION ZINTHOS!
ALL RIGHT-- FREEDOM! AND BACK IN MY CLEAN DUDS. THANK YOU, MAMA!
DON'T MAKE ME PUT YOU BACK.

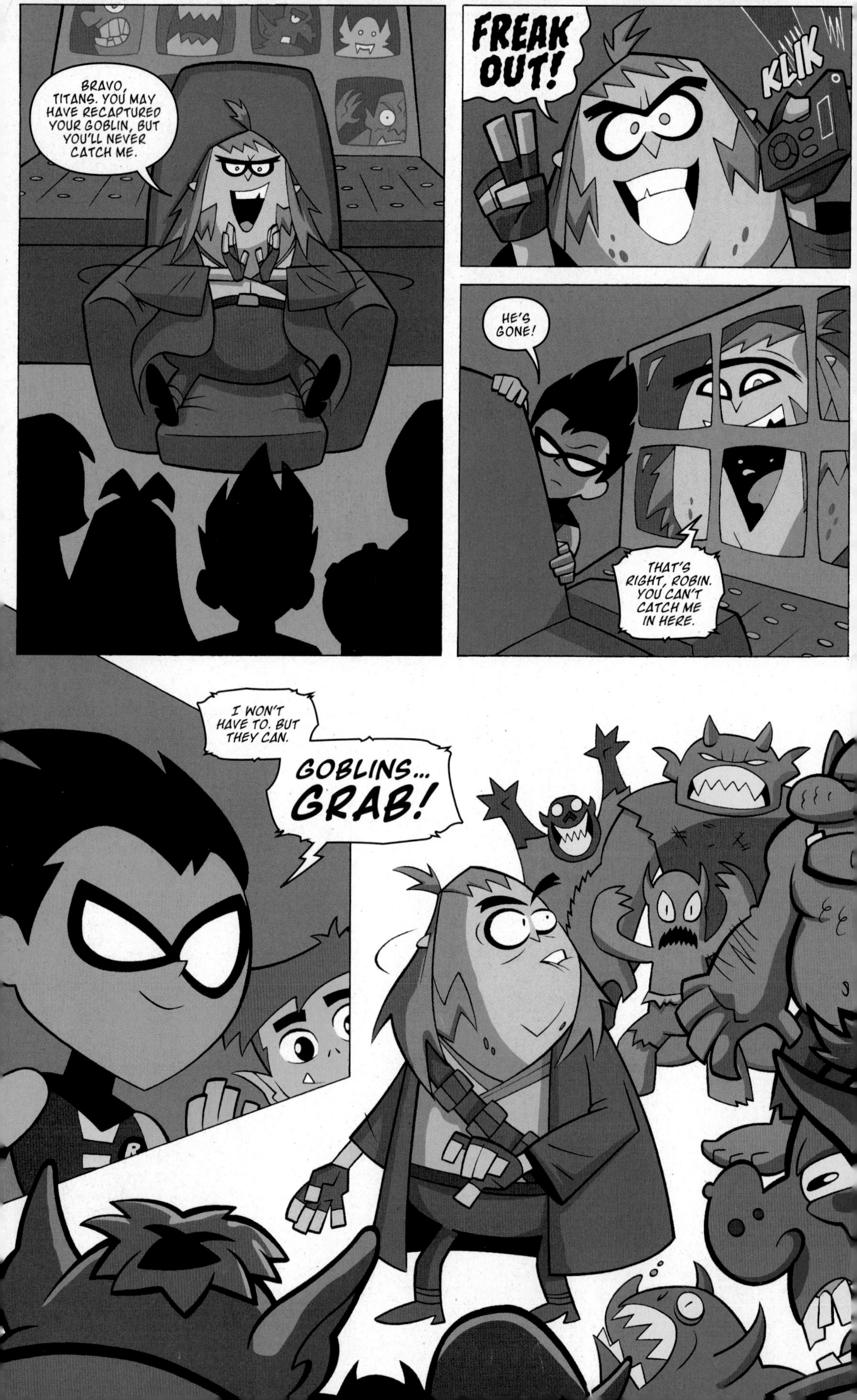
BRAVO, TITANS. YOU MAY HAVE RECAPTURED YOUR GOBLIN, BUT YOU'LL NEVER CATCH ME.
FREAK OUT!
KLIK
HE'S GONE!
THAT'S RIGHT, ROBIN. YOU CAN'T CATCH ME IN HERE.
I WON'T HAVE TO. BUT THEY CAN.
GOBLINS... GRAB!

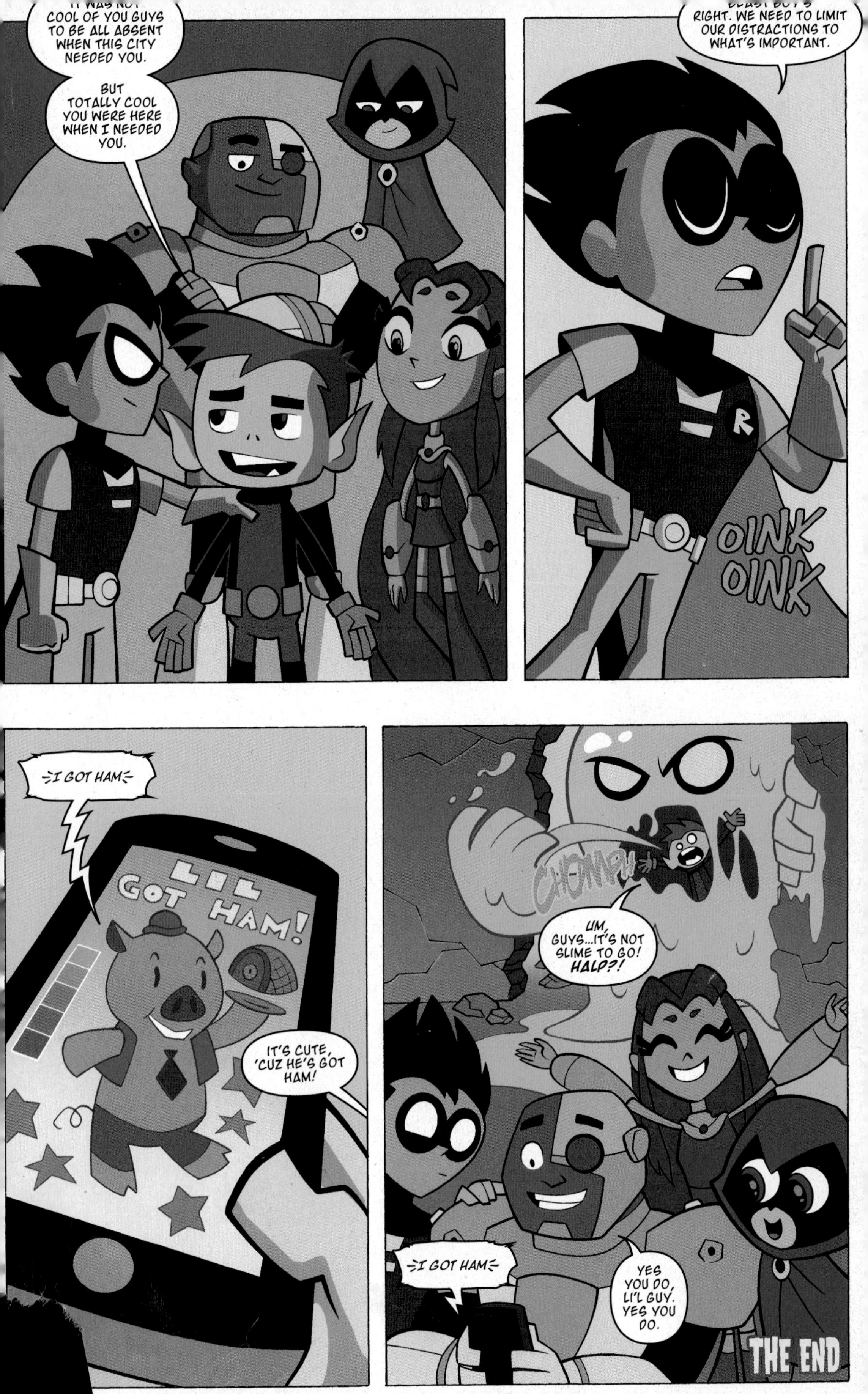
COOL OF YOU GUYS TO BE ALL ABSENT WHEN THIS CITY NEEDED YOU.
BUT TOTALLY COOL YOU WERE HERE WHEN I NEEDED YOU.
RIGHT. WE NEED TO LIMIT OUR DISTRACTIONS TO WHAT'S IMPORTANT.
OINK OINK
I GOT HAM
LIL GOT HAM!
IT'S CUTE, 'CUZ HE'S GOT HAM!
CHOMPH
UM, GUYS...IT'S NOT SLIME TO GO! HALP?!
I GOT HAM
YES YOU DO, LI'L GUY. YES YOU DO.
THE END

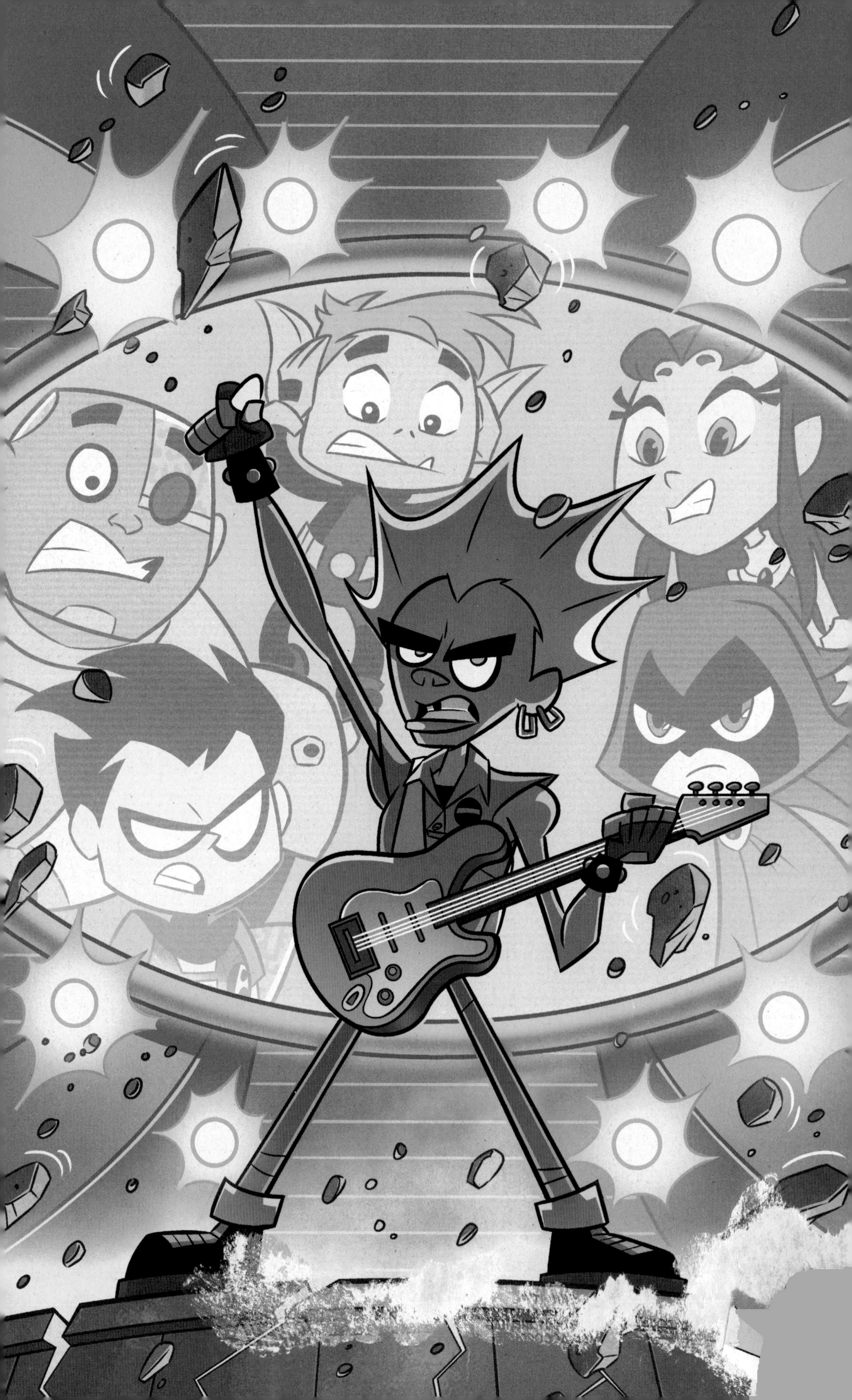

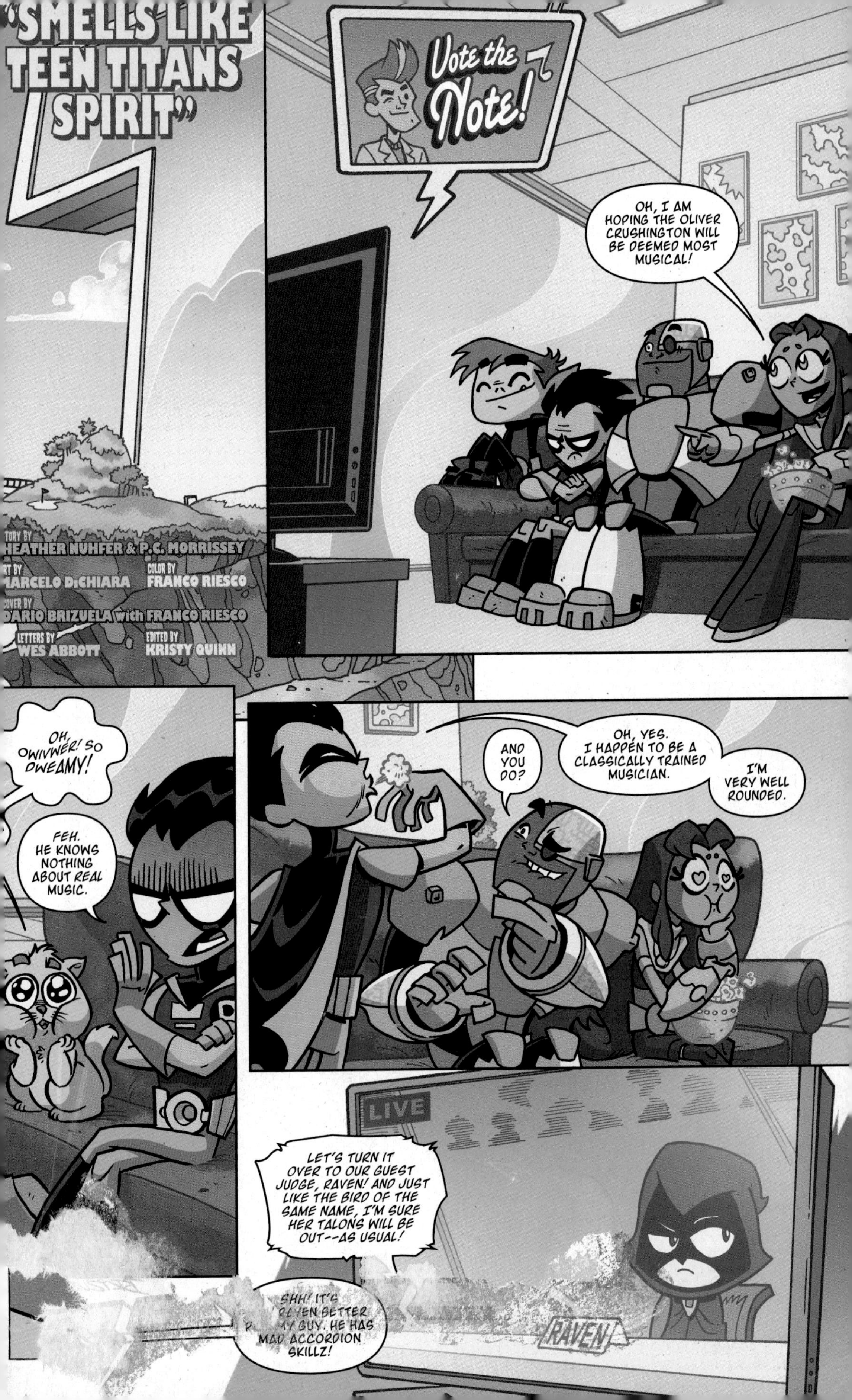
"SMELLS LIKE TEEN TITANS SPIRIT"
TORY BY
HEATHER NUHFER & P.C. MORRISSEY
RT BY
MARCELO DiCHIARA
COLOR BY
FRANCO RIESCO
OVER BY
DARIO BRIZUELA with FRANCO RIESCO
LETTERS BY
WES ABBOTT
EDITED BY
KRISTY QUINN
Vote the Note!
OH, I AM HOPING THE OLIVER CRUSHINGTON WILL BE DEEMED MOST MUSICAL!
OH, OWIVWER! SO DWEAMY!
FEH. HE KNOWS NOTHING ABOUT REAL MUSIC.
AND YOU DO?
OH, YES. I HAPPEN TO BE A CLASSICALLY TRAINED MUSICIAN.
I'M VERY WELL ROUNDED.
LIVE
LET'S TURN IT OVER TO OUR GUEST JUDGE, RAVEN! AND JUST LIKE THE BIRD OF THE SAME NAME, I'M SURE HER TALONS WILL BE OUT--AS USUAL!
SHH! IT'S
EN BETTER
GUY. HE HAS
MAD ACCORDION SKILLZ!
RAVEN

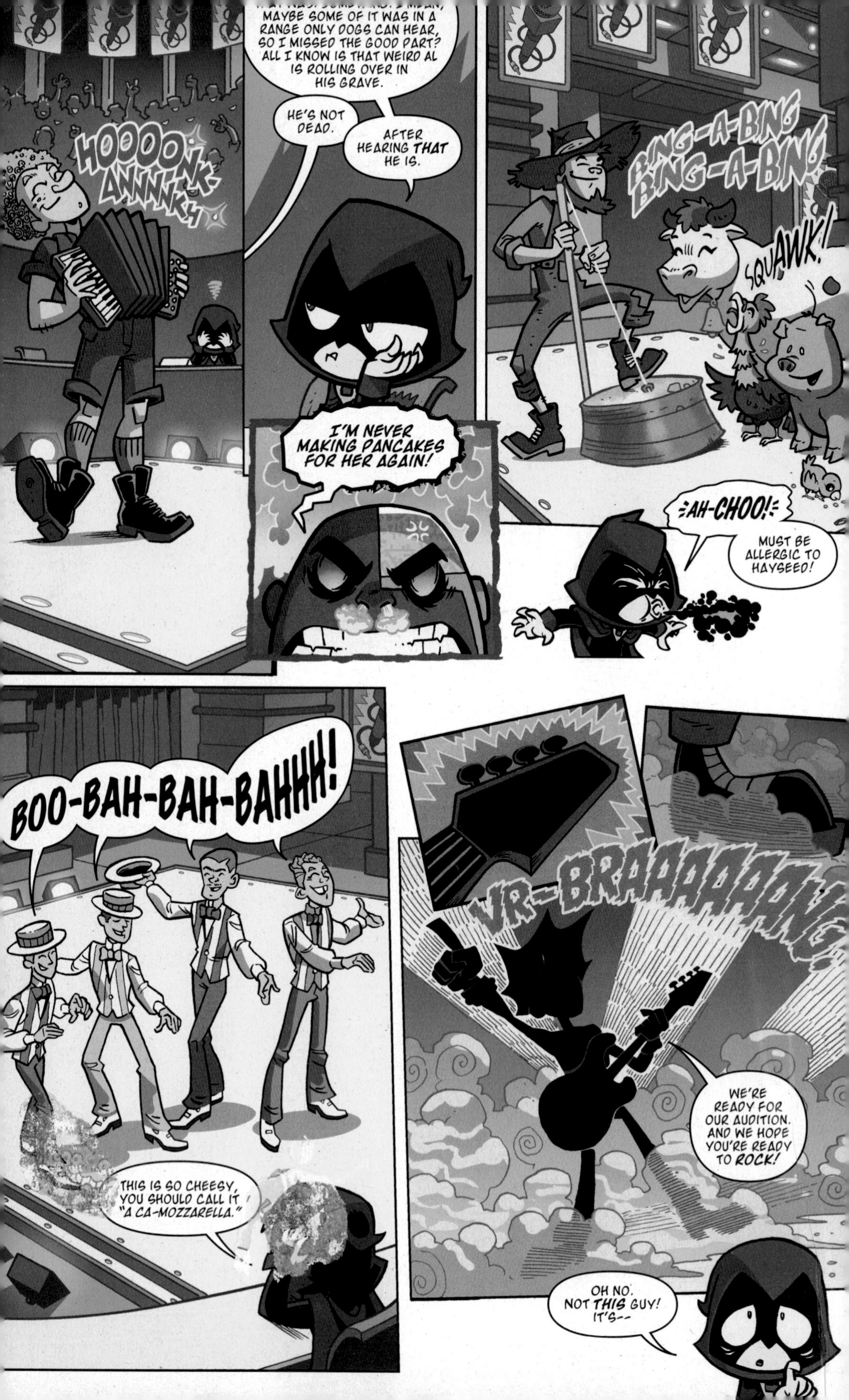
HOOOONK ANNNNK
MAYBE SOME OF IT WAS IN A RANGE ONLY DOGS CAN HEAR, SO I MISSED THE GOOD PART? ALL I KNOW IS THAT WEIRD AL IS ROLLING OVER IN HIS GRAVE.
HE'S NOT DEAD.
AFTER HEARING **THAT** HE IS.
I'M NEVER MAKING PANCAKES FOR HER AGAIN!
BING-A-BING BING-A-BING
SQUAWK!
AH-CHOO!
MUST BE ALLERGIC TO HAYSEED!
BOO-BAH-BAH-BAHHH!
THIS IS SO CHEESY, YOU SHOULD CALL IT "A CA-MOZZARELLA."
VR-BRAAAAAANG
WE'RE READY FOR OUR AUDITION. AND WE HOPE YOU'RE READY TO *ROCK!*
OH NO. NOT **THIS** GUY! IT'S--

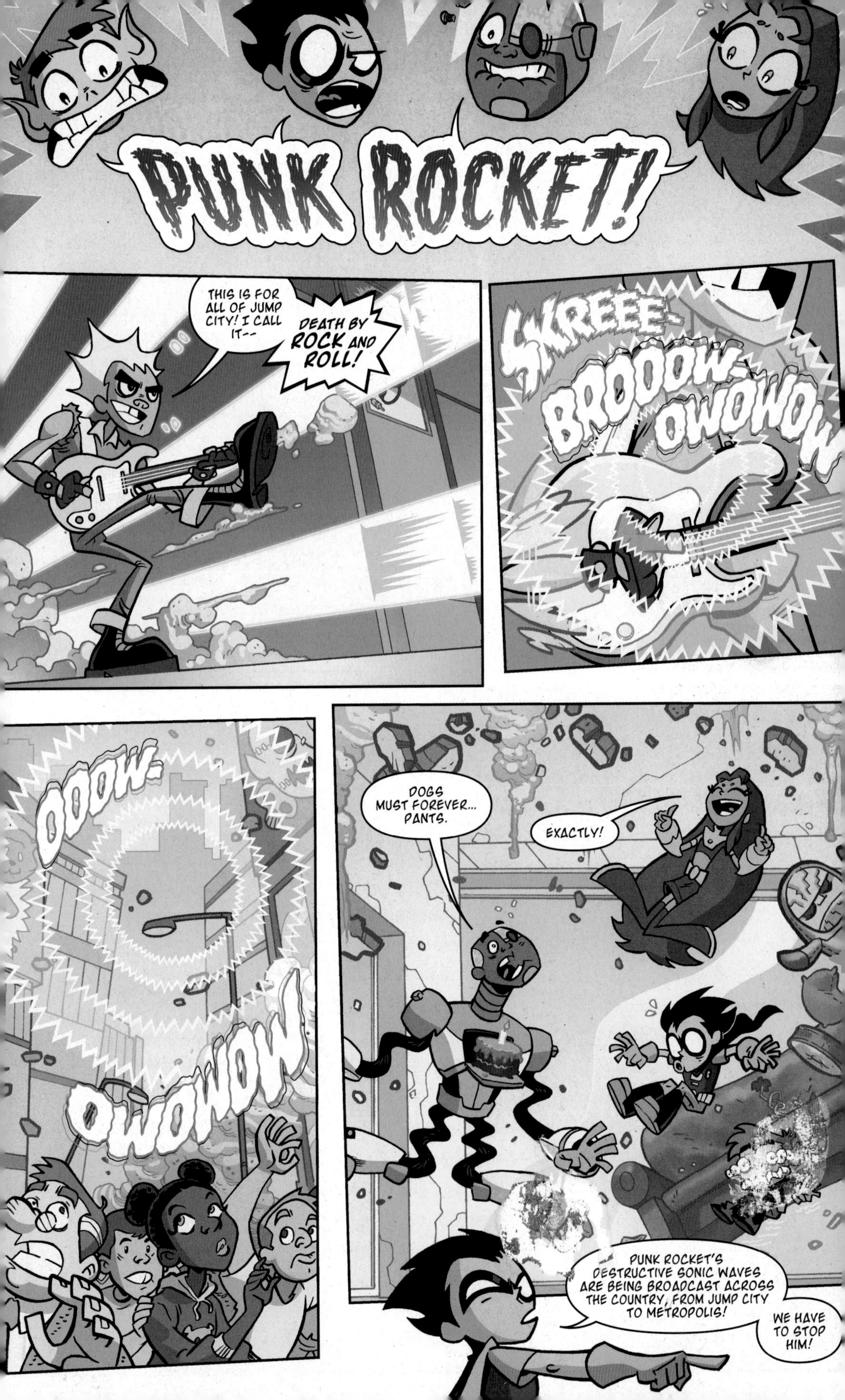
PUNK ROCKET!
THIS IS FOR ALL OF JUMP CITY! I CALL IT--
DEATH BY ROCK AND ROLL!
SKREEE-
BROOOW-
OWOWOW
OOOW-
OWOWOW
DOGS MUST FOREVER... PANTS.
EXACTLY!
PUNK ROCKET'S DESTRUCTIVE SONIC WAVES ARE BEING BROADCAST ACROSS THE COUNTRY, FROM JUMP CITY TO METROPOLIS!
WE HAVE TO STOP HIM!

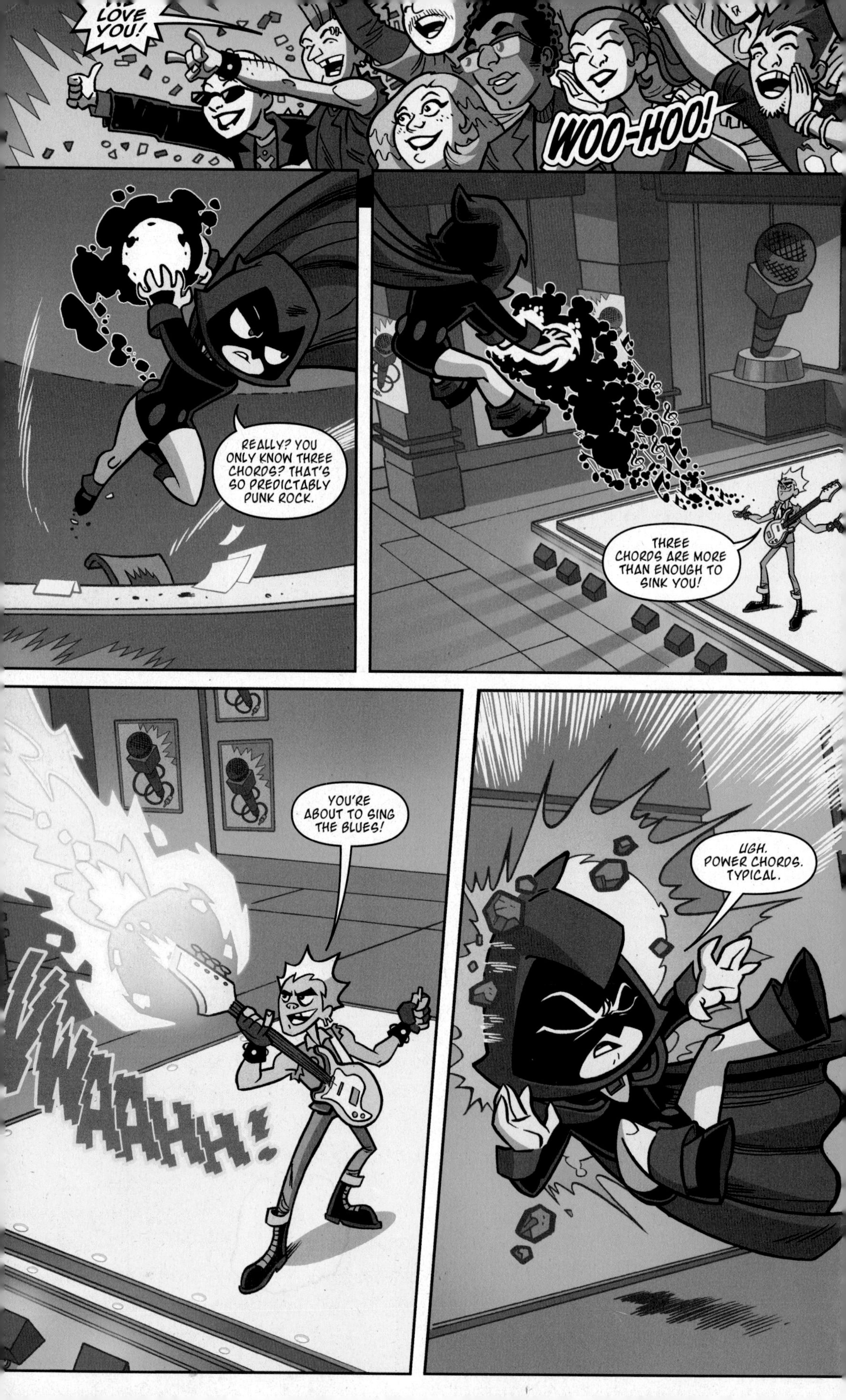
LOVE YOU!
WOO-HOO!
REALLY? YOU ONLY KNOW THREE CHORDS? THAT'S SO PREDICTABLY PUNK ROCK.
THREE CHORDS ARE MORE THAN ENOUGH TO SINK YOU!
YOU'RE ABOUT TO SING THE BLUES!
WAAHH!
UGH. POWER CHORDS. TYPICAL.

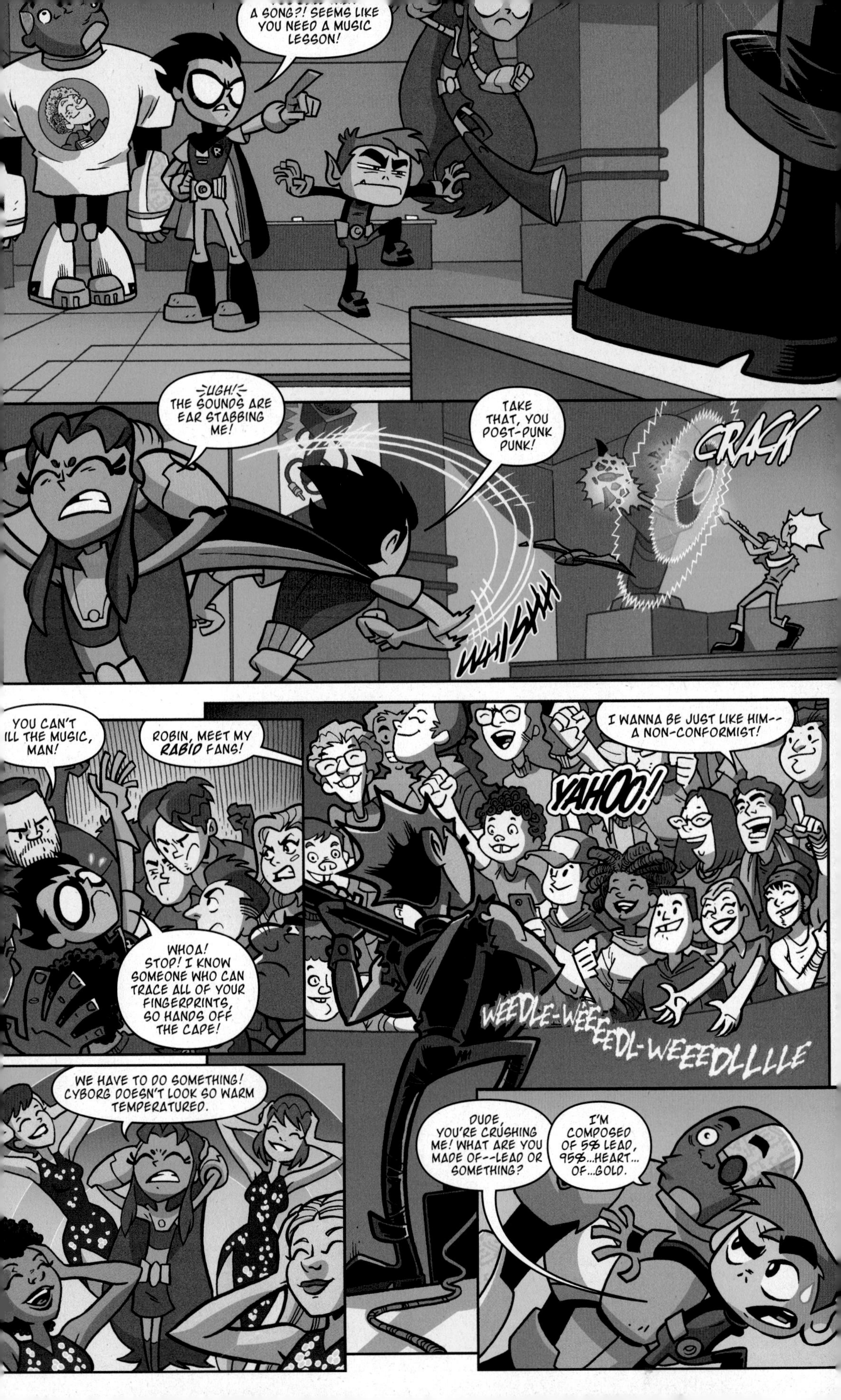
A SONG?! SEEMS LIKE YOU NEED A MUSIC LESSON!
UGH! THE SOUNDS ARE EAR STABBING ME!
TAKE THAT, YOU POST-PUNK PUNK!
CRACK
WHISHH
YOU CAN'T ILL THE MUSIC, MAN!
ROBIN, MEET MY RABID FANS!
WHOA! STOP! I KNOW SOMEONE WHO CAN TRACE ALL OF YOUR FINGERPRINTS, SO HANDS OFF THE CAPE!
I WANNA BE JUST LIKE HIM-- A NON-CONFORMIST!
YAHOO!
WEEDLE-WEEEEDL-WEEEDLLLLE
WE HAVE TO DO SOMETHING! CYBORG DOESN'T LOOK SO WARM TEMPERATURED.
DUDE, YOU'RE CRUSHING ME! WHAT ARE YOU MADE OF--LEAD OR SOMETHING?
I'M COMPOSED OF 5% LEAD, 95%...HEART... OF...GOLD.

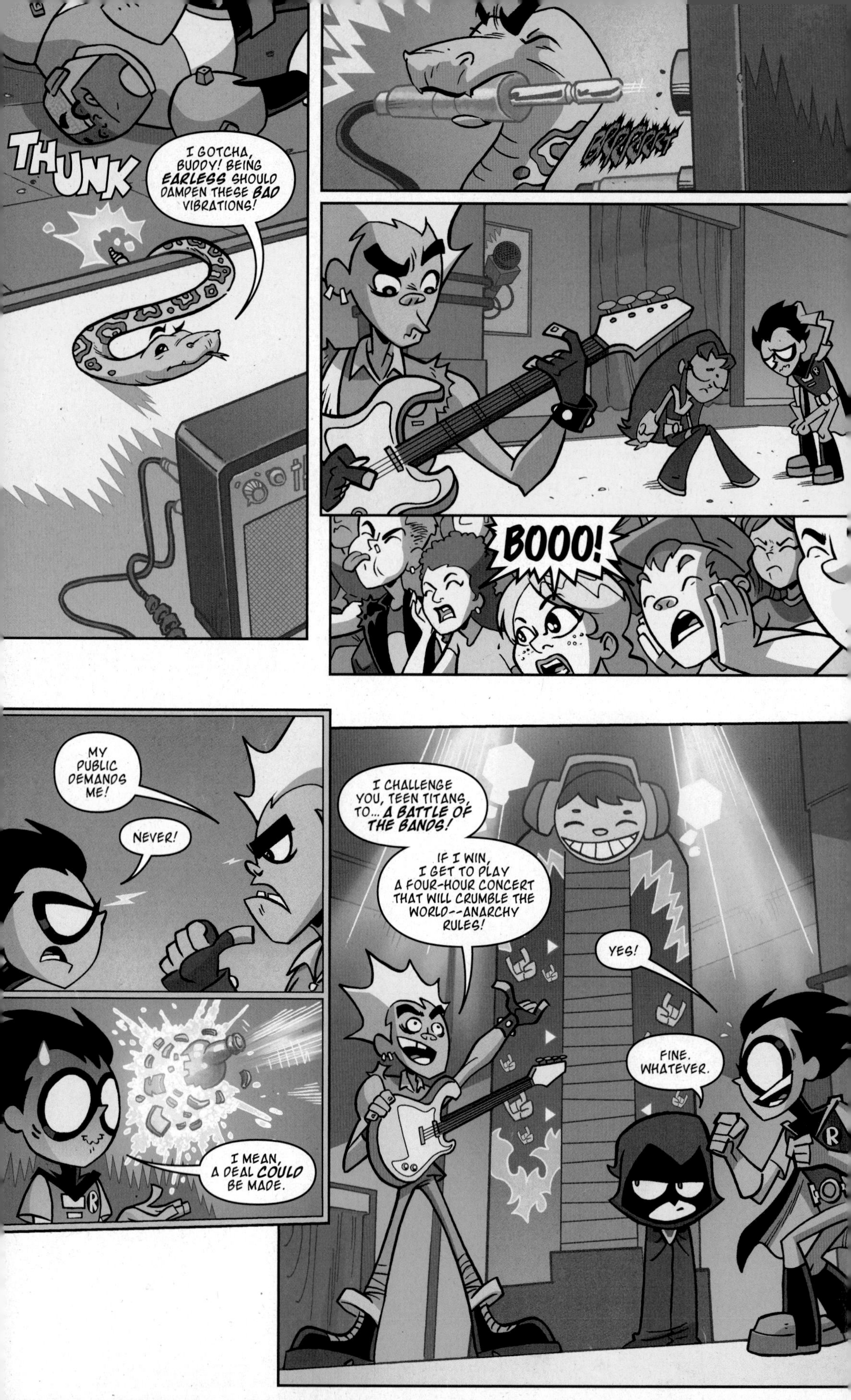
THUNK
I GOTCHA, BUDDY! BEING EARLESS SHOULD DAMPEN THESE BAD VIBRATIONS!
BOOO!
MY PUBLIC DEMANDS ME!
NEVER!
I MEAN, A DEAL COULD BE MADE.
I CHALLENGE YOU, TEEN TITANS, TO... A BATTLE OF THE BANDS!
IF I WIN, I GET TO PLAY A FOUR-HOUR CONCERT THAT WILL CRUMBLE THE WORLD--ANARCHY RULES!
YES!
FINE. WHATEVER.

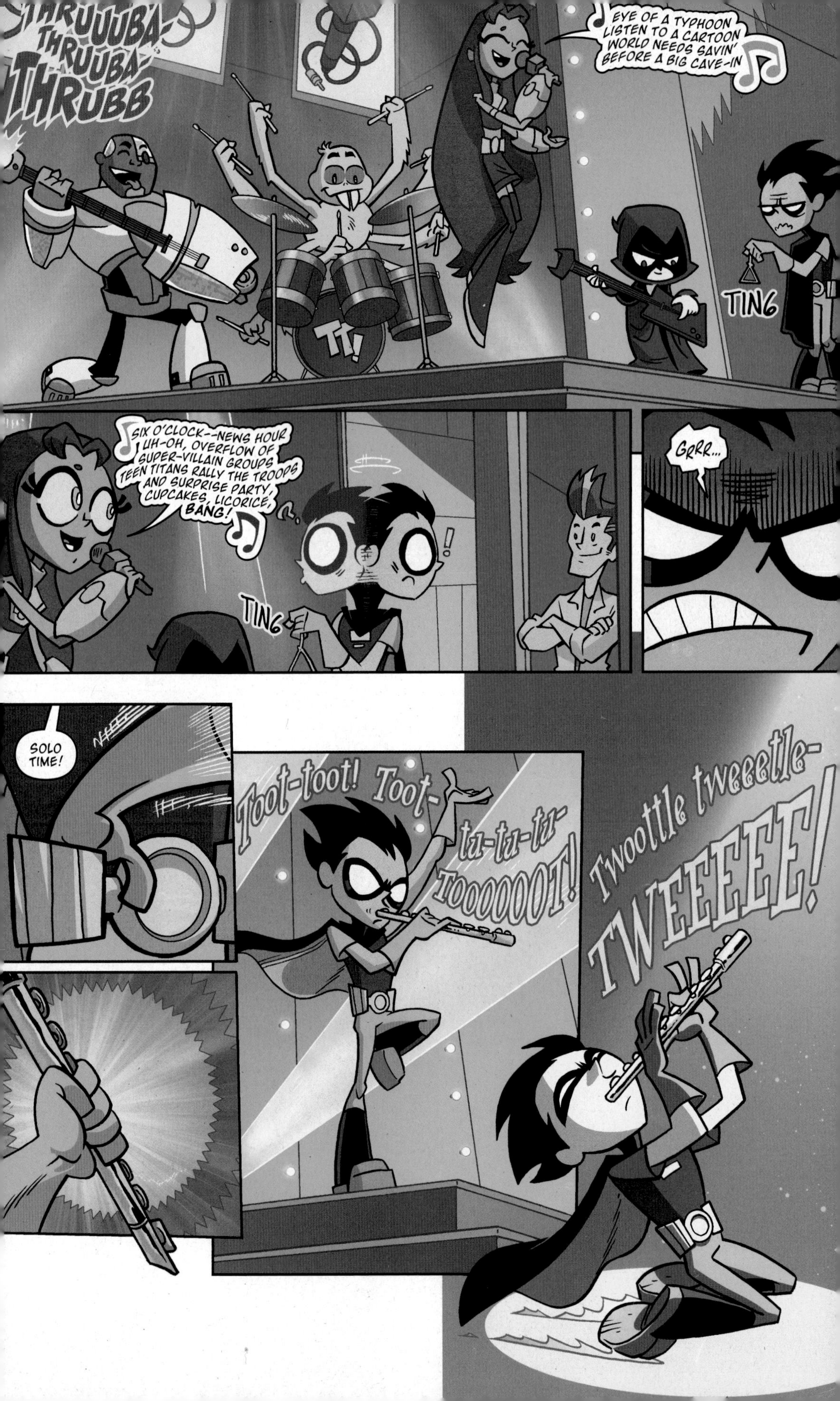
THRUUUBA-THRUUBA-THRUUBA-THRUBB
EYE OF A TYPHOON LISTEN TO A CARTOON WORLD NEEDS SAVIN' BEFORE A BIG CAVE-IN
TT!
TING
SIX O'CLOCK--NEWS HOUR UH-OH, OVERFLOW OF SUPER-VILLAIN GROUPS TEEN TITANS RALLY THE TROOPS AND SURPRISE PARTY, CUPCAKES, LICORICE, BANG!
TING
GRRR...
SOLO TIME!
Toot-toot! Toot-ta-ta-ta-TOOOOOOT!
Twoottle tweeetle-TWEEEEE!

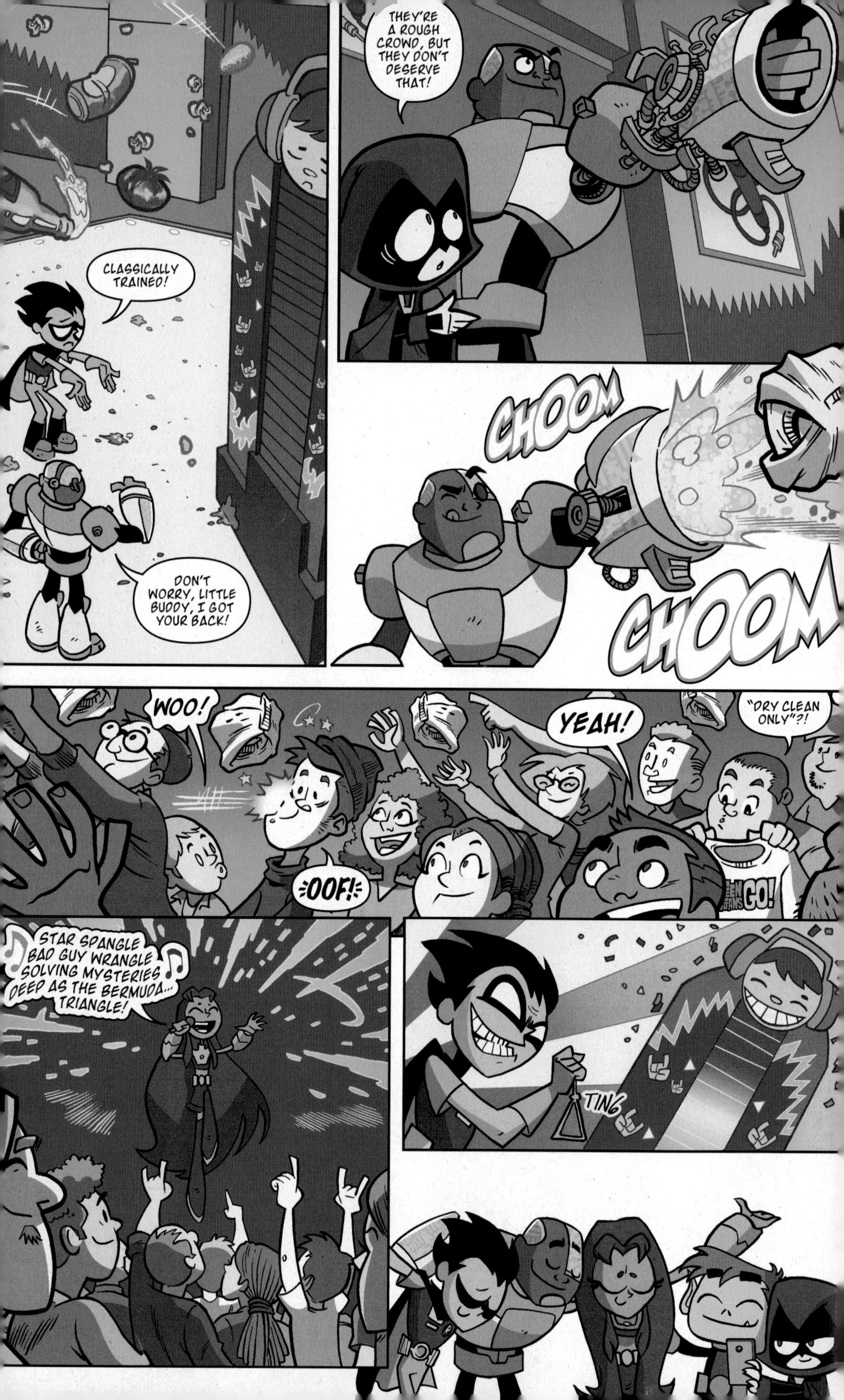
THEY'RE A ROUGH CROWD, BUT THEY DON'T DESERVE THAT!
CLASSICALLY TRAINED!
DON'T WORRY, LITTLE BUDDY, I GOT YOUR BACK!
CHOOM
CHOOM
WOO!
YEAH!
"DRY CLEAN ONLY"?!
OOF!
TEEN TITANS GO!
STAR SPANGLE BAD GUY WRANGLE SOLVING MYSTERIES DEEP AS THE BERMUDA... TRIANGLE!
TING

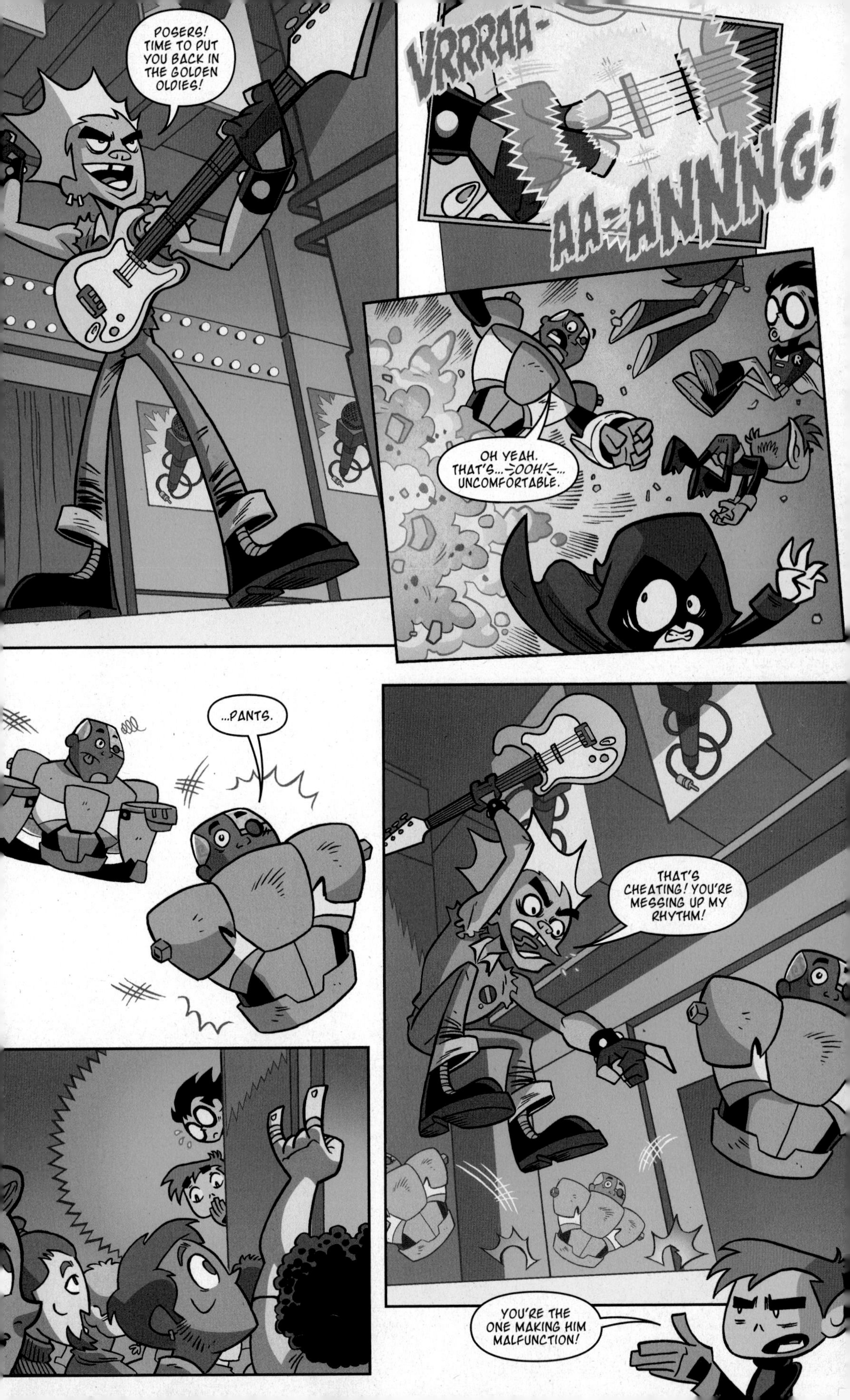
POSERS! TIME TO PUT YOU BACK IN THE GOLDEN OLDIES!
VRRRAA-
AA-ANNNG!
OH YEAH. THAT'S... OOH! ... UNCOMFORTABLE.
...PANTS.
THAT'S CHEATING! YOU'RE MESSING UP MY RHYTHM!
YOU'RE THE ONE MAKING HIM MALFUNCTION!

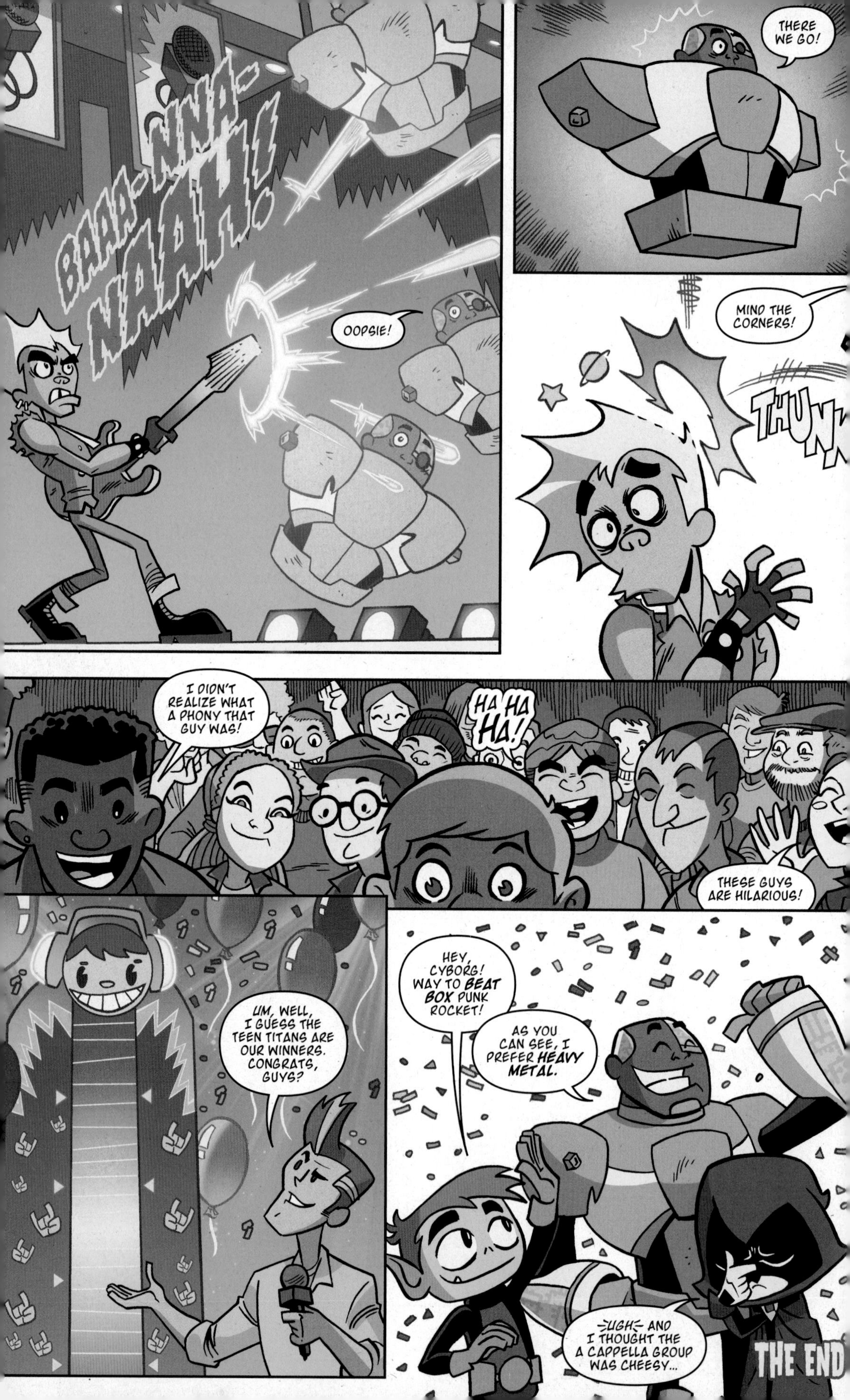
BAAA-NNA-NAAH!
OOPSIE!
THERE WE GO!
MIND THE CORNERS!
THUNK
I DIDN'T REALIZE WHAT A PHONY THAT GUY WAS!
HA HA HA!
THESE GUYS ARE HILARIOUS!
UM, WELL, I GUESS THE TEEN TITANS ARE OUR WINNERS. CONGRATS, GUYS?
HEY, CYBORG! WAY TO BEAT BOX PUNK ROCKET!
AS YOU CAN SEE, I PREFER HEAVY METAL.
UGH AND I THOUGHT THE A CAPPELLA GROUP WAS CHEESY...
THE END

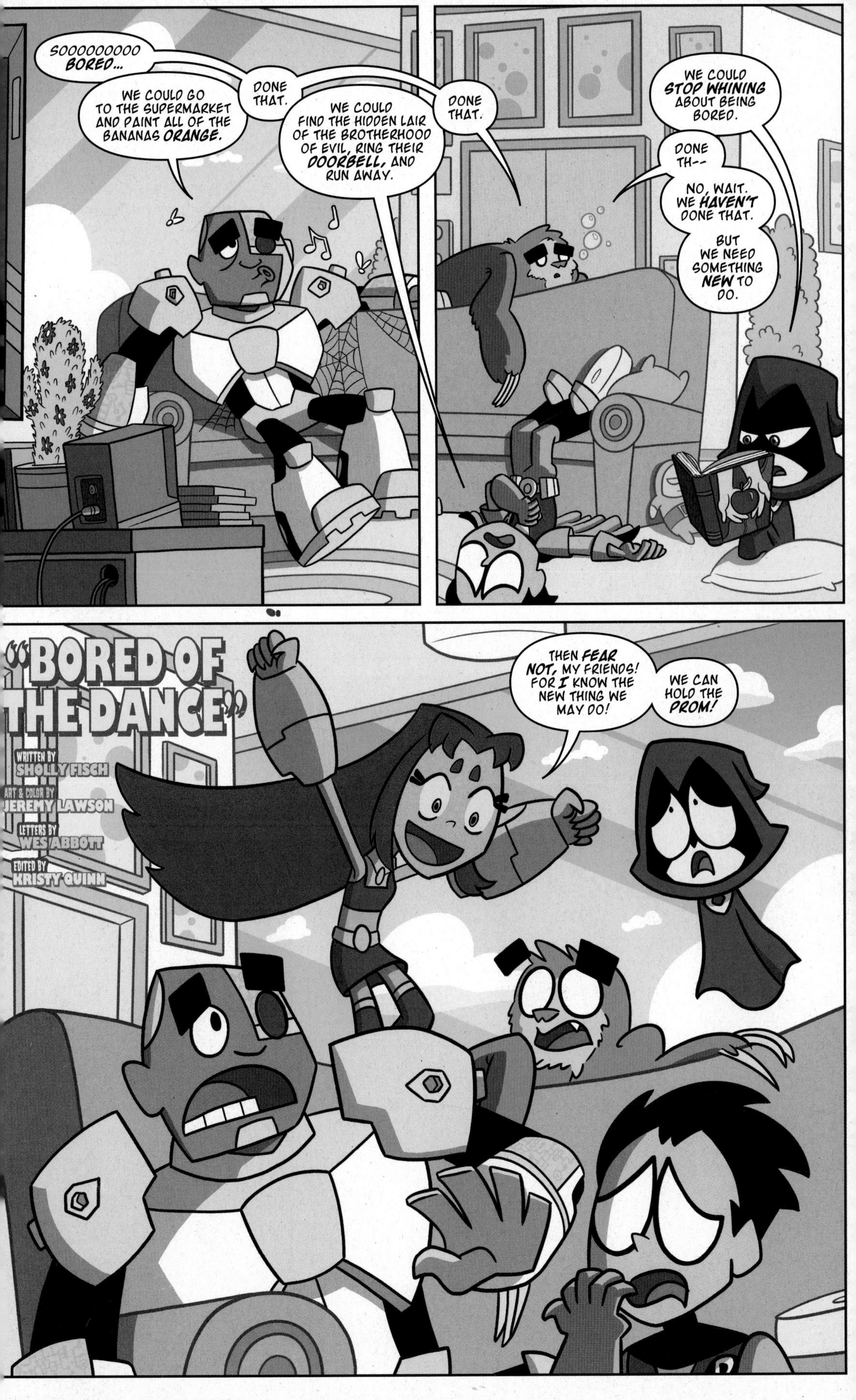
SOOOOOOOOO BOREO...
WE COULD GO TO THE SUPERMARKET AND PAINT ALL OF THE BANANAS ORANGE.
DONE THAT.
WE COULD FIND THE HIDDEN LAIR OF THE BROTHERHOOD OF EVIL, RING THEIR DOORBELL, AND RUN AWAY.
DONE THAT.
WE COULD STOP WHINING ABOUT BEING BORED.
DONE TH--
NO, WAIT. WE HAVEN'T DONE THAT.
BUT WE NEED SOMETHING NEW TO DO.
"BORED OF THE DANCE"
WRITTEN BY SHOLLY FISCH
ART & COLOR BY JEREMY LAWSON
LETTERS BY WES ABBOTT
EDITED BY KRISTY QUINN
THEN FEAR NOT, MY FRIENDS! FOR I KNOW THE NEW THING WE MAY DO!
WE CAN HOLD THE PROM!

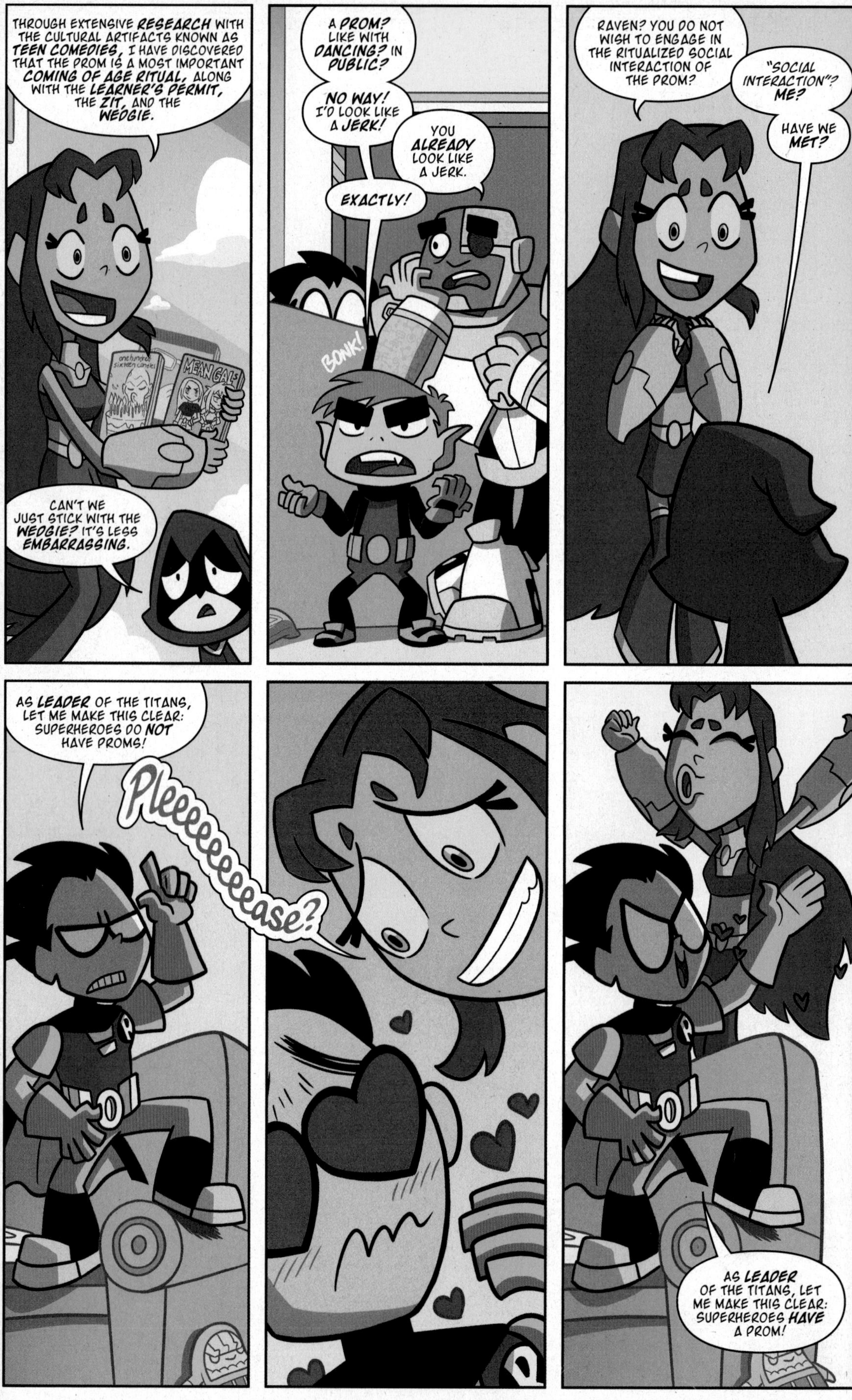

THROUGH EXTENSIVE RESEARCH WITH THE CULTURAL ARTIFACTS KNOWN AS TEEN COMEDIES, I HAVE DISCOVERED THAT THE PROM IS A MOST IMPORTANT COMING OF AGE RITUAL, ALONG WITH THE LEARNER'S PERMIT, THE ZIT, AND THE WEDGIE.
one hundred sixteen candles
MEAN GALS
CAN'T WE JUST STICK WITH THE WEDGIE? IT'S LESS EMBARRASSING.
A PROM? LIKE WITH DANCING? IN PUBLIC?
NO WAY! I'D LOOK LIKE A JERK!
YOU ALREADY LOOK LIKE A JERK.
EXACTLY!
BONK!
RAVEN? YOU DO NOT WISH TO ENGAGE IN THE RITUALIZED SOCIAL INTERACTION OF THE PROM?
"SOCIAL INTERACTION"? ME?
HAVE WE MET?
AS LEADER OF THE TITANS, LET ME MAKE THIS CLEAR: SUPERHEROES DO NOT HAVE PROMS!
Pleeeeeeeeease?
AS LEADER OF THE TITANS, LET ME MAKE THIS CLEAR: SUPERHEROES HAVE A PROM!

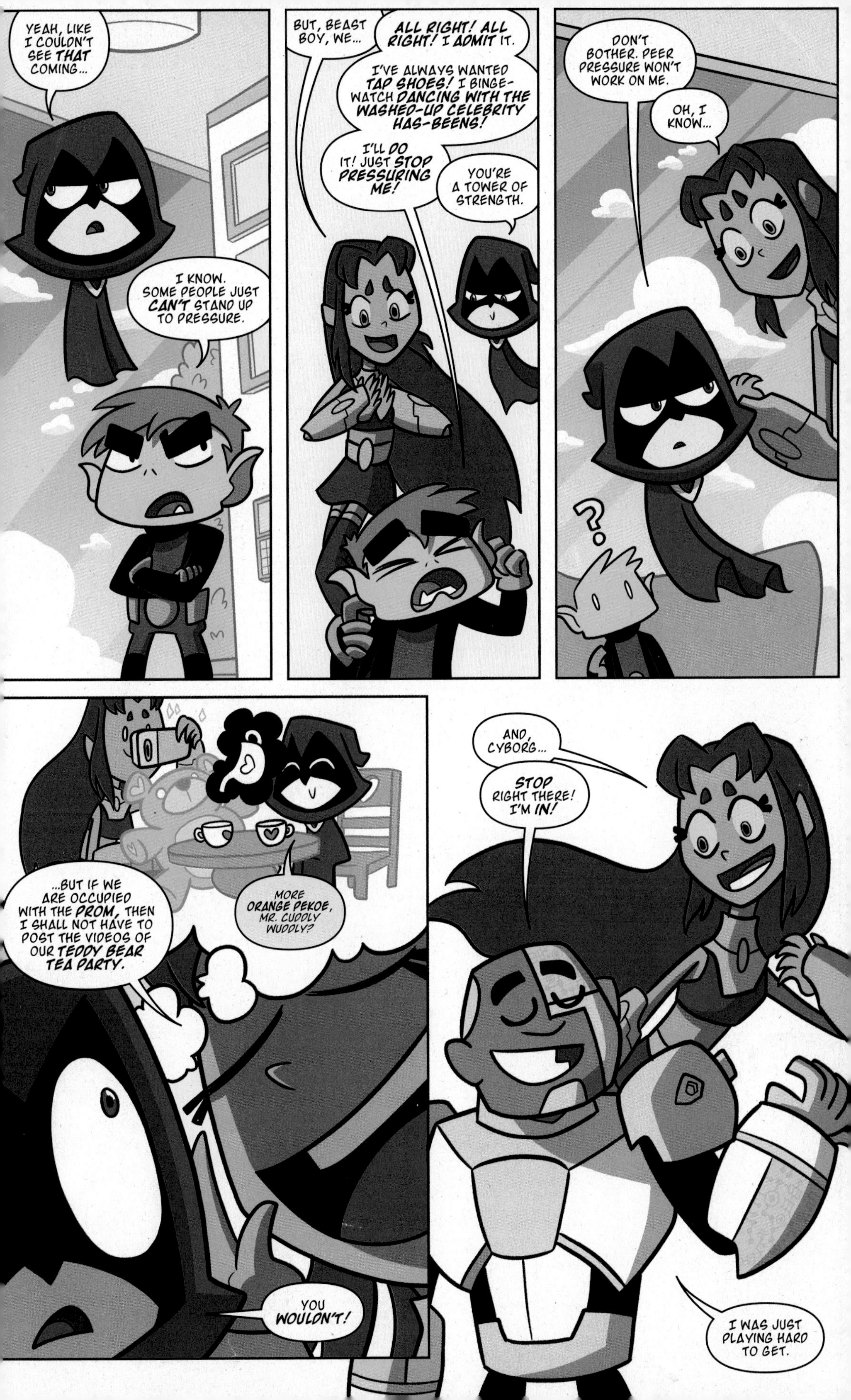

YEAH, LIKE I COULDN'T SEE THAT COMING...
I KNOW. SOME PEOPLE JUST CAN'T STAND UP TO PRESSURE.
BUT, BEAST BOY, WE...
ALL RIGHT! ALL RIGHT! I ADMIT IT.
I'VE ALWAYS WANTED TAP SHOES! I BINGE-WATCH DANCING WITH THE WASHED-UP CELEBRITY HAS-BEENS!
I'LL DO IT! JUST STOP PRESSURING ME!
YOU'RE A TOWER OF STRENGTH.
DON'T BOTHER. PEER PRESSURE WON'T WORK ON ME.
OH, I KNOW...
?
...BUT IF WE ARE OCCUPIED WITH THE PROM, THEN I SHALL NOT HAVE TO POST THE VIDEOS OF OUR TEDDY BEAR TEA PARTY.
MORE ORANGE PEKOE, MR. CUDDLY WUDDLY?
YOU WOULDN'T!
AND, CYBORG...
STOP RIGHT THERE! I'M IN!
I WAS JUST PLAYING HARD TO GET.

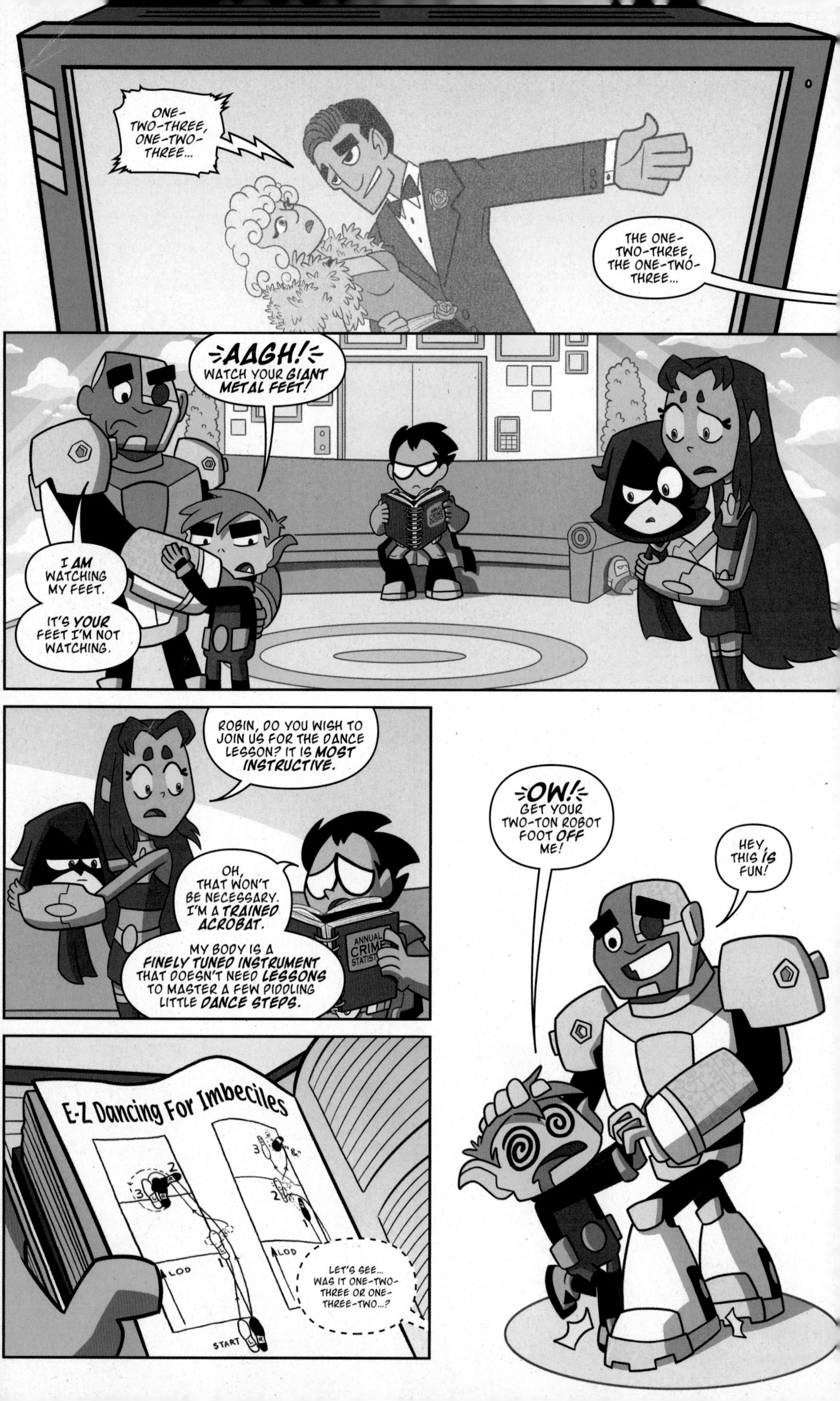
ONE-TWO-THREE, ONE-TWO-THREE...
THE ONE-TWO-THREE, THE ONE-TWO-THREE...
AAGH! WATCH YOUR GIANT METAL FEET!
I AM WATCHING MY FEET.
IT'S YOUR FEET I'M NOT WATCHING.
ANNUAL CRIME STATISTICS
ROBIN, DO YOU WISH TO JOIN US FOR THE DANCE LESSON? IT IS MOST INSTRUCTIVE.
OH, THAT WON'T BE NECESSARY. I'M A TRAINED ACROBAT.
MY BODY IS A FINELY TUNED INSTRUMENT THAT DOESN'T NEED LESSONS TO MASTER A FEW PIDDLING LITTLE DANCE STEPS.
E-Z Dancing For Imbeciles
START
LOD
LET'S SEE... WAS IT ONE-TWO-THREE OR ONE-THREE-TWO...?
OW! GET YOUR TWO-TON ROBOT FOOT OFF ME!
HEY, THIS IS FUN!

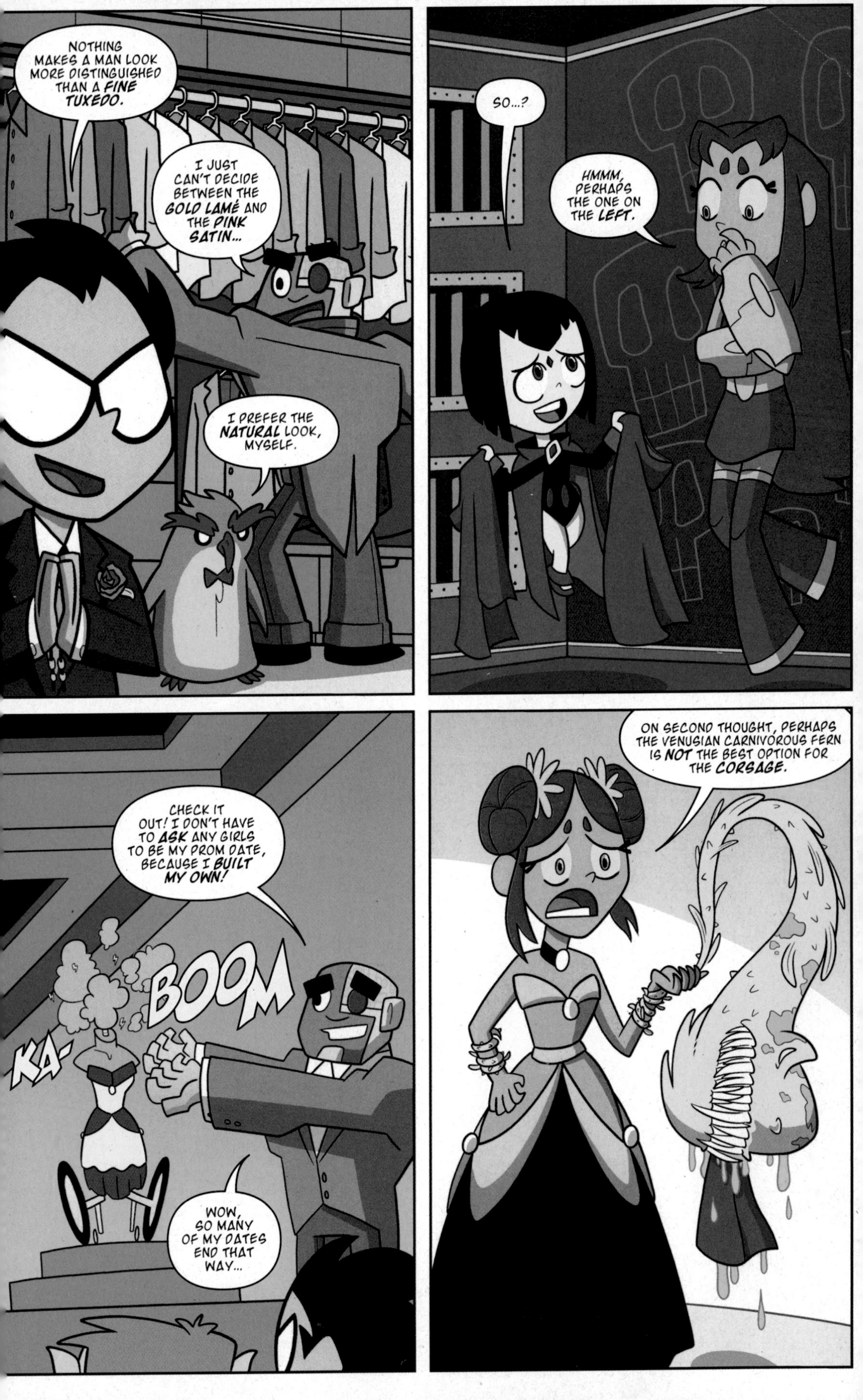
NOTHING MAKES A MAN LOOK MORE DISTINGUISHED THAN A FINE TUXEDO.
I JUST CAN'T DECIDE BETWEEN THE GOLD LAMÉ AND THE PINK SATIN...
I PREFER THE NATURAL LOOK, MYSELF.
SO...?
HMMM, PERHAPS THE ONE ON THE LEFT.
CHECK IT OUT! I DON'T HAVE TO ASK ANY GIRLS TO BE MY PROM DATE, BECAUSE I BUILT MY OWN!
KA-BOOM
WOW, SO MANY OF MY DATES END THAT WAY...
ON SECOND THOUGHT, PERHAPS THE VENUSIAN CARNIVOROUS FERN IS NOT THE BEST OPTION FOR THE CORSAGE.

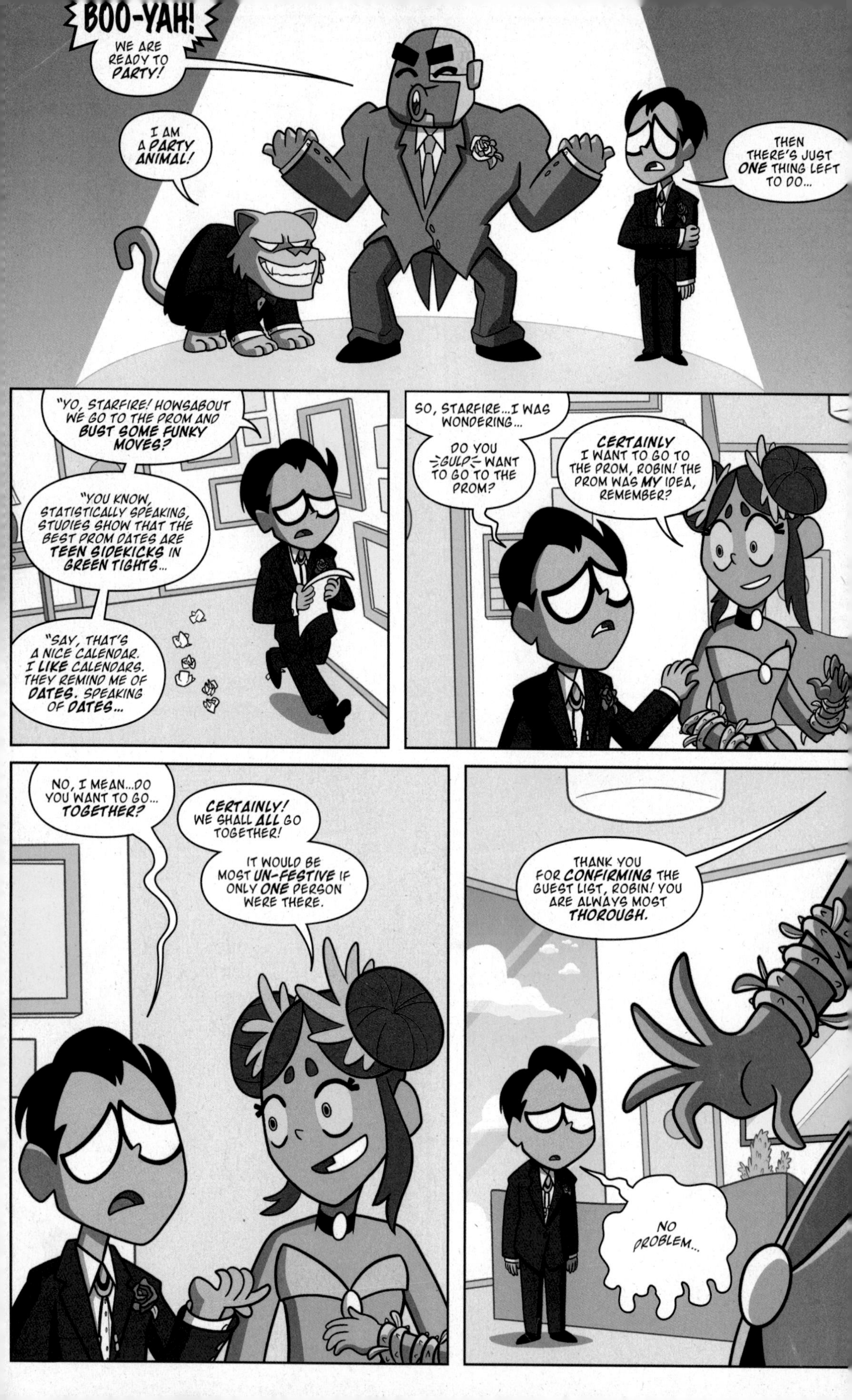
BOO-YAH!
WE ARE READY TO PARTY!
I AM A PARTY ANIMAL!
THEN THERE'S JUST ONE THING LEFT TO DO...
"YO, STARFIRE! HOWSABOUT WE GO TO THE PROM AND BUST SOME FUNKY MOVES?
"YOU KNOW, STATISTICALLY SPEAKING, STUDIES SHOW THAT THE BEST PROM DATES ARE TEEN SIDEKICKS IN GREEN TIGHTS...
"SAY, THAT'S A NICE CALENDAR. I LIKE CALENDARS. THEY REMIND ME OF DATES. SPEAKING OF DATES...
SO, STARFIRE...I WAS WONDERING...
DO YOU -GULP- WANT TO GO TO THE PROM?
CERTAINLY I WANT TO GO TO THE PROM, ROBIN! THE PROM WAS MY IDEA, REMEMBER?
NO, I MEAN...DO YOU WANT TO GO... TOGETHER?
CERTAINLY! WE SHALL ALL GO TOGETHER!
IT WOULD BE MOST UN-FESTIVE IF ONLY ONE PERSON WERE THERE.
THANK YOU FOR CONFIRMING THE GUEST LIST, ROBIN! YOU ARE ALWAYS MOST THOROUGH.
NO PROBLEM...

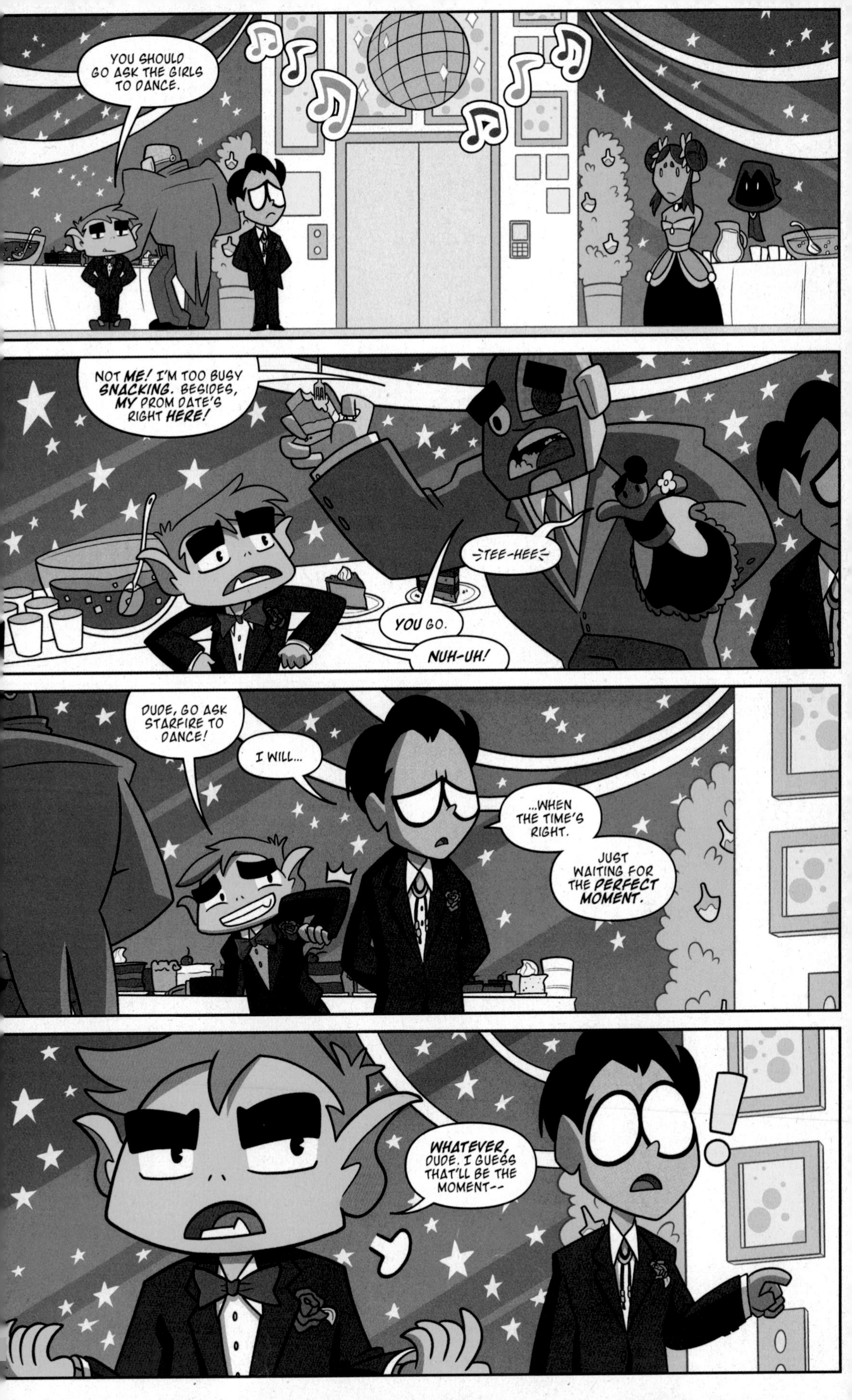
YOU SHOULD GO ASK THE GIRLS TO DANCE.
NOT ME! I'M TOO BUSY SNACKING. BESIDES, MY PROM DATE'S RIGHT HERE!
TEE-HEE
YOU GO.
NUH-UH!
DUDE, GO ASK STARFIRE TO DANCE!
I WILL...
...WHEN THE TIME'S RIGHT.
JUST WAITING FOR THE PERFECT MOMENT.
WHATEVER, DUDE. I GUESS THAT'LL BE THE MOMENT--

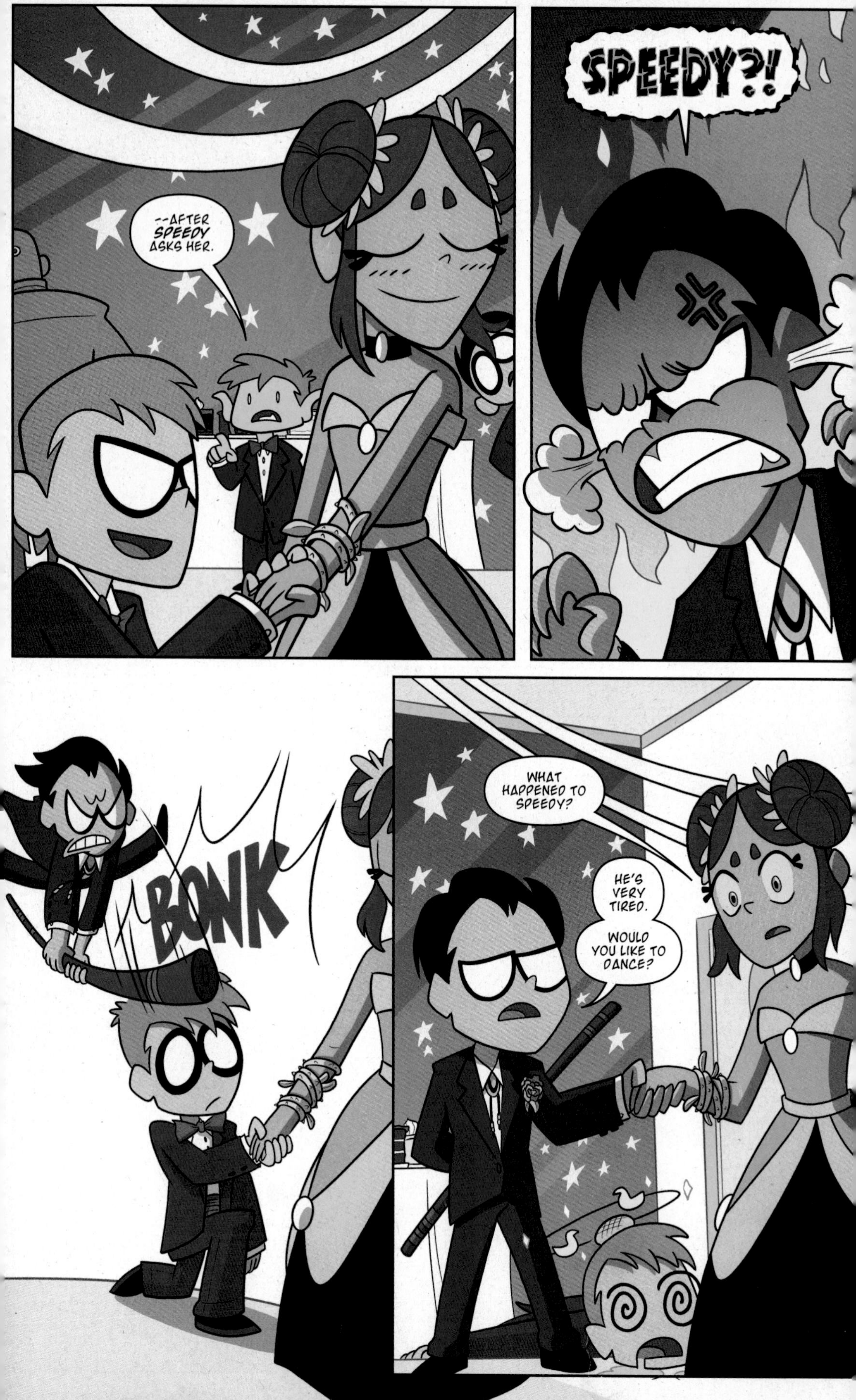
--AFTER SPEEDY ASKS HER.
SPEEDY?!
BONK
WHAT HAPPENED TO SPEEDY?
HE'S VERY TIRED.
WOULD YOU LIKE TO DANCE?

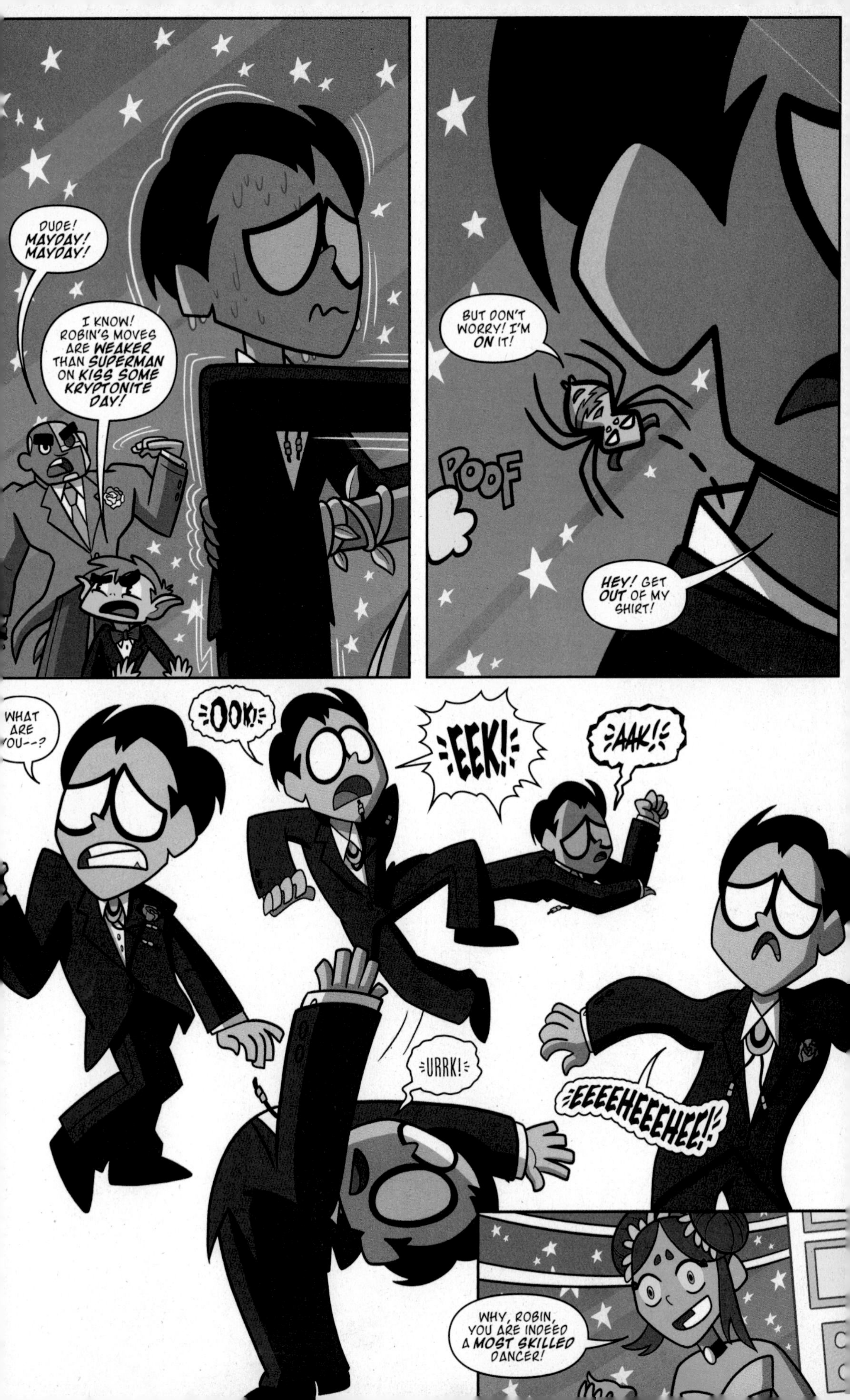
DUDE! MAYDAY! MAYDAY!
I KNOW! ROBIN'S MOVES ARE WEAKER THAN SUPERMAN ON KISS SOME KRYPTONITE DAY!
BUT DON'T WORRY! I'M ON IT!
POOF
HEY! GET OUT OF MY SHIRT!
WHAT ARE YOU--?
OOK!
EEK!
AAK!
URRK!
EEEEHEEEHEE!
WHY, ROBIN, YOU ARE INDEED A MOST SKILLED DANCER!

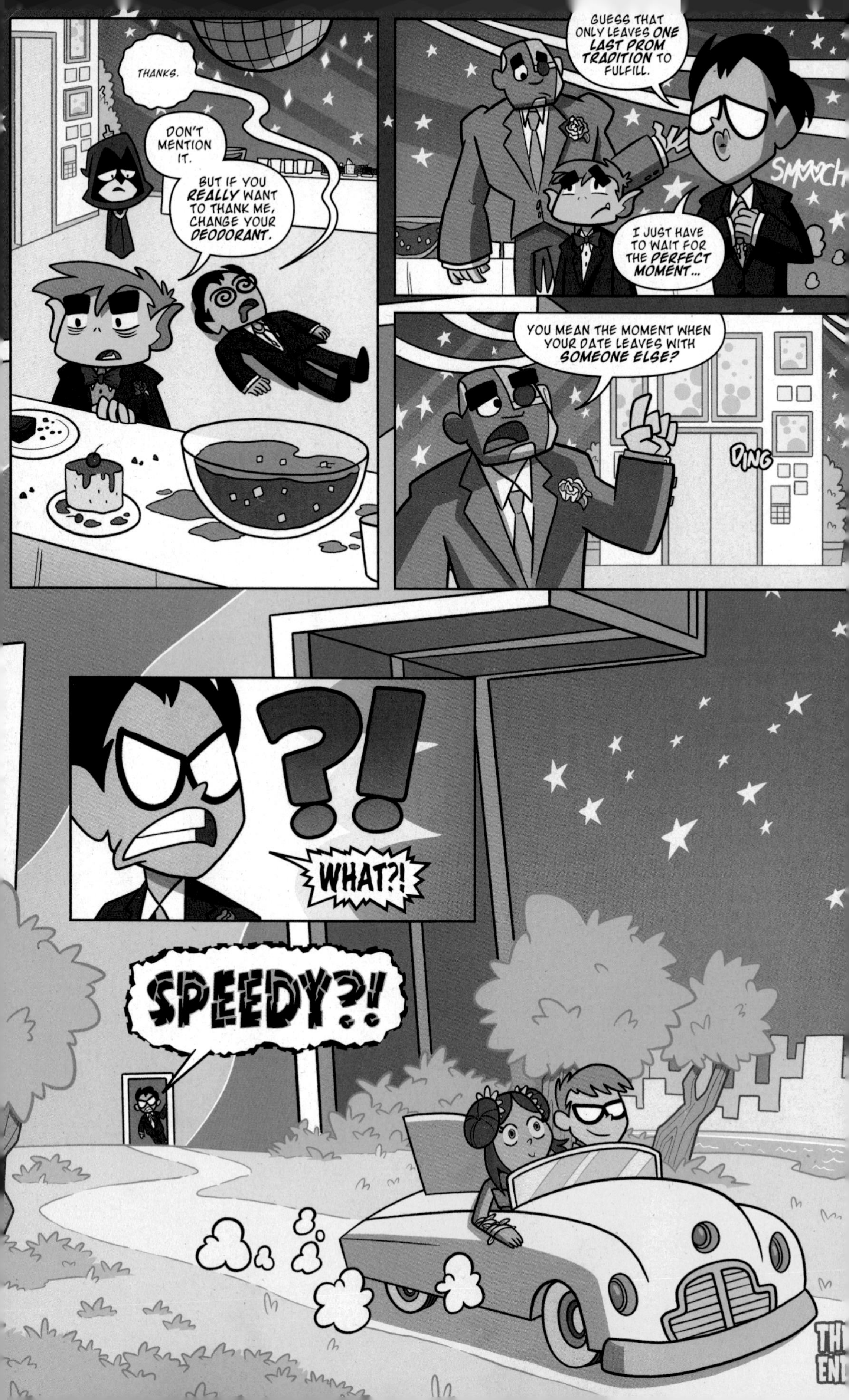
THANKS.
DON'T MENTION IT.
BUT IF YOU REALLY WANT TO THANK ME, CHANGE YOUR DEODORANT.
GUESS THAT ONLY LEAVES ONE LAST PROM TRADITION TO FULFILL.
SMOOCH
I JUST HAVE TO WAIT FOR THE PERFECT MOMENT...
YOU MEAN THE MOMENT WHEN YOUR DATE LEAVES WITH SOMEONE ELSE?
DING
?!
WHAT?!
SPEEDY?!

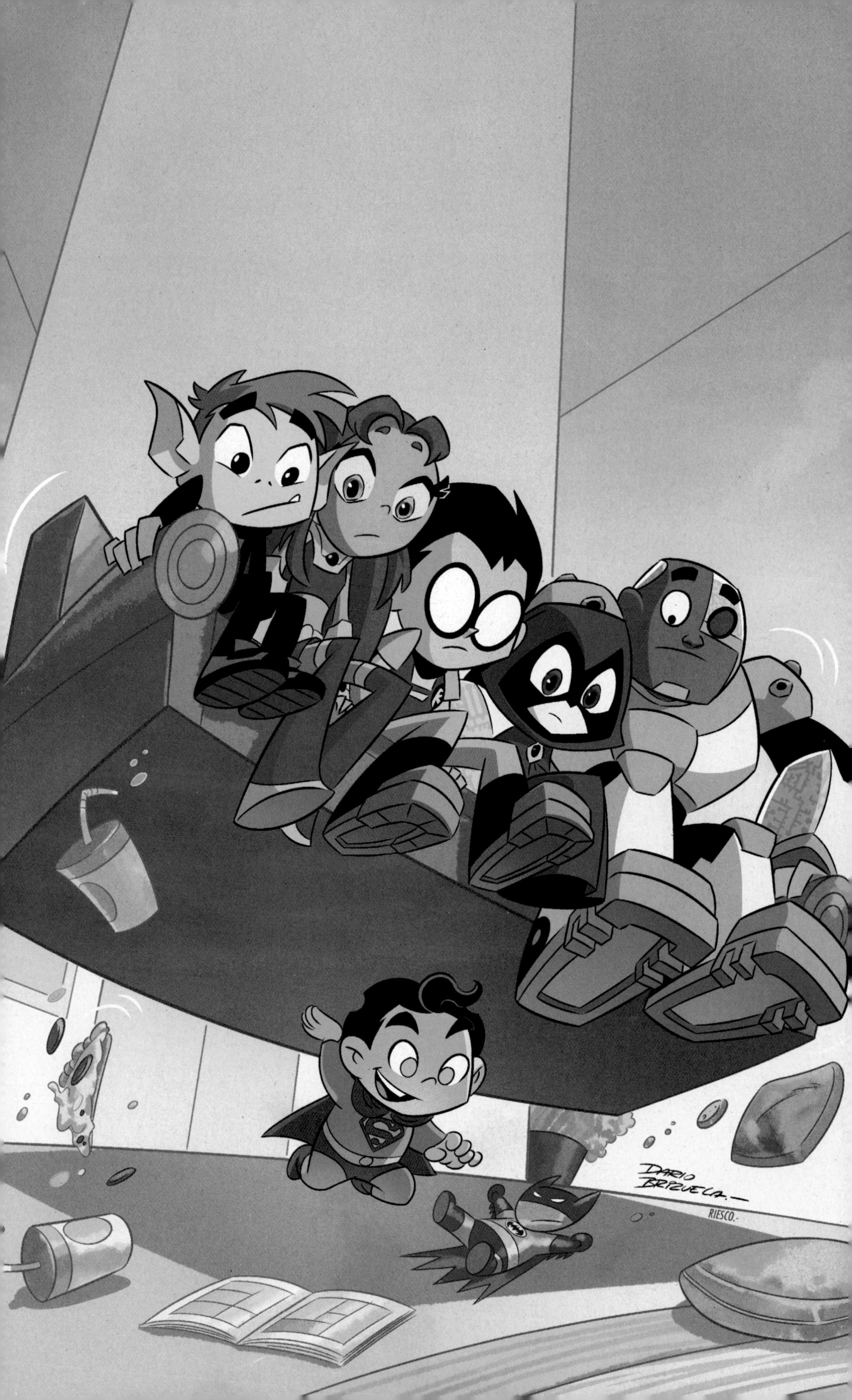
DARIO BRIZUELA
RIESCO.

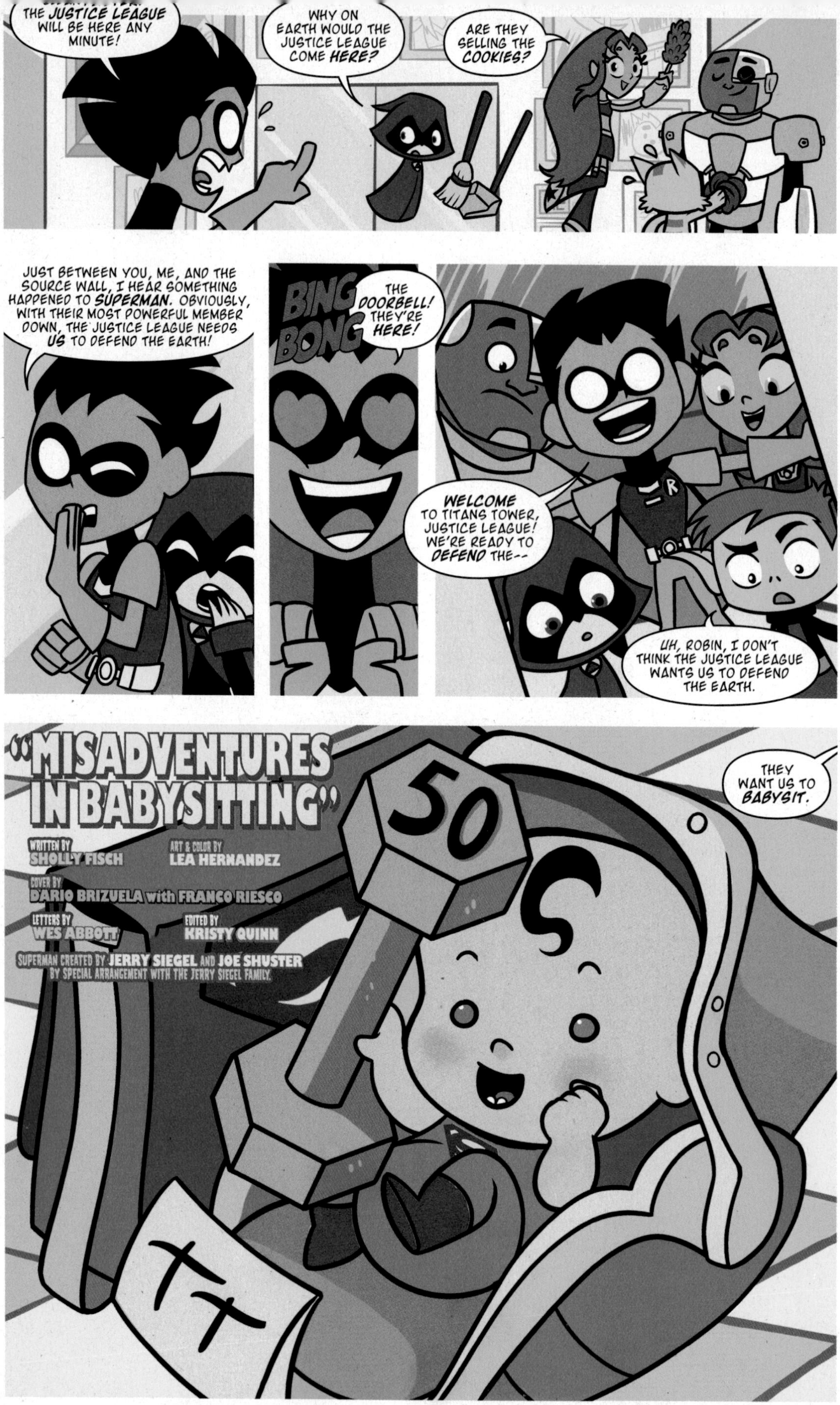
THE JUSTICE LEAGUE WILL BE HERE ANY MINUTE!
WHY ON EARTH WOULD THE JUSTICE LEAGUE COME HERE?
ARE THEY SELLING THE COOKIES?
JUST BETWEEN YOU, ME, AND THE SOURCE WALL, I HEAR SOMETHING HAPPENED TO SUPERMAN. OBVIOUSLY, WITH THEIR MOST POWERFUL MEMBER DOWN, THE JUSTICE LEAGUE NEEDS US TO DEFEND THE EARTH!
BING BONG
THE DOORBELL! THEY'RE HERE!
WELCOME TO TITANS TOWER, JUSTICE LEAGUE! WE'RE READY TO DEFEND THE--
UH, ROBIN, I DON'T THINK THE JUSTICE LEAGUE WANTS US TO DEFEND THE EARTH.
"MISADVENTURES IN BABYSITTING"
WRITTEN BY SHOLLY FISCH
ART & COLOR BY LEA HERNANDEZ
COVER BY DARIO BRIZUELA with FRANCO RIESCO
LETTERS BY WES ABBOTT
EDITED BY KRISTY QUINN
SUPERMAN CREATED BY JERRY SIEGEL AND JOE SHUSTER BY SPECIAL ARRANGEMENT WITH THE JERRY SIEGEL FAMILY.
THEY WANT US TO BABYSIT.
50
TT

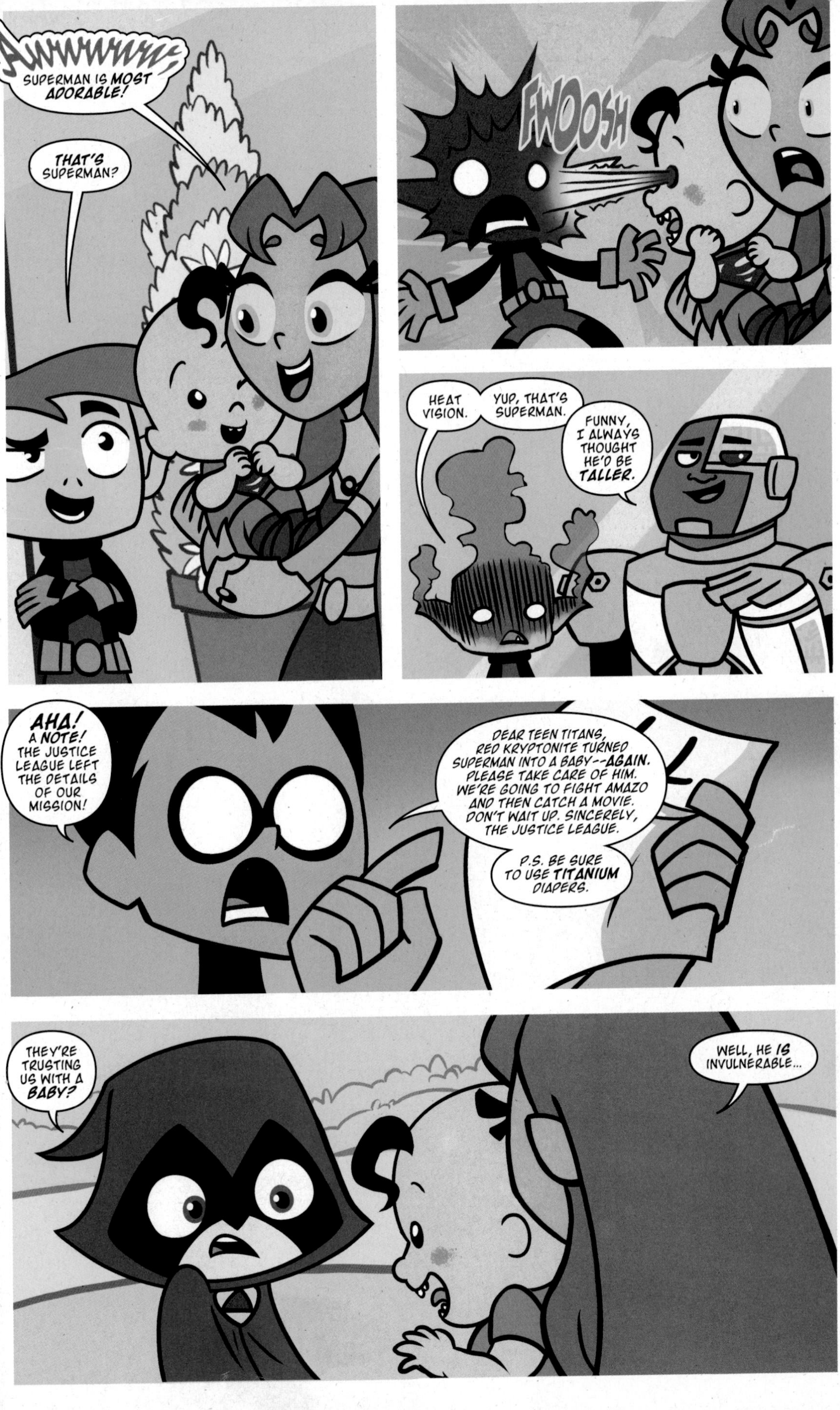
AWWWWW!
SUPERMAN IS MOST ADORABLE!
THAT'S SUPERMAN?
FWOOSH
HEAT VISION.
YUP, THAT'S SUPERMAN.
FUNNY, I ALWAYS THOUGHT HE'D BE TALLER.
AHA! A NOTE! THE JUSTICE LEAGUE LEFT THE DETAILS OF OUR MISSION!
DEAR TEEN TITANS, RED KRYPTONITE TURNED SUPERMAN INTO A BABY--AGAIN. PLEASE TAKE CARE OF HIM. WE'RE GOING TO FIGHT AMAZO AND THEN CATCH A MOVIE. DON'T WAIT UP. SINCERELY, THE JUSTICE LEAGUE.
P.S. BE SURE TO USE TITANIUM DIAPERS.
THEY'RE TRUSTING US WITH A BABY?
WELL, HE IS INVULNERABLE...

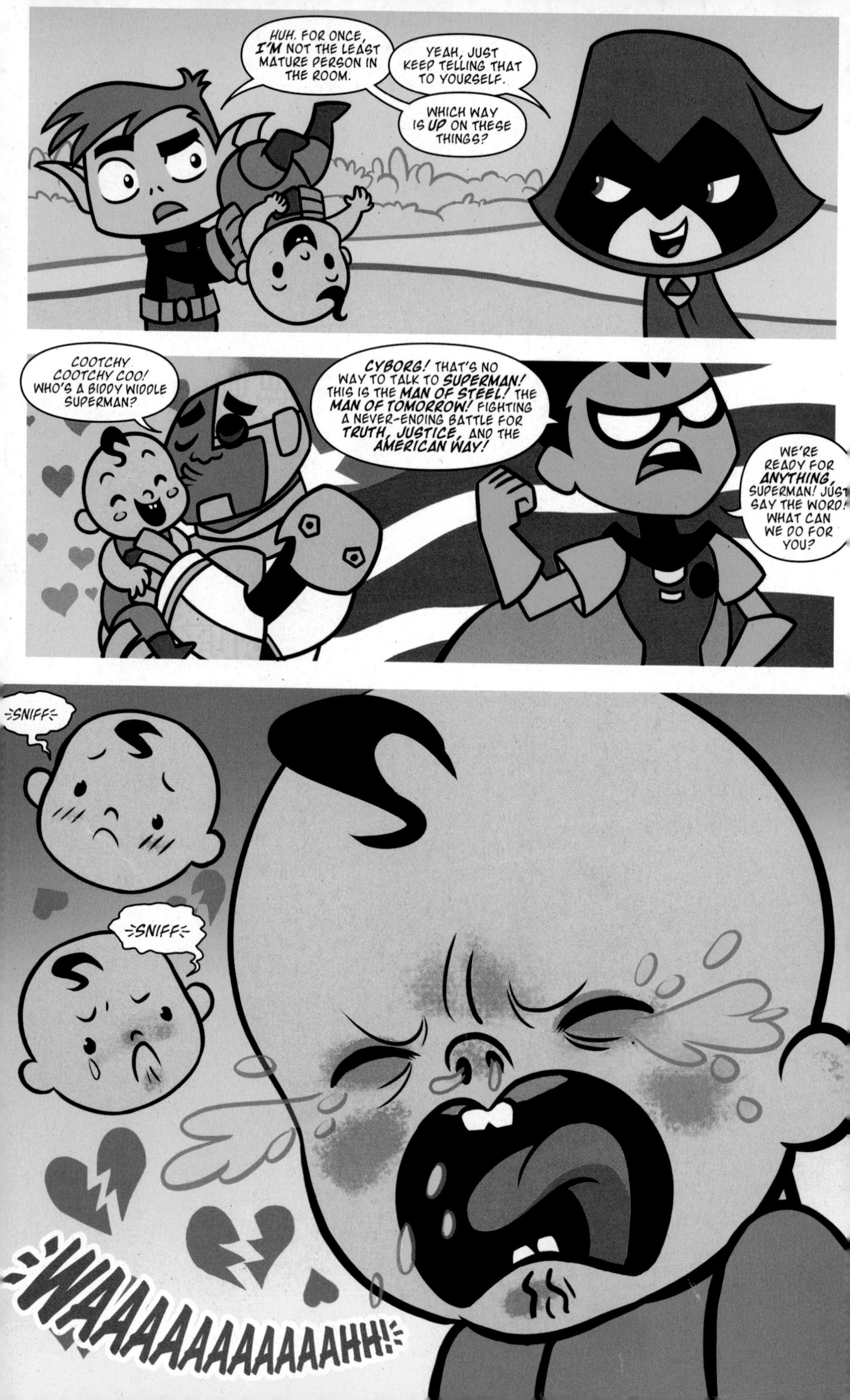
HUH. FOR ONCE, I'M NOT THE LEAST MATURE PERSON IN THE ROOM.
YEAH, JUST KEEP TELLING THAT TO YOURSELF.
WHICH WAY IS UP ON THESE THINGS?
COOTCHY COOTCHY COO! WHO'S A BIDDY WIDDLE SUPERMAN?
CYBORG! THAT'S NO WAY TO TALK TO SUPERMAN! THIS IS THE MAN OF STEEL! THE MAN OF TOMORROW! FIGHTING A NEVER-ENDING BATTLE FOR TRUTH, JUSTICE, AND THE AMERICAN WAY!
WE'RE READY FOR ANYTHING, SUPERMAN! JUST SAY THE WORD! WHAT CAN WE DO FOR YOU?
SNIFF
SNIFF
WAAAAAAAAAAAHH!

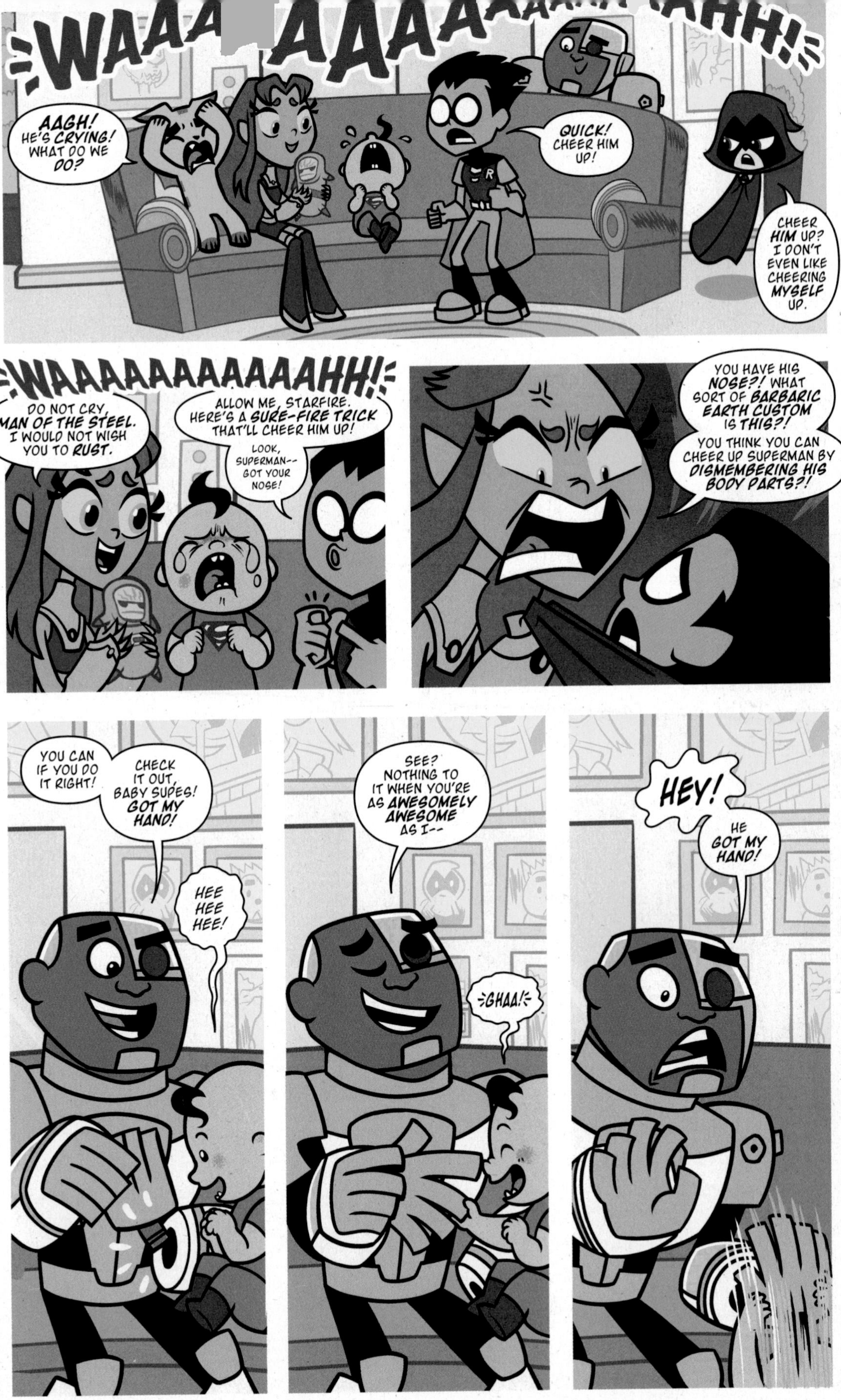

WAAA AAAAAAAAHH!
AAGH! HE'S CRYING! WHAT DO WE DO?
QUICK! CHEER HIM UP!
CHEER HIM UP? I DON'T EVEN LIKE CHEERING MYSELF UP.
WAAAAAAAAAAAHH!
DO NOT CRY, MAN OF THE STEEL. I WOULD NOT WISH YOU TO RUST.
ALLOW ME, STARFIRE. HERE'S A SURE-FIRE TRICK THAT'LL CHEER HIM UP!
LOOK, SUPERMAN-- GOT YOUR NOSE!
YOU HAVE HIS NOSE?! WHAT SORT OF BARBARIC EARTH CUSTOM IS THIS?!
YOU THINK YOU CAN CHEER UP SUPERMAN BY DISMEMBERING HIS BODY PARTS?!
YOU CAN IF YOU DO IT RIGHT!
CHECK IT OUT, BABY SUPES! GOT MY HAND!
HEE HEE HEE!
SEE? NOTHING TO IT WHEN YOU'RE AS AWESOMELY AWESOME AS I--
GHAA!
HEY!
HE GOT MY HAND!

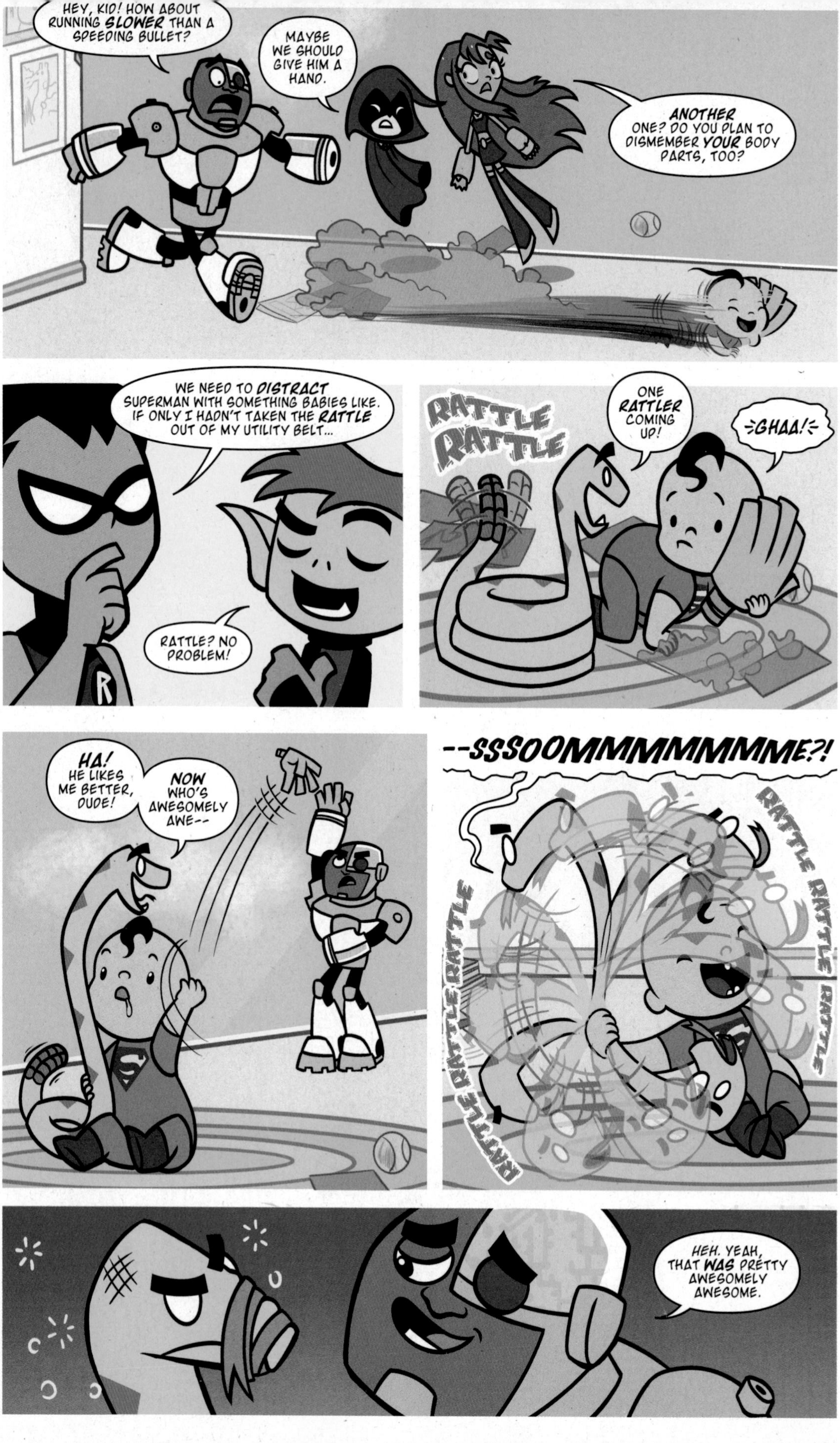
HEY, KID! HOW ABOUT RUNNING SLOWER THAN A SPEEDING BULLET?
MAYBE WE SHOULD GIVE HIM A HAND.
ANOTHER ONE? DO YOU PLAN TO DISMEMBER YOUR BODY PARTS, TOO?
WE NEED TO DISTRACT SUPERMAN WITH SOMETHING BABIES LIKE. IF ONLY I HADN'T TAKEN THE RATTLE OUT OF MY UTILITY BELT...
RATTLE? NO PROBLEM!
RATTLE RATTLE
ONE RATTLER COMING UP!
GHAA!
HA! HE LIKES ME BETTER, DUDE!
NOW WHO'S AWESOMELY AWE--
--SSSOOMMMMMMMME?!
RATTLE RATTLE
RATTLE RATTLE RATTLE
HEH. YEAH, THAT WAS PRETTY AWESOMELY AWESOME.

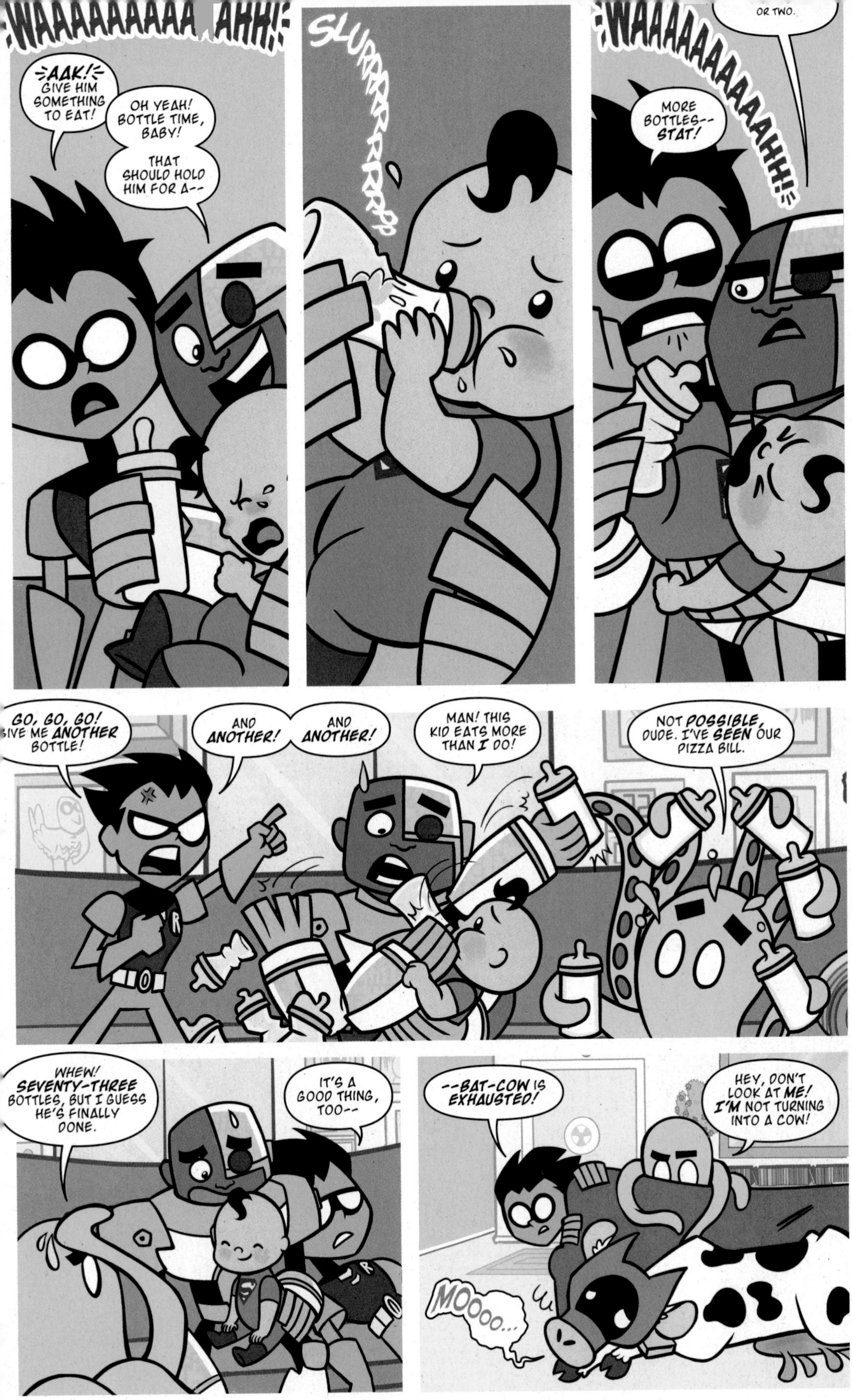
WAAAAAAAAAAAHH!
AAK! GIVE HIM SOMETHING TO EAT!
OH YEAH! BOTTLE TIME, BABY!
THAT SHOULD HOLD HIM FOR A--
SLURRRRRRRRRP
OR TWO.
MORE BOTTLES--STAT!
WAAAAAAAAAAAHH!
GO, GO, GO! GIVE ME ANOTHER BOTTLE!
AND ANOTHER!
AND ANOTHER!
MAN! THIS KID EATS MORE THAN I DO!
NOT POSSIBLE, DUDE. I'VE SEEN OUR PIZZA BILL.
WHEW! SEVENTY-THREE BOTTLES, BUT I GUESS HE'S FINALLY DONE.
IT'S A GOOD THING, TOO--
--BAT-COW IS EXHAUSTED!
HEY, DON'T LOOK AT ME! I'M NOT TURNING INTO A COW!
MOOOO...

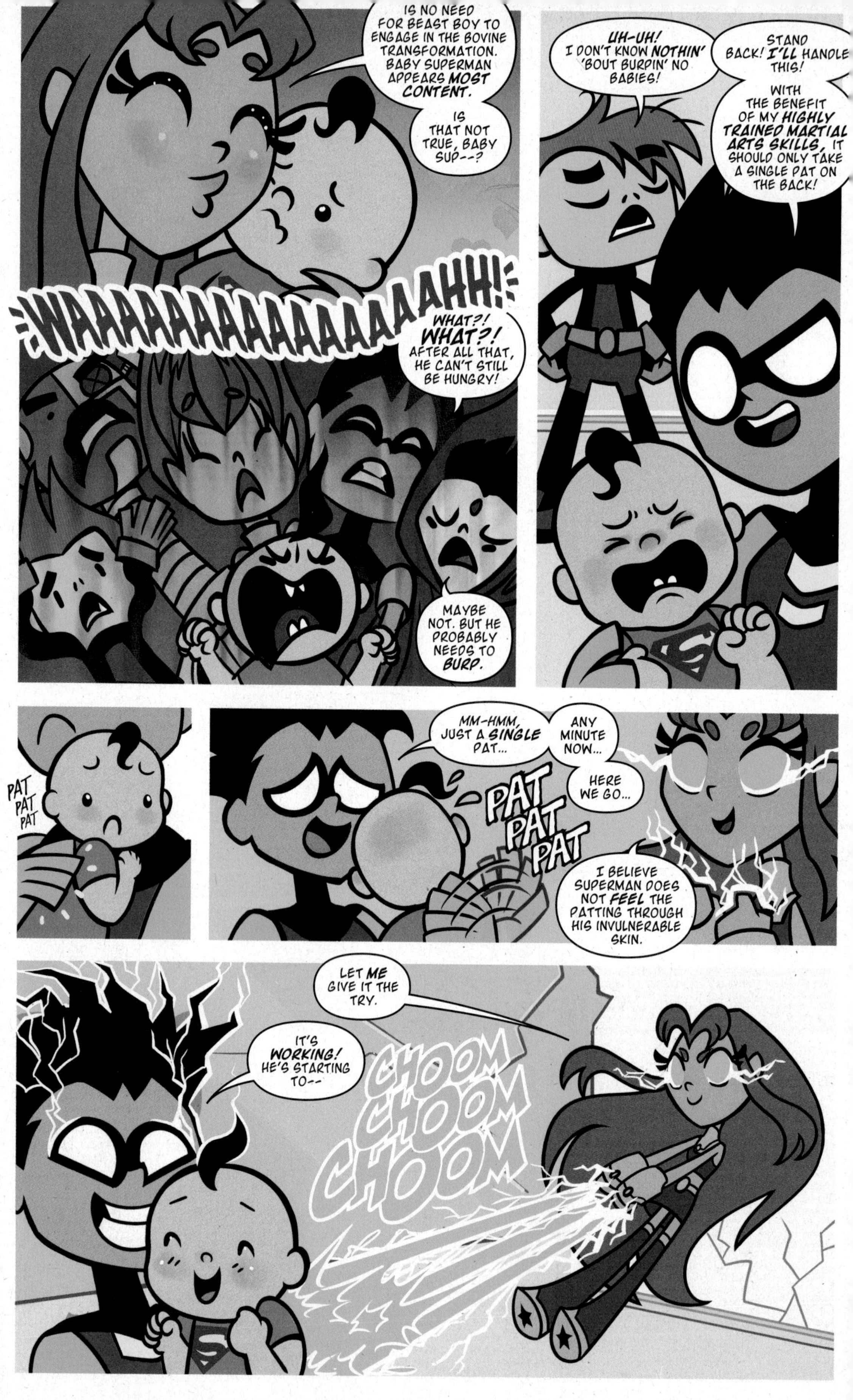
IS NO NEED FOR BEAST BOY TO ENGAGE IN THE BOVINE TRANSFORMATION. BABY SUPERMAN APPEARS MOST CONTENT.
IS THAT NOT TRUE, BABY SUP--?
WAAAAAAAAAAAAAAAAAAHH!
WHAT?! WHAT?! AFTER ALL THAT, HE CAN'T STILL BE HUNGRY!
MAYBE NOT. BUT HE PROBABLY NEEDS TO BURP.
UH-UH! I DON'T KNOW NOTHIN' 'BOUT BURPIN' NO BABIES!
STAND BACK! I'LL HANDLE THIS!
WITH THE BENEFIT OF MY HIGHLY TRAINED MARTIAL ARTS SKILLS, IT SHOULD ONLY TAKE A SINGLE PAT ON THE BACK!
PAT PAT PAT
MM-HMM, JUST A SINGLE PAT...
ANY MINUTE NOW...
HERE WE GO...
PAT PAT PAT
I BELIEVE SUPERMAN DOES NOT FEEL THE PATTING THROUGH HIS INVULNERABLE SKIN.
LET ME GIVE IT THE TRY.
IT'S WORKING! HE'S STARTING TO--
CHOOM CHOOM CHOOM

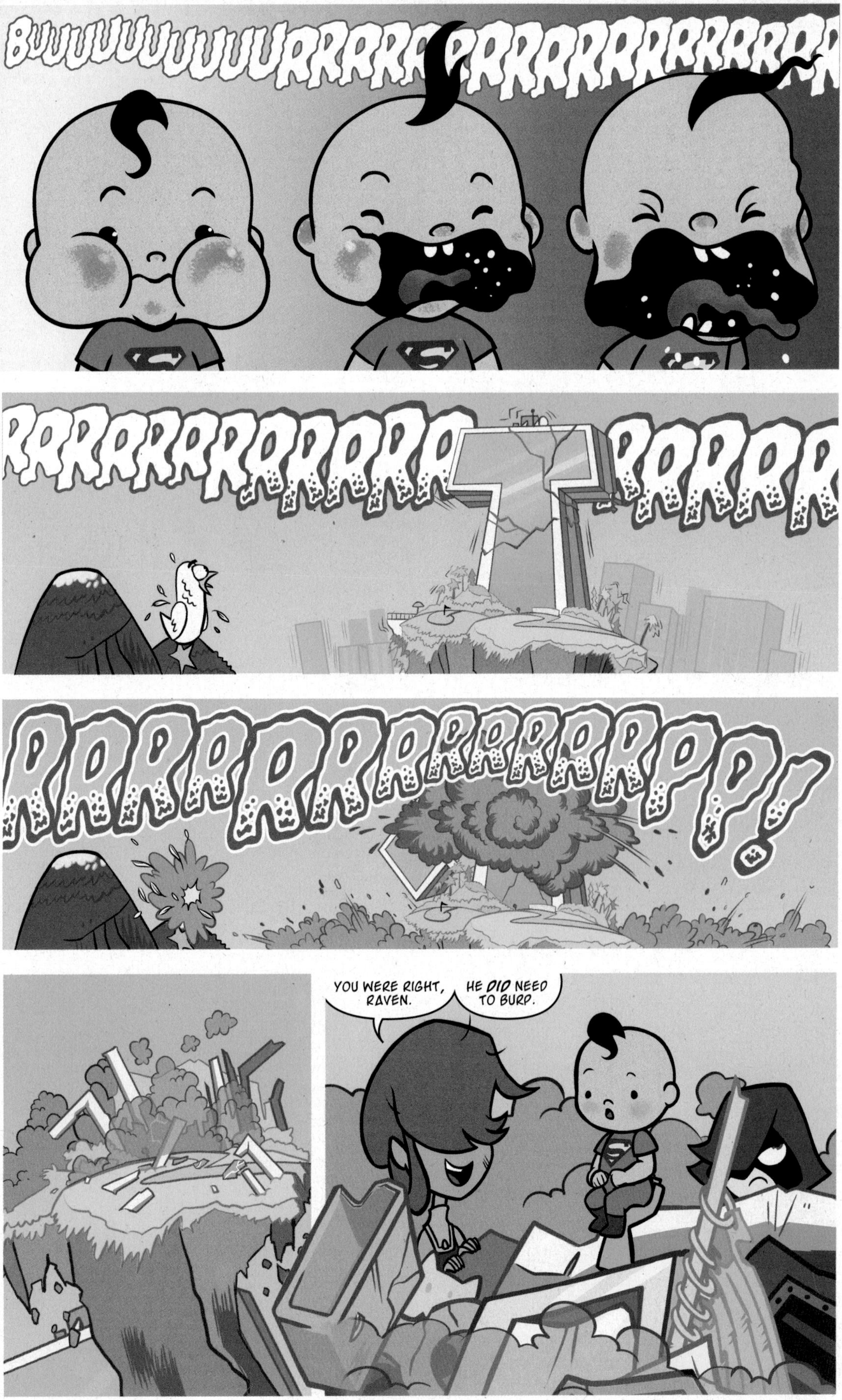
BUUUUUUUUUURRRRRRRRRRRRRRRR
RRRRRRRRRRRRRRR
RRRRRRRRRRRRRRRRP!
YOU WERE RIGHT, RAVEN.
HE DID NEED TO BURP.

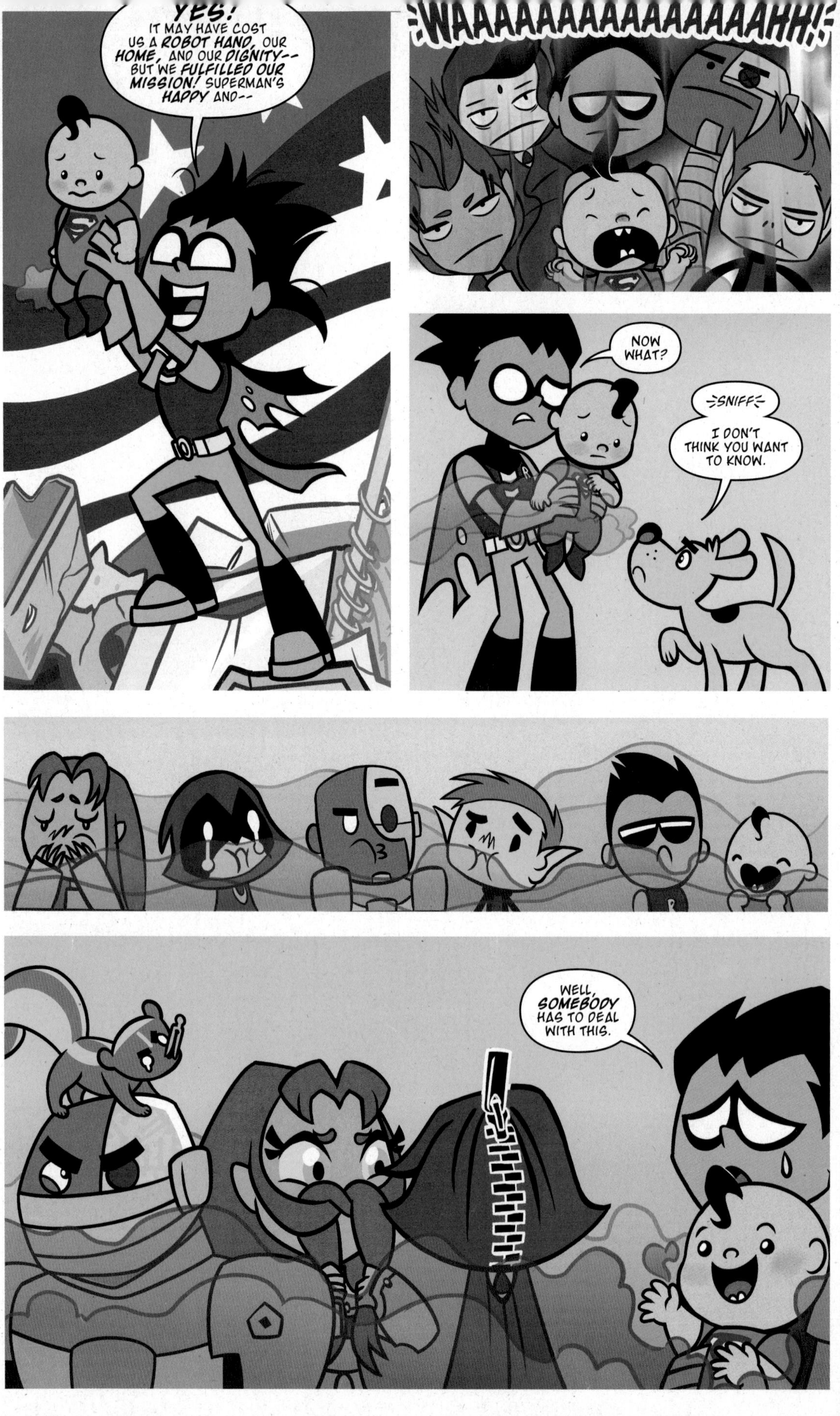
YES! IT MAY HAVE COST US A ROBOT HAND, OUR HOME, AND OUR DIGNITY-- BUT WE FULFILLED OUR MISSION! SUPERMAN'S HAPPY AND--
WAAAAAAAAAAAAAAAHH!
NOW WHAT?
SNIFF
I DON'T THINK YOU WANT TO KNOW.
WELL, SOMEBODY HAS TO DEAL WITH THIS.

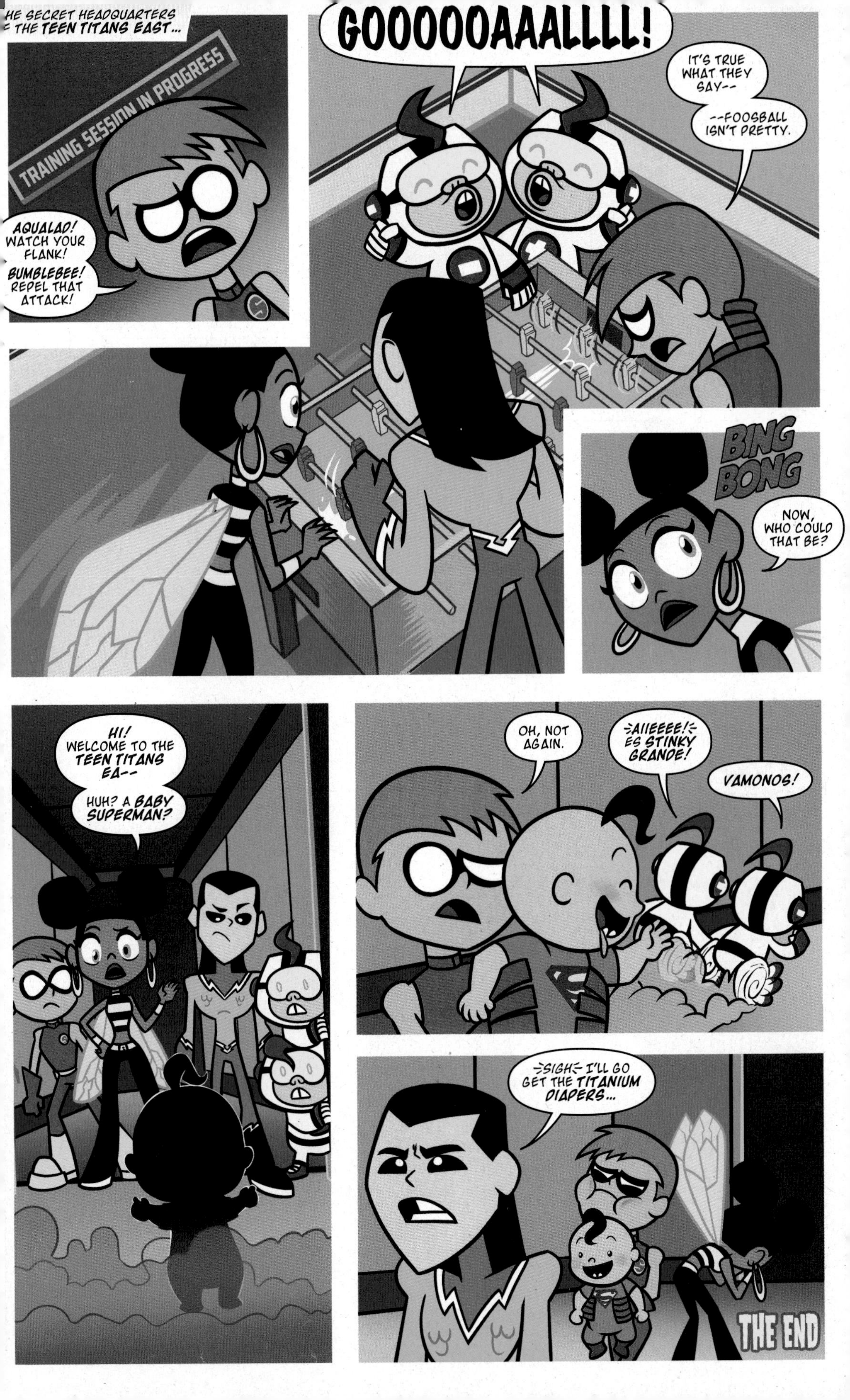
HE SECRET HEADQUARTERS
= THE TEEN TITANS EAST...
TRAINING SESSION IN PROGRESS
AQUALAD! WATCH YOUR FLANK!
BUMBLEBEE! REPEL THAT ATTACK!
GOOOOOAAALLLL!
IT'S TRUE WHAT THEY SAY--
--FOOSBALL ISN'T PRETTY.
BING BONG
NOW, WHO COULD THAT BE?
HI! WELCOME TO THE TEEN TITANS EA--
HUH? A BABY SUPERMAN?
OH, NOT AGAIN.
=AIIEEEE!= ES STINKY GRANDE!
VAMONOS!
=SIGH= I'LL GO GET THE TITANIUM DIAPERS...
THE END

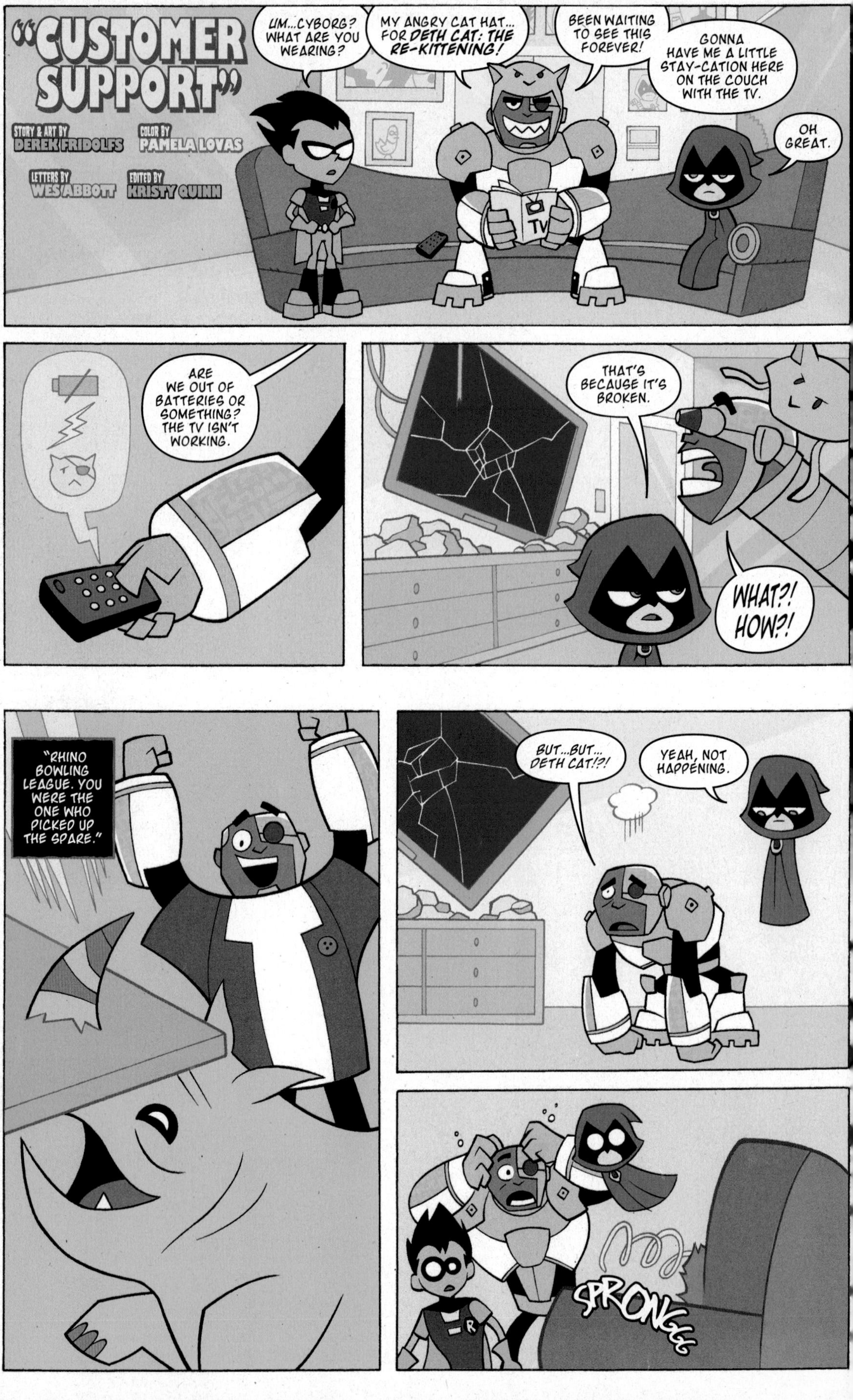
"CUSTOMER SUPPORT"
STORY & ART BY DEREK FRIDOLFS
COLOR BY PAMELA LOVAS
LETTERS BY WES ABBOTT
EDITED BY KRISTY QUINN
UM...CYBORG? WHAT ARE YOU WEARING?
MY ANGRY CAT HAT... FOR DETH CAT: THE RE-KITTENING!
BEEN WAITING TO SEE THIS FOREVER!
GONNA HAVE ME A LITTLE STAY-CATION HERE ON THE COUCH WITH THE TV.
OH GREAT.
TV
ARE WE OUT OF BATTERIES OR SOMETHING? THE TV ISN'T WORKING.
THAT'S BECAUSE IT'S BROKEN.
WHAT?! HOW?!
"RHINO BOWLING LEAGUE. YOU WERE THE ONE WHO PICKED UP THE SPARE."
BUT...BUT... DETH CAT!?!
YEAH, NOT HAPPENING.
SPRONGGG

WHAT'S WRONG, B? WHY ARE YOU CRAWLING LIKE THAT?

PANT! PANT! PANT!

THE... ELEVATOR... WAS...BROKEN... DUUUUDE...

THAT TOO?! I NEVER NOTICED.

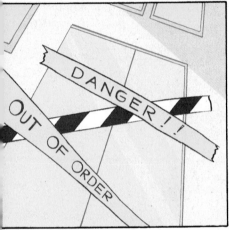

DANGER!!
OUT OF ORDER

HOW'D YOU GET UP HERE?

IT WAS HORRIBLE. I HAD TO USE...THE STAIRS!

WHAT ARE THESE "STAIRS" YOU SPEAK OF? EXPLAIN.

"THERE ARE LIKE, A LOT OF STEPS THAT GO UP. AND YOU HAVE TO USE WALKIE THINGIES."

"YOU MEAN FEET?"

"THAT'S RIGHT, MAMA!"

ALSO THERE'S A STAIR TROLL!

"YOU CAN'T BE SERIOUS."

"DON'T BE HEARTLESS. WITH THE BRIDGE OUT, IT HAD NOWHERE ELSE TO GO."

STARFIRE, WHAT'S WRONG?

THE FRIDGE THAT DOES THE RATORING, HOLDS NOTHING. IT'S... EMPTY!

SPRONGG

SPRONGG

SPRONGG

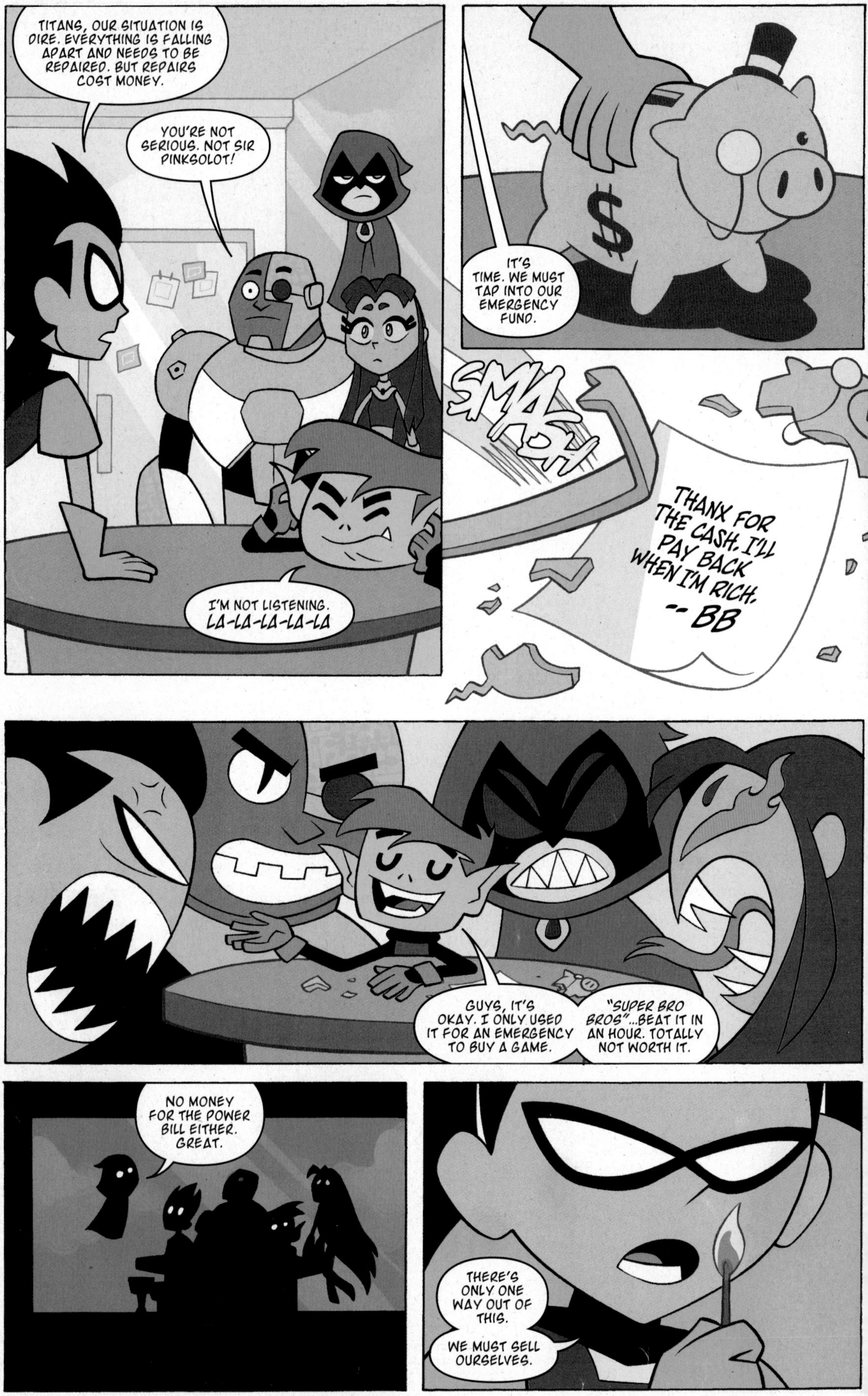
TITANS, OUR SITUATION IS DIRE. EVERYTHING IS FALLING APART AND NEEDS TO BE REPAIRED. BUT REPAIRS COST MONEY.
YOU'RE NOT SERIOUS. NOT SIR PINKSOLOT!
I'M NOT LISTENING. LA-LA-LA-LA-LA
IT'S TIME. WE MUST TAP INTO OUR EMERGENCY FUND.
SMASH
THANX FOR THE CASH. I'LL PAY BACK WHEN I'M RICH. -- BB
GUYS, IT'S OKAY. I ONLY USED IT FOR AN EMERGENCY TO BUY A GAME.
"SUPER BRO BROS"...BEAT IT IN AN HOUR. TOTALLY NOT WORTH IT.
NO MONEY FOR THE POWER BILL EITHER. GREAT.
THERE'S ONLY ONE WAY OUT OF THIS.
WE MUST SELL OURSELVES.

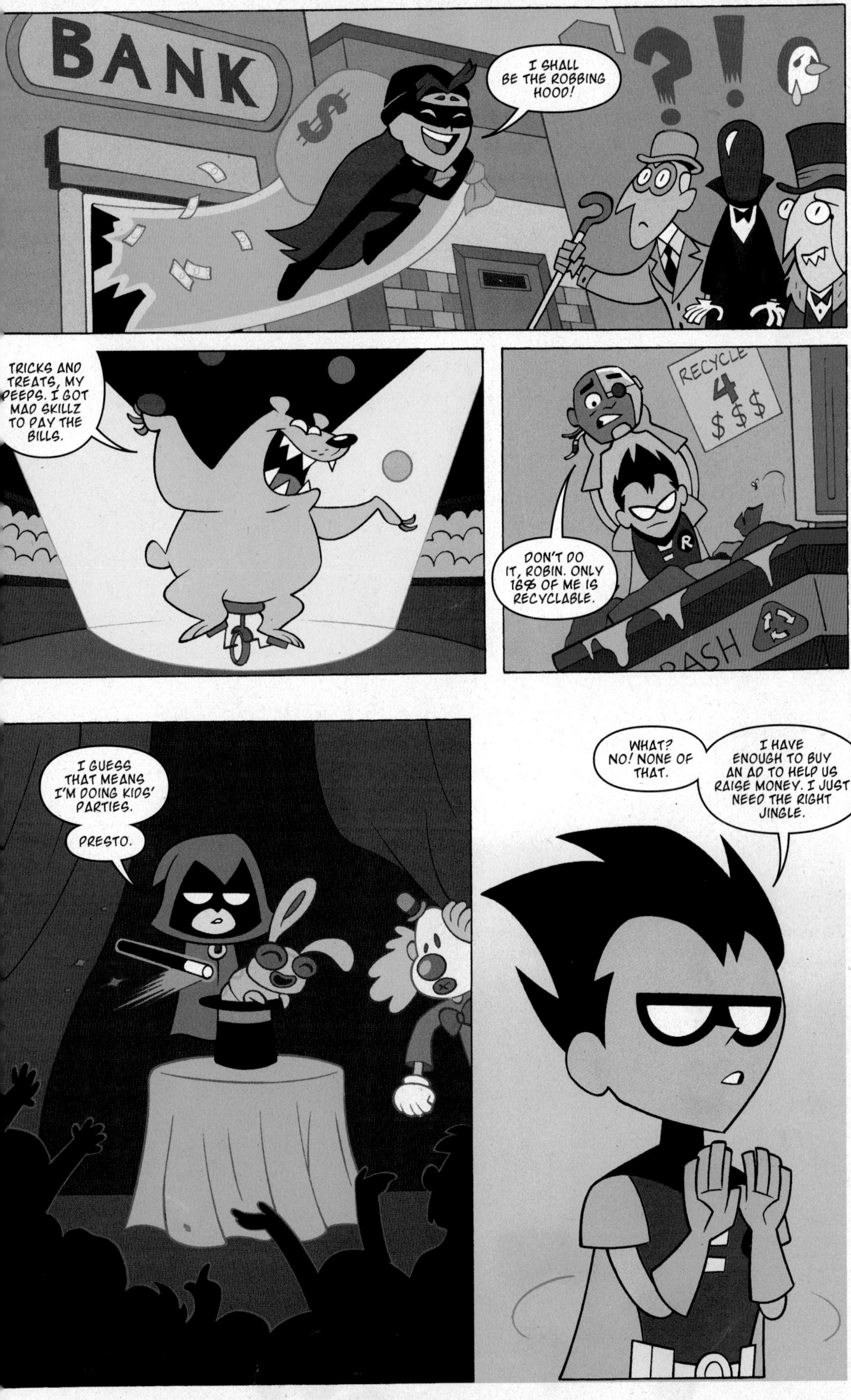
BANK
I SHALL BE THE ROBBING HOOD!
TRICKS AND TREATS, MY PEEPS. I GOT MAD SKILLZ TO PAY THE BILLS.
RECYCLE 4 $$$
DON'T DO IT, ROBIN. ONLY 16% OF ME IS RECYCLABLE.
I GUESS THAT MEANS I'M DOING KIDS' PARTIES.
PRESTO.
WHAT? NO! NONE OF THAT.
I HAVE ENOUGH TO BUY AN AD TO HELP US RAISE MONEY. I JUST NEED THE RIGHT JINGLE.

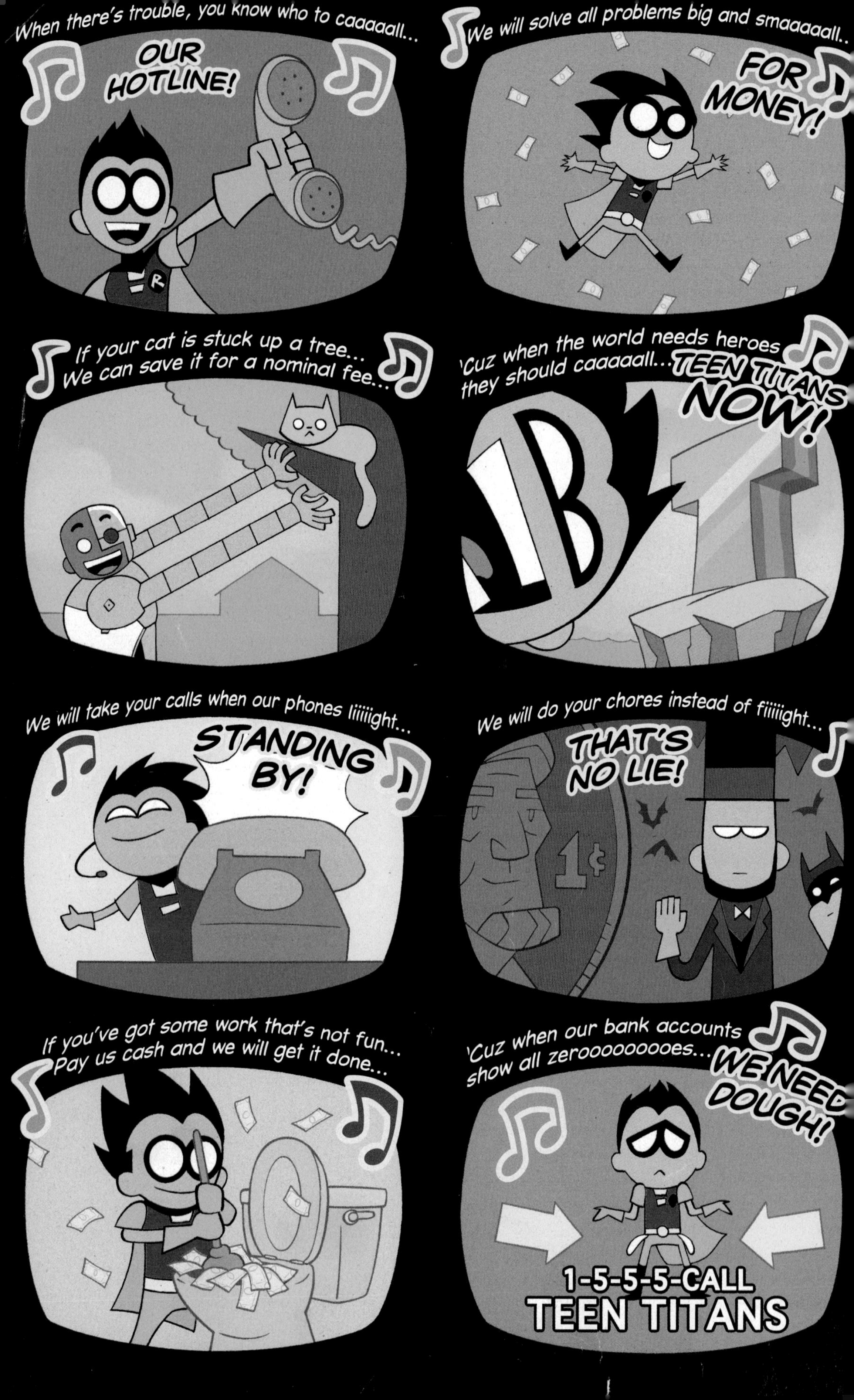
When there's trouble, you know who to caaaaall...
OUR HOTLINE!
We will solve all problems big and smaaaaall...
FOR MONEY!
If your cat is stuck up a tree...
We can save it for a nominal fee...
'Cuz when the world needs heroes they should caaaaall...
TEEN TITANS NOW!
We will take your calls when our phones liiiiight...
STANDING BY!
We will do your chores instead of fiiiiight...
THAT'S NO LIE!
1¢
If you've got some work that's not fun...
Pay us cash and we will get it done...
'Cuz when our bank accounts show all zeroooooooes...
WE NEED DOUGH!
1-5-5-5-CALL
TEEN TITANS

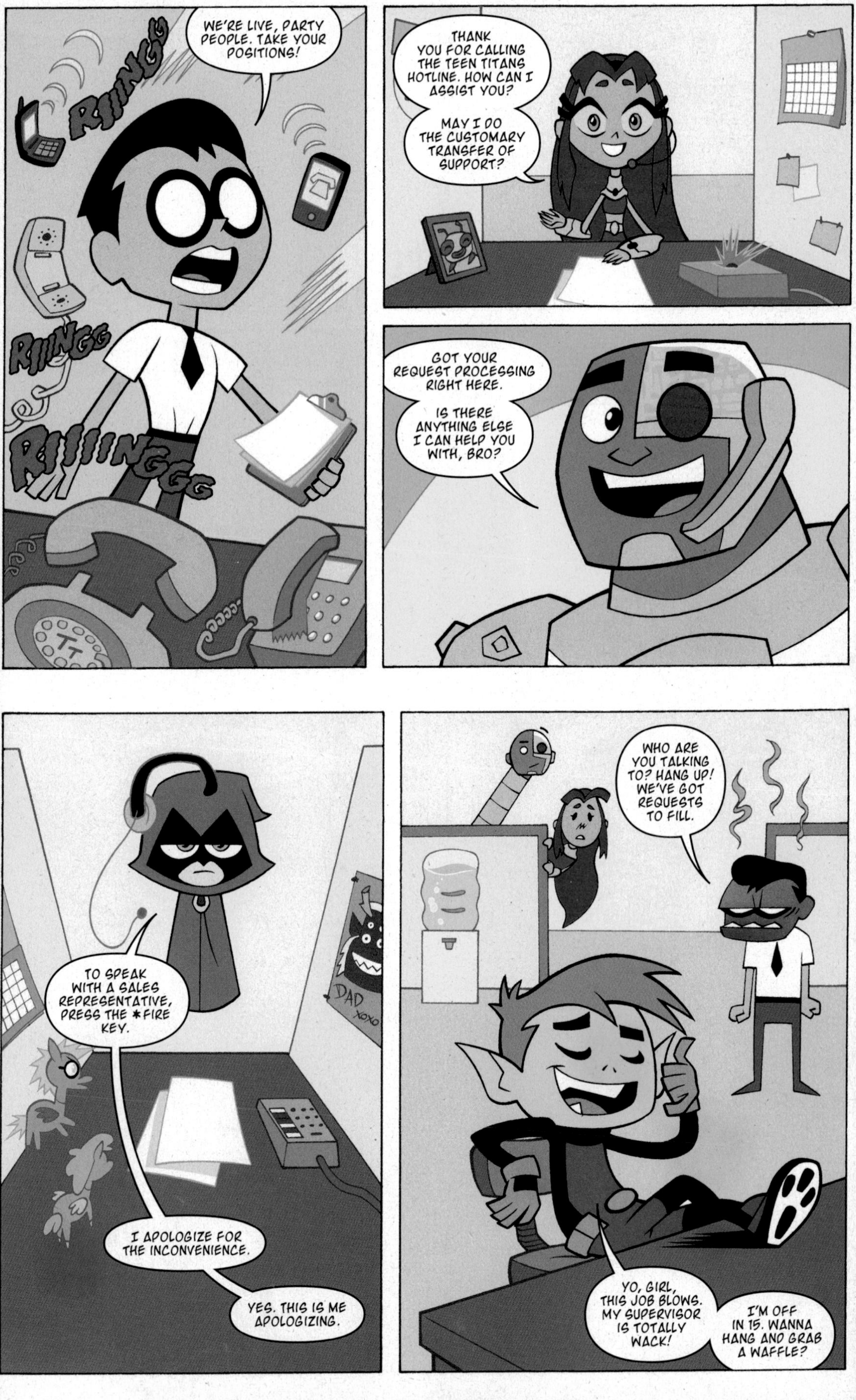
WE'RE LIVE, PARTY PEOPLE. TAKE YOUR POSITIONS!
RIIINGG
RIIINGG
RIIIINGGG
THANK YOU FOR CALLING THE TEEN TITANS HOTLINE. HOW CAN I ASSIST YOU?
MAY I DO THE CUSTOMARY TRANSFER OF SUPPORT?
GOT YOUR REQUEST PROCESSING RIGHT HERE.
IS THERE ANYTHING ELSE I CAN HELP YOU WITH, BRO?
TO SPEAK WITH A SALES REPRESENTATIVE, PRESS THE *FIRE KEY.
I APOLOGIZE FOR THE INCONVENIENCE.
YES. THIS IS ME APOLOGIZING.
DAD XOXO
WHO ARE YOU TALKING TO? HANG UP! WE'VE GOT REQUESTS TO FILL.
YO, GIRL, THIS JOB BLOWS. MY SUPERVISOR IS TOTALLY WACK!
I'M OFF IN 15. WANNA HANG AND GRAB A WAFFLE?

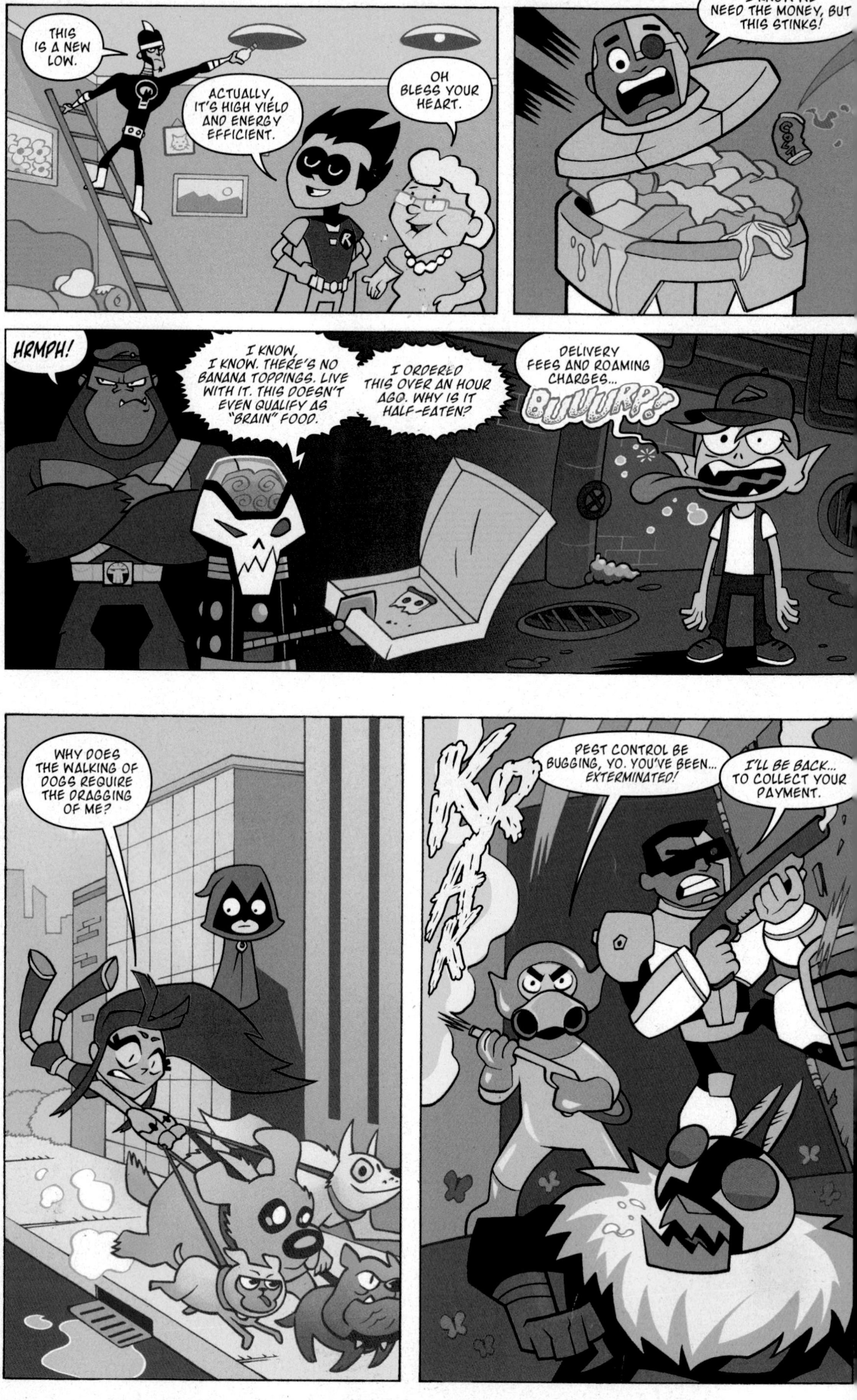
THIS IS A NEW LOW.
ACTUALLY, IT'S HIGH YIELD AND ENERGY EFFICIENT.
OH BLESS YOUR HEART.
I KNOW WE NEED THE MONEY, BUT THIS STINKS!
HRMPH!
I KNOW, I KNOW. THERE'S NO BANANA TOPPINGS. LIVE WITH IT. THIS DOESN'T EVEN QUALIFY AS "BRAIN" FOOD.
I ORDERED THIS OVER AN HOUR AGO. WHY IS IT HALF-EATEN?
DELIVERY FEES AND ROAMING CHARGES...
BUUURP!
WHY DOES THE WALKING OF DOGS REQUIRE THE DRAGGING OF ME?
KRAK
PEST CONTROL BE BUGGING, YO. YOU'VE BEEN... EXTERMINATED!
I'LL BE BACK... TO COLLECT YOUR PAYMENT.

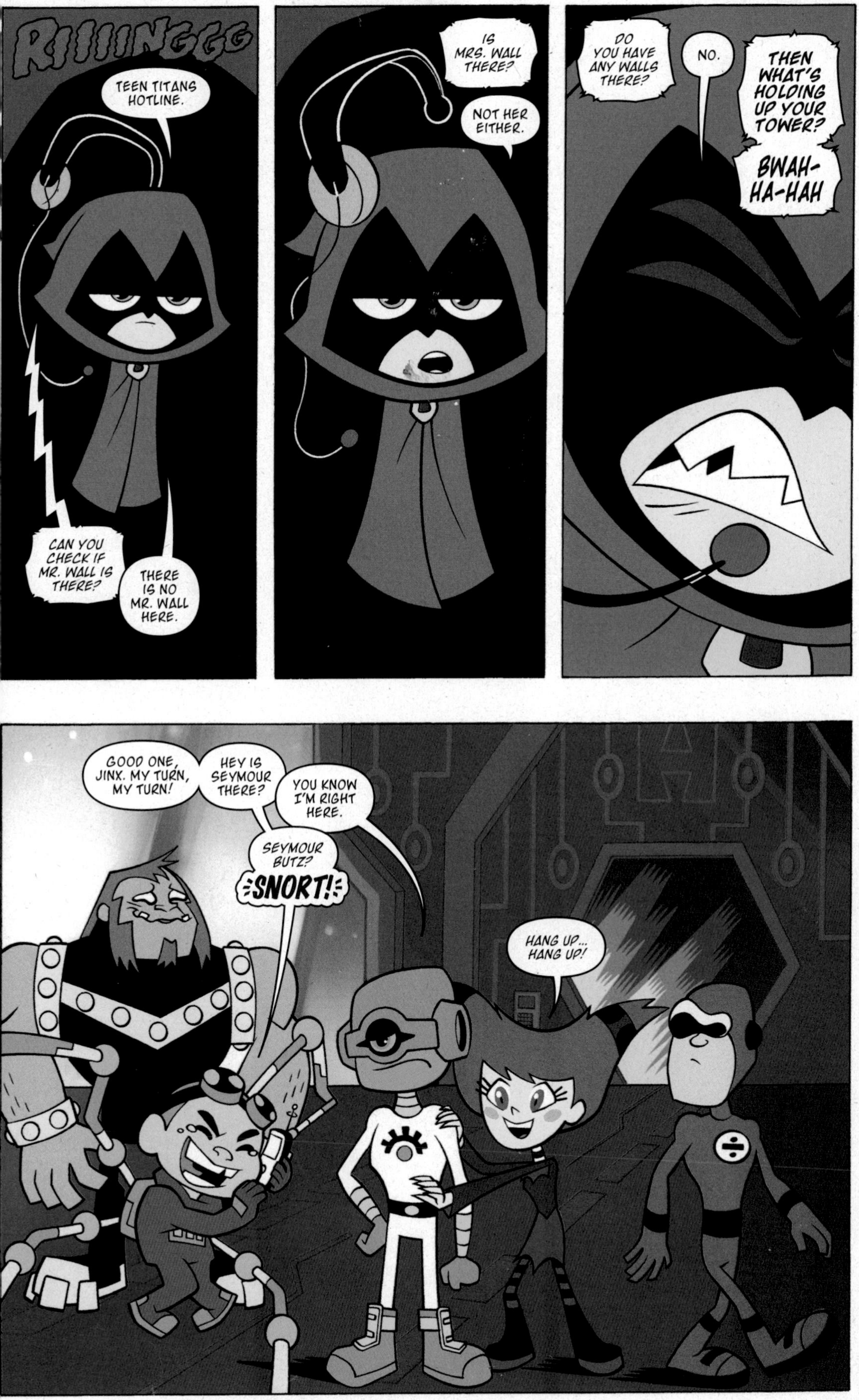
RIIIINGGG
TEEN TITANS HOTLINE.
CAN YOU CHECK IF MR. WALL IS THERE?
THERE IS NO MR. WALL HERE.
IS MRS. WALL THERE?
NOT HER EITHER.
DO YOU HAVE ANY WALLS THERE?
NO.
THEN WHAT'S HOLDING UP YOUR TOWER?
BWAH-HA-HAH
GOOD ONE, JINX. MY TURN, MY TURN!
HEY IS SEYMOUR THERE?
YOU KNOW I'M RIGHT HERE.
SEYMOUR BUTZ?
SNORT!
HANG UP... HANG UP!

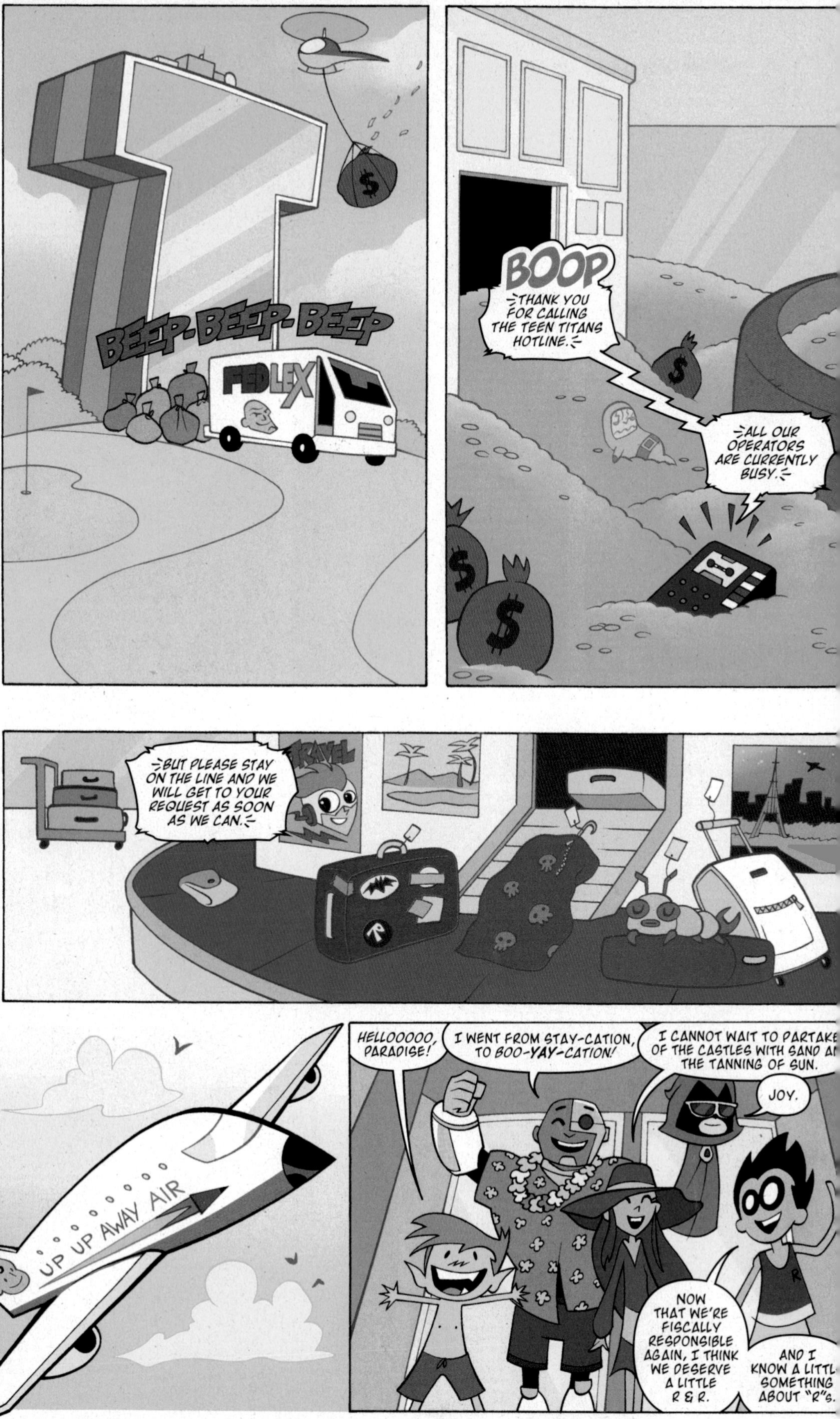
BEEP-BEEP-BEEP
FEDLEX
BOOP
THANK YOU FOR CALLING THE TEEN TITANS HOTLINE.
ALL OUR OPERATORS ARE CURRENTLY BUSY.
BUT PLEASE STAY ON THE LINE AND WE WILL GET TO YOUR REQUEST AS SOON AS WE CAN.
TRAVEL
UP UP AWAY AIR
HELLOOOOO, PARADISE!
I WENT FROM STAY-CATION, TO BOO-YAY-CATION!
I CANNOT WAIT TO PARTAKE OF THE CASTLES WITH SAND AN THE TANNING OF SUN.
JOY.
NOW THAT WE'RE FISCALLY RESPONSIBLE AGAIN, I THINK WE DESERVE A LITTLE R & R.
AND I KNOW A LITTL SOMETHING ABOUT "R"s.

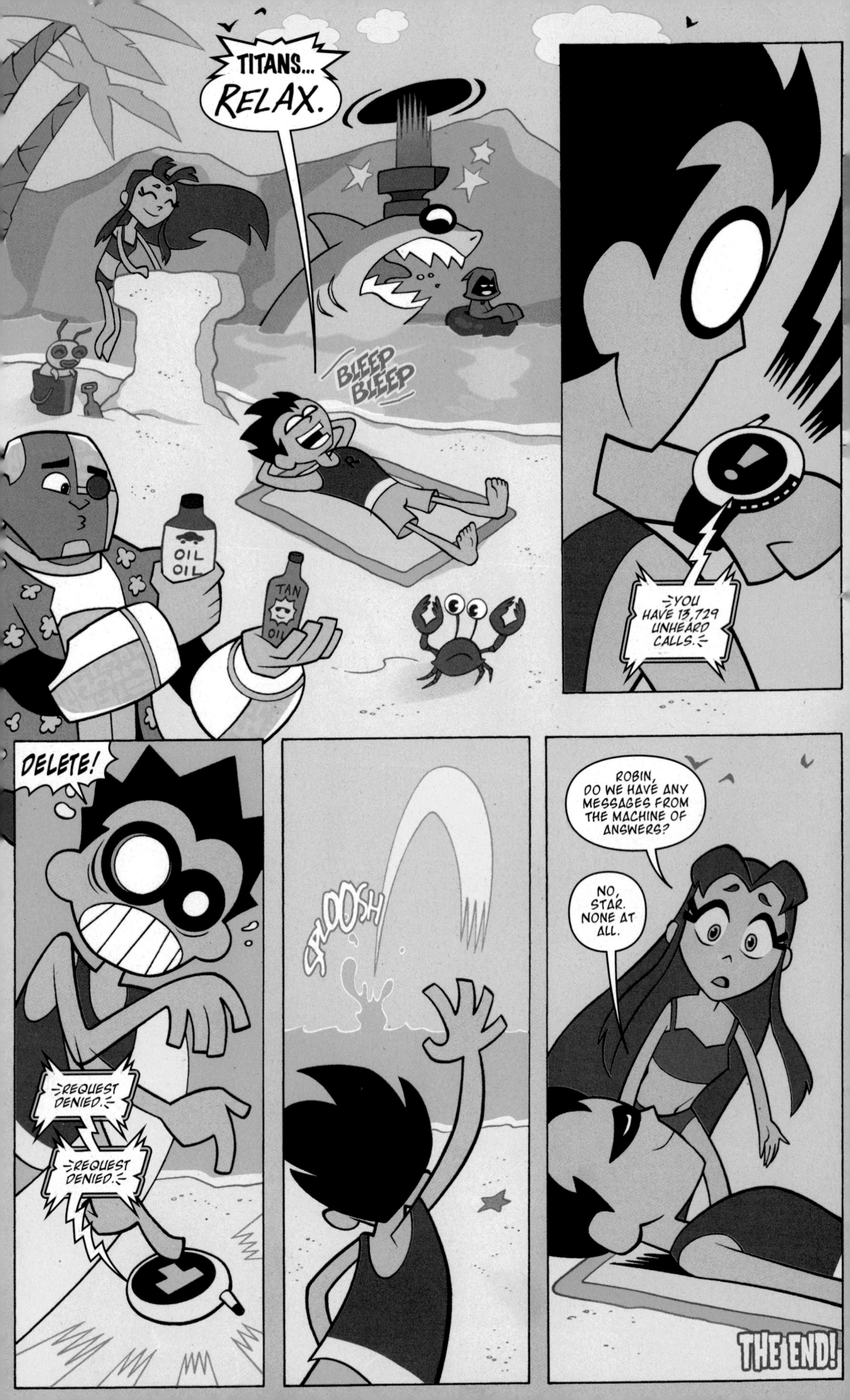
TITANS... RELAX.
BLEEP BLEEP
OIL OIL
TAN OIL
YOU HAVE 13,729 UNHEARD CALLS.
DELETE!
REQUEST DENIED.
REQUEST DENIED.
SPLOOSH
ROBIN, DO WE HAVE ANY MESSAGES FROM THE MACHINE OF ANSWERS?
NO, STAR. NONE AT ALL.
THE END!

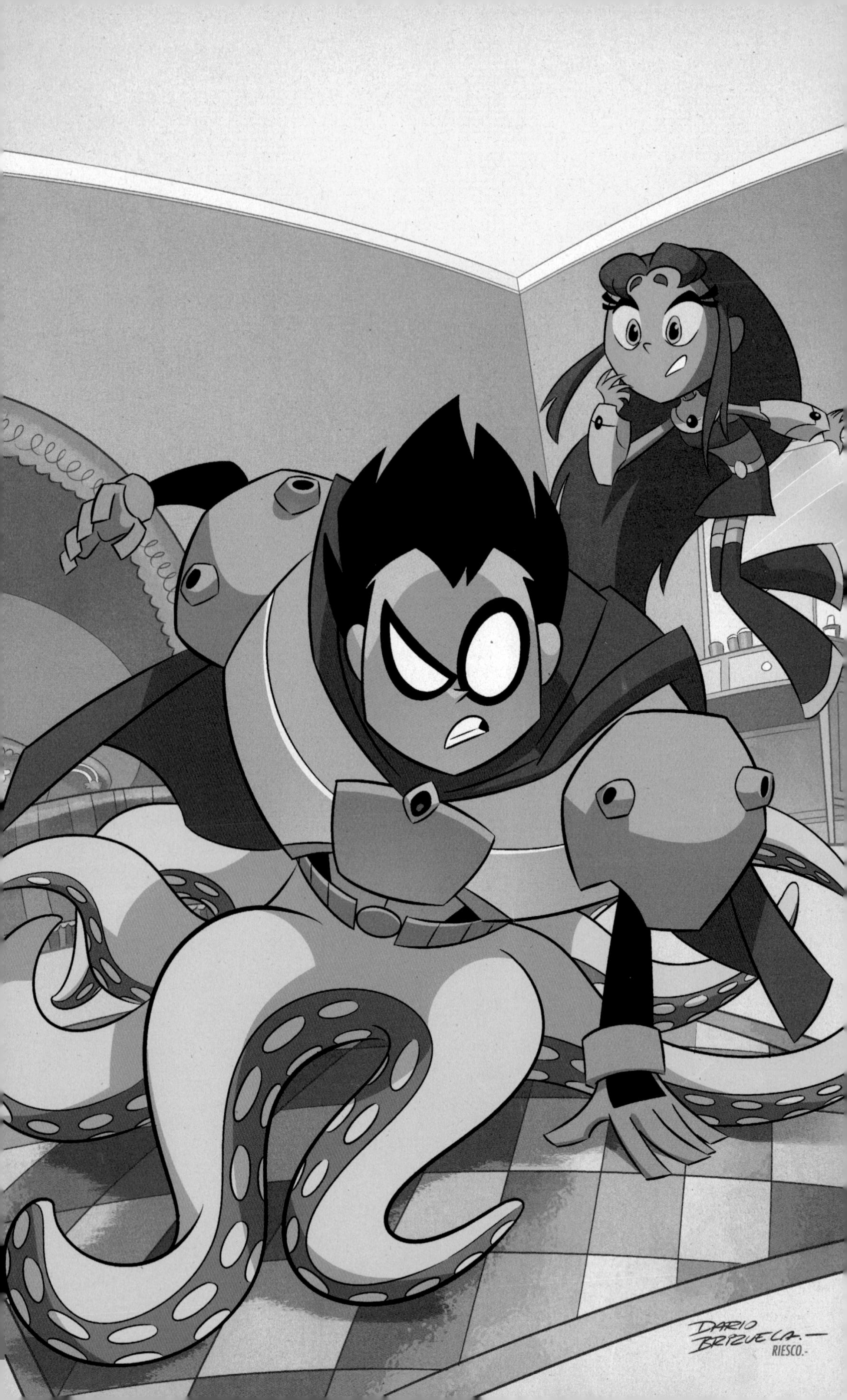
DARIO BRIZUELA
RIESCO.

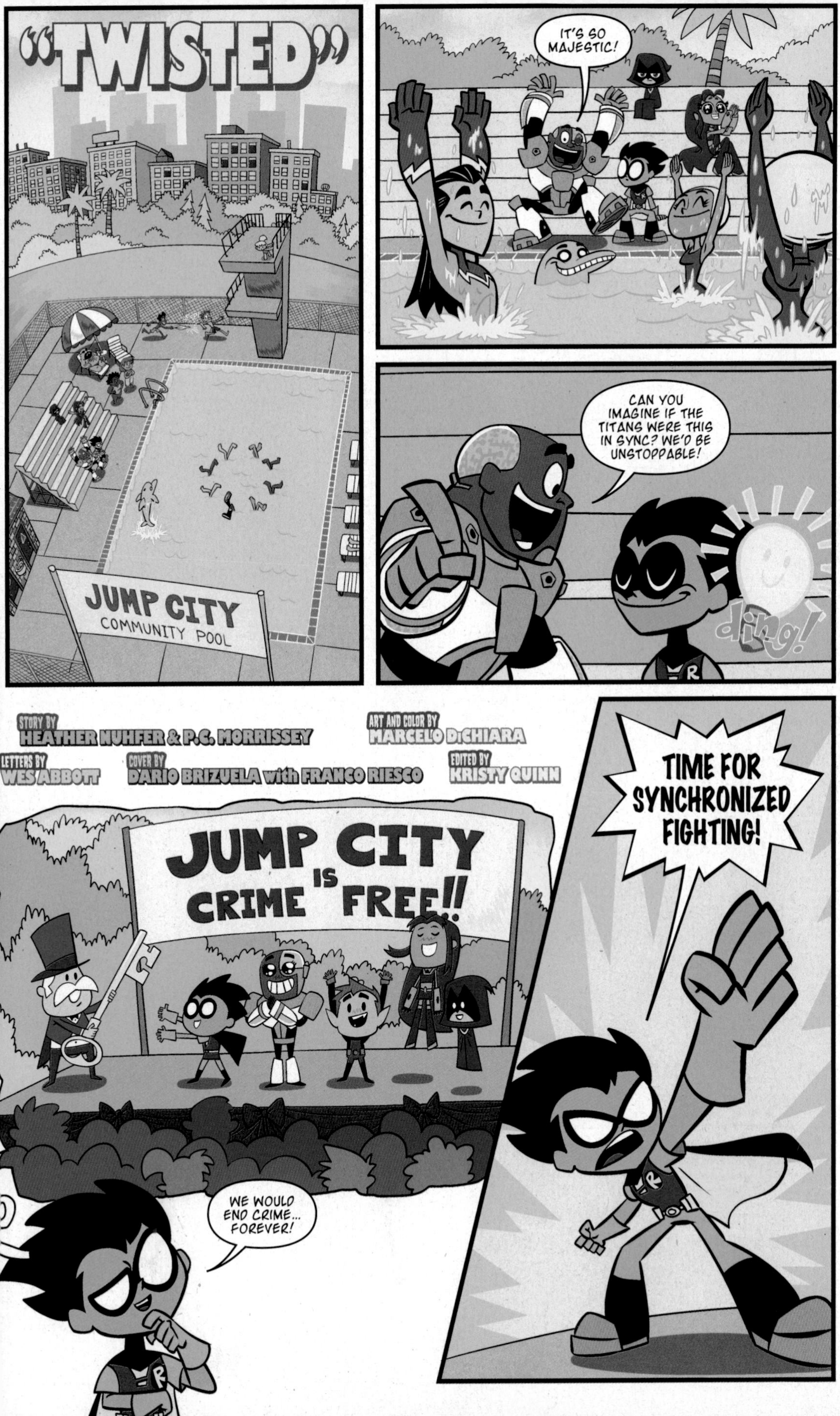
"TWISTED"
JUMP CITY
COMMUNITY POOL
IT'S SO MAJESTIC!
CAN YOU IMAGINE IF THE TITANS WERE THIS IN SYNC? WE'D BE UNSTOPPABLE!
ding!
STORY BY HEATHER NUHFER & P.C. MORRISSEY
ART AND COLOR BY MARCELO DiCHIARA
LETTERS BY WES ABBOTT
COVER BY DARIO BRIZUELA with FRANCO RIESCO
EDITED BY KRISTY QUINN
JUMP CITY IS CRIME FREE!!
WE WOULD END CRIME... FOREVER!
TIME FOR SYNCHRONIZED FIGHTING!

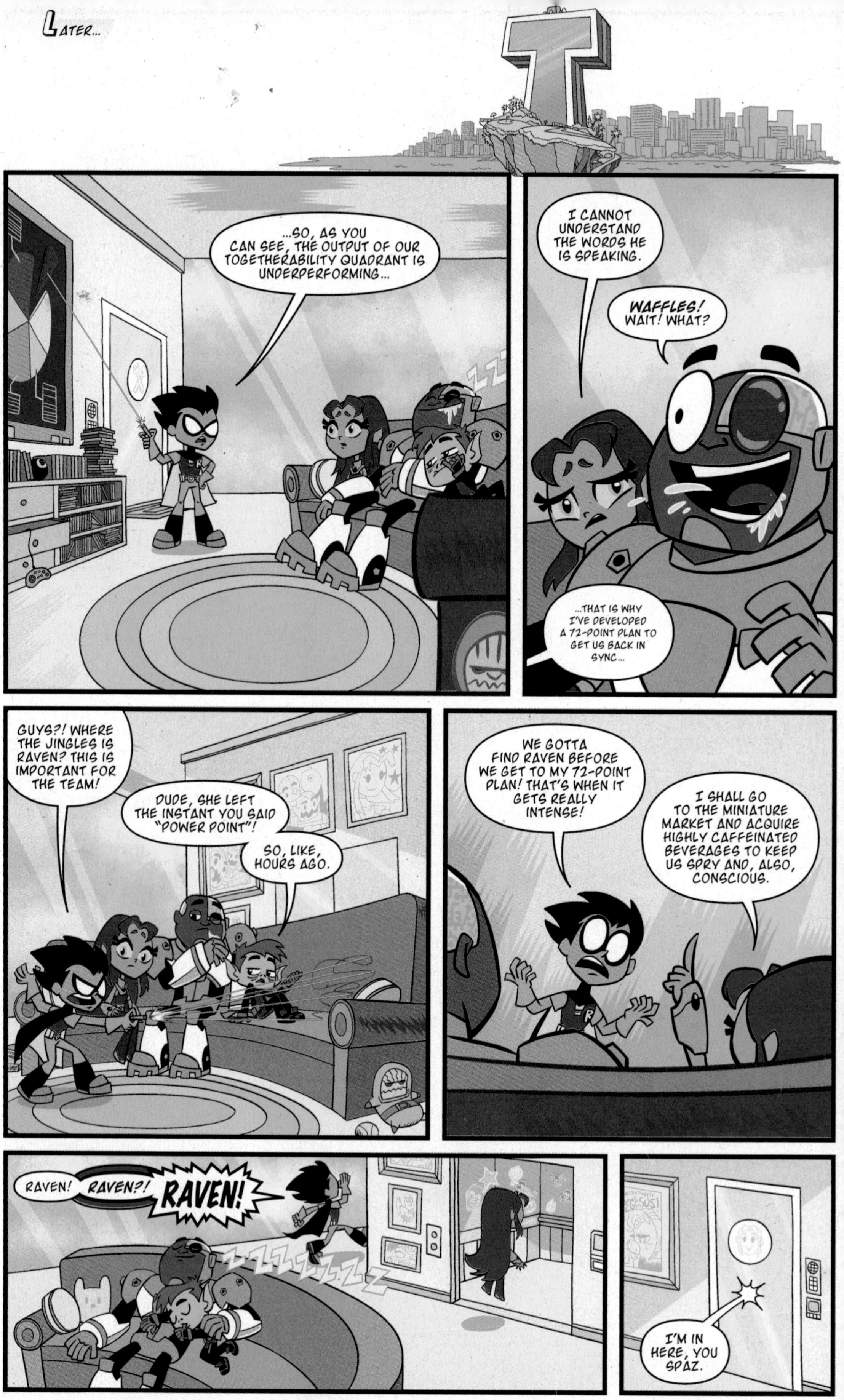
LATER...
...SO, AS YOU CAN SEE, THE OUTPUT OF OUR TOGETHERABILITY QUADRANT IS UNDERPERFORMING...
I CANNOT UNDERSTAND THE WORDS HE IS SPEAKING.
WAFFLES! WAIT! WHAT?
...THAT IS WHY I'VE DEVELOPED A 72-POINT PLAN TO GET US BACK IN SYNC...
GUYS?! WHERE THE JINGLES IS RAVEN? THIS IS IMPORTANT FOR THE TEAM!
DUDE, SHE LEFT THE INSTANT YOU SAID "POWER POINT"!
SO, LIKE, HOURS AGO.
WE GOTTA FIND RAVEN BEFORE WE GET TO MY 72-POINT PLAN! THAT'S WHEN IT GETS REALLY INTENSE!
I SHALL GO TO THE MINIATURE MARKET AND ACQUIRE HIGHLY CAFFEINATED BEVERAGES TO KEEP US SPRY AND, ALSO, CONSCIOUS.
RAVEN!
RAVEN?!
RAVEN!
I'M IN HERE, YOU SPAZ.

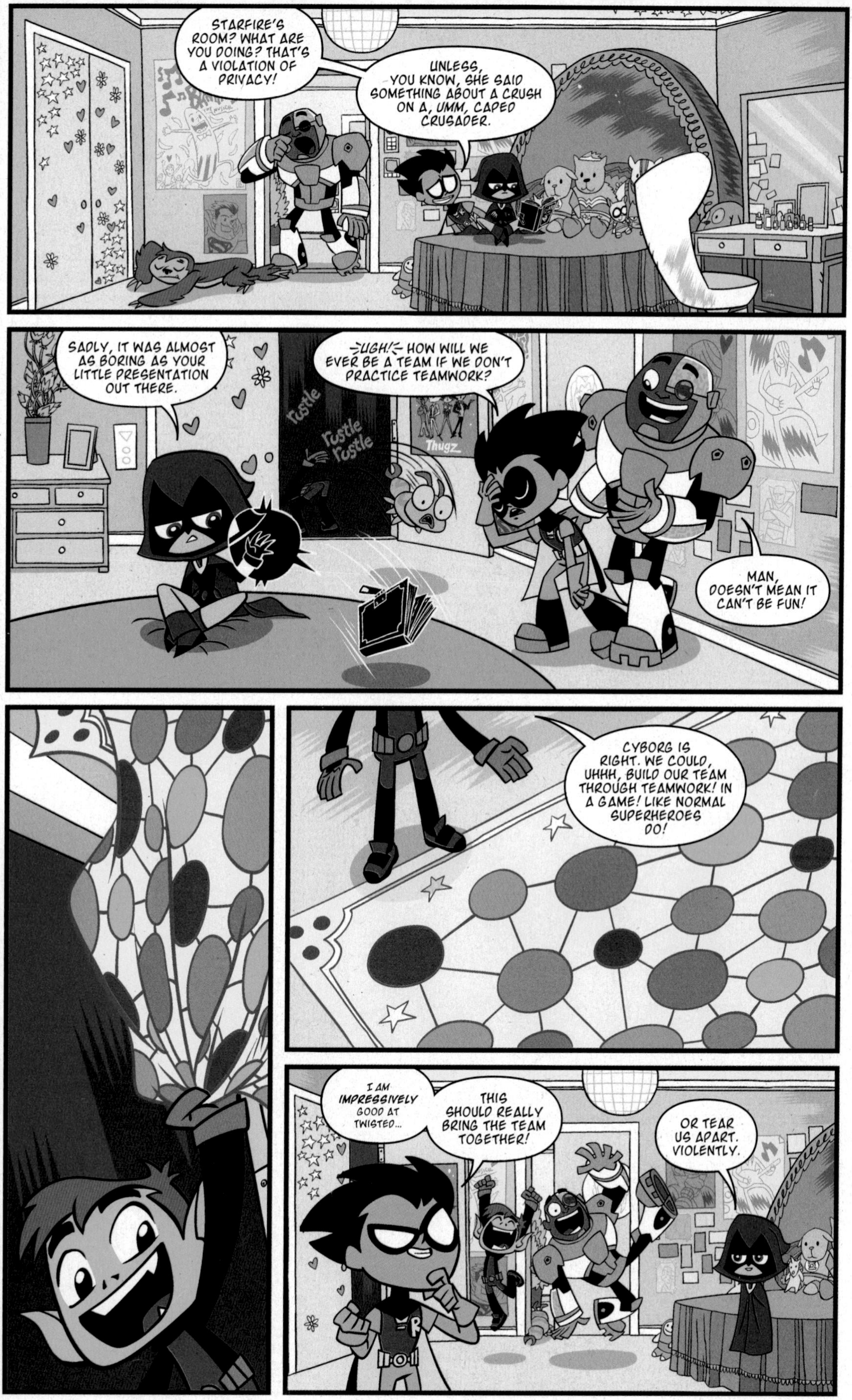
STARFIRE'S ROOM? WHAT ARE YOU DOING? THAT'S A VIOLATION OF PRIVACY!
UNLESS, YOU KNOW, SHE SAID SOMETHING ABOUT A CRUSH ON A, UMM, CAPED CRUSADER.
SADLY, IT WAS ALMOST AS BORING AS YOUR LITTLE PRESENTATION OUT THERE.
-UGH!- HOW WILL WE EVER BE A TEAM IF WE DON'T PRACTICE TEAMWORK?
rustle
rustle rustle
Thugz
MAN, DOESN'T MEAN IT CAN'T BE FUN!
CYBORG IS RIGHT. WE COULD, UHHH, BUILD OUR TEAM THROUGH TEAMWORK! IN A GAME! LIKE NORMAL SUPERHEROES DO!
I AM IMPRESSIVELY GOOD AT TWISTED...
THIS SHOULD REALLY BRING THE TEAM TOGETHER!
OR TEAR US APART. VIOLENTLY.

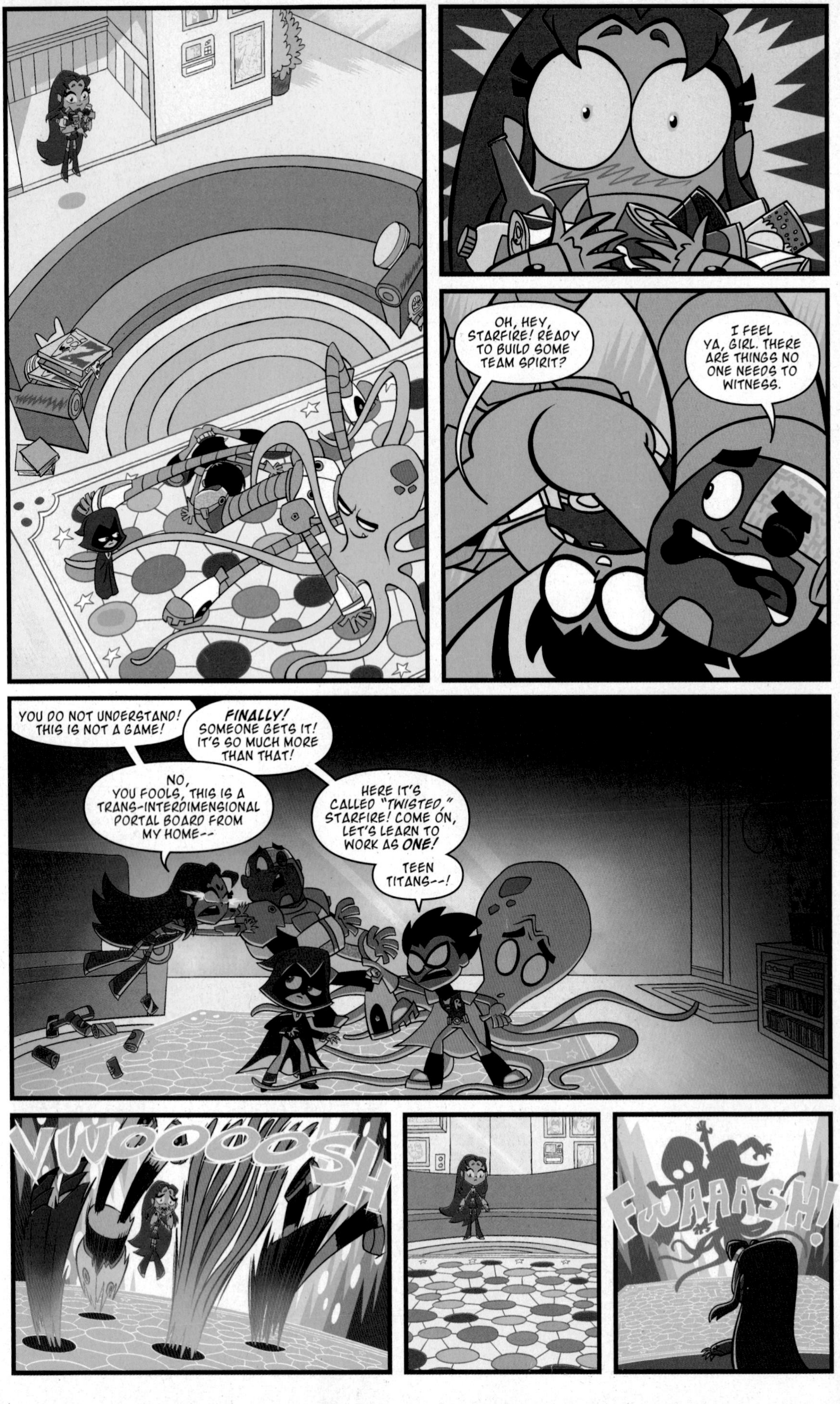
OH, HEY, STARFIRE! READY TO BUILD SOME TEAM SPIRIT?
I FEEL YA, GIRL. THERE ARE THINGS NO ONE NEEDS TO WITNESS.
YOU DO NOT UNDERSTAND! THIS IS NOT A GAME!
FINALLY! SOMEONE GETS IT! IT'S SO MUCH MORE THAN THAT!
NO, YOU FOOLS, THIS IS A TRANS-INTERDIMENSIONAL PORTAL BOARD FROM MY HOME--
HERE IT'S CALLED "TWISTED," STARFIRE! COME ON, LET'S LEARN TO WORK AS ONE!
TEEN TITANS--!
VWOOOOOSH
FWAAASH!

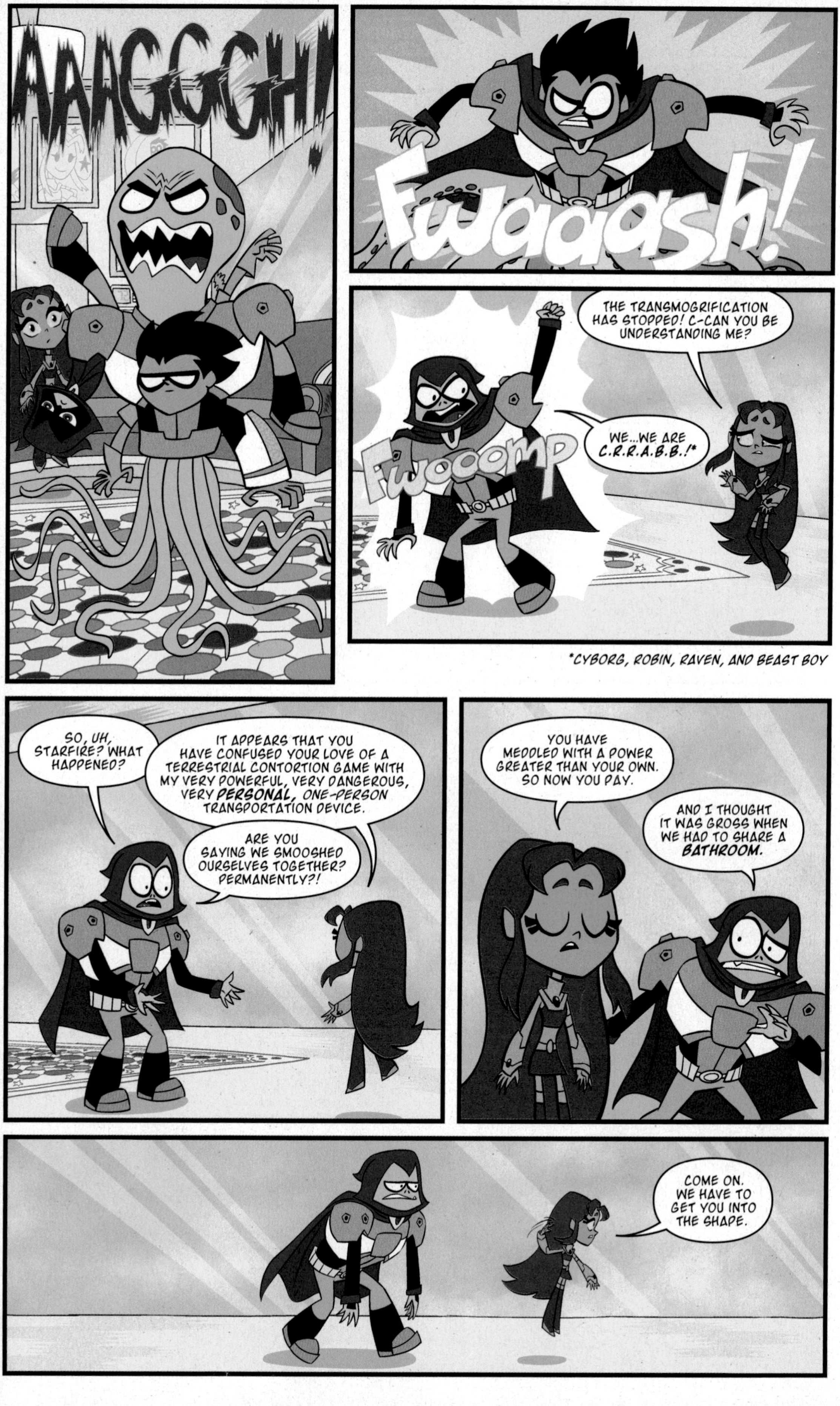
AAAGGGH!
FWAAASH!
THE TRANSMOGRIFICATION HAS STOPPED! C-CAN YOU BE UNDERSTANDING ME?
FWOOOMP
WE...WE ARE C.R.R.A.B.B.!*
*CYBORG, ROBIN, RAVEN, AND BEAST BOY
SO, UH, STARFIRE? WHAT HAPPENED?
IT APPEARS THAT YOU HAVE CONFUSED YOUR LOVE OF A TERRESTRIAL CONTORTION GAME WITH MY VERY POWERFUL, VERY DANGEROUS, VERY PERSONAL, ONE-PERSON TRANSPORTATION DEVICE.
ARE YOU SAYING WE SMOOSHED OURSELVES TOGETHER? PERMANENTLY?!
YOU HAVE MEDDLED WITH A POWER GREATER THAN YOUR OWN. SO NOW YOU PAY.
AND I THOUGHT IT WAS GROSS WHEN WE HAD TO SHARE A BATHROOM.
COME ON. WE HAVE TO GET YOU INTO THE SHAPE.

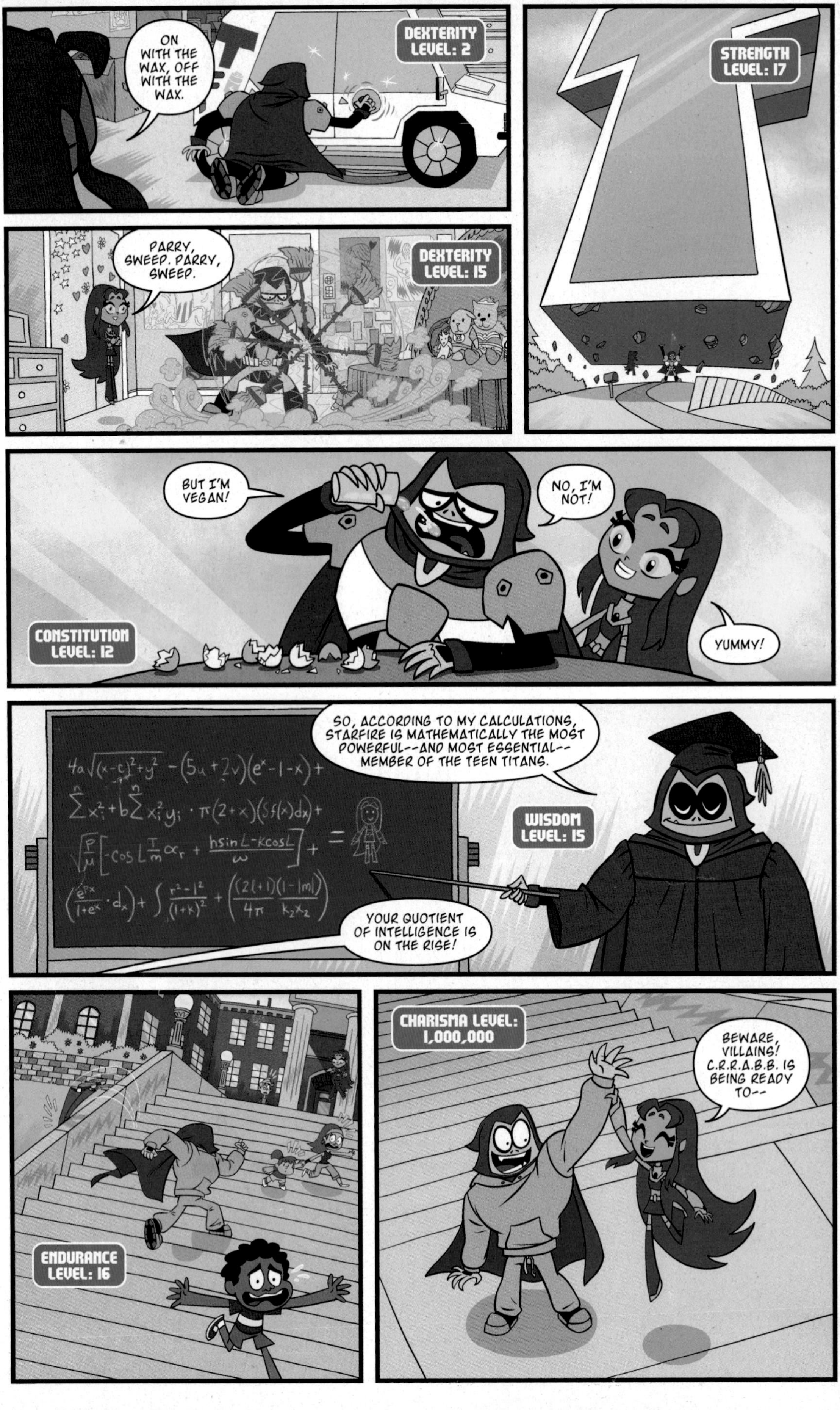
ON WITH THE WAX, OFF WITH THE WAX.
DEXTERITY LEVEL: 2
STRENGTH LEVEL: 17
PARRY, SWEEP. PARRY, SWEEP.
DEXTERITY LEVEL: 15
BUT I'M VEGAN!
NO, I'M NOT!
CONSTITUTION LEVEL: 12
YUMMY!
SO, ACCORDING TO MY CALCULATIONS, STARFIRE IS MATHEMATICALLY THE MOST POWERFUL--AND MOST ESSENTIAL--MEMBER OF THE TEEN TITANS.
WISDOM LEVEL: 15
YOUR QUOTIENT OF INTELLIGENCE IS ON THE RISE!
ENDURANCE LEVEL: 16
CHARISMA LEVEL: 1,000,000
BEWARE, VILLAINS! C.R.R.A.B.B. IS BEING READY TO--

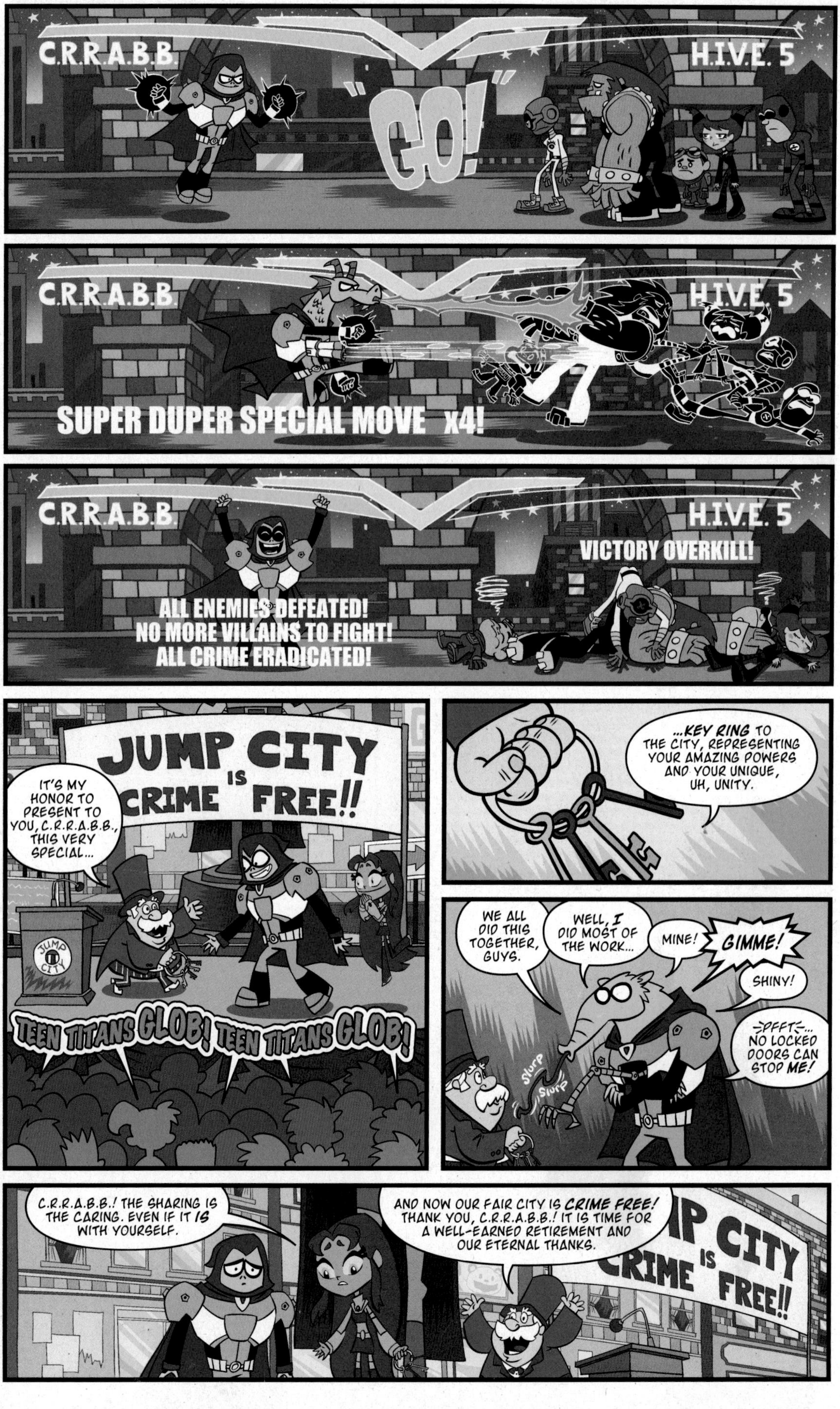
C.R.R.A.B.B.
H.I.V.E. 5
"GO!"
C.R.R.A.B.B.
H.I.V.E. 5
SUPER DUPER SPECIAL MOVE x4!
C.R.R.A.B.B.
H.I.V.E. 5
VICTORY OVERKILL!
ALL ENEMIES DEFEATED!
NO MORE VILLAINS TO FIGHT!
ALL CRIME ERADICATED!
JUMP CITY IS CRIME FREE!!
IT'S MY HONOR TO PRESENT TO YOU, C.R.R.A.B.B., THIS VERY SPECIAL...
JUMP CITY
TEEN TITANS GLOB! TEEN TITANS GLOB!
...KEY RING TO THE CITY, REPRESENTING YOUR AMAZING POWERS AND YOUR UNIQUE, UH, UNITY.
WE ALL DID THIS TOGETHER, GUYS.
WELL, I DID MOST OF THE WORK...
MINE!
GIMME!
SHINY!
-PFFT-... NO LOCKED DOORS CAN STOP ME!
SLURP
SLURP
C.R.R.A.B.B.! THE SHARING IS THE CARING. EVEN IF IT IS WITH YOURSELF.
AND NOW OUR FAIR CITY IS CRIME FREE! THANK YOU, C.R.R.A.B.B.! IT IS TIME FOR A WELL-EARNED RETIREMENT AND OUR ETERNAL THANKS.
JUMP CITY IS CRIME FREE!!

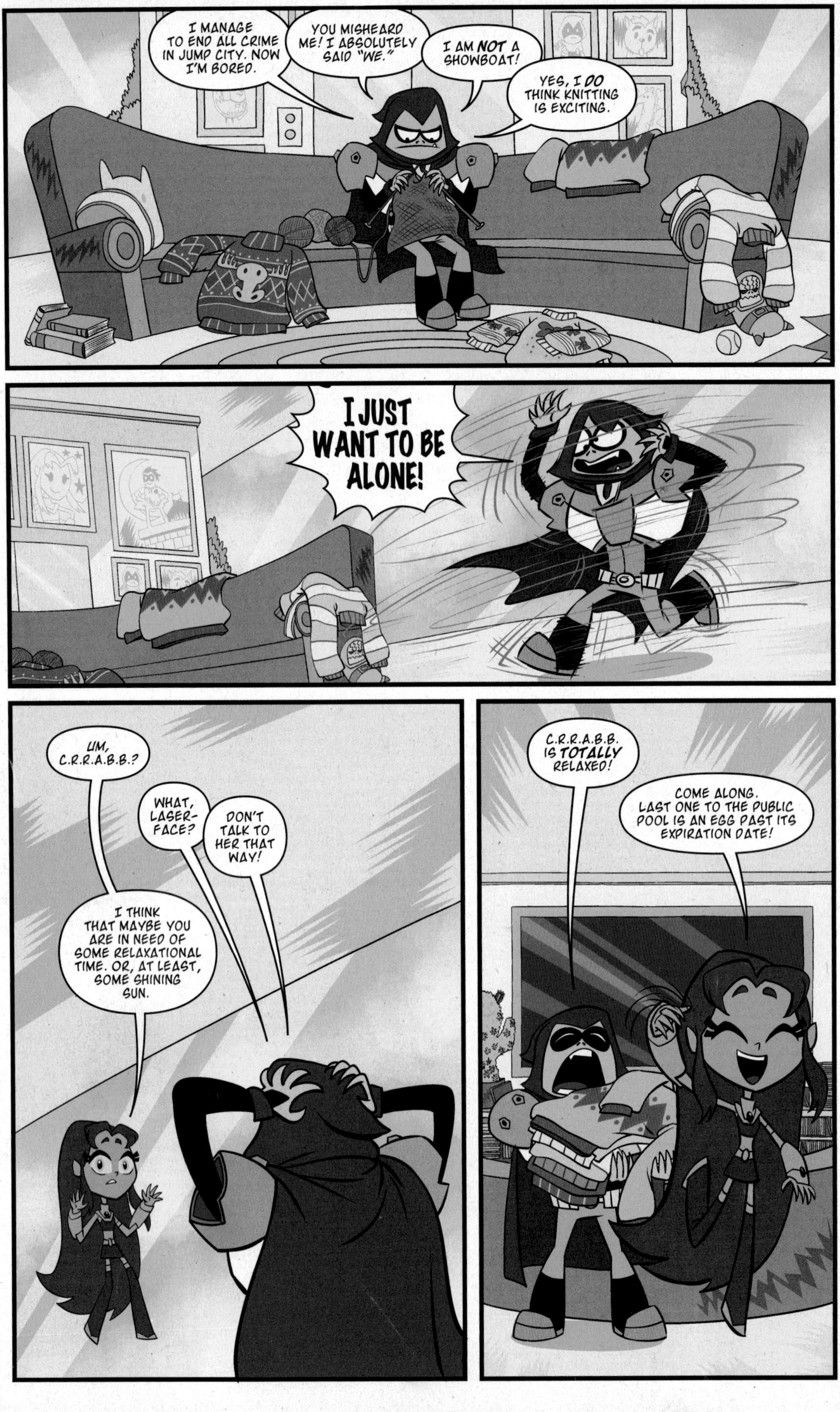
I MANAGE TO END ALL CRIME IN JUMP CITY. NOW I'M BORED.
YOU MISHEARD ME! I ABSOLUTELY SAID "WE."
I AM NOT A SHOWBOAT!
YES, I DO THINK KNITTING IS EXCITING.
I JUST WANT TO BE ALONE!
UM, C.R.R.A.B.B.?
WHAT, LASER-FACE?
DON'T TALK TO HER THAT WAY!
I THINK THAT MAYBE YOU ARE IN NEED OF SOME RELAXATIONAL TIME. OR, AT LEAST, SOME SHINING SUN.
C.R.R.A.B.B. IS TOTALLY RELAXED!
COME ALONG. LAST ONE TO THE PUBLIC POOL IS AN EGG PAST ITS EXPIRATION DATE!

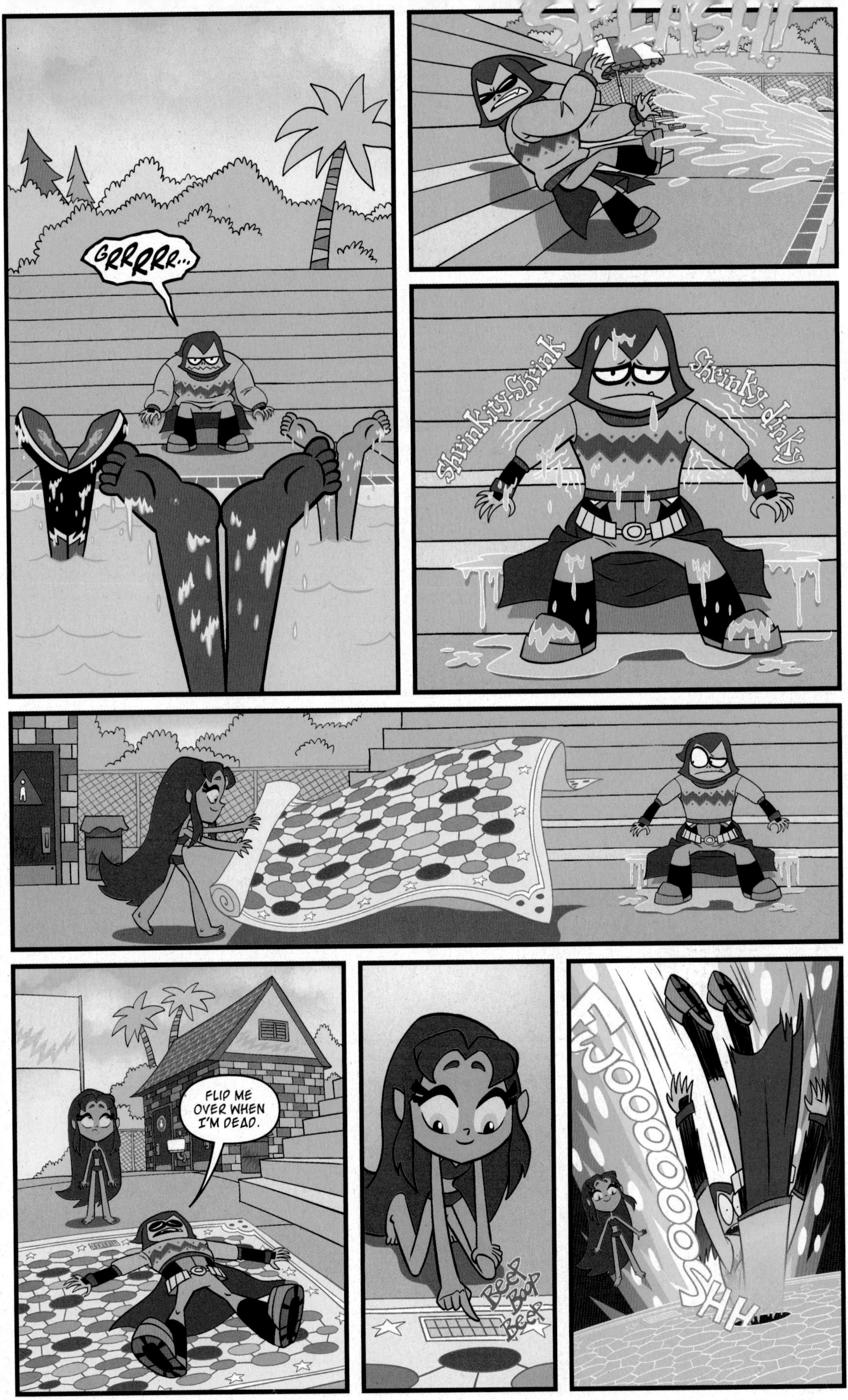
GRRRRR...
SPLASH!
Shrinkity-Shrink
Shrinky-dinky
FLIP ME OVER WHEN I'M DEAD.
BEEP BOOP BEEP
FWOOOOOOOSHH

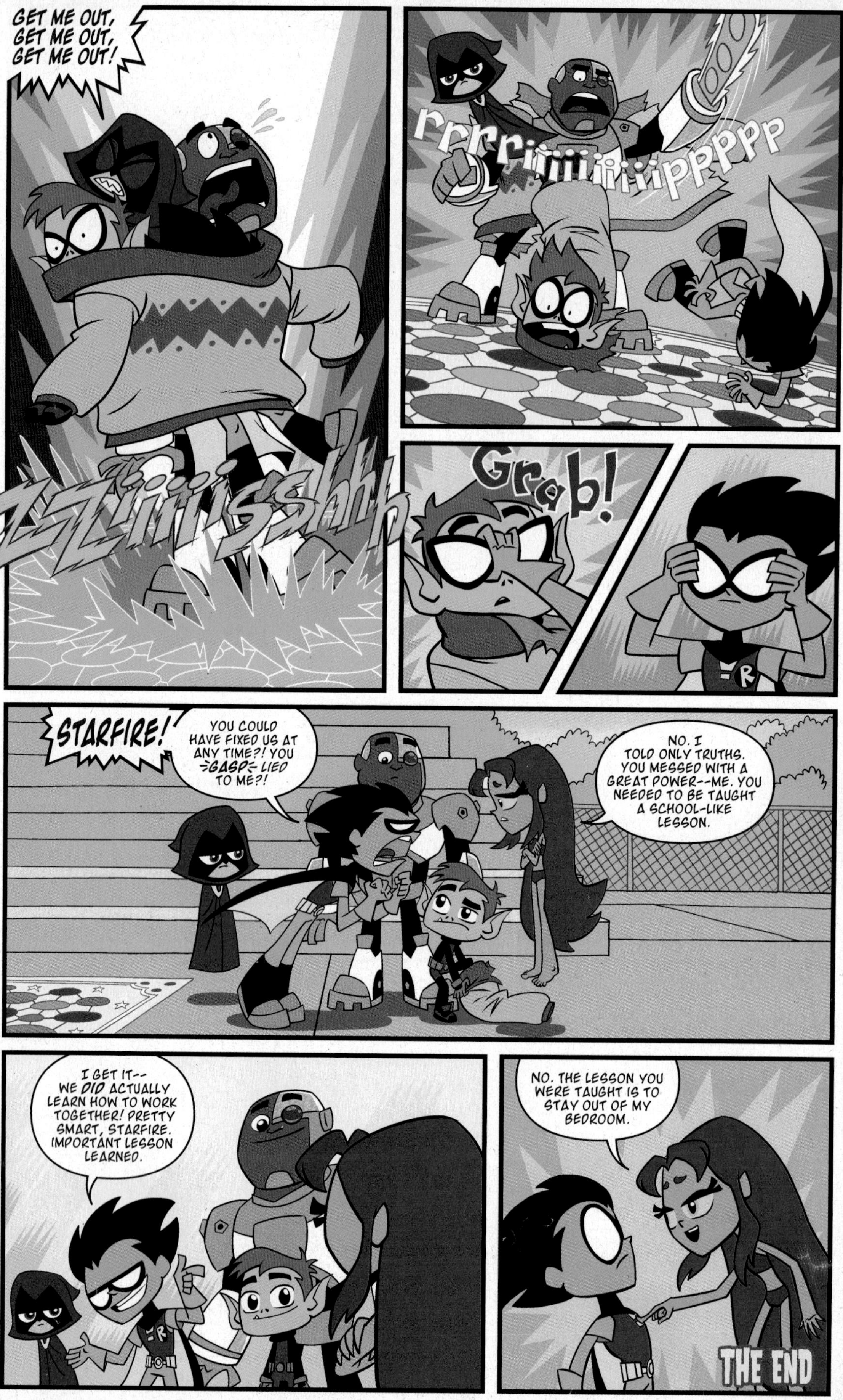
GET ME OUT, GET ME OUT, GET ME OUT!
ZZZiiiiiSShhh
rrrrriiiiiiiiiiipPPPPP
Grab!
STARFIRE!
YOU COULD HAVE FIXED US AT ANY TIME?! YOU =GASP= LIED TO ME?!
NO. I TOLD ONLY TRUTHS. YOU MESSED WITH A GREAT POWER--ME. YOU NEEDED TO BE TAUGHT A SCHOOL-LIKE LESSON.
I GET IT--WE DID ACTUALLY LEARN HOW TO WORK TOGETHER! PRETTY SMART, STARFIRE. IMPORTANT LESSON LEARNED.
NO. THE LESSON YOU WERE TAUGHT IS TO STAY OUT OF MY BEDROOM.
THE END

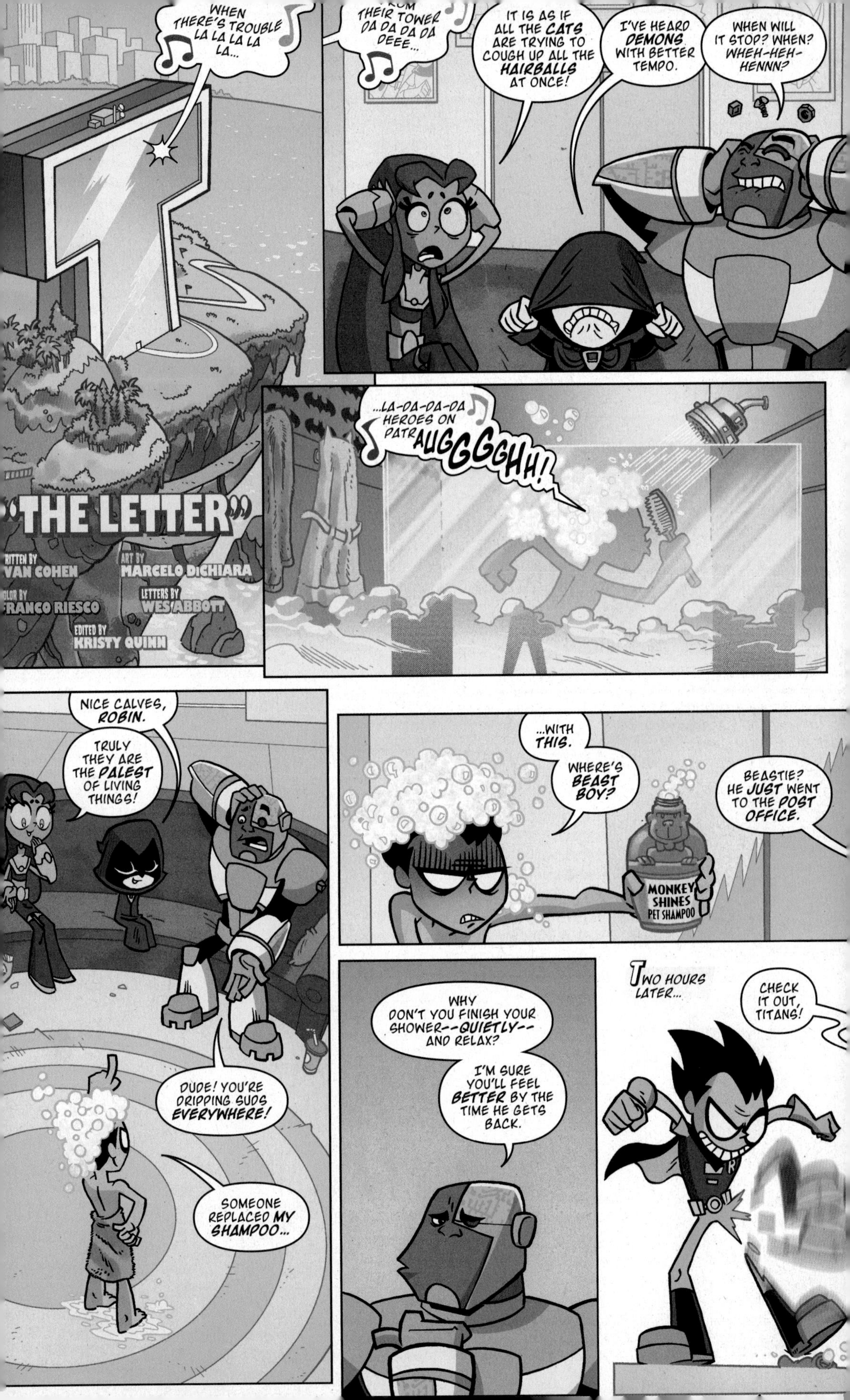

WHEN THERE'S TROUBLE LA LA LA LA LA...
THEIR TOWER DA DA DA DA DEEE...
IT IS AS IF ALL THE CATS ARE TRYING TO COUGH UP ALL THE HAIRBALLS AT ONCE!
I'VE HEARD DEMONS WITH BETTER TEMPO.
WHEN WILL IT STOP? WHEN? WHEH-HEH-HENNN?
"THE LETTER"
RITTEN BY
VAN COHEN
ART BY
MARCELO DiCHIARA
OLOR BY
FRANCO RIESCO
LETTERS BY
WES ABBOTT
EDITED BY
KRISTY QUINN
...LA-DA-DA-DA HEROES ON PATRAUGGGGHH!
NICE CALVES, ROBIN.
TRULY THEY ARE THE PALEST OF LIVING THINGS!
DUDE! YOU'RE DRIPPING SUDS EVERYWHERE!
SOMEONE REPLACED MY SHAMPOO...
...WITH THIS.
WHERE'S BEAST BOY?
MONKEY SHINES PET SHAMPOO
BEASTIE? HE JUST WENT TO THE POST OFFICE.
WHY DON'T YOU FINISH YOUR SHOWER--QUIETLY--AND RELAX?
I'M SURE YOU'LL FEEL BETTER BY THE TIME HE GETS BACK.
TWO HOURS LATER...
CHECK IT OUT, TITANS!

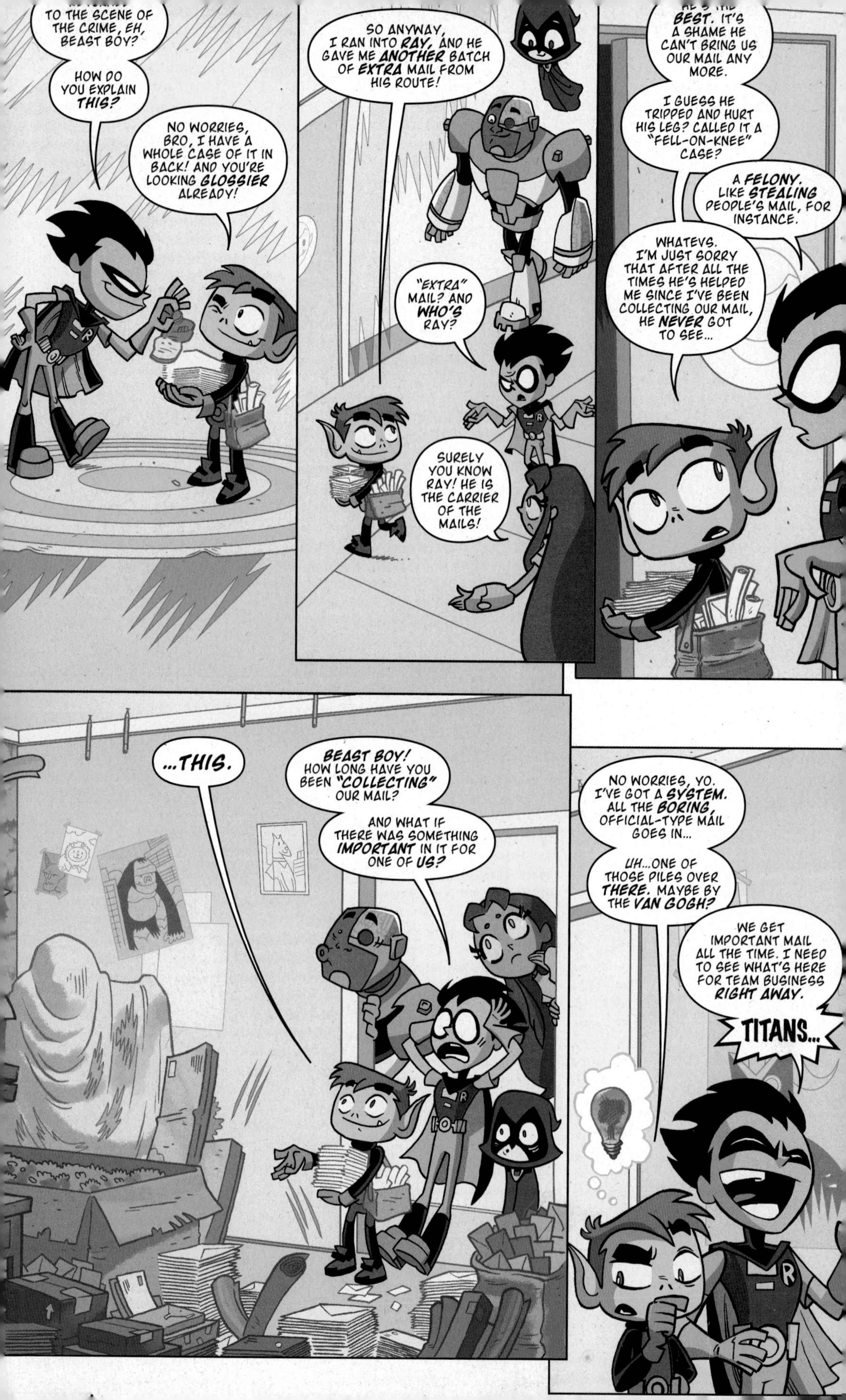
TO THE SCENE OF THE CRIME, EH, BEAST BOY?
HOW DO YOU EXPLAIN THIS?
NO WORRIES, BRO, I HAVE A WHOLE CASE OF IT IN BACK! AND YOU'RE LOOKING GLOSSIER ALREADY!
SO ANYWAY, I RAN INTO RAY, AND HE GAVE ME ANOTHER BATCH OF EXTRA MAIL FROM HIS ROUTE!
"EXTRA" MAIL? AND WHO'S RAY?
SURELY YOU KNOW RAY! HE IS THE CARRIER OF THE MAILS!
BEST. IT'S A SHAME HE CAN'T BRING US OUR MAIL ANY MORE.
I GUESS HE TRIPPED AND HURT HIS LEG? CALLED IT A "FELL-ON-KNEE" CASE?
A FELONY. LIKE STEALING PEOPLE'S MAIL, FOR INSTANCE.
WHATEVS. I'M JUST SORRY THAT AFTER ALL THE TIMES HE'S HELPED ME SINCE I'VE BEEN COLLECTING OUR MAIL, HE NEVER GOT TO SEE...
...THIS.
BEAST BOY! HOW LONG HAVE YOU BEEN "COLLECTING" OUR MAIL?
AND WHAT IF THERE WAS SOMETHING IMPORTANT IN IT FOR ONE OF US?
NO WORRIES, YO. I'VE GOT A SYSTEM. ALL THE BORING, OFFICIAL-TYPE MAIL GOES IN...
UH...ONE OF THOSE PILES OVER THERE. MAYBE BY THE VAN GOGH?
WE GET IMPORTANT MAIL ALL THE TIME. I NEED TO SEE WHAT'S HERE FOR TEAM BUSINESS RIGHT AWAY.
TITANS...

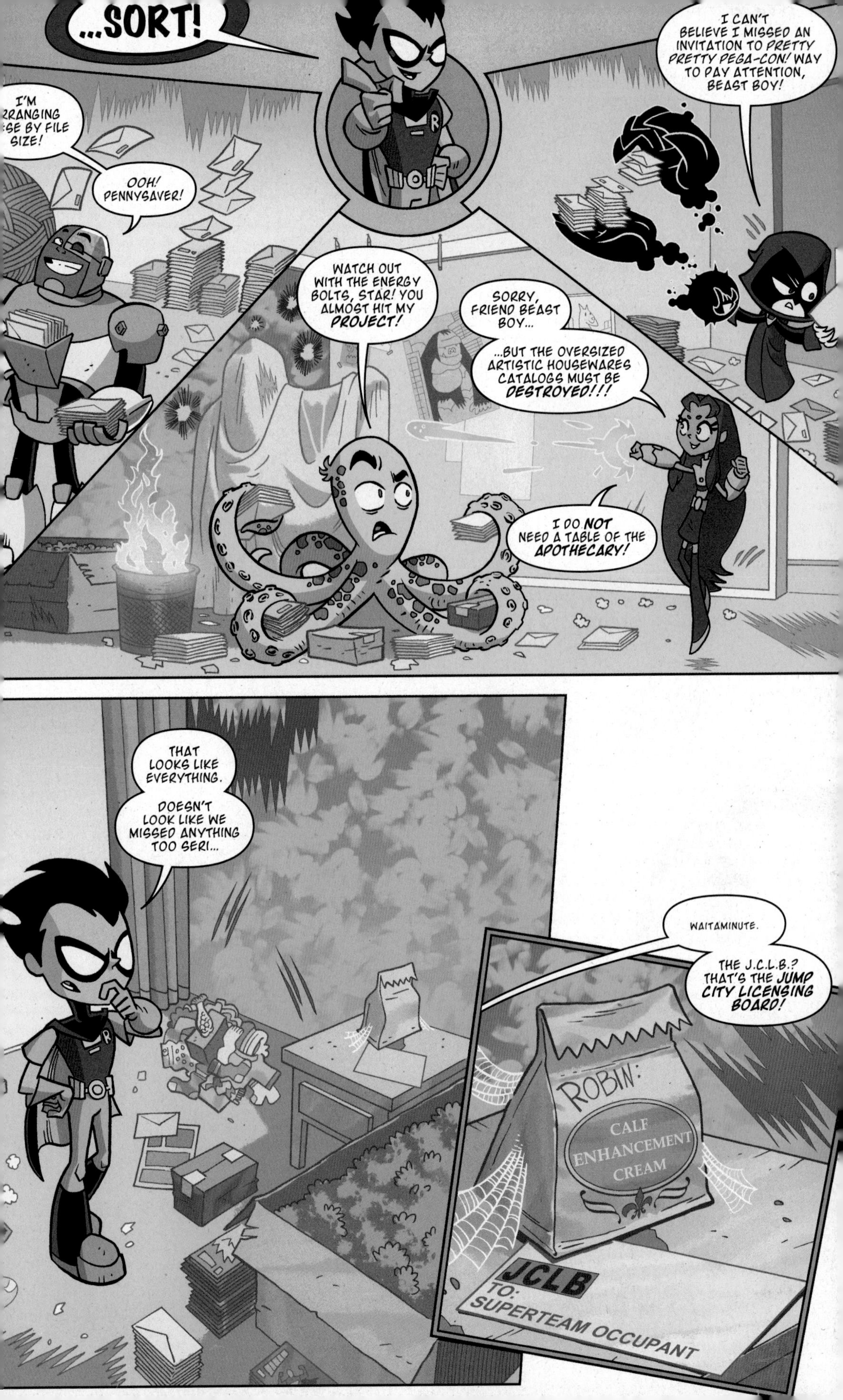

...SORT!
I'M RRANGING ESE BY FILE SIZE!
OOH! PENNYSAVER!
I CAN'T BELIEVE I MISSED AN INVITATION TO PRETTY PRETTY PEGA-CON! WAY TO PAY ATTENTION, BEAST BOY!
WATCH OUT WITH THE ENERGY BOLTS, STAR! YOU ALMOST HIT MY PROJECT!
SORRY, FRIEND BEAST BOY...
...BUT THE OVERSIZED ARTISTIC HOUSEWARES CATALOGS MUST BE DESTROYED!!!
I DO NOT NEED A TABLE OF THE APOTHECARY!
THAT LOOKS LIKE EVERYTHING.
DOESN'T LOOK LIKE WE MISSED ANYTHING TOO SERI...
WAITAMINUTE.
THE J.C.L.B.? THAT'S THE JUMP CITY LICENSING BOARD!
ROBIN:
CALF ENHANCEMENT CREAM
JCLB
TO: SUPERTEAM OCCUPANT

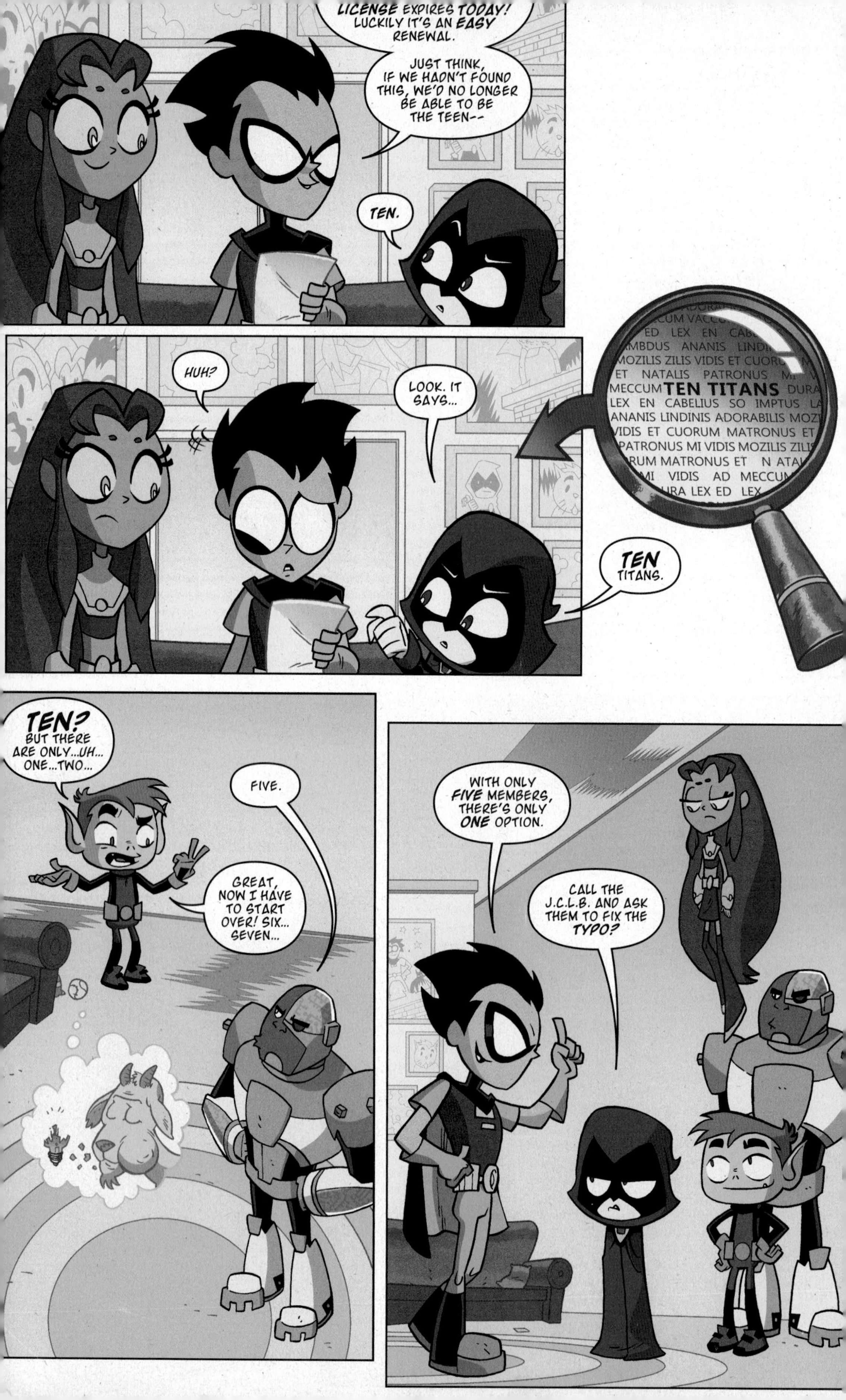
LICENSE EXPIRES TODAY! LUCKILY IT'S AN EASY RENEWAL.
JUST THINK, IF WE HADN'T FOUND THIS, WE'D NO LONGER BE ABLE TO BE THE TEEN--
TEN.
HUH?
LOOK. IT SAYS...
TEN TITANS
TEN TITANS.
TEN? BUT THERE ARE ONLY...UH... ONE...TWO...
FIVE.
GREAT, NOW I HAVE TO START OVER! SIX... SEVEN...
WITH ONLY FIVE MEMBERS, THERE'S ONLY ONE OPTION.
CALL THE J.C.L.B. AND ASK THEM TO FIX THE TYPO?

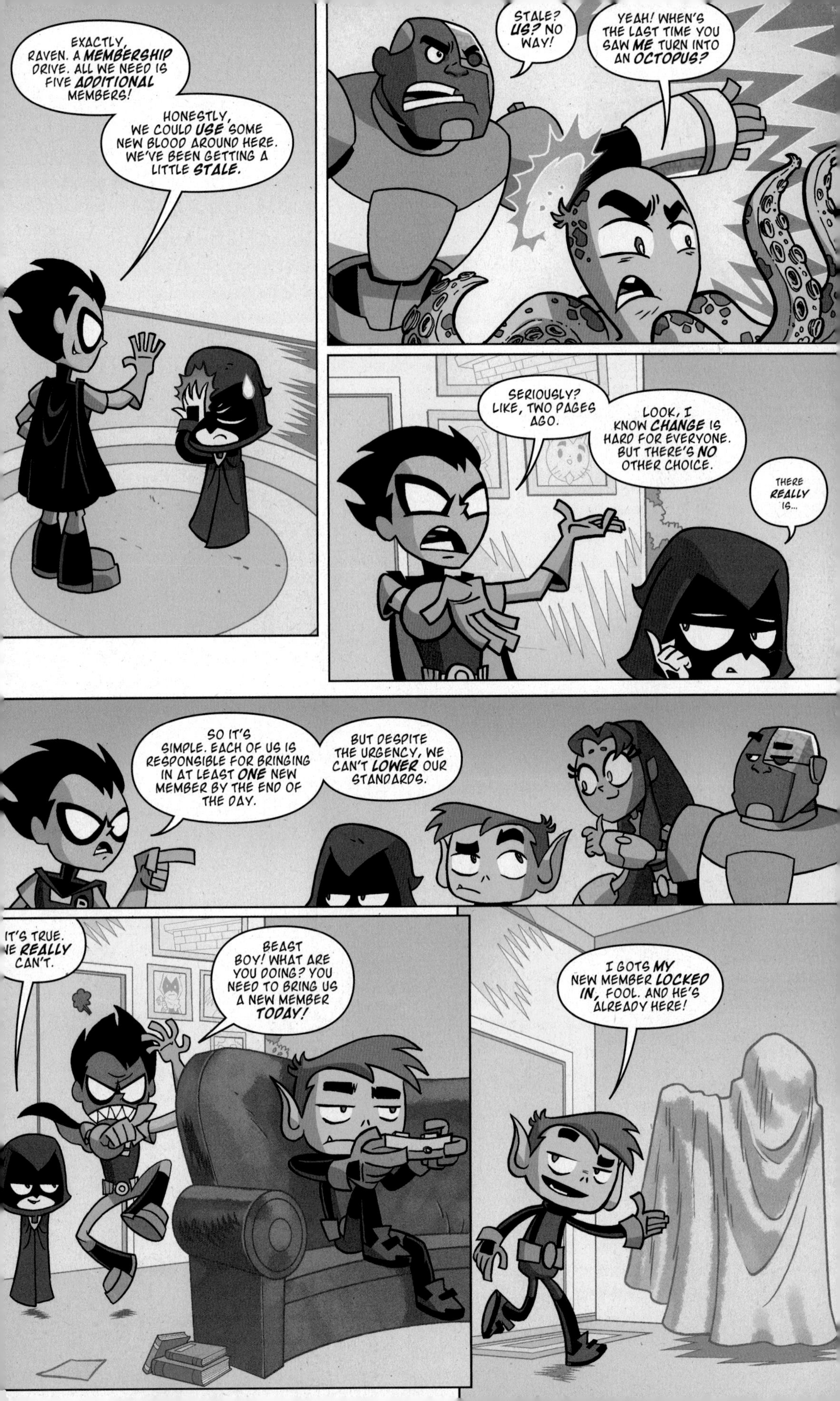
EXACTLY, RAVEN. A MEMBERSHIP DRIVE. ALL WE NEED IS FIVE ADDITIONAL MEMBERS!
HONESTLY, WE COULD USE SOME NEW BLOOD AROUND HERE. WE'VE BEEN GETTING A LITTLE STALE.
STALE? US? NO WAY!
YEAH! WHEN'S THE LAST TIME YOU SAW ME TURN INTO AN OCTOPUS?
SERIOUSLY? LIKE, TWO PAGES AGO.
LOOK, I KNOW CHANGE IS HARD FOR EVERYONE. BUT THERE'S NO OTHER CHOICE.
THERE REALLY IS...
SO IT'S SIMPLE. EACH OF US IS RESPONSIBLE FOR BRINGING IN AT LEAST ONE NEW MEMBER BY THE END OF THE DAY.
BUT DESPITE THE URGENCY, WE CAN'T LOWER OUR STANDARDS.
IT'S TRUE. WE REALLY CAN'T.
BEAST BOY! WHAT ARE YOU DOING? YOU NEED TO BRING US A NEW MEMBER TODAY!
I GOTS MY NEW MEMBER LOCKED IN, FOOL. AND HE'S ALREADY HERE!

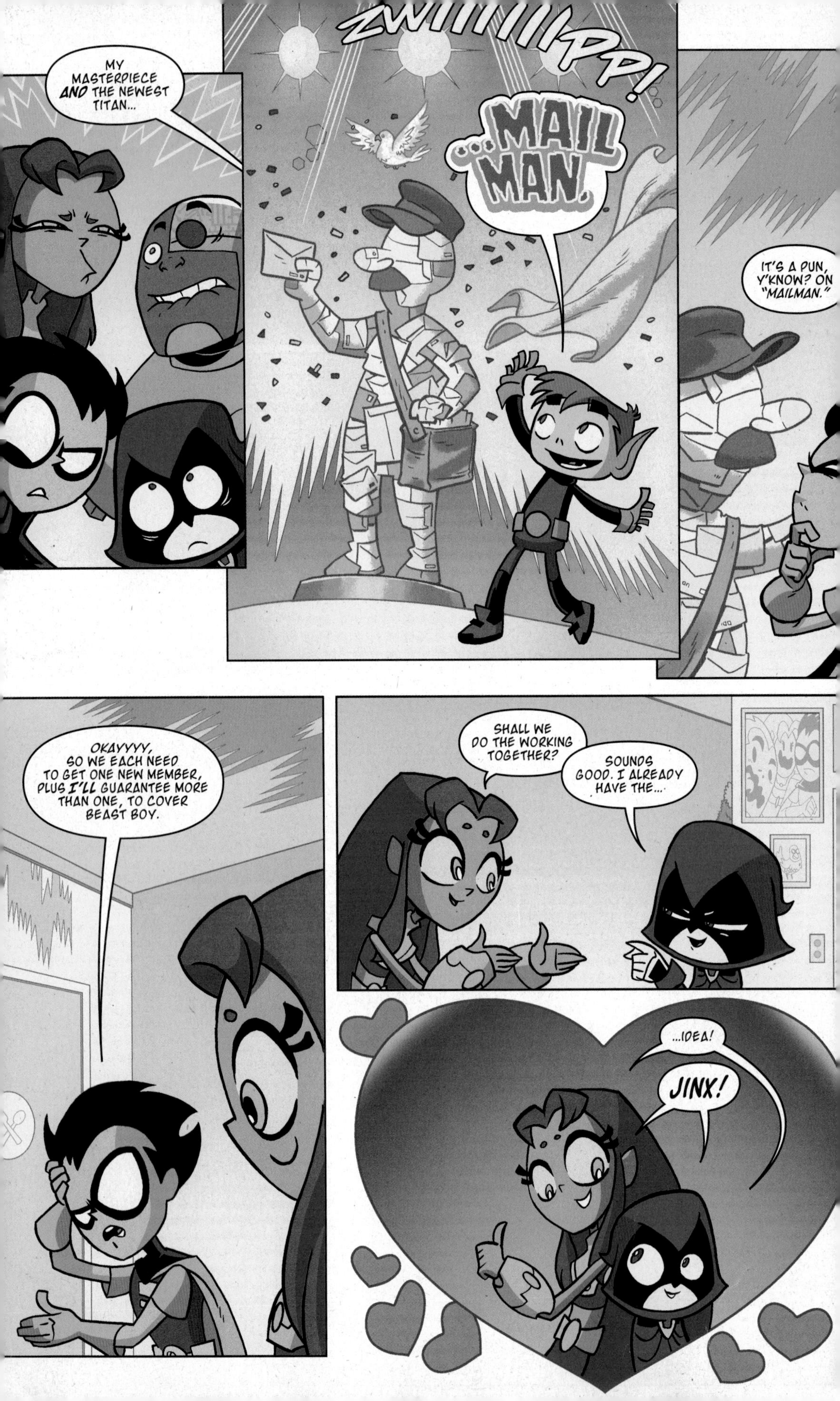

MY MASTERPIECE AND THE NEWEST TITAN...
ZWIIIIIIPP!
...MAIL MAN.
IT'S A PUN, Y'KNOW? ON "MAILMAN."
OKAYYYY, SO WE EACH NEED TO GET ONE NEW MEMBER, PLUS I'LL GUARANTEE MORE THAN ONE, TO COVER BEAST BOY.
SHALL WE DO THE WORKING TOGETHER?
SOUNDS GOOD. I ALREADY HAVE THE...
...IDEA!
JINX!

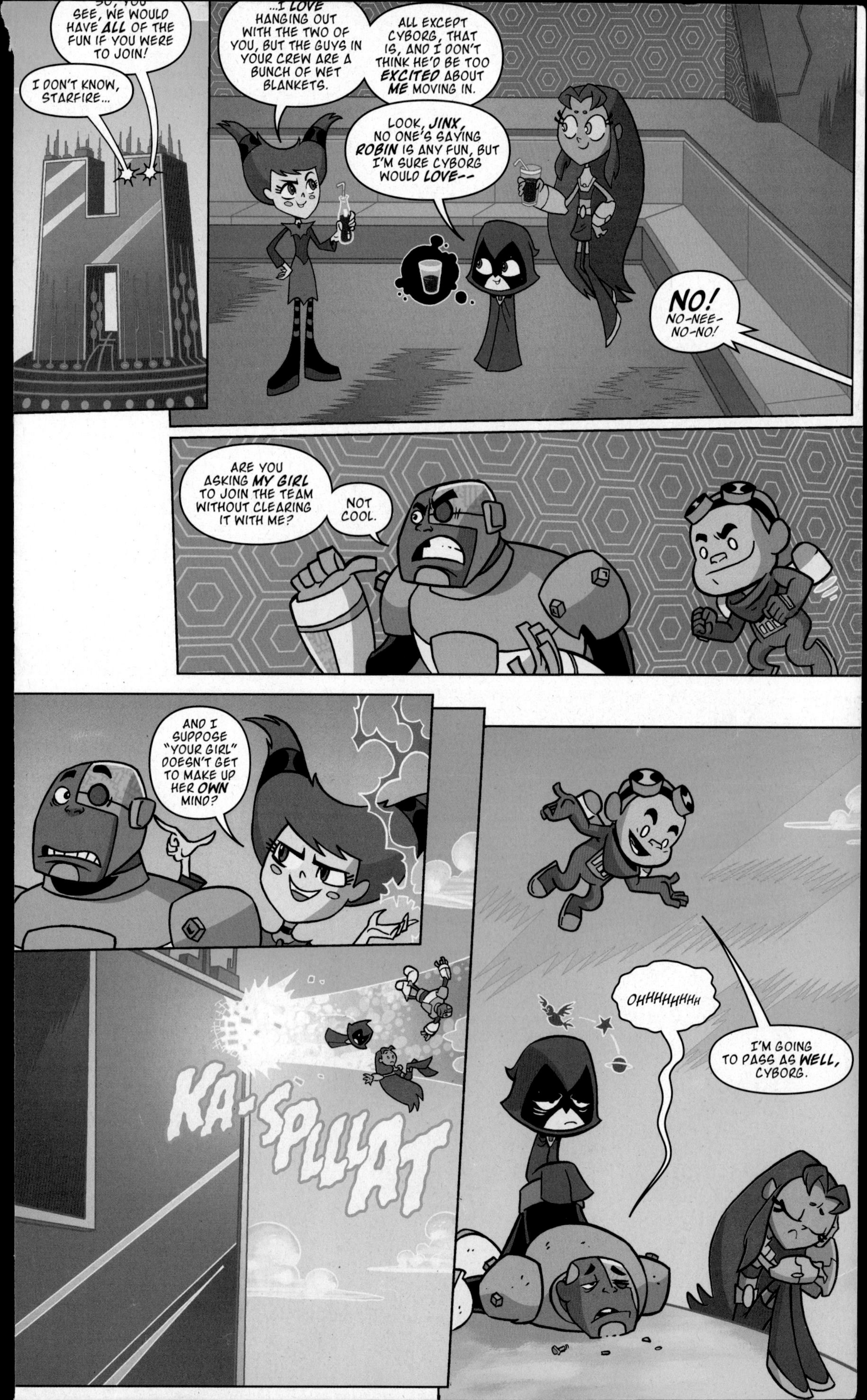
SEE, WE WOULD HAVE ALL OF THE FUN IF YOU WERE TO JOIN!
I DON'T KNOW, STARFIRE...
...I LOVE HANGING OUT WITH THE TWO OF YOU, BUT THE GUYS IN YOUR CREW ARE A BUNCH OF WET BLANKETS.
ALL EXCEPT CYBORG, THAT IS, AND I DON'T THINK HE'D BE TOO EXCITED ABOUT ME MOVING IN.
LOOK, JINX, NO ONE'S SAYING ROBIN IS ANY FUN, BUT I'M SURE CYBORG WOULD LOVE--
NO! NO-NEE-NO-NO!
ARE YOU ASKING MY GIRL TO JOIN THE TEAM WITHOUT CLEARING IT WITH ME?
NOT COOL.
AND I SUPPOSE "YOUR GIRL" DOESN'T GET TO MAKE UP HER OWN MIND?
KA-SPLLLAT
OHHHHHHHH
I'M GOING TO PASS AS WELL, CYBORG.

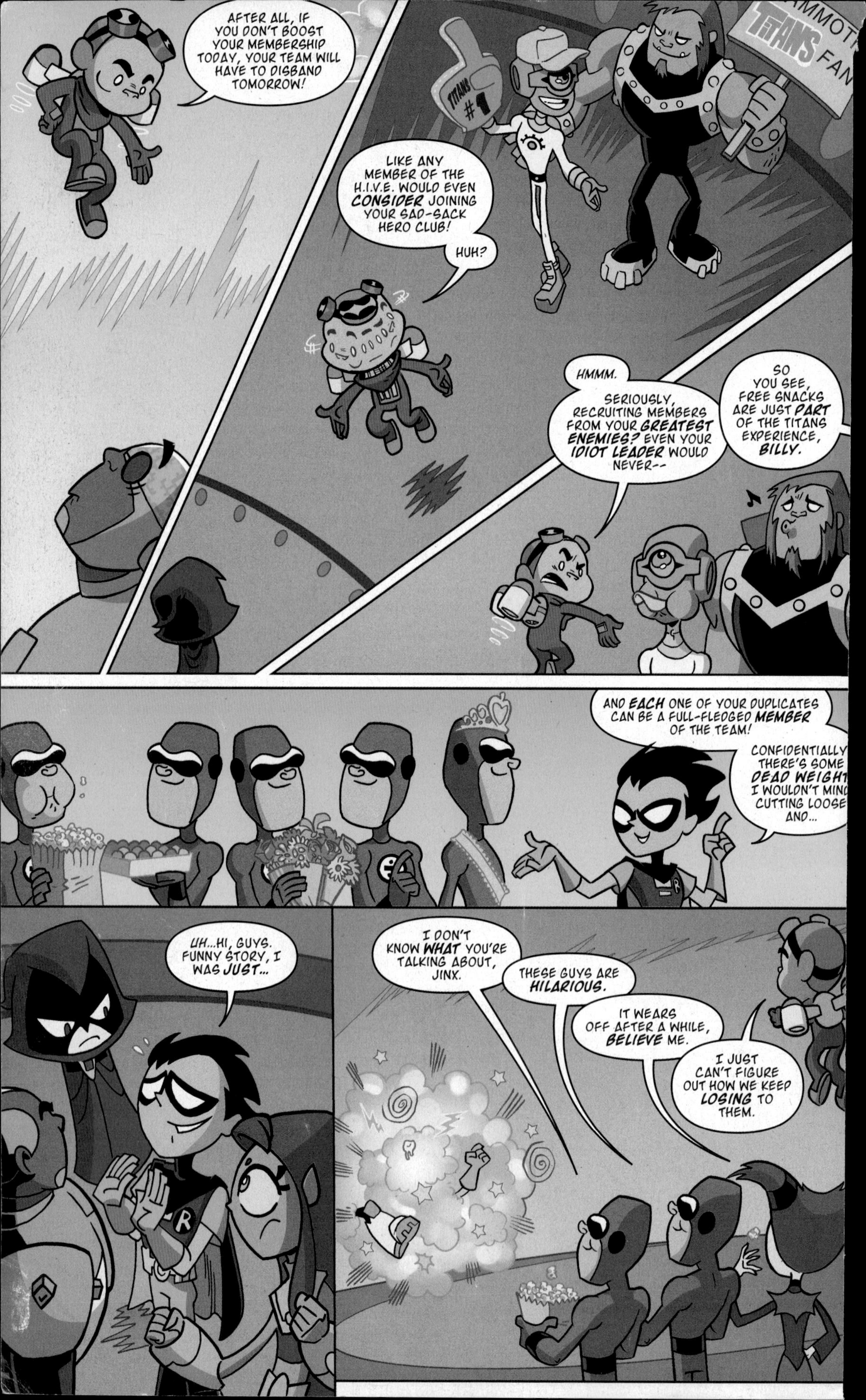
AFTER ALL, IF YOU DON'T BOOST YOUR MEMBERSHIP TODAY, YOUR TEAM WILL HAVE TO DISBAND TOMORROW!
TITANS #1
TITANS FAN
LIKE ANY MEMBER OF THE H.I.V.E. WOULD EVEN CONSIDER JOINING YOUR SAD-SACK HERO CLUB!
HUH?
HMMM.
SERIOUSLY, RECRUITING MEMBERS FROM YOUR GREATEST ENEMIES? EVEN YOUR IDIOT LEADER WOULD NEVER--
SO YOU SEE, FREE SNACKS ARE JUST PART OF THE TITANS EXPERIENCE, BILLY.
AND EACH ONE OF YOUR DUPLICATES CAN BE A FULL-FLEDGED MEMBER OF THE TEAM!
CONFIDENTIALLY, THERE'S SOME DEAD WEIGHT I WOULDN'T MIND CUTTING LOOSE AND...
UH...HI, GUYS. FUNNY STORY, I WAS JUST...
I DON'T KNOW WHAT YOU'RE TALKING ABOUT, JINX.
THESE GUYS ARE HILARIOUS.
IT WEARS OFF AFTER A WHILE, BELIEVE ME.
I JUST CAN'T FIGURE OUT HOW WE KEEP LOSING TO THEM.

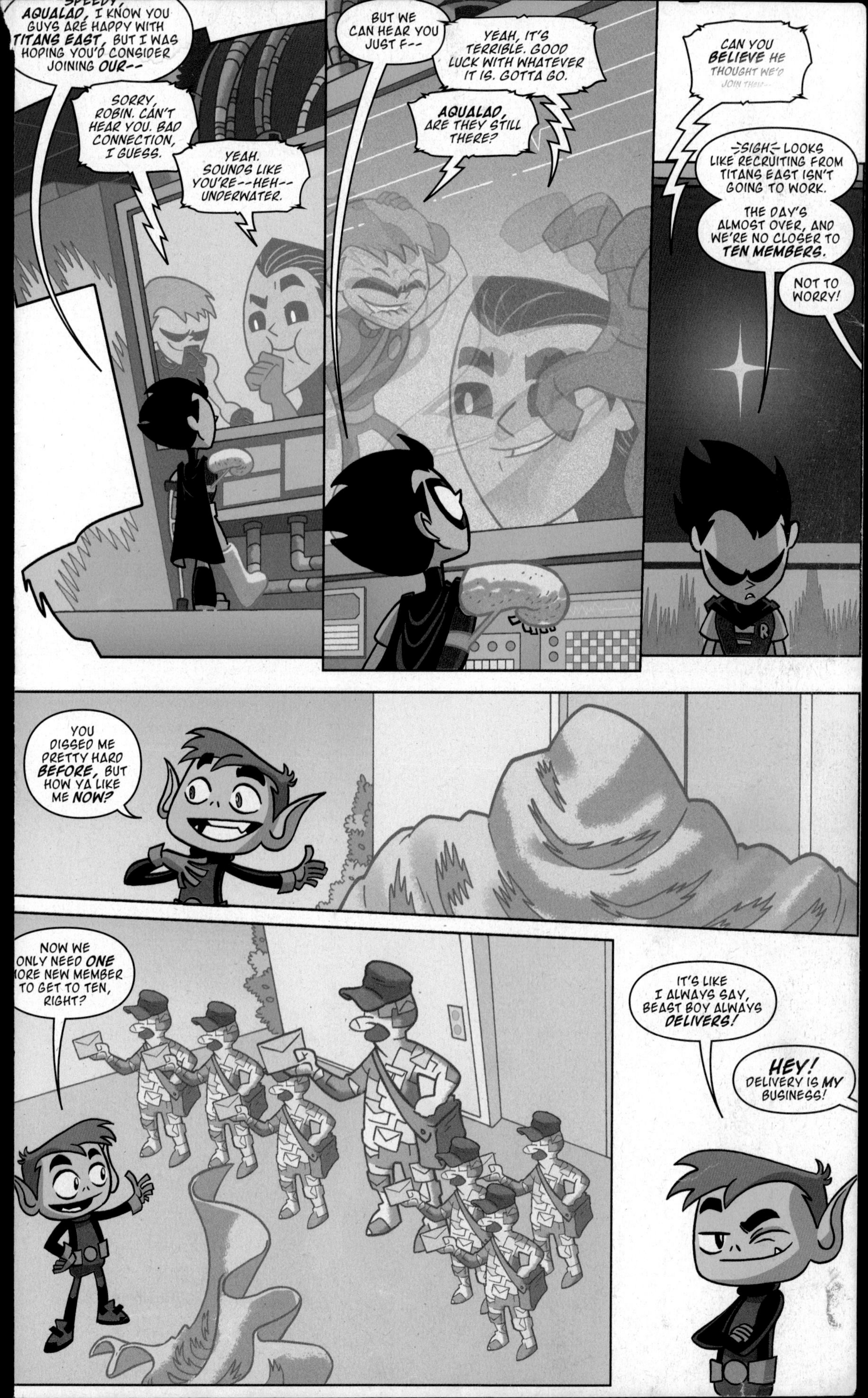
SPEEDY, AQUALAD, I KNOW YOU GUYS ARE HAPPY WITH TITANS EAST, BUT I WAS HOPING YOU'D CONSIDER JOINING OUR--
SORRY, ROBIN. CAN'T HEAR YOU. BAD CONNECTION, I GUESS.
YEAH. SOUNDS LIKE YOU'RE--HEH--UNDERWATER.
BUT WE CAN HEAR YOU JUST F--
YEAH, IT'S TERRIBLE. GOOD LUCK WITH WHATEVER IT IS. GOTTA GO.
AQUALAD, ARE THEY STILL THERE?
CAN YOU BELIEVE HE THOUGHT WE'D
-SIGH- LOOKS LIKE RECRUITING FROM TITANS EAST ISN'T GOING TO WORK.
THE DAY'S ALMOST OVER, AND WE'RE NO CLOSER TO TEN MEMBERS.
NOT TO WORRY!
YOU DISSED ME PRETTY HARD BEFORE, BUT HOW YA LIKE ME NOW?
NOW WE ONLY NEED ONE MORE NEW MEMBER TO GET TO TEN, RIGHT?
IT'S LIKE I ALWAYS SAY, BEAST BOY ALWAYS DELIVERS!
HEY! DELIVERY IS MY BUSINESS!

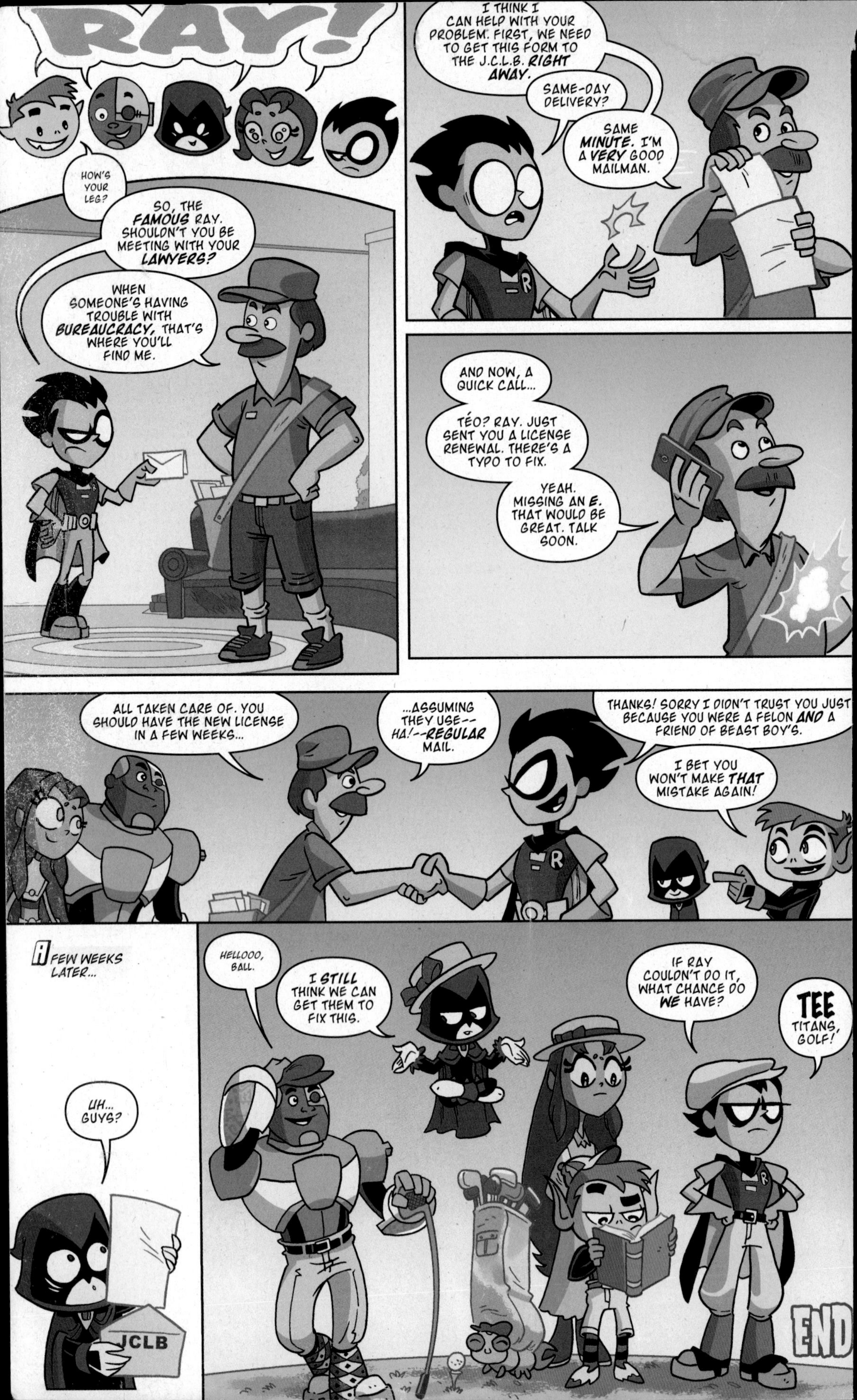
RAY!
HOW'S YOUR LEG?
SO, THE FAMOUS RAY. SHOULDN'T YOU BE MEETING WITH YOUR LAWYERS?
WHEN SOMEONE'S HAVING TROUBLE WITH BUREAUCRACY, THAT'S WHERE YOU'LL FIND ME.
I THINK I CAN HELP WITH YOUR PROBLEM. FIRST, WE NEED TO GET THIS FORM TO THE J.C.L.B. RIGHT AWAY.
SAME-DAY DELIVERY?
SAME MINUTE. I'M A VERY GOOD MAILMAN.
AND NOW, A QUICK CALL...
TÉO? RAY. JUST SENT YOU A LICENSE RENEWAL. THERE'S A TYPO TO FIX.
YEAH. MISSING AN E. THAT WOULD BE GREAT. TALK SOON.
ALL TAKEN CARE OF. YOU SHOULD HAVE THE NEW LICENSE IN A FEW WEEKS...
...ASSUMING THEY USE-- HA!--REGULAR MAIL.
THANKS! SORRY I DIDN'T TRUST YOU JUST BECAUSE YOU WERE A FELON AND A FRIEND OF BEAST BOY'S.
I BET YOU WON'T MAKE THAT MISTAKE AGAIN!
A FEW WEEKS LATER...
UH... GUYS?
JCLB
HELLOOO, BALL.
I STILL THINK WE CAN GET THEM TO FIX THIS.
IF RAY COULDN'T DO IT, WHAT CHANCE DO WE HAVE?
TEE TITANS, GOLF!
END